RUNE OF SECRETS

ENCHANTED SHADOWS - BOOK 1

TALES OF EDENIA 1

KELLY N. JANE

Title: Rune of Secrets (Enchanted Shadows) book 1

Copyright © 2022 by Kelly N. Jane

All rights reserved.

No part of this book may be reproduced in any form or by any electronic or mechanical means, including information storage and retrieval systems, without written permission from the authors, except for the use of brief quotations in a book review.

All characters, places, and incidents are either the product of the authors' imagination or are used fictitiously. Any resemblance to actual persons, living or dead, events, or locales is entirely coincidental.

Published by 18th Avenue Press

Cover by Bewitching Book Covers by Rebecca Frank

Editing by Jen McDonnell of Bird's Eye books; Candy Skinner of Valkyrie Publishing; Enchanted Quill Press

Updated 2024

ISBN 978-1-947695-24-5

ISBN 978-1-947695-20-7

Check out Kelly's website for a free story!

https://www.kellynjane.com

For everyone who chases their dreams in the middle of the storms

THE ENCHANTED LANDS
OF
EDENIA

AETERNUS SEA

GALLINAR SEA

RULAVA
PENUMAR
KAZNA
KUR
MORTUS
THE BARROWS
AETHERCREST
SAGANUS
SIGHTLESS VALE
ORA
FANGHOLT
VEILRUNE MOUNTAINS
ANOMIE
HAVILAR
ACLANUS
SYLPHRA
BAILARA
THALASSAR
VATARA
KESTURU
ZANDIRI
TIXAMAR
ILLUSION PASS
THE BLUFFS
ERIDAR

ONE

IN THE EIGHTEENTH SUMMER OF THE SPINDLE AGE

Only one burly Telana warrior stood in Rowena's way.

Her match was the last one for the day. A determined drizzle made her braid heavy down her back. Long shadows from the forest's edge reached across the open field like fingers ready to snatch her prize. She risked having to postpone the fight until morning if she didn't finish it soon. That would waste too much strength and risk her chance to compete for the championship later in the day. She had to end this now.

"If you're just going to stand there, it's not much of a show for the crowd." She lunged, her linden wood competition sword held firm . . . and missed her massive target. The warrior swatted away her attack with a lazy back stroke of his blunted blade.

The force of his swing rattled her arm, giving Rowena a momentary pause. She glanced at her weapon. The leather-wrapped hilt was still tight in her grip. She must have misjudged the distance. She licked her lips, salty from the sweat of previous matches. A flutter of apprehension filled her belly. Perhaps she wasn't ready to face challengers from other lands?

No. Her mother was wrong.

Rowena raised her gaze to the elven warrior. Tattoos etched his forehead, trailing down the side of his face and disappearing under his tunic. Steam rose from his sweating frame. A head taller than most other men, with a longer reach. It made him overconfident. He pivoted in the center of their twelve-foot competition circle, never leaving his position. His feet seemed rooted to the soil.

That's how she would win. She was quicker, more agile. Rowena stayed on the balls of her feet, scooting backward with her stare locked on the warrior's sullen face.

His nostrils flared, and he curled one side of his lips into a sneer. He lifted his practice blade, muscles tense. Rowena rocked from side to side, ready to take advantage of his exaggerated swing.

Something caught the man's eye over Rowena's shoulder. He hesitated a moment, then spat on the ground with a grumble before returning his attention to her. "You should be wary, princess. Many watching have set hopes for your defeat."

Of course, there were some who wished her to lose. Those who'd traveled from Ibern with her uncle, no doubt. That was an old feud. If her father put it behind him, so should everyone else.

"I'll disappoint your companions if they bet against me, I'm afraid." She danced around, searching for an opening to dart in and earn another point.

"Their coin is safe."

"We'll see." Rowena glided sideways, staying within the circle's limits, which were well defined after all the earlier rounds from the day. Her leather-clad feet squelched in the trampled mud, signaling her kick before she made it.

The warrior snatched her ankle from the air, yanking Rowena off her feet. She twisted, landed partially on her back, and rolled to her side. The point of his sword pressed, harder than necessary, against the square metal patch sewn into her armor a heartbeat later.

"I guess we will," her opponent said, looming over her.

She hurried to stand, flinging the mud from her fingers and swiping her fake sword's hilt free from the slippery gunk. That attack had been so quick. He hadn't projected signals to warn her of movements like that. At least she'd worn her trousers and tunic like all the other entrants, rather than staying in her working serk. How much more humiliating it would have been in a skirt that exposed her to the waist when she fell.

Rowena straightened her shoulders. It was only one point. No harm done.

She glanced to her left, where her parents stood, watching with the visiting king and queen from Ibern. Her mother's golden crown shone in Sawel's lowering sunlight as she adjusted her nalbinding shawl against the dropping temperatures. But her father met her gaze and winked with a grin. That was all the encouragement Rowena needed.

Two more points—she'd have her victory. She'd make it to the final round the next day. Her father would have to take her with him to collect rents in the outer villages if she became champion. She could finally train for her duties as his heir and the future queen.

"Still want to put on a good show?" Her opponent asked. "Or have you had enough?"

Rowena's stomach clenched. His looming size cast a shadow over her, despite the distance between them. And she wasn't a short woman. He kept the tip of his sword pointed at the ground while they circled each other, completely disrespecting her as a worthy opponent.

The others she'd faced had as well. They always did.

Rowena faked a lunge to her left and then jabbed straight ahead, landing her sword against the Ibern's chest. "That's two."

The man roared and charged. Rowena threw her arms up to block his swing. His sword crashed into hers. She shook from the effort of keeping her own blade from slamming into her nose. His foot slipped. She spun and swung from the right. He gained his footing; crashed his sword into hers. He dodged right and threw a downward cut. Rowena raised her sword, twisting her wrists, letting her blade slide down his until she parried and thrust.

The man leaned away. Her sword sliced through the air. He lurched forward, forcing her to duck. He cut down on her with a grunt. All she could do was lift her sword once more, using both hands to block. The competition faded from her mind. Instead, she pictured her lessons. Her heartbeat slowed; movements more fluid. Bar. Parry. Dodge. Counter.

Sweat rolled into Rowena's eyes, burning them. The man charged, lowered his shoulder, and smashed into her chest. She flew and landed on her back. Her head hit the ground, splashing mud onto her face. She sputtered and spit. The gritty, melted dirt coated her tongue. She couldn't roll away fast enough to prevent the elven warrior from slapping the side of his blade over her middle.

He'd evened the score.

Stunned, she heaved herself to her side. It would be fine. She could still win. Rowena inhaled, rolled to her knees, clenched her fists.

Something solid cracked against her ribs. Her elbows gave way, and she landed on her back. She gaped, useless to gather air back into her lungs. The low, gray clouds danced overhead, teasing her stomach to retch.

A figure stepped into view. His shadow loomed over her, blotted out the sky. She blinked against the sudden darkness as a blunt sword's edge pressed against her neck.

"You lose." The Telana's gravelly words battered her heart worse than her bruised ribs.

He hadn't given her time to get to her feet. To reset herself and prepare. That had to be wrong. Cheating. The guards always gave her rest between points during practice.

Strong fingers gripped her upper arm and hauled her to her feet. Hot breath blew over her face as the man pulled her closer.

"Someone like you shouldn't think so highly of yourself," he whispered into her ear.

Rowena yanked at her arm. "Let go."

He twisted her to face the royals, then smacked his meaty hand against her back. "A worthy opponent, for sure! In a year or two, we shall all live in fear of her blade!"

His bellow must have reached the farthest corner of the open field. Even those who'd watched other events, now privy to her loss. The surrounding crowd roared with cheers and laughter, misunderstanding his mocking comment as sincerity. There was no choice but to nod to the victor and accept her defeat. Though, Rowena's stomach churned, and she desired nothing more than to fall to her knees and vomit.

The warrior strode away, swarmed by his fellow countrymen, laughing. Congratulating.

Rowena waited until the crowd dispersed before she left the circle. She swiped at her face and spat the foul taste of mud mixed with blood from where she'd bit the inside of her cheek.

Thankfully, others huddled around her parents, and kept them preoccupied. She wouldn't have to face them until later.

Her friend, Hann, ambled closer. The king's sigil emblazoned on his mud-free tunic. It fit him well. He'd become a member of her father's personal guard two days ago. Perhaps his competition hadn't started yet.

"You almost had him," he said, offering a cloth.

"He didn't give me rest between points. Clearly, from the cheering, no one cares he cheated."

"There is no rule against his actions."

She flashed a glare at her friend. "It was a competition, not actual battle. Decency should apply."

Rowena used the cloth to wipe her face, then cleaned her blade, wooden though it was. She'd won three earlier matches and earned two points against the visiting warrior. Perhaps it was enough. "My father had better allow me to travel with him."

"To collect the rents?" Hann scratched at the short stubble emerging along his jaw.

Rowena stuffed her sword through the loop on her belt. "What else have I spoken about in the last weeks?"

Hann huffed a chuckle. "I'm positive he will."

They made their way toward the last competition for the day—axe throwing. Throngs of farmers, merchants, servants, and guards milled about. Some pushed small hand carts full of wares to sell. Some hung leather straps around their necks, supporting trays full of hand pies and honey cakes. The week-long King's Day celebrations had drawn folk from every village in Skandan. All had made the pilgrimage to Taesing to honor her father.

Then his own daughter disgraced herself in front of everyone. Rowena swallowed, the bitter tang of bile rising in her throat at how disappointed he must be.

The evening feast would start soon. She could use the excuse of cleaning up for a moment alone to brace her nerves before facing too many others. Mud caked her hair and stiffened her fighting clothes. She didn't relish exchanging her trousers for a dress at the moment, but a warm bath and dry attire would suit her fine.

Hann adjusted his axe, so it hung further back on his hips. He'd not competed in the contest against her. She'd itched to ask him why, not that it mattered any longer. Though he'd beaten her the last time they sparred, she'd hoped to settle the score. One more disappointment.

Rowena kicked a rock out of her path. "How did the stone lift go?"

"Perhaps you should have watched me, instead of trying to best battle-hardened men twice your size. No matter. You can watch me tomorrow." Hann bumped against her shoulder, forcing her to wobble sideways for a step.

So, he'd won. She snuck a peek at him. Not that she'd forgotten his wavy dark curls, rich brown eyes or how his ear tips pointed just right. The way he'd started looking at her in the last year made fire sizzle up her spine. His simple touch as they strolled caused her skin to pebble, like being caught in the snow without a cloak.

But wasn't he just like her parents? Eager to marry, to build a longhouse, to start a family. Rowena shuddered. Her parents met and married within weeks—at Rowena's age.

Seventeen winters weren't enough time to do all she planned. She'd traveled no farther than to her grandmother's village near the fjords on the other side of the island. Hardly an adventure. They hadn't even sailed around. Instead, they'd hiked through the mountains on the same trails they used for hunting.

She wasn't ready for marriage.

Hann couldn't possibly understand her need to stay independent. The year before, he'd gone with her father to the continent. Now he was part of the King's Guard. He would travel everywhere her father did, while she stayed behind . . . tending the village like her mother. She had more to do before that became her life.

"I lost coin because of you," a smooth voice, hinting at laughter, called from behind.

Rowena spun, coming face to face with Prince Daenon, her uncle's foster son. Only half a summer older than her, his full lips quirked upward at one corner when she turned. The cerulean color of his eyes seared into her, startling her heart into kicking like a frolicking colt. She'd had a few moments to speak with him when he'd first arrived, but not a word since.

"Know your place, unsket," Hann spat, forcing his way between her and the golden-haired elf.

She'd told Hann multiple times that she could defend herself. He needed to respect that about her. Especially when it wasn't necessary, as with the prince. She pushed against Hann's corded upper arm.

He twisted and winked. "Impressed?"

She glared, hoping to hide that she was. "Stop being an arse. Father welcomed my uncle and all his men. We need to do the same." Despite them showing up unannounced. So far, tensions had stayed calm. They should be considerate, so it continued.

Daenon dipped his head in a shallow bow, the pointed tips of his ears peeking through his unbound hair, before meeting her gaze. "I'm forever grateful for the king's hospitality."

As was she. So much so she had to turn away to hide the heat blooming in her cheeks like a fool. They'd just met. She mentally shook herself. "Even when it costs you coin?"

Daenon let out a hearty laugh. It floated through the air like chimes. So caught up in the rhythm, she almost missed Hann's huff. Gah, her friend was giving her a headache. She dropped her gaze and stomped to the axe throwing competition.

Mid-stride an elfling toddled into her path and Rowena nearly plowed over her.

Rowena scooped the girl into her arms and wiggled their noses together. "Where do you belong? It's not safe here, even for such a brave shieldmaiden."

"She likes you." Hann placed a hand gently between Rowena's shoulder blades and grinned at the small girl.

"Why wouldn't she?" Rowena kept her focus on the child, ignoring how her friend's soft touch made tingles flutter through her belly.

"Why should you care is the bigger question. A peasant's child holds no value."

Rowena twisted to gape at Daenon. "A queen cares for all her people. This child is as important as anyone else."

Daenon shrugged and leaned closer to the elfling, wrinkling his nose. "Then I offer you some advice. They give bad little elflings as offerings to the Seeker. He digs into them with sharp claws and devours them as snacks. It's not good to wander alone."

"You're despicable," Hann said, scooting closer to Rowena's other side once more. "That's not a true story, nor one you tell a child."

"Why not? The realm is full of dangers. Why shouldn't she

learn of them? True or not." Daenon stood to his full height, squaring off with Hann despite how Rowena stood between them.

She ducked out from between the rutting males, rubbed the girl's back, and scanned the area. Fifty yards away, a woman darted one way and then the next, searching for something near the ground.

"I think I found where you belong," she whispered into the girl's ear. She kissed the girl's forehead, waving her free arm to gain the distraught mother's attention.

"Thank you," gasped the harried woman as she rushed to the group. The girl leaned out to her mother and settled on the woman's hip. "You need to stay put, Malia. Now, say goodbye to the princess. I've got to get inside before all these hungry stomachs arrive for supper."

"Bye, bye."

Rowena chuckled and wiggled Malia's foot. "You listen to your mother."

"From your lips." The woman sighed, curtsied first to her queen who'd strolled near, and then to the Ibern queen, arriving with her.

When the mother had gone, Rowena slid next to her mother.

"Good advice you gave that elfling. I wonder where you might have heard such a sentiment before?" The edges of her mother's mouth fought to stay straight.

Rowena rolled her eyes. "It's a worthy goal for one so young. As you keep reminding me, my prime day is approaching. Perhaps my wisdom is overflowing in preparation."

The queen chuckled, but it was short-lived.

The kings were due to take part in axe throwing as the last competition for the day, but her father left the area and strode over, sliding in next to her mother with his gaze caught on a spot behind them.

Rowena twisted to find the crowd rolling to an eerie silence, separating for someone heading for the royals.

Moments later, Asta came into view.

TWO

Her father's broad back blocked Rowena's view as he slid in front of her and her mother while they waited for the druid to approach. Asta lived on the outskirts of the village and had advised the king for as long as Rowena could remember.

A shiver prickled Rowena's spine for reasons she didn't understand. The air seemed heavier somehow. More so when silence rolled over the meadow as everyone took notice of the new arrival.

"I thought she was coming tomorrow, Olve." Rowena's mother spoke low to her father while keeping her queenly smile in place. She remained behind the king's shoulder, but slid over enough to be in the druid's view.

Her father twisted his neck to keep his voice from carrying, yet his gaze also stayed locked on the approaching woman. "She comes when she pleases."

Asta's long glossy-white hair fluttered in the breeze while she glided closer. Her long white robe and pale skin made her nearly glow against the patches of mud and grass. Rowena swallowed hard and twisted the edge of her tunic between her fingers. Not for the first time, Rowena wondered if her mother's enchanted powers could match a druid's.

"Asta, I'm grateful you've arrived," Olve said with a nod to the druid.

"I am happy to serve my king." The druid dipped her head slightly, but kept her back tall and straight, her hands folded within the wide sleeves of her flowing robe. She slid her gaze to Rowena's mother. "And you as well, Queen Jarah."

"We are pleased to have you join us. The celebrations would not be complete without you."

"It is with a heavier heart that I arrive this year."

Rowena's heart pounded so hard she could feel the veins in her neck pulse. She glanced at her father. He stood tall and regal. Rowena did her best to emulate him, but couldn't keep her hands from shaking. There was something in the stoic presence of the druid that had her on edge.

"Please share your news; hopefully, it will unburden you and you can enjoy your time with us." The king kept his tone calm and easy.

"If it were so simple." Asta's shoulders rose and fell with a deep breath before she continued. "Rumors of the one called Seeker have circulated since your last King's Day, and I must confirm them to be true."

Gasps and murmurs rippled through the crowd. Rowena slid her hand over her stomach, willing herself to stay steady.

"For what purpose would they unleash such a being upon our world?" her mother asked, shifting from behind her father's shoulder to stand at his side.

"The Heptad has lost contact with the Armor of Caelus. They fear they will not have all the pieces together with their proper heartstones secured before the next Reaping." Asta's mouth twisted as if she'd eaten something sour, and her nostrils flared as she continued. "It has been nearly eighteen years since the first Burning Moon. The second will happen this year on the same day, and if all the stones are not within their proper piece of the Armor before that begins, it will bring about destruction, rather than unification."

"How does that connect to a shadowy being with claws and horns? If rumors of the monster are true." Olve asked.

"Of that, I'm not informed. Nor am I versed on why they would take such an action." Asta paused, took a deep breath, and continued. "It has been so long since the Chasm forced us out of the god realm. My guess is the Heptad has become complacent about their duties. Pride has risen among them and they are quick to believe only others make mistakes."

Rowena nibbled at her bottom lip. The seven druids were the judges, the keepers of the laws for every race in Edenia. Including their own. They disavowed druids, like Asta, and forced them from their homeland to live off the charity of others. Rowena stood tall, every bone in her spine rigid, as Asta stared at her for an uncomfortable moment before she continued.

"The Primary Spring feeds enchanted power to the gems as conduits to all the realms. The armor's purpose is to protect the heartstones from improper use. Yet, long before I became disavowed, it was common knowledge that some had removed the gems from the Armor. They may have called upon the Seeker to cover their failure. However, no one can hide their secrets forever."

Rowena wasn't sure which was more terrifying—what the woman said or the way her expression glittered hard and dark as she spoke.

"What does that mean for those born during the Burning Moon—for the prophecy?" Jarah asked. Her mother had a way of keeping herself regal in all matters, yet her voice faltered slightly during the question. Others may not have noticed. But Rowena did.

Her skin pebbled with a chill. She kept her eyes trained on the grass in front of her, feeling the weight of many stares shift in her direction. Everyone knew when she'd been born.

"The Sight has always failed me in that regard. I have learned they tasked the Seeker with finding the moon-born who will fulfill the prophecy as well."

"There are others, then?" Her father voiced the same question floating through Rowena's mind.

Hope dared flow through Rowena. Surely, the Heptad would have simply come for her if she had anything to do with that cryptic prophecy. If there were others, it had to be someone else. That she was born during the Burning Moon meant nothing, after all.

"What is this prophecy?" Daenon strolled to a stop at Rowena's side.

Asta's words held Rowena's attention so much, she'd forgotten anyone else stood nearby. Rowena glanced at the prince. No one other than the king and queen was to speak to the druid when she came for a blessing. He had to know that. And how could he not have heard the prophecy?

"Be silent," Uther snarled at his foster son.

Rowena glanced around. Many others had pressed into a semicircle behind her family to listen.

Asta slowly slid her gaze to meet Daenon's, who hadn't moved or given Uther any acknowledgment. She narrowed her eyes, scrutinizing the prince with an unnerving stare that would make Rowena shrivel like a grape in the heat of summer.

"It is unwise to be so bold yet so ignorant. Though I will answer you to correct one of your flaws." Asta spread her hands wide, palms up, exposing her long slender fingers and recited the words Rowena had learned as an elfling. "The sparrow of silver fire will strike the owl from above and below, when thrice the seven gather before the prime goes dark."

Daenon let out a huff and leaned back into his heels. "How can anyone decipher that? Or know that it is about the Burning Moon?"

Rowena's aunt twisted to Daenon. "Enough. Say no more, please." Even the frosty Ibern queen seemed rattled.

He clamped his lips together but gave her a tight nod.

Asta ignored Daenon's questions, returning her hands to her sleeves and her gaze to Rowena's father. "Endings always create a path for beginnings."

"Is that my blessing?" The king offered a polite smile that barely moved his lips and didn't dull the worry floating over his face.

The druid bowed her head deeper than when she'd arrived. "Only in part."

Rowena's shoulders curled in another inch. She wanted Asta to turn and leave, saying nothing more. But the woman again removed her hands from her sleeves with a small leather pouch she cradled in both palms.

"Danger lies ahead, but your line is strong. What is to come will set things right. Fear not." Asta sprinkled the contents of her pouch into one hand, whispered silent words, and then blew the contents into the air toward Rowena's father.

The king placed his hand over his heart, letting the powder float around him. When it had settled, he dropped his arm. "Thank you. I will hold your words close and accept this blessing, no matter what occurs."

Asta nodded before turning and striding back through the crowd to a path that led into the woods.

Rowena let out a heavy sigh, dropping her shoulders an inch. Several minutes dripped by with only her heartbeat to mark the time. The king remained silent.

Someone a few steps to Rowena's right shifted their feet. From the corner of her eye, she caught sight of another warrior grip the handle of his dagger, still sheathed. She hadn't noticed until that moment how the Ibernians seemed ready for a true melee, dressed in fighting leathers and their hair bound tightly away from their faces—even Fidessa.

A knot formed in Rowena's belly.

Her aunt's sour, prickly attitude didn't seem any different

from the last two days. Then there was her uncle. He had a similar laugh as her father's, and he used it liberally as well, yet it seemed forced somehow. Perhaps she'd not spent enough time with him to understand his mannerisms.

After Hann and Daenon's face-off earlier, Rowena avoided studying either of them too much.

She mentally shook herself. The week had been long, and she needed more rest, nothing more. The king would call for the competition to resume and all would be well.

As king, her father commanded so much respect, yet he kept a casual appearance, as if he was just Olve, no different from the average farmer. He wore a pair of trousers with a sleeveless tunic wrapped by his leather belt, the same as Hann. He had a calm personality that welcomed all, yet it was a fool who stood against him. It was why everyone in Skandan loved him.

"After that, I need fun. Let's throw some axes!" Olve shouted, releasing the crowd from its tense silence.

A loud cheer filled the wide meadow, all went back to as it was before the druid arrived. Both kings strode to their designated area where painted targets leaned against stumps five paces from where the competitors were to stand. They had laid a selection of axes out on a cloth for the two kings to choose from.

"It appears I'll have to dig deep for my skills today, brother." Olve smirked as he lifted his chosen axe. "I didn't realize axe throwing required armor."

"A competition is like a battle, is it not?" Uther called, followed by a booming laugh. "Or have your forgotten all the training of our youth? Always stay prepared!"

"I have not. Perhaps you don't remember our long afternoons practicing with swords and axes." Olve tossed his axe, letting it flip in the air before adroitly catching the handle. "Stay on the balls of your feet so you can dodge and duck. The one who wins a battle is not always the most armed, but the one who avoids death."

Uther nodded and offered his hand to Olve. They shook to

begin the competition in good will. "How could I forget such teachings, when you were always so quick to inform me whenever I failed?"

"You will not fail today, husband," Fidessa called out.

The queen's ash-brown hair and sharp nose reminded Rowena of a coyote, cunning and sly, waiting for the opportunity to strike.

The knot tightened in Rowena's stomach. As a mage, Fidessa could conjure spells or incantations to cause havoc. Based on the continual sneer she flashed, it seemed more likely the longer the Ibernians visited.

Rowena became so lost in her thoughts she hadn't noticed how close Fidessa had moved. When the Ibern queen leaned in, she brushed against Rowena's shoulder, speaking low so only she and her mother could hear.

"Uther will be high king of Ibern soon. Your time to rule is ending."

Rowena sucked in a breath. The knot in her belly tightened, binding her in surety she hadn't imagined the looming trouble. She slid a peek sideways at her mother, waiting for her response.

Jarah kept her head high and answered without looking at Fidessa. "We did not invite your husband back to Skandan for a reason. Only Olve's generosity has allowed him to stay. You, and he, need to remember your place."

Rowena licked her lips and did her best to control her breathing. She'd only strapped the small knife around her thigh out of habit. It was only talk. Her aunt had a nasty disposition. That was all it was. Rowena did her best to choke down her growing dread and focus on the competition ahead of her, but the sly grin her aunt gave made the hairs on Rowena's neck rise.

THREE

"After today's display, it's a surprise you're not testing yourself against the men in this competition as well, princess," Honey dripped from the queen's words, but they were a hive full of stingers.

"I've not yet excelled at throwing axes, though I can swing one well enough." Rowena straightened her shoulders and clenched her fists.

"I can attest to that," Hann said. He leaned just enough to brush Rowena's arm. His support calmed her nerves.

"It's a fine quality in a woman who can fight as well as a man," Daenon said, a hint of challenge in his tone that gave Rowena pause. The surrounding air suddenly chilled and she wished to end the conversation.

"For one going off to battle, I suppose. Not one soon to be wed," Fidessa cooed.

"Thank Caelus; I don't have to face either." Marriage was the last topic of conversation Rowena wished to have at that moment, especially with the prickly aunt she'd just met.

"So like your mother." Fidessa flattened her lips.

"That's enough, Fidessa." Her mother hissed the other queen's name, her nostrils flaring. The sight sent a jolt of satisfaction through Rowena. Perhaps she and her mother were more alike than she'd thought.

"Probably best that you don't marry, anyway, I would guess." Fidessa clasped her hands in front of her and tightened her gaze on Rowena. "With so many concerned about your curse."

"She's not cursed," Hann spat.

Rowena tried to swallow the rising knot, scratching its way up her throat. She had heard no one speak of such things in years. The occasional guest would hint at a question, but her parents tossed it aside as nonsense—as it was.

"I'm sure she isn't. However, when one is born during a Burning Moon, and that rare event occurs on the same night as the Reaping, it's inevitable that some will make assumptions."

"It was just an eclipse, nothing more." Jarah echoed the words she'd told Rowena many times, but her voice wobbled, betraying her. "A baby comes when it's time. There's no control over that."

The area seemed to darken, blocking out the competition, so that only Fidessa shown with the orange firelight glowing brighter behind her. "Time grows short until the truth comes out. You are the curse whose weapon will destroy kingdoms and bring darkness into the realm. The love protecting you will end. Though you grasp for it, it will slip through your fingers like shadows."

"Lies. No one would believe such things about her. Rowena will have true love forever." Hann slid his shoulder in front of Rowena's.

The queen smirked. "Perhaps—if the shadows kiss back."

The queen's words made no sense. Yet . . . after the way Asta had stared at her . . . Her shoulders curled in and she longed for it to be dark. Run into the woods, hide, let the moon's silvery beams wash over her. Yet, she couldn't run, couldn't move, couldn't deny the ache in her chest that accepted the queen's words as truth.

Olve and Uther had begun their competition, unaware of the clash taking place behind them. Hopefully, afterward, they could help diffuse the tension bubbling between the two queens. Both simmered quietly after Fidessa's outrageous comment.

Rowena's mind raced, searching for answers, for a way to dispel the queen's comments and prove they did not destine her for such horrible things. She glanced around at the others, but found no reassurance. Hann stood with his arms crossed over his chest and lips pursed, fixated on the field where two teams were finishing a ball game. All the other events had concluded, making the meadow oddly empty and silent. The crowd surrounding the axe-throwing grew, pressing closer.

Dried mud crumbled out of Rowena's hair and stuck to the sweat trickling down her neck.

Uther's next axe hit the center of the target, and Rowena's mother clapped. "Well done!" Jarah had a knack for understanding how to soothe tempers beyond her enchanted powers.

"He doesn't need your encouragement. You've done enough of that for a lifetime."

Rowena snapped her gaze to Fidessa. The queen's nostrils flared, and she glared so hard at Jarah it seemed she had tried to sear her in two.

"It was a good throw, deserving of praise regardless of who tossed the axe." Jarah turned to stand face-to-face with the mage. "I tire of your insults."

It took a lot to make her mother truly angry. Rowena knew the measurement well. She probably should have stepped back to give them space, but she couldn't uproot her feet. Instead, she slipped her hand into her mother's palm, offering support.

"You are a beetle that burrowed yourself into his heart and then abandoned him when he had nothing left to give. Keep to your own husband." Fidessa clenched her fists at her side, as if wanting to draw her dagger.

Too focused on their match, neither king noticed how their wives squared off against each other. Her mother still looked pale and drained from a day spent in Sawel's light, but her eyes were alight with fire. This would not end well.

Uther prepared to send his next axe.

Fidessa twisted her neck to stare at the match. "Let your aim be true." She spoke to no one in particular, but returned her gaze to Jarah. "Find the target to finish this battle in victory."

A stiff wind picked up and blew over Rowena's neck, trailing down her spine like ice.

A moment later, Uther swung his axe over his shoulder, but the sharp blade's bindings fell away. Distracted by choosing a new axe, Olve leaned over, and the loose axe-head sailed safely over his back.

Too confused to acknowledge the danger, Rowena watched as the sharp edge came directly at her.

A heartbeat later, her mother shoved against Rowena's shoulder, knocking her sideways. She grasped for her mother's hand, but her fingernails only dragged across Jarah's palm as they both hit the ground.

"Mor!" Rowena scrambled to her knees alongside her mother, snatching hold of her hand once again.

The axe head stuck out from where it had embedded into Jarah's chest. Dumbfounded, Rowena couldn't make sense of the sight, and twisted to call for her father. Her gaze met her uncle's wide-eyed stare, the empty axe handle held frozen in his hand.

Her father straightened abruptly, briefly meeting Rowena's stare. "Healers, now!"

Her father skidded onto his knees opposite of Rowena, grabbing his wife's hand.

"Rowena," Jarah whispered between gasps. "My sparrow . . ."

Rowena reached for the axe-head with her free hand, but her father grabbed her wrist. "Don't pull it free. It will worsen."

"I don't know what happened," Uther said, standing over them. "It's one I've used the whole time."

Jarah squeezed Rowena's hand and forced her to meet her

mother's gaze again. She tried to speak, but only a wet gurgle came from her throat.

"Jarah, hold on, my love." Olve brushed his fingers over his wife's face, clutching her hand until his knuckles turned white.

Rowena tightened her grip to match. They'd break her hands, but whatever it took to keep her with them was all that mattered. If she could hold on with enough strength, she could keep her mother alive. Keep her from slipping away to return to Caelus.

Her mother grimaced, but turned a weak smile to Olve before gasping once and then no more. A powerful jolt sparked into Rowena's palm and bore into her veins, racing up her arm and into her chest right before her mother's hand went limp.

"Jarah!" her father yelled, wrapping his arms around her and pulling her to his chest.

But it was no use. Rowena's mother would never respond. Tears flowed down Rowena's cheeks and she folded over so that her forehead nearly touched the dirt.

The world went silent and her mind went numb until her father screamed into the sky. His pain created another fissure in Rowena's heart.

"No. This isn't right. It can't be." Her uncle's voice echoed somewhere over her head, but she shoved it aside.

Her father startled her when he jumped to his feet and faced his brother. "You did this!"

She followed his stare to where her uncle stood, pale and shaking. His gaze fixated on her mother's lifeless form.

Olve charged and grabbed Uther's tunic, punching him so hard he stumbled backward, wrenching from Olve's grip.

The action spurred Rowena's mind, but she gently arranged her mother's hands over her stomach before rising to her feet.

"Far. Wait!" she yelled.

Olve twisted to her. Fury simmered in his eyes. She understood, but he directed his actions toward the wrong source.

"It was her." Rowena pointed at Fidessa. "She called the axe with a spell—" Tears choked out more words, but there was no doubt her aunt had caused her mother's death.

Fidessa shook her head.

All activity had halted, and a circle formed around her family. Goetz, her father's advisor, grabbed hold of Fidessa's upper arm, glancing at both kings. Good. He would ensure the mage paid for her crime. "Let's not be too hasty to cast blame until we hear all the facts," he said.

What? "You don't believe me?" Rowena called out to her father's advisor.

"We need to stay calm before words or actions send us all down a path we can't return." Goetz held out his hand, palm up, as if her mother's murder was a simple dispute.

"We are beyond words." Olve spoke in a low tone. A growling wolf would not sound so terrifying.

"Call for the weapons master," Uther yelled. Blood smeared his teeth from a cut on his lip. "Find out how he made such an inferior weapon."

Olve stalked closer to Fidessa, but Uther hurried to stand in front of his wife.

"Do not protect her, brother," Olve said. "I'll have to believe you sanctioned her actions."

"There is no proof she was involved," Uther said. "We are all upset by this. Jarah has always been the voice of love and reason. She would have us remain calm right now; you know she would. Rowena is confused."

"I'm not. She said angry things, just before . . ." Rowena's gaze dropped to her mother.

"I'm a simple mage, trained in potions and charms. How could I have done anything that would overpower Jarah's Lunara enchantment?" Fidessa rested her hand over her heart and waited for Olve's answer.

Her feigned innocence would fool no one. Jarah's power came from the moons, and she had been too weak to be a threat after a day spent in the sun. No one would believe the foreign mage over Rowena.

Hann and Daenon pushed through the crowd, each standing near his own king. Others shifted around, some with ease, some shoving their way to stand on their king's side.

The air grew thick with the scent of wet leather and boiling rage.

Olve glanced at Fidessa and licked his lips. He couldn't be confused, no one could. Could they?

"She did it, Far. Don't believe her lies."

"It's Rowena's word against my queen." Uther's arms hung slack at his side, and his voice softened as he stared at Jarah's body. "We have to treat this as an accident and nothing more, brother. There's no way to judge."

"They came here for this. Their guise of friendship was a ruse," Hann said, speaking to Olve, but glaring at Daenon. "They intended to overthrow you all along, my king."

Uther raised his hands against the accusation. "Jarah held a great place in my heart, too, Olve. I'm sure you remember. Let's honor her and put aside this talk of blame."

"You fool." Fidessa twisted to Uther, her voice emotionless and hard. "You're so weak where your brother and his wife are concerned. You want to become king of all Skandan and Ibern, yet it was love that drew you back to these lands. My help was worthless."

The air became too heavy. A lump grew in Rowena's throat. Her knees gave out. Strong arms grabbed hold of her to keep her from falling, but she didn't care right then. *Mor, don't leave me. I need you.* Her mother had to wake up.

She didn't. She never would again.

Rowena had been right about Fidessa, but it changed nothing. Fidessa had sent that axe flying and now her mother was dead.

"You will hang," Olve said.

The viciousness in his tone chilled Rowena's skin, yet the

pronouncement roused her from her grief. She brushed off whoever helped her and stood tall beside her father.

"Foolish woman!" Uther yelled. "This was not the way."

"Did you want me dead, too? It would have been me if my mother hadn't pushed me out of the way." Rowena shook her head. "This was no accident."

Olve lunged at Fidessa, but his brother blocked him. Goetz yanked the queen away and disappeared behind a wall of Uther's men.

For a heartbeat, Rowena stood motionless while the hiss of metal rang through her ears. Bodies slammed against each other and the crowd erupted, taking sides as everyone dissolved into battle.

Rowena threw herself over her mother to keep others from trampling her, but rough hands yanked her to her feet.

"We need to get you to safety," Hann said.

She fought to release herself, but her attention couldn't focus enough on the hand encircling her wrist. Her gaze kept watch over her mother. The fighters kicked up dirt, but momentum carried them away from where Jarah lay on the ground, alone and untouched.

One of Uther's men slammed into Hann's side and sent the three of them sprawling into the dirt. Hann burst up from the ground and buried his axe into the man's skull.

"Come, Rowena. We have to hurry," Hann said, holding out his hand to her.

The dead man had a quiver of arrows on his belt. There were too many unanswered questions. She reached down, untied the quiver, and then grabbed the bow that had fallen near the body.

"What are you doing? Don't waste time. I'll get you away from here."

"I'm not leaving." She couldn't trust anyone to protect her except herself. She tossed her wooden sword and replaced it with a fallen seax. "My father will bring these dregs to justice, and I will help him do it."

She spun and raced closer to the melee that had erupted. Her first arrow lodged into the ground and the man she missed struck a killing blow to one of her father's men.

Rowena screamed into the air and nocked another arrow. The next one flew into the neck of her targeted warrior. She slowed, taking aim carefully at those who gained an advantage over the warriors fighting with her father. Her heart slowed and her vision cleared. All the training she'd received finally had a solid purpose. Her next arrow plunged into the chest of an Ibernian woman with her sword in the air, ready to strike.

With the next arrow on her string, she scanned the fighters. She had only four arrows left. One of her father's guards fought off two of Uther's men. She aimed for one to even the odds. As she released the string, someone bumped into her shoulder. The arrow missed her target and stuck into the back of the guard's calf.

"No!" Rowena threw her elbow into the fighters near her to make more room, but she was too late to send another arrow. The guard had fallen to one knee and the other warriors overpowered him. She retched, but swallowed the vomit rising in her throat. Two of her countrymen were dead because she didn't help them.

There wasn't time for her to wallow. She had to pull herself together. Wiping her mouth with her sleeve, she readied her next arrow. It sailed true; the attacker she aimed for fell dead.

Once more, she struck down an enemy before they could blindside an ally from a nearby village. Her last arrow rested against the bow, ready. She would make it count.

The fighting had moved Hann farther to her right, and he fought well, wasting no movements, slicing through his opponents one by one. She scanned left and witnessed Daenon stab a man from Ibern—his own man. Why? That made no sense. He should have been fighting against her family. He caught her eye and nodded, forcing his way closer to her.

There wasn't time to figure out his motives. She searched for her next target.

Her father stood in the center of the field, fighting with another warrior nearly as skilled as well as he. The two matched each other blow for blow, an exercise in fluid precision. So captivated, she let her arm relax. The ready arrow slipped out of position.

Until she spotted a man charging toward her father's back.

Rowena raised her bow and shot in one fluid motion. It flew straight, but so did another arrow alongside of it—one that had come from over her shoulder.

She ignored how her arrow struck deep into her target, because the second arrow plunged into her father's chest a heartbeat later. His eyes widened, and he twisted to meet her gaze. Rowena wanted to scream, to call his name, to run to him, but her chest caved in, offering her no such choice. Silence descended on her like a shroud. The harried field faded away. Only her father stayed in her view. His brows pinched together just before he dropped his sword and crumpled to the ground.

A wail ripped out of Rowena, as if it carried her entire insides with it. No, no, no. Not her father, too. Please Osric, don't let them both be gone. Her father's body remained motionless, broken. A numbing chill gripped Rowena. She flung her bow away. There was nothing left to fight for.

Slowly, she tore her gaze from her father and twisted to find who had shot the second arrow. Only Goetz, honorable, loyal Goetz, stared at her father's defeated form.

Her vision swirled. Her chest tightened. "Why?"

Her father's advisor glared; a bitter expression. He didn't answer, yet a slight glint shone in his eyes before he hollered over the din of fighting. "The king is dead! Princess Rowena has killed the king!"

"I didn't." She breathed the words so low she wasn't sure if they came out. This was wrong. Everything was wrong. She screamed, louder, primal, tipping at the waist, unaware of anything but her pain until she couldn't breathe. She wobbled but didn't fall. Why not? How was she alive and her parents were not?

Hann gathered her by both shoulders, staring into her face, saying something, but his words came to her ears as if she floated underwater. He snatched her hand and yanked her after him.

Daenon arrived at her other side, helping to keep her from falling. Her feet barely touched the ground between the two of them as they raced away from the battle.

She couldn't speak, couldn't think, couldn't care for anything anymore, and stumbled along wherever they led.

FOUR

Nothing made sense. Her father's stare, dazed by pain and betrayal, ground through Rowena's mind like a millstone. He'd never seen the man coming up behind him—or the traitor hiding behind her.

Now he'd never know the truth. He was dead.

Tears clawed down her face.

"Keep running." Hann tugged Rowena's arm, forcing her to stay moving. If he let go, she'd drop to the ground and care nothing for what happened next.

Goetz. The leader of the king's council. Why had he done it? He'd been at her father's side forever; if his loyalty wasn't true, was anyone's?

Fingers dug into her skin and brought screams and clanging metal back into her awareness. Behind her, the battle raged on while Hann pulled her away from it.

"No!" She yanked her arm free, surprising her friend, who skidded to a stop. Daenon twisted sideways to avoid tripping over her.

It wasn't right to leave. Her parents were dead, but she still lived. Taesing was her home. It was up to Rowena to wear the crown and avenge her parents. She would kill everyone who'd taken them from her.

She spun and ducked out of reach from both men, who tried to prevent her from going back into the fray.

Goetz would be her first target. There would be no mercy for his treachery. Next would be her aunt. She'd started everything by killing her mother. But Rowena would find her last. She wanted no distractions when she faced the mage.

A warrior sprawled dead on the ground with his bloody sword poking out from under him. Through the mud, Rowena couldn't determine where he'd been from. Friend or foe, it didn't matter—she would put the elf's sword to good use. She used her heel to roll him enough to find the handle of the weapon and grabbed it in time to dive out of the way from a blow aimed at her head.

"Rowena!" Hann called, but she ignored him.

Her pilfered sword was longer and heavier than she'd trained with, but she would make it sing. She hopped to her feet and swung in an arc. Her blade bit into the side of the attacker's leg. He fell to one knee and her next slice left a gash across his neck.

She charged forward, swallowing the bile that threatened her throat. It was her first time killing someone with direct contact. It didn't matter, nothing did. She'd swing her blade at anyone who struck first. Except, her vision tunneled clear in the center. Most warriors on the field wore armor.

The attack wasn't some random accident. But the Ibernians hadn't brought that many fighters with them. Rowena dodged the thrusting blade of a male wearing a scarf tied to his belt. She recognized the woven pattern as from a village near to Taesing.

"Traitor." She curled her lip into a snarl, charging, weapon raised. Her blade was heavy, too heavy, but her rush had been enough to startle the man. She swung her with all her might and the sword cleaved into the man's side until he crumpled to the ground.

When she found herself alone, surrounded only by dead

bodies, she dropped her sword arm, chest heaving, and let the blade tip land in the mud.

This wasn't a battle between armies, but between family and friends. Many waged against each other with only their fists, having not had a weapon at the ready when the melee had started.

Her gaze snagged on a male racing her way. She raised the sword, arms shaking. It had grown heavier. When she recognized Daenon, she let the tip of the blade fall to the ground.

"This is madness. Come and survive," he yelled through gritted teeth.

She nodded, suddenly too exhausted to speak or fight. Daenon held out his hand, and she took it. Together, they sprinted for the forest once again.

"Rowena!" Hann called her name, and she twisted her neck in time to see him cut down a hammer-swinging enemy.

"Wait," she called to Daenon, dragging her feet to force him to stop.

Daenon spun to face her, keeping hold of her hand. Deep lines dug into his forehead. "Now, what is it?"

Hann called to her again, this time closer.

"Fool!" Daenon yelled toward Hann and then focused on Rowena. "If he continues to bellow out your name, it will draw attention to those who may want you dead."

She held the prince's gaze, letting his words sink in. It made sense. It didn't matter, though, because Hann arrived before she could speak.

"Do you want to get her killed? Never use her name again," Daenon spat.

Hann sneered at their clasped hands, but a flash of what seemed indecision crossed his face. He turned away from Daenon and faced Rowena. "You are our queen now. I know where we can hide, to keep you safe until we figure out what to do next."

She nodded to each man, unable to form words.

"Not him. He came with your uncle. We can't trust him," Hann said. "I'll protect you."

"You just pointed out her location for all who could hear." Daenon tightened his grip, squishing Rowena's palm against his.

Someone screamed in the distance. The noise mixed with the scent of churned up earth and blood. It was too overwhelming. Both men made sense, and she decided.

She squeezed back. "We'll all go together."

Daenon didn't wait for Hann's reply and hurried off toward the trees. Hann grumbled, but his heavy footprints pounding behind her said he followed.

They'd made it only twenty feet before shouts rang out, voices calling her name.

"Run faster! They've spotted you," Hann called.

She tried to turn and find who it was, but Daenon tugged her along, increasing his momentum. Her toe stubbed on a rock, so she grabbed hold of his arm with her free hand. Daenon kept her from falling, taking all of her weight upon his forearm, without a stumble.

A moment later, she gathered herself enough to keep up. Though it took two strides to match his one, she doubled her effort, refusing to fall again. Her father had taken her with him on short hunting trips over the years, where they'd played games of tag through the woods. She pushed aside all else and focused as if this moment was just another game, a test to see if her skills were sharp enough. Because if she thought of it any other way, she wouldn't want to go on. She'd want to curl up and die along with them.

She wasn't a quitter. Failure made her feel weak and vulnerable. It allowed others to treat her as incapable, underestimated. That would not happen. Her parents led Taesing with honor and integrity. She would do everything she could to continue their legacy.

They charged between the trees at the edge of the surrounding forest. The dim light forced her to adjust her sight quickly. The ground masked risen tree roots under a thin spongy layer of composted leaves as summer's thawing temperatures fought winter for control. Branches grabbed at them like claws from a mountain imp, tearing at their tunics and Rowena's loose hair.

A path used by varsler deer appeared and they took advantage, sprinting left. The narrow passage forced Daenon to release Rowena, but she stayed right on his heels. Hann's presence provided a comfort she wouldn't have guessed she needed before.

When the path forked ahead, Hann shouted to Daenon. "Go right!"

She gained a quarter step closer as the prince hesitated. His shoulders stiffened as if he wouldn't listen, but he veered right and they kept their momentum. The trail descended into a ravine, causing the need to lean back to keep their balance. Rowena recognized the area; she'd collected picha mushrooms nearby with her mother.

"Where are we headed?" Daenon flashed his square-jawed profile as he called back to Hann. "We need to keep the high ground. This path loses our advantage."

"We'll run through a shallow stream at the bottom to cover our tracks," Rowena answered for her friend.

Hann snorted behind her in a way that seemed to approve of her recognition of their surroundings. "There's a hunting cabin this way. No one knows of it but me."

They hopped down the path in silence after that, using tree roots like a staircase until the bubbling water came into view.

Daenon called out just before he reached the creek. "Which way?"

"West," Hann answered.

Of course, he had to say it that way. With the cloud-cover, there was no way to tell which direction Sawel's light came from, and Rowena had never learned to navigate with directions like that. She muttered a curse word under her breath, but followed

Daenon left, against the current, when he splashed into the water first.

The rocks were smooth, but that made them slippery. She stumbled more than once, but stayed moving forward on her own despite Hann's attempts to help. The challenge would not force her to act like a simpering female in need of rescue. She would honor her parents and survive to avenge them.

"Turn north where that birch hangs over the water ahead," Hann called to Daenon, who nodded his understanding.

For all her efforts, Rowena had to concentrate on her footing so much she could only follow. She lost track of the forest and any familiar landmarks and simply stayed upright. The path they'd traveled would be easy enough to follow back to Taesing when the time was right.

The cold water had soaked through her soft leather boots and numbed her feet. By the time they left the stream, she had to trust they were still under her, pushing for each step, and ignore the shooting needles as she regained feeling.

The hillside rose steeper on the opposite side of the creek, requiring her to take hold of branches for a boost now and then as she climbed. Daenon stopped ahead, and she sighed quickly at the prospect of a rest.

"How much farther?" he asked once they'd gathered.

The air from their heavy breathing fogged into the cool air. Steam rose from each of them, yet a chill prickled over Rowena's skin at the same time. It was afternoon, but winter still had a grip on the mountains the higher they went.

"There's a trail not far ahead. We follow it up the mountain until we reach a small open valley. The cabin is on the leeward edge of the meadow." Hann's tone had calmed, perhaps because of the exertion of their flight away from Taesing, or Daenon's willingness to follow his directions. Either way, it brushed a small amount of tension from Rowena's shoulders. "The cabin is rough, but solid. There's dry firewood inside."

Rowena quirked her lips at the added comment, understanding he meant it for her. Hann knew her so well—how she'd savor the prospect of warmth. "Let's get going then. Daylight is waning."

Before any of them moved, a noise echoed from the other side of the ravine. Distant voices. They were too far away to make out the words, but too close for them to take another second of rest.

"Go!" Hann whisper-yelled, spurring all of them to scramble into action.

A burst of fear jolted through Rowena, masking the way her muscles screamed. She raced after Daenon without hesitation.

Animals had worn the trail Hann mentioned into a ledge along the mountain's side. The only way to reach it forced them to hoist themselves over the edge. Daenon crawled over first and then twisted back to aid Rowena. But the steep angle caused him to topple. On his knees, he threw his hands up, trying to regain his balance, but he slid off the edge and rolled like a barrel.

Rowena lunged to the side, grabbing a branch to save herself from being taken down with him. A heavy grunt echoed below her. When she had a firm grip on a solid tree branch, she glanced over her shoulder to find Hann's arm wrapped around the prince, keeping him from tumbling farther through the trees.

Her friend strained to pull Daenon toward a protruding root so he could grab hold. A moment later, both men were on solid ground, huffing with relief, each supporting himself. Rowena's shoulders dropped an inch as she released a heavy sigh.

Daenon nodded and squeezed Hann's shoulder before he ascended back to the trail. He passed Rowena without a word. She wasted no time following in the same footholds he used to get herself onto the path. Hann emerged behind them seconds later, and they sped single file along the steep cliff.

The slip had cost them precious time. Though neither man had yelled out, the crashing rocks and branches had been enough to alert the group pursuing them. They hustled along the narrow trail, jogging faster on the somewhat smoother terrain. Exposed more, the wind cut at Rowena's cheeks and the colder temperatures at the higher elevation frosted her lungs as her legs burned with the incline.

A faint whisper in the back of her mind called to her desire for adventure. Despite the circumstances, she'd trained for just such a moment. It could be the spark she needed for her enchantment to begin as it had for her mother. Her heart beat a little harder in anticipation.

Except this wasn't a new land, and those chasing her weren't strangers. Her parents were dead, and she had to survive. She forced herself to concentrate on the current moment only.

The misty drizzle returned and formed into a light rain, creating puddles and slippery footing. Sometimes, there was enough room where Rowena couldn't touch the side of the mountain, or peek over the edge to the ravine below. Then, other times, her shoulder rubbed along the hillside with the steep drop-off impossible to ignore.

No one spoke. Puffs of mist exploded from each of them. As hard as she tried, the continual incline took its toll. Rowena slowly fell behind; a step at first and then two. Daenon rounded a corner, out of sight, and she forced herself to close the space between them. She dug her feet deeper into the soft soil to gain speed.

Without warning, the ground gave way beneath her. A scream erupted into the air. She scratched for anything to hold on to, but the dirt only crumbled between her fingers.

"Oof." All air burst from her in a grunt when she halted.

Strong hands held one of her wrists, but she gasped as she slipped again. Daenon dropped to his knees, tightening his grip. His wide eyes met hers as she dangled over the washed-out trail.

Her chest tightened, and her vision swirled. He'd never be able to pull her up . . . she was going to fall.

FIVE

"Don't let me fall." She heard the pitifulness in her plea, but her mind went blank of all else but survival.

Daenon didn't answer, but flattened his lips, emitting a low grunt as he fought to dig his heels into the mud, keeping them both in place without expanding the landslide. The misty air kept everything slick since the last rain.

Pressure against the bottom of Rowena's boot triggered her thoughts, a fissure of hope yawning. She may have found a foothold.

She slowly glanced down, careful of her movements. No! A choking wine left her throat. Her heart seized within her chest, afraid to beat. Hann's gaze met hers, deep brown, piercing. He clung to a branch below, lodged under his armpit, his elbow bent to hold on with one hand while he used his other to brace her foot in his palm. Her vision misted, and she blinked rapidly to keep sight of her friend, gasping as her body forced a breath.

"Climb, Rowena. Get to safety," Hann said calmly, yet the branch he clung to quivered and bent from his weight. "Move slow and steady. I'll follow."

"You have to," she called, tears freely rolling down her cheeks.

Hann's fingers were white from his effort to remain in place, even as his hold on her remained steady. Far below, exposed by the landslide, sat jagged boulders among tall sharp pine trees, waiting like silent assassins.

Steady and protective, Hann. She'd seen his nature as an attempt to stifle her desires, to hinder her freedom. But there he was, risking his precarious safety to keep her aloft. She was a fool to ignore her feelings for him.

"You climb first." His expression softened, and his gaze roved over her face. "I'll be fine."

Her arm wrenched as Daenon made progress, dragging her over the edge. She kept Hann's gaze as long as she could. "Hold on!"

"Go. Be safe, my queen." There wasn't any fear on Hann's face as he smiled. "Follow your destiny. Promise me."

"Don't say that. I need you." It was the tone of one who believed his life wouldn't continue.

"Rowena." His deep voice was soft, loving, pleading.

"I promise."

A heartbeat later, Daenon scrambled backward, dragging her over the ledge to safety.

"We need a branch . . . a rope . . . something," she cried and slipped in the mud as she scrambled to her feet, away from the ledge.

Most of the trail had fallen away in a large semi-circle, leaving a precarious section about a half-foot wide to scoot across. Daenon had pulled her to the downhill side, and she'd worry about getting across the gaping divide after they had helped Hann.

"Rowena, slow down." Daenon grabbed both shoulders and forced her to face him. "You'll slip again. You stay put, and I'll find something."

"He can't hold on much longer!"

"If you don't stop, you'll cause more damage and he'll fall for sure."

An icy chill flowed over her shoulders like a cloak and she glanced to the edge, nodding her understanding. She slipped from Daenon's grip.

The prince raced back the way they'd come, while she crawled slowly on hands and knees closer to the edge, but mud gave way under her palms and she had to retreat.

"Don't come any closer," Hann called out.

Her body shook from the cold or fear she couldn't tell. Rain drops blended with her tears while she stayed back.

Daenon arrived with a long, thin branch. He still held the axe he'd pulled from his belt and quickly knocked off several smaller branches and then lowered to the ground on his stomach. "Hold on to my feet, and I'll reach over the edge to him."

"Be careful. The edge will crumble." She braced her back against the mountain and wrapped her arms around the prince's feet, gritting her teeth to hold tight. Her arms trembled and her pulse raced, sounding like rolling thunder in her ears.

Daenon shimmied his way to the edge and lowered the branch. "Grab this."

Rowena jerked, folding over Daenon's boots when Hann's extra weight lurched the prince forward an inch.

She couldn't lose Hann as well. His warm brown eyes, glittering with mischief, asking her to play a game of tafl the night before, flashed through her mind. What she wouldn't do to have that moment back. She'd ignore her duties as a royal host and follow him. And when he said they were good together, she'd agree. Maybe even let him pull her close . . . she wouldn't waste another chance with him.

Daenon muttered something to Hann. Her friend's voice might have answered, but she couldn't tell. It wasn't the time for discussion. She doubled her efforts to pull both men from the ledge.

Then, in a blink, the prince's legs relaxed. As if in slow motion, she moved her gaze to stare at the edge.

Hann yelled out once.

Branches crashed.

Silence.

"Hann!" Rowena released Daenon and lunged toward the drop-off.

Daenon whirled and snatched her, flinging them both to safety. "Don't look. He's gone." He held her tight, too tight to move.

"Let me go." Rowena squirmed and kicked her heels into the ground. "I need to see him."

"You don't. Trust me." Daenon sagged and loosened his arms enough so she could meet his gaze.

Her body melted. Hann couldn't be gone. He was her best friend, her confidante. Even though she wasn't ready to marry, it was Hann she pictured standing beside when the time came. Her vision swirled and her limbs were heavy. She loved him. She had always loved him. Now he was gone before she could tell him.

They were all gone.

First, her mother. Over what? Jealousy? Or had they had planned it all along? Goetz had been the leader of the king's council her whole life. Yet he killed her father—and made it seem as if she'd done it. Why? Her father's pained expression as he stared at her before he collapsed would never leave her mind, or her heart. And now Hann. An image of a broken body, twisted and destroyed, came to mind. She swiped at her tears, smearing the idea away with them.

She had no one left. Tears streamed down her cheeks. Daenon wrapped his arms tighter around her shoulders. It was right that he hadn't allowed her to peer over the edge. She'd remember Hann as he'd always been. Strong, vibrant, protective, loving. Fresh tears filled her eyes.

Daenon whispered close to her ear. "The others are coming."

The reminder struck the part of her brain grasping for reason and forced her to rise alongside the prince. She glanced once more at the slippery edge and then to the washed-out trail. They had to go back the way they came.

She nodded without looking at Daenon. A heartbeat later, he dragged her by the hand down the trail, heading toward the oncoming attackers.

"We'll be outnumbered." Her voice echoed into the air as if from someone else. Some of her sense returned without her permission. She wasn't ready to function, but there wasn't time to grieve. She would, though, for them all. Later.

"The trail keeps going the other way, but we have to get past where we emerged from the trees before they do." Daenon yanked on her hand for her to pick up speed. His effort only made her stumble.

Rowena leaned back, using the prince's forward momentum to help her tear herself from his grip. He skidded to a halt. "There isn't time. Come, now!"

His nose wrinkled, anger burning through his cerulean eyes. It caused the tiny hair on her neck to rise as if a winter's storm approached. Why had he helped her get away?

"They're coming. Take my hand." He stretched out his palm, wiggling his fingers impatiently.

"I'll follow on my own," she spat, his glare sizzling darker, but she didn't care. Whatever his reason for running, she had her own. She would be strong for all of them. For everyone she loved who could no longer fight for themselves. No one would treat her as an incapable elfling. Not anymore.

"Fine, but keep up." He spun and raced away, but not before she saw the way he curled his lip in disgust.

She stayed a half step behind, her mind focused on the trail and nothing more. If she gave in to her pain, her loss, she'd never make it to safety.

They sprinted past the spot where they'd climbed onto the trail and voices rose from below to confirm the others were near—too close.

A hundred yards later, a running waterfall poured from a crevice on the mountain's side, cascading over the trail. The hillside had become a steep, craggy rock face, with a sheer drop-off on the other side.

Heavy footsteps thudded up the trail. It was too late. They had no choice but to turn and face the enemy with fist and dagger.

Three warriors rounded the corner and slipped to a halt in the mud.

"Here's your little princess, Soren," the first in line called over his shoulder.

The oaf she'd fought earlier arrived next and slid past the man to smirk at Rowena.

"You've nowhere to run and no one to help you this time," Soren said. His brows pinched for a moment as he glanced at the prince. "They have cast the runes. You can't change fate."

"Perhaps that's true." She glared at Soren. An hour ago, he'd beaten her with a practice sword. Now, he faced her with a true blade, which he would use to kill her if she gave him the chance. "But the druids of the Heptad do the weaving, and they may still change the spindle."

Her gaze drifted to the wall of stone at her left, where a flutter of movement caught her attention. On a tree branch, growing from a gap between boulders, a small white bird perched so pristine among the gray skies and muddy surroundings. It hopped up the branch closer to the wall and turned its head to stare directly at Rowena.

Follow, it seemed to say.

Rowena scanned the vertical hillside. Her heart lightened, and a peace settled over her, before she stared at the bird once more. A small grin tugged at the corner of her mouth. She dipped her chin in understanding and the bird instantly fluttered to a higher branch.

So caught in her reverie, Rowena hadn't heard three more warriors arrived. When she faced them again, Goetz snagged her stare. Her mouth went dry as if she'd stuffed it full of lamb's wool. Both terror and a fury she'd never experienced before flooded through her body, making her want to charge and flee at the same time.

"You've nowhere to run, Rowena. Come back with us and speak to the king," Goetz said.

"The king is dead. You killed him." She'd hoped that the revelation would surprise the men behind the advisor. Perhaps they hadn't known of their leader's betrayal. Except, none of them reacted.

"It's time for a new era. Come, be a part of it."

She narrowed her eyes at the traitor. He'd sided with Uther to overthrow her father. Fidessa had killed her mother. They could only want to kill her too—leave the throne for Uther to claim.

Her uncle would die for what he did, and his wife. She wouldn't let them destroy her parents' legacy.

Without another word, she pivoted. Facing the mountain, she dug her fingers into a crack in the rocks, and hauled herself up the side with as much haste as she dared.

"Row—" Daenon called for her. His fingers grazed her boot. But his grunts rang out a moment later as he climbed after her.

There were enough hand and footholds that she had scrambled too high to reach from the ground in only seconds. Without a doubt, Soren and the men with him would follow. It made little sense to put herself in a position to fall if they got hold of her, but she trusted that the white bird had urged her to follow it to safety.

She shoved her toes into a new foothold, but as she pushed herself up, her foot slipped, dangling by only her hands. A yelp ripped from her throat.

Daenon's firm hand caught her. Fingers wrenched around her foot; he pressed her toes back between the stones.

Chest heaving, she resumed her climb.

SIX

The climb was harder than Rowena expected. She hadn't paid attention to the steep grade or the effort it would take when she followed the bird. Despite how her arms and legs shook or her fingers bled, it had been the right thing to do.

"Keep going. They're following," Daenon grunted out below her.

He stayed just to the side, at her heels, while they worked their way up the slippery cliff. It made little sense why the prince would continue to help her, especially since he'd come to Taesing with his foster father, and probably knew about the planned attack. But he'd kept her from falling twice, and stayed by her. She couldn't ask for more in the current situation.

"Go!" he yelled.

She glanced over her shoulder; dizziness washed over her in a wave as she peered down. It spiraled into a surge of energy. The third man who'd arrived with Soren, smaller and wiry, reached close enough to grab Daenon's foot. The prince kicked and swiped at the man.

Rowena forced herself to find the next handhold, and the next. Blood rushed past her ears, quickly dulling the sounds of Daenon's fight below. All that mattered was the next step, the next few inches higher, one hand after the other.

Until fingers wrapped around her heel.

She screamed and recoiled as her heart raced in her chest.

"You're coming with us, princess," Soren's voice snapped. He tried to tug her foot out of the crevice where her toes clung.

The crack was long. One foot became secured enough that she could let go of her right hand and grab the seax on her belt. She swallowed and counted her breaths to slow her heart and mind as she worked her hand between her body and the cliff to the handle.

Her knuckles scraped against the rock as the weapon came free. She swung her arm down, slashing through the air without aim, hoping she hit any part of the oaf.

His scream and the momentary lifting of his fingers told her she had found her mark. She slammed her blade down once again. The reverberation in her arm needed no explanation. The man fell away, nearly taking the seax with him. Rowena had to grip harder to dislodge it from above Soren's ear. She watched him fall, and a pit formed in her gut. None of her training had prepared her for the violence of true combat. The coppery scent of blood combined with the sticky residue on her hands and face made her gag. But she couldn't stop to cry or care. She had to press on.

The big man, who'd led the three originally, remained on the trail below. His glare burned into her as Soren's limp body landed in a heap. A moment later, the wiry man Daenon fought also hit the path near Soren, but rolled and kept going over the edge, to the forest below.

She returned her focus to the climb and shoved the long knife back into her belt. Wiping her fingers on her tunic, she took a breath and then reached for the next hold. Hand over hand, she didn't stop until she reached a small ledge. The men hadn't continued to follow and as she rolled herself to her stomach along what had to be a mountain goat trail. She caught sight of the remaining three men hustling back toward Taesing.

"Rowena, make room," Daenon said as he reached the ledge.

She inched her way to her feet, holding the rocky side to steady herself. The small path wouldn't allow her to have both feet side by side. Keeping her midsection against the stone, she edged higher along the trail.

Daenon's hand wrapped around her own a few steps later. She twisted her neck to meet his gaze.

"You did well." He held her stare for several heartbeats.

His compliment warmed through her, but also muddled her thinking. They were still in danger. It was an odd reason to stop her right then. She gave him a confused nod and turned back to inching along the narrow trail.

What seemed like hours later, the path ended on top of a large, flat boulder. Rowena dropped to her knees and crawled out of the way for Daenon to rest beside her. Her parched throat and lips begged for more air and her limbs fell to her sides like wilted rampion.

Daenon's heavy breathing matched her own as they lay in silence.

The skies overhead stayed the rain, but remained the same gray they'd been all day, only darker with the fading light. Early afternoon had turned to evening as she and Daenon raced away from her home.

It wasn't her home any longer. How could it be? Tears rolled down her temples and into her hair.

"We can't stay here overnight. We'll need shelter before it gets too dark." Daenon spoke into the air from the sounds of it, and he was correct.

"Let's go before my body tightens to match this stone," she said. She understood the process well from all her training. After a hard sword practice, it would sometimes become difficult to lift a mug to her lips. If they didn't keep moving, her legs would stiffen, unable to maneuver along the terrain. She might as well have stayed in Taesing and let someone kill her if that happened.

She rolled to her stomach and brought in her knees, pushing herself to stand. Daenon matched her movements. Then they both scanned the mountains. From their height, the view stretched to the bay and the sea beyond. Sharp pines covered the steep mountainside, ending at the plains that surrounded Taesing. Smoke from meal fires rose above the rooftops like dancing ribbons, as if nothing far below had changed.

Her eyes stung, and mist covered her vision. She spun away before she crumpled into a tear-filled heap. Rowena pointed at a small opening in the rocks higher up. "There."

Daenon nodded and then led the way. They moved just in time as a light, misty rain fell. The boulder would have proved too slippery if they'd waited any longer. As it was, they moved slow and steady, moving along a more uneven trail than before. Step-like stones provided the way, but were difficult to manage scooting sideways.

Drenched and exhausted, they finally reached the opening of a small, triangular-shaped cave cut between large boulders.

Daenon stepped aside at the opening and motioned for Rowena to go in first. She hesitated. The skies grew darker by the minute as evening closed in. Little of the day's remaining light penetrated inside the space, so any number of beasts could have already bedded down in the cozy shelter. She squatted to pick up a palm-sized stone and tossed it into the dark space.

The prince raised his brows and nodded in approval of her gesture. When nothing but the echo of stone on stone met their ears, she ducked into the space. The tight quarters required dropping to her knees to scoot around and sit with her back against the side.

The floor of the cave would be long enough for them to lie down sideways to the opening, but it wasn't any higher than her shoulders, if that. For Daenon, that would only be mid-chest, most likely. However, the small space would trap enough heat to keep them warm through the night.

A heartbeat later, Daenon landed next to her with a deep sigh. She pulled her knees to her chest and allowed herself to relax as much as was possible. If not for the exertion of the climb, she wouldn't have been capable of it. And without Daenon's help, she never would have made it to safety at all.

"Thank you." Her quiet words disappeared into the dark.

Daenon reached over and took one of her hands into his, at the same time he worked his other arm around her shoulders. He pulled her against his chest, snuggled and secure. "I'm sorry about your mother."

"And my father." And Hann. Her friend's name lodged in her throat.

Daenon's chest tightened as he held his breath and then squeezed her tighter. "Him too."

They sat in silence, their bodies giving off warmth and steam with an unwashed musk. Rowena's thoughts turned to Hann. The night before, she'd teased him he needed a bath, and he'd playfully edged closer to her. She'd thought he was going to kiss her, but then he'd only whispered in her ear how much he'd been sure she liked his scent.

If he'd known about the way her skin had pebbled at his touch, or how he'd captured her breath being so close, maybe he wouldn't have walked away. Now, she'd never feel his lips on hers again. Why had she pushed him away so hard?

"Rowena?"

"Hmm?" Daenon's voice brought her out of her thoughts, and she pulled her hand free of his, vaguely realizing he'd said something else. "What was that?"

A chuckle rumbled under her cheek. "I was asking what made you decide to climb the cliff instead of going through the water? It was a daring move."

"Did you see the bird? It was so stark white against the rock, and it stared at me as if peering into my mind."

Daenon didn't answer for a long moment. "I had my focus trained on the men with swords."

"Goetz would sometimes lead my training. He was tough, but fair. I didn't think he'd really try to hurt me." What had made him turn against her family? It was another spike to her heart, another loss.

"I don't think you can count on your father's councilman any longer."

"I don't understand why everyone insists on trying to decide my fate for me. Runes or weaving, it makes no difference. I'll find my own way." She wriggled, trying to get more comfortable on the hard ground, and Daenon tightened his arm around her shoulders.

"Uther tosses runes every morning, and Fidessa scoffs at him each time. She says the fae were all one once and will be again. She believes the old ways of Caelus will return soon."

"How? I doubt the gods will allow that."

"Probably true." Daenon let out a heavy sigh. "I don't think it matters, anyway. What we see is what there is. We live, and we die. Nothing more. We take what we want or lose out. There's no other bigger purpose."

That might have been easier to think, but she didn't believe him. Her mother believed the same as Fidessa did about the fae, oddly. If they were right and there was a bigger fate to look forward to, it was too much for her to think about right then. Her heart continued to beat while her family lay dead. Nothing made sense.

Not even why the prince had helped her.

Rowena frowned into the dark. "Goetz has sided with Uther, and you defied him to help me. Why?"

"Perhaps I'm charmed by you. Did you use Lunara magic on me?"

A sarcastic laugh bubbled out of her. "I couldn't if I tried. Besides, mages use charms. Enchanted magic doesn't work that way."

"Your mother, and you, are the only enchanted I've ever met."

She tried to search for the magic she'd felt earlier. The kernel that would prove she'd inherited her mother's Lunara abilities. But she was hollow. Numb. "I'm not like my mother."

"Uther says that you were born during the Burning Moon. That it makes you dangerous. Does he have that wrong?"

Uther said that? She huffed, adjusting her back against the hard stone wall. "It means nothing."

Daenon swiped a pebble toward the cave entrance. "Some say it might tie you to the prophecy."

"I'm sure it doesn't." Who said such things? Her father had always stopped the conversation if he heard anyone speak of her connection to the Burning Moon or the Reaping. He'd say to leave things be. Yet, she'd overheard her parents arguing about it once. He'd told her mother to wait until Rowena's prime day to say more. She needed to think about that, but it wasn't something to share with the prince.

"Hmm." Daenon leaned his cheek on top of her head, and ran his free hand down the side of her face, letting his thumb caress her jaw.

His caress muddled her thinking. It was so soft and kind, but odd. She had gotten no hints that the prince cared for her. Not that she'd asked him to comfort her. In the darkness, his cinnamon scent with hints of pepper burrowed their way into her senses. His fingers found their way to her ear, slipping up to the point and back down the other side. It wasn't unpleasant, yet there was a danger in it. A sense of need that she neither expected nor wanted.

She wiggled to remove herself out from under his arm, but Daenon gripped her shoulder tighter. "I'll rest against the stone now. Alone."

"What makes you mourn your father? Was he kind?"

His questions caught her off guard. She stilled. "Of course. He loved me." She didn't want to speak of her father with him. Her feelings were too raw to share with someone she barely knew. At the moment, though, she had more concerns about Daenon's intentions. She forced herself to breathe even.

"What was that like? Do you think he was proud of you?" He didn't wait for her to answer, continuing on as if he spoke more to himself than to her. "Time is running out for me to make my father proud. Another month. That's all I've got left."

Rowena pushed against his chest. Yet again Daenon dug his fingers stronger. She was a warrior, she could fight, but this was . . . different? He seemed lost in his own troubles. Perhaps he didn't realize what he was doing. "Let me go, Daenon."

"There has to be a reason he sent me to that gods-forsaken place. Uther thinks himself a king, but has no control over Forsa. The place is a boil on a bonnacon's arse."

"You're hurting me." Daenon had coiled her hair in his fingers, yanking against her scalp as he spoke. She slapped him with her free hand.

"He thinks he can force me to marry a stinking Lunara. Join the might of Velmeg and Taesing, giving him control over both islands."

Lunara? Did he mean her? She pounded her fist against his ribs over and over, squirming to get out from under him. "Stop! Go away."

Daenon brought his lips closer to her ear. "I won't let him gain more power than my father. That has to be why he traded me away. It's up to me to keep that dimwit from gaining control over both islands."

Time slowed down. Why couldn't she save herself? If she could reach for her knife, she would slit his throat.

Daenon pulled her hair, making her neck bend backward to meet his gaze. His eyes were hard and glittered with hate, nostrils flaring. "Uther thinks you're the key to his success."

Rowena's heart pounded against her chest. Her mouth grew dry. The small space restricted her ability to fight. She had to get out of his grip. She kicked.

Daenon slammed his knee into her thigh. "You won't be a compliant wife, will you?"

"Get off." Rowena pinched her lips closed and turned her head from one side to the other as Daenon tried to kiss her. Her shoulders rubbed against the wall as her body shifted farther down to the floor. Her thigh hurt, bruising deep enough she feared he'd crush her bone.

Daenon shifted his weight and grabbed her under the knee, yanking her flat onto her back. Pebbles from the stone floor dug into her spine. She couldn't breathe. This wasn't happening. Once, a few years ago, she'd accidentally walked around a corner to witness a maid, leaning against a barrel with a guard, plunging himself into her like a horse in spring. For a moment back then she'd stood, unable to turn away, frozen with indecision. Her mind found that same spot for a split second.

Daenon had her arms pinned over her head with one hand, his knee still digging into her thigh, while he worked her belt with his other hand. He let out a guttural roar, unable to get the buckle unlatched. In the middle of everything so heinous, his effort seemed amusing. As if the whole thing was so ridiculous, it couldn't really be happening. She must have fallen asleep. It was an outlandish dream gone bad.

Except the stone in her back felt all too real. Her tunic stuck to her skin from the blood oozing from cuts. Fingers pinched her wrists, probably leaving bruises.

Daenon grunted and growled out a curse as he finally released the buckle, allowing his hand access to lift her tunic and cup his hand over her breast.

Rowena gasped and froze. The action was so egregious she couldn't move. But when he dragged his fingers down to the edge of her trousers, her mind cleared. He'd left one of her legs free and she thrust it up hard between his legs. The prince moaned, but didn't move. Still trapped, she wriggled and fought the best she could, unable to free herself.

She screamed out, more from anger than fear. How could she be so helpless? She had a weapon . . . stuck under her hip where she couldn't reach it. Tears stung the back of her eyes as she lost hope. She tried to thrust her knee again, but he maneuvered his other knee between her legs.

In a last attempt, she forced her head into his, cracking her skull into his nose. Daenon grabbed his nose, lifting the pressure on her wrists enough that she pulled one arm free. She slapped against his shoulder, and when she connected, a jolt of energy surged through her arm into her palm. It wasn't a sensation she'd ever experienced. Instead of giving it any more thought, she pressed her hand against the prince's ribs and screamed.

Power built in her chest and raced through her arm like fire. When it hit Daenon, the force threw him into the rough stone wall. Silver light sparked, lighting the cave in a flash. Rowena scrambled backward, pinning herself against the corner of the cave, knees bent, hands outstretched, ready if he came closer.

Daenon rolled to his knees, staring at Rowena.

"Witch."

"Get out."

The prince's chest heaved. Even in the low light, she could see his face had a feverish flush. Without another word, Daenon hurried out of the cave. The sudden emptiness left her feeling hollow, unsure, terrified.

She wrapped her arms around her knees and tried to steady her breathing. Tears came then. A small trickle that turned steady until she rested her forehead against her knees and sobbed.

SEVEN

A deep, penetrating cold forced Rowena awake. She shoved herself to a sitting position from where she lay on the cold stone floor. Her shoulder ached, but that was nothing compared to the sharp sting on her back or the throbbing pain in her thigh. Somehow, she'd fallen asleep, and stayed that way for some time. The skies were the deep purple of dawn, lighting the cave enough to discover that she was still alone.

She scrambled to her knees and crawled to the edge, listening. No rustling or noises other than early morning bird calls echoed through the forest. Tentatively, she emerged to stand upright on the slim trail. She groaned and rubbed at her shoulder and then her wrists.

Daenon wasn't anywhere in sight. Wherever he'd gone, she needed to be away before he came back. The prince was as bad as the rest of them. She'd only jogged a few paces, but had to stop, crossing her arms over her chest, huddling down in a crouch. What he'd done—what he'd tried to do—the images came flooding back. The dark cave, the stones cutting into her back, the feeling of helplessness . . . she turned and heaved. There wasn't anything left in her stomach, but she retched as if there were.

If she just lay down and gave up, eventually she'd end up with everyone else. Wouldn't she? No. She'd done nothing of valor to make it to the hero fields. She had no enchantment like her mother. The Primary Fae of Caelus would want nothing to do with her. She'd end up spending eternity with the King of Kur under the mounds of Mortus. Forever reliving her mistakes, able to see every choice she should have made but didn't. She'd never get a rest from her pain; it would only grow worse and never end. Those like Daenon would paw at her every moment and she wouldn't be able to stop them.

Her chest tightened again. She straightened and clenched her fists until she willed her heartbeat to slow. After everything else Uther, Fidessa, and Daenon had taken from her, she still had her own mind, her own will. They would not break her. She would survive. She set her gaze on the path ahead and took a trembling step, and then another.

The trail continued in a steep trajectory, forcing her progress to a crawl. Sawel had lifted above the horizon and colored the skies in pink and brilliant blue before the clouds rolled in again, cloaking the day in the usual dull gray. On the side of the trail, she spotted several small bushes clumped together, each one weighed down with bilberries. On one branch, a little white bird chirped before fluttering away. It couldn't be the same one from before. Surely not. However, her stomach rumbled at the sight of the berries.

"Thank you." She said the words aloud to the bird, just in case someone had sent it to help her once again. Rowena plucked a handful of the ripe berries, showing a slight shade of purple as the smooth, round fruit piled into her palm. The juices coated her parched tongue, creating a sigh of relief.

After another handful, she took a moment to study her surroundings. Not far to her left, she halted, and her breath froze. A beautiful rowan tree rose above the brush near the trail only a few paces from where she'd rested. Myth said the first fae planted the sacred tree when they arrived in Edenia as a tribute to the Great

Guardian Osric, who'd provided a haven for them after The Chasm.

It was the perfect place to give a tribute to her parents and Hann. She'd never have the chance to take part in the formal offerings and rituals that Asta would have led her through, but she could do as much as she could on her own to help guide their way to the god realm.

Rowena returned to the bilberry bushes and plucked a handful. After checking the trail in both directions, where nothing seemed out of place, she kneeled near the tree. She withdrew her seax, thanked the tree for an offering, and then cut a small branch.

"I've found these small tributes to help you on your way." She used the branch to draw three interconnecting upside-down triangles. "May all three of you find your way to the hero grounds in Caelus."

Tears pricked at Rowena's eyes until they blurred her vision and dribbled down her cheeks, where they fell into the soft soil. "Since I have no ale, please accept my tears as refreshment on your journey. These berries will sustain you. I remember how much you love them, Mor."

Her shoulders shook, and she huddled over her lap. She wasn't a druid. It was no use trying to hide her feelings. She spoke to aloud to her parents, hoping they could hear. "How will I go on without you? I need you both. Hann is there. Look for him. Tell him I loved him. I should have honored your wishes and accepted his betrothal."

She lay the rowan branch on the ground near the tribute, folding herself over her knees. Tears fell like a winter storm, her nose dripping without care. Nothing would ever be the same.

Sawel ambled higher in the sky while she cried herself dry, and even after that. She left everything there in the dirt until her mind went blank. All she could do was sit, numb. For how long, she didn't know or care. Nature continued to thrive regardless of her crushed life. Small creatures rustled through the brush. Birds took flight and landed again, calling to each other with cheery tunes. None of it held any consequence.

But, after a time, she heard a whistle. Not the kind that came from nature. Rowena's senses stirred, despite how she wanted to fade away. She forced herself to listen more intensely, realizing that the natural sounds had halted.

Instincts kicked in. She jumped to her feet, swiping her face clean, and flattened herself to the cliff side, dragging her seax from her belt. A rock tumbled from the trail in front of her, clattering against the rocks as it bounced downhill. Daenon must have been ahead of her. She spun and hurried back the way she'd come, searching for any place she could get off the rocky goat trail.

Not more than ten paces later, she noticed a break between some vines crawling up the side of the rocks. She slipped her hand between them to reveal a narrow passage through a crevice in the mountain. The walls were steep on both sides, but it would be wide enough for her to ease through. Deer tracks were visible in the mud, proving it must have another way out.

The idea of placing herself into such a tight space made her hands and legs shake. Perhaps she only had to hide behind the vines for a short time. The white bird arrived again, twittering while it hopped on a branch farther down the trail. She swallowed hard, breathing slowly through her mouth, and stepped into the dark passage.

She didn't go far, hoping Daenon passed her by. The wet earth smell overpowered the few plants that dared to grow out the side of the fissure. Between that and the chill, Rowena couldn't wait to find the end to the slim path. Tight places never used to bother her, but after the night before, it would take time to feel comfortable again . . . if she ever could.

Mud covered her shoulders from where she kept scraping along the walls. She had to shuffle sideways in spots.

Finally, more light shined up ahead, signaling she'd reached the end. She exited into an area where the trees had changed from pine to aspen mixed among hawthorn and bilberry bushes. Such relief washed over her; she didn't see the warrior until he stepped in front of her with Daenon at his side.

She spun to head back the way she'd come, but a large, gloved hand wrapped around her mouth from behind.

"Too late, princess," a voice whispered into her ear. The scent of onion stew mixed with the rank leather nearly made her gag.

Rowena kicked and bucked, but the man pinned her arms to her sides with his thick arm. He smashed her to his chest and lifted her off her feet.

Spots covered her vision as her heart pounded against her chest with an erratic beat. Her breath came in quick shallow gasps, while she felt faint. Not again. The large hands touching her body gave her chills. She kicked and bucked.

"Don't let her touch you." She recognized that voice. A whine escaped her throat without her consent. Goetz had found her. And brought guards with him.

Her captor pinched his grip harder, one arm snaking around the front of her shoulders, while a second guard stepped into view. He grabbed her hands and smashed her palms together. Then, he wrapped rope tightly around her wrists, leaving a long tail like a lead for a horse.

"You're coming back home, princess," Goetz said. He had the audacity to give her a half smile.

"Why?" It was the only word she could squeeze out, muffled behind the man's glove. It was the only answer she needed.

Goetz inhaled, his nostrils flaring before he spoke. "Because your father refused to listen. He should have left you in the woods the day you were born. Time has run out and he would allow all of Taesing to suffer for your sake."

He made no sense. How could he think her father would ever harm her—or that he had a reason to? She spat, but all that came out was a scrawny spattering that didn't come near the advisor her father had trusted.

Daenon ambled next to Goetz, giving Rowena a pitying grin. "Did you really think I wanted you? I just needed to see if you had your mother's enchantment. You obviously don't know what you're doing, but your efforts were helpful."

He'd done all that just to test her? Somehow, she doubted it had all been an act. If she held her mother's enchantment, then what he'd said—what he'd done—had been his desire; she'd only enhanced his emotional state. Perhaps, he didn't know how it worked.

"I am sorry about last night. Let's put all that business behind us, shall we? Besides, what I said was most likely from your doing, anyway."

Interesting that that was his concern. Not that he'd touched her in ways he shouldn't have or that he'd tried to do worse to her body while she fought and told him not to. She'd been right that he didn't understand enchantments. The information he shared may serve her later, but she certainly wouldn't forgive him. She flattened her lips and said nothing.

"We're going home where a stronger king will do what we have needed for far too long." Goetz motioned for her captor to let her go and turned to Daenon, slapping him on the back like a friend.

It made no sense. They'd at least took her silence for compliance and left her feet free. The large man who'd grabbed her tugged on the rope, pulling her free from the large man at her back. The movement dragged her closer to Goetz like an animal.

"Make no more trouble, Rowena. I only need to deliver you. Your uncle didn't say in what condition."

She didn't bother with an answer and just turned away from the traitor . . . both traitors?

Goetz led the group through the trees and down a trail that wound around easier than the other side of the mountain had been. She learned quickly to watch her step, otherwise her designated watchdog picked her up.

They made it to the creek at the bottom of the valley and

stopped for a rest near midday. Rowena kept her mouth clamped tight when they offered her a piece of salted fish, despite how her stomach screamed. She wouldn't acknowledge her discomfort and give them any satisfaction. Anger would fill her belly well enough.

The men talked amongst themselves, but Daenon sat to the side, alone. She had so many questions, but the only one that mattered was why? Had they found him when he went scouting and forced him to betray her? That was an easier answer to swallow than the alternative that she'd been dim, allowing herself to be duped.

It seemed an unreasonable response from her rejection of his kiss. The rational part of her mind tried to tell her he'd never cared for her. But none of it really mattered. They were dragging her back to Taesing, where her uncle had murdered her parents and most likely would kill her too.

They arrived in the village by late afternoon. A few sheep rambled through the village unattended. No merchants or children milled about. No mothers shouted, no men shared ale and laughed.

When they shoved her through the longhouse doors, her stomach recoiled and her feet became too heavy to move. At the far end, Uther sat on her father's throne. Beside him, sitting in her mother's, Fidessa grinned.

"Get moving, girl," her guard said, using his huge hand to shove her forward.

Goetz spun and grabbed her arm. He dragged her past the hearth fires to stand before her uncle.

"That took longer than I expected."

"We had to find out if she'd use her magic," Goetz said.

Uther nodded and twisted to stare at Daenon. "And did she?"

"Yes. She's every bit Lunara," the prince answered.

Rowena shook her head. Daenon had been working with them all along. Her shoulders wilted, and she stared at the floor.

"Your mother was powerful, a royal from Penumar," Uther

said. "It makes sense she passed her abilities to you, even with only half the heritage, based on when you were born."

Fidessa scoffed. "The Burning Moon only lasted a day. She could have been born before or after."

Uther narrowed his eyes as if trying to peer into Rowena's essence. "She was born early in the day, but I'm positive the event had begun."

He didn't know for sure? Had he come here just because of that stupid prophecy? It made no sense. All he had to do was ask. Everyone knew she lacked enchantment. Until it showed up in the cave. Why commit treason before he confirmed her status?

"You killed my parents, your own brother. What makes you think I'd ever help you?" Rowena snapped.

"True." Uther scratched his beard. "But if you have anything to do with the prophecy, you won't be able to stop yourself from using your power. My brother would have held you back. He would have feared your full range of skills. I won't."

A grumbled oath muttered from Fidessa. So unlike Rowena's mother's refinements—she didn't deserve to sit on the queen's throne.

They would both regret sitting in those chairs.

"If I am who you think, you should have thought twice about killing everyone I loved."

Uther threw his head back and laughed. The sound ricocheted off the walls and pelted her like an ice storm. Try as she might, she couldn't call upon the powers she'd summoned the night before. Not that it would do her any good unless she could touch the traitorous fool.

"So feisty. Perhaps, to put me in my place, we should have a demonstration of your skills?" Her uncle leaned forward. "Or do you not yet possess the Lunastone?"

The what? Rowena's head was spinning over all that kept happening. This wasn't something she understood.

"Did your parents tell you nothing?" Fidessa asked. "Or are you too simple-minded to understand?"

Rowena gritted her teeth, her fists tightened at her side. If not for Goetz's hand that took hold of her arm, she may have launched herself at the insolent woman.

"I can vouch for her in this," the former councilman said. "Her father did not wish for her to carry the burden of her fate, hoping he could spare her from it. It's unlikely she knows anything of the heartstones."

Uther fell back into the throne, leaning against one arm as he studied her. "Well then, I supposed there's nothing to fear from her after all. Search my brother's bedchambers. He would have kept the armor close, and it wasn't on his body."

Rowena lost all ability to breathe as if a hammer had smacked her in the stomach. Uther spoke of her father as if he wasn't the most powerful man in Skandan. Nothing more than a deer felled for the winter stores.

Three men hurried around the wall behind the thrones, into her parents' chambers, to follow his orders. The idea of their things ransacked and tossed about added another weight to her shoulders.

Her uncle would pay for what he'd done. She wasn't sure how, but he would.

An icy wind blew through the longhouse, causing the hearth fires to flicker higher and dance in eerie shadows on the walls. Several men's voices and the sound of scuffling feet reached her ears, but she didn't turn. She kept watch for what they might find among her parent's belongings.

Someone bumped against her shoulder and forced her to stumble a step sideways and pay attention to the newcomers.

Five of Uther's men forced a group of Taesing warriors closer to the thrones. "We found these gathered in the forest at the edge of the village," a brutish man said, his scraggly dark hair hanging over his shoulders.

"I offered pardons to any who would pledge their fealty to me on the battlefield. I made myself clear about the consequences if they refused. Why would you drag these before me?" Uther asked.

"They begged to change their minds and ask for your forgiveness." There was a hint of humor in the big man's voice.

Bile crept up Rowena's throat. As much from the scene as from the men who would switch loyalties so easily. She recognized one who she'd sparred with before. "Petr, you would dishonor your true king and pledge to this usurper? I remember when you arrived in Taesing, hungry and poor. My father brought you in—you slept right here in this room. You apprenticed with the smithy so you could earn a wage when you returned home. After all that, you turn your back on his memory?"

The man, only a few years her senior, perhaps twenty summers, darted a glance in her direction, then over her shoulder at Goetz before he returned his gaze to the floor.

"Is that true? Did my brother give you so much hospitality?" Uther asked.

Petr nodded, speaking in a low, quivering voice, "King Olve was very kind to me."

"He was an excellent king to everyone," one of the other men spoke up. She recognized his face but couldn't remember meeting him personally.

"Yet, you wish to beg mercy from me."

"We wish to spare our families further heartbreak," the same man answered.

Uther drummed his fingers on the arm of the throne. "That is a noble sentiment that I can appreciate. However, if my brother treated you so well, and now you're here to beg mercy from me, how are you to be trusted?"

Rowena snapped her gaze to her uncle. Something about his calm tone reminded her of a predator about to strike. Goosebumps rose on her arms.

Uther raised his chin in a silent command to one of his men.

"No!" she yelled, but her voice disappeared among the screams of her father's men as swords ran through their backs or knives slit their throats.

Their blood soaked into the wooden floor as the warm, coppery scent filled the air. Rowena's breath caught before she leveled a glare at the man responsible.

The men from her parents' chambers returned just then. Two carried a large trunk between them, and others were laden down with smaller items. One carried a locked box, carved with intricate patterns of stars with Edenia's two moons on the top. Rowena nearly gasped, but caught herself.

In the box was her great-grandfather's sword. The blade her mother had smuggled out of Penumar when she fled for her life alongside her mother, Jarl Unna. It was a family heirloom, one that Uther had no claim upon. As much as it pained her, he may claim his brother's title by heredity. But he had no right to her mother's things.

They deposited all the items at the base of the dais.

"Take this garbage away," Uther said, waving to the dead men and then turned his attention to those who'd searched the bed chambers. "Well? What did you find?"

"We filled the bigger trunk with all the gold, silver, and jewels, but found nothing magical. Though we could not break the lock on that box," one man said.

"I've never seen that box open," Goetz said. He'd stayed silent during the murder of men he should have considered friends. "It was to be given to Rowena on her prime day."

If Rowena still had her seax, she would bury it in his belly. She'd make sure none of these traitors ever touched her mother's sword.

EIGHT

Rowena sat on the edge of her bed, staring at the room she'd lived in her entire life, yet it was no longer hers. She found Bia under the furs where she'd left her, running her fingers over the doll's embroidered smile. Never had she feared for her life, or felt so alone.

Uther had posted a guard outside her door. His shadow covered the wooden floorboards just beneath the door. What was he waiting for? Wasn't she next to be murdered?

Her door opened without a knock.

"King Uther commands you to come," the guard said.

He wanted a spectacle most likely. Kill her in front of everyone to prove there was no one left to challenge his rule. "I don't follow his commands."

"I'm to bring you, no matter what. If you'd like to put up a fight, I wouldn't mind." He dragged his gaze down over her body with a leering smirk. Pig.

She rose and ambled closer. "Keep looking at me like that and you'll find your throat cut."

A big grin opened between his bushy black beard and

mustache. Yellowed teeth matched his foul breath. Ibernians were disgusting—did they never use a comb or tooth sticks?

She arched a brow and waited for the man to move out of her way. If he hadn't entered to kill her, there wasn't any chance she'd get closer and allow him to touch her.

He grumbled, stepped aside, and followed her a little too close to the main room. Next time, she'd remember to keep her enemy in front of her. She should have known better.

"Keep your dogs at a distance, Uther," she said when she strolled to the front of the dais.

"Be thankful I kept them outside your door."

She glared at her uncle. His gaze matched her own and never wavered. All hints of the man who'd arrived in Taesing with promises of peace and family reunions had disappeared.

Twenty others, perhaps more, sat at tables or milled around in the longhouse. All of them were restless, speaking in low tones with furtive glances to the thrones.

A man, thin and weasel-featured, entered the hall, hurrying toward Uther without diverting his gaze from the floor.

Rowena tracked him. He was one of Uther's men and should be relaxed now that his king controlled Taesing. What was his hurry?

The man didn't bow before the throne, but hurried straight up the three steps and whispered into Uther's ear. The king leaned back and said nothing after the man finished with his message, inviting Rowena's curiosity. When someone had done that with her father, it always meant trouble.

Uther nodded to the man. "Let's get on with things, then."

The man gave a shallow bow and scurried back the way he came, leaving a trail of discontent like bouncing dust motes in a ray of sunshine.

"Come," Uther said to no one. Everyone strode down the steps and through the longhouse.

Fidessa rose and followed along with all the others seated at tables. Rowena stayed where she was. Until the same dreg that had been at her door arrived at her side.

"You too, princess," the man spat.

"I've no interest in his plans."

"You'll want to see this, I'll bet." He grabbed her upper arm and yanked along next to him. His touch made bile rush up to rest in the hollow of her throat. Her knee knocked against a bench, causing her feet to tangle. The man let her fall before reaching to haul her up by the back of her tunic.

She twisted out of his grip. "Don't touch me again."

He sneered and stood upright, resting his hand on the axe in his belt, waiting.

Rowena righted herself and strode for the door of her own accord, though the bruise blooming on her leg screamed and her hands shook from how easily men could toss her around.

When they made it outside, the skies had turned the dark gray with purple and tangerine streaks, sneaking through the heavy clouds during the last vestige of dusk. Sawel was giving way to Masah. The gentle waning moon already glowed on the horizon as the fortune tide reached its height.

The rains held back, but the misty air made Rowena's trousers damp against her legs. Mud squelched under her boots as she marched in front of the Ibernian guard. They'd made it to the open square where her father made village announcements. Rowena slowed, expecting they would stop.

When she scanned the area and didn't see anyone gathering, she turned her gaze to movement in the distance. Peering between the blacksmith hut and a family lodging, two men dug a hole at the apex of a small rise. Dirt mounded in the grasses.

No, it wasn't dirt. It was a shrouded body—her father. The King of Skandan lay on the ground without honor. Where were his men? Was there no one left to pray to the gods for his carriage to the hero grounds?

Rowena raised her arms and tilted her chin to the clouds,

adding another prayer to the ones she'd given on the trail earlier. "May the druids carry you through the Primary Spring and escort you—"

"None of that," the guard growled. The flat top of his axe butted into Rowena's kidney. "Get moving."

Folding over, Rowena coughed and fought to catch her breath. When the pain subsided, she spun and swung her fist through the air at the man. He stood a head taller and outweighed her by double. "He's my father and your king!" she screamed.

The man avoided her punch and lunged forward. He knocked the back of his knuckles across Rowena's face and sent her sprawling to the mud.

Blinding light followed by shooting pain disoriented Rowena until the wet ground soaked into her clothes and cleared her senses. She pushed to her hands and knees, spitting out the slimy muck she'd bitten. Her cheek was already swelling, and it felt like an arrow pierced through her skull.

A rough hand jerked her the rest of the way to her feet. "No more of that or I'll drag you by your hair. Walk."

She glanced once more at the field in time to see the two men drop her father's body into the shallow grave. An anvil's weight crushed her chest, but she closed her eyes, swiping at the mud on her face to give herself time for a few shallow, calming breaths. Uther would pay for what he'd done. Fidessa would pay. Daenon would pay. She'd make sure of it.

The butt of the axe shoved between her shoulders. She stumbled forward, one eye clear, the other blurry, as they headed toward the docks.

A crowd had gathered. "Out of the way!" Her captor used her like a battering ram to forge a path.

Rowena's knees threatened to buckle when they reached the front. Her uncle stood halfway out on the main dock, next to a longboat decorated in flowers. A moan crept out of her throat and tears fogged away the rest of her vision even as her feet carried her over the wooden planks.

Her mother's body rested in a small fishing boat, on her back, shrouded, serene and regal. A wreath of primrose and jasmine encircled her head over the gauzy fabric. A simple bundle of phlox, moonflower, and evening lilies nestled in her hands that laid on her stomach. The moonlight scents were perfect for the queen. They were her favorites. The ones she and Rowena would have picked together if they'd been able to go out the night before the world turned bleak.

Someone had dressed her mother in the ceremonial gown she wore for special occasions, and all three of her golden neck rings rested in place. They placed candles all around her body, along with a basket of bread and a jug of wine for her journey. Straw lined the edges of the boat to help it burn. At least her mother was prepared for her welcome into Caelus.

"Your mother was a good woman," Uther said, his voice thick with emotion. "She wasn't supposed to get hurt."

Her eye, half swollen, kept her from viewing her uncle on her right. Someone shuffled on his far side, but she didn't care who it was. Maybe Uther hadn't intended to kill her mother, but his wife had. It made little difference anymore. Her parents were dead. Hann was dead. She was alone.

"I will avenge you," she whispered in the ancient Penumar tongue her mother had taught her, hoping Uther might not understand.

A hand took hold of Rowena's elbow and she yanked herself away, spinning to face her uncle.

"Step back and allow the druid to finish," Uther said softly.

She held his gaze with her good eye. "My father should be next to her."

"I can't allow that."

"You shouldn't allow this," Fidessa spat in a whisper, moving into Rowena's view to Uther's other side.

"Hush, woman." Uther slid back a step and gently pulled Rowena with him.

Asta stepped in front of them and spoke to Rowena. "Osric will welcome both of your parents this day. We will remember them with honor."

The druid turned her back without waiting for a response. Asta raised her arms and prayed. Fresh tears streamed down Rowena's cheeks at the knowledge that the druid would bless both of her parents.

Asta's words were in the Primary fae language. Rowena understood most of them, but her mind wandered to the brooch pinned to the cloak around her mother's shoulders. The golden twisting vines had been a gift from her father after he'd come home from a trading journey in Penumar a few years before. Her mother had held the piece of her homeland in her hand so tenderly. She'd fled with her mother to Skandan when she was younger than Rowena.

"I'd hoped you'd like it," she'd heard her father say as he wiped a tear from her mother's cheek.

They'd celebrated that night and seemed happier than Rowena had ever seen them.

Someone bumped her shoulder, and Rowena's mind cleared of her memories. Men were untying the boat and pushing it into the bay. The fortune tide was at its peak and would begin its slow retreat to the sea, carrying her mother with it.

When Uther ambled to the end of the docks, Rowena went with him as if in a dream. The ship floated to the center of the bay until Jarah's body was no longer visible. Three burning arrows sailed overhead and landed on the ship.

Rowena's breath hitched as flames burst into the air and engulfed the ship. Smoke billowed. She wanted to fall to her knees, for the pain was too great. But she stood firm and didn't turn from the orange glow brightening the darkening skies. Masah's light fell onto the waters in a long shimmering path, guiding her mother. Rowena soaked it all in, determined to remember every moment.

The ship rocked as it moved closer to Siren Straight that led to the sea. It would find the current and sail out of sight soon enough.

"Come, Rowena," Uther said.

She didn't move. "I'll wait."

Uther released a heavy sigh at her side, but his boots scraped against the wooden boards as he left her alone to mourn. She didn't budge, but her tears fell harder when the silence wrapped around her. It took all of her strength to keep her shoulders from shaking.

They had taken everything from her. How could she go on alone? For a moment, she wanted to let herself fall off the edge of the dock. Slip below the surface and join her loved ones.

The ship rounded the corner of the bay and floated out of sight as she watched. Smoke still rose over the hillside for another few moments before it, too, disappeared.

If she gave in, if she let herself collapse, the pain might stop, but no one would remember what happened. No one would honor her parents and restore the kingdom her father had ruled with fairness and integrity. No one would put the world back into order.

The breeze dried Rowena's face. It was her task now. She would take the crown and avenge her parents. No one would stop her. She pulled her shoulders back and stared at the empty bay. "I will remember and honor you."

She spun and strode for the longhouse, ignoring Uther, Fidessa, and everyone else who'd gone back to their duties as if it was any other night in the village. It wasn't.

A burly man, different from the one who'd bothered her before, stepped into Rowena's path. She skidded to a stop.

"Get out of my way."

Two women walked past, each carrying the end of a heavy trunk.

"Where are you taking that?"

"We're leaving Taesing," Uther said.

Rowena rocked back on her heels. Why would he leave? "To go where?"

"Back to Forsa," Fidessa answered.

"For what purpose? Isn't Taesing what you wanted?" Rowena darted a glance at another man carrying out the carved box holding her great-grandfather's sword. It was the last connection Rowena had to her mother and her Lunara heritage.

"We leave in the morning with the fury tide." Uther called out.

They were leaving Taesing. And during the fastest and most dangerous of tides. The reality of it weighted Rowena's shoulders like a cloak.

NINE

Rowena paced inside her room, unable to rest. The rest of the night had been a blur of activity. Her smallest trunk, filled only with essentials, sat waiting to be loaded onto the ship as Fidessa had ordered. Though the queen insisted Rowena had to include her finest dress for Daenon's celebration, which took up most of the space. It had given her a chance to slip Bia within the folded fabric, at least. She understood how silly it was to keep the doll her mother had given her years ago. But taking the small token comforted her.

She'd also pinned a simple brooch to the inside of her stocking, just above her knee. Her mother had let her borrow it for the celebrations. It was nothing special, gold with an oval carnelian gemstone, but it would serve as a reminder—inspiration—for her vengeance.

Uther had already loaded her family's other possessions onto his ship, including the sword box he still couldn't open.

When it left the longhouse, she could sense it, somehow. A force washed over her, making her dizzy, similar to how it had been before she sent Daenon into the cave wall. She had to get that sword. If it called to her enchantment, which had to explain what was happening to her, it didn't belong in the hands of her unenchanted Telana relatives.

She paced the length of her room and back, thinking. Moonlight shone through the single window, illuminating the sanctuary of her past. It also filled her with a sense of purpose. She grabbed her cloak hanging from a peg on the wall.

When she peeked out the door, no guards came into view. They were surely in the open hall, but they could also be watching the bathhouse as well. She would have to stand on a trunk and wriggle her shoulders through her window, which would take all of her attention. If anyone came by, they would catch her easily. There wasn't any better choice; she had to try.

Uther had forced her to hand over her seax and cleared her chambers of her axe and bow as well. But no one bothered to check under her bedding where she kept a dagger. She wrapped the weapon into her cloak and stuffed the package out the window, holding her breath as it landed with a quiet thud against the grass outside.

She would have to slide through the window like diving into the bay. Otherwise, she'd risk getting her shoulders stuck. Sword lessons had taught her how to fall and roll out of the way of her opponent. This would be the same . . . just from a higher distance. Rowena bit her lip and took a deep breath to steady her racing pulse. The night was as dark as it would get. Soon, both moons would be high. If she was going to go, it had to be right now. She lowered as much as she dared into a squat and then launched herself through the opening.

The night air brushed against her cheeks. A slight grin played at her lips when her shoulders made it through, but her toes hit the windowsill, knocking her off balance. She flailed her hands out of position for the landing, barely tucking her chin before her shoulder hit the ground with full force. Instead of gracefully rolling to her feet, she crumpled in on herself and fell sideways with an audible oof.

She lay still, listening, waiting for the shooting pain radiating from her neck to subside. Somehow, the night remained quiet. Rowena rolled her knees, inhaled deeply, and let it fall back out, forcing her pulse to slow. She brought her feet under her, grabbing her cloak. The dagger fit through a loop on her belt, and she pulled her hood low to hide her hair and face.

After a quick roll of her shoulders, she grinned. She could do this. Uther and Fidessa thought they could take everything from her, and she'd break. She'd show them how wrong they were.

At the corner of the longhouse, she listened once again. Two men spoke in hushed tones to the left. There weren't any shuffled feet or steps—they were sitting on the bench out front where she sometimes helped spin wool for her mother. Her breath caught for a moment at the memory. There would be time to think of those things later; she had to stay focused.

If she kept to the shadows and headed right, she could hide behind the cart out in front of Sven's place. It would be easy enough to get behind the barrels of salted herring he hadn't moved to the store house yet.

She bit her lip and leaned sideways to glimpse the talking men. Neither looked her direction. Once again, the games she and her father had played shielded her like armor. His play had been training.

Slide one foot. Wait . . . slide the next, breathe. Stay in the shadows. Listen.

The backs of her eyes stung as Far's voice mentally led her through the steps, but she blinked, forcing herself to concentrate. She made it to the wagon without being seen. Some of the tightness in her chest released.

She made it far enough, but she stood completely still, back against the wall, unseen in plain sight.

That was the trick to winning the game. She never sought the best hiding spot, just the one most likely overlooked. Usually, that meant the closest spot where the shadows were darkest. She'd keep her hair wrapped up so the light color wouldn't give her away, and wait. Patience, that was the key.

The men hadn't moved. They still conversed on the bench with no concern. Rowena lowered herself to a squat. There were only two exposing steps she had to make to reach a wagon that would put a barrier between her and the men. If she moved too fast, it would draw attention. If she moved too slowly, she'd leave herself vulnerable. She swallowed and steadied her racing heart. Stay low, move in one fluid motion.

She twisted and stretched one leg, bracing one hand on the ground, drawing her dagger into her other palm, stare fixed on the men. She stayed low, stretching one leg and then brought her feet back under her, creeping along. Stretch, feet together, stretch, feet together. When she made it back into the shadows, she released a heavy exhale.

The wagon would be excellent cover until she reached the small pig pen outside of Grandma Myrna's. She wasn't anyone's real grandmother; her husband and children had died long ago, and she'd never remarried, but everyone had adopted her and she treated them as her own. What would life be like for her now?

Thoughts of Myrna gave Rowena one more reason to claim the sword. It could help her avenge her parents and rid Taesing of the usurpers and all their filth—she had to retrieve it. She was the rightful queen and the village's only hope. Keeping low, she raced for the pig shed.

Lungol's teasing moonlight bounced between the smaller lodgings, weaving out from the center of Taesing like a spiderweb. The further she moved away from the meeting square, and her home, the more things appeared normal, as if nothing had changed. But it had. They would subject everyone to Uther's rule, carried out by whatever puppet he set up. That would change everything. No one was safe, despite how peaceful it seemed.

The salty air signaled the bay before she could see it. The glittering waves, lapping on the shore in the distance, were a nighttime melody for her heart. There would be guards watching the ships, of course. Uther had arrived in just one—large enough for forty warriors. For all the trunks he'd hauled away, the warriors wouldn't all fit again when he left. Either his intent was to leave half of those fighters behind, or steal one of her father's ships. Whichever it was, it meant camped warriors would fill the shore; ready to shove off quickly during the fast-moving morning tide.

When she reached the beach, Rowena ducked behind a pile of fishing nets sitting next to some barrels, filled with ale from the smell of it. Clouds moved through the sky and dimmed the smaller moon's light, but the view confirmed her suspicions. Sleeping bodies lay scattered along the shore or propped against storage huts. A scattering of small warming fires flickered along the pebbled shoreline. One group of three men and two women sat awake, huddled together on some crates near the longest dock, talking amongst themselves. The same dock where her mother's burial boat had been earlier. Uther's ship had moved into that position since then.

She huffed. What she'd give to send Uther's ship into the bay for the same purpose—but she'd show him more respect and lay his wife alongside of him as the ship burned. That those two had shown up and destroyed so much in so short of time fired up her need to make them pay. Which started with getting her family's sword.

The clouds shifted again, revealing the brilliantly waxing crescent moon. Only Lungol raced across the star-scattered sky. Masah had already traveled his path and gone to rest until the next night. Rowena tipped her chin up and let the exuberant rays wash over her. For as long as she could remember, she'd gone on night walks with her mother. They'd search for moon flowers or picha mushrooms they could only harvest during the darkness. But mostly, it was time for her mother to soak up the energy, preferring the softer resonance of the larger Masah to the feisty, smaller moon, Lungol.

Try as she might, after all those years, Rowena couldn't feel what her mother did.

She huffed a laugh when her skin tingled and a series of bubbles wiggled through her stomach. Tears leaked out of the edges of her eyes. She missed her mother so much she almost caused herself to believe she had some enchantment. But of course, she didn't.

She shook her head and swiped at her eyes. The reality before her was all that mattered in that moment. How was she going to get past all those warriors, stroll down the docks, and board the ship without being caught? That was the only question—and it had her stumped.

No matter what, she couldn't sneak through the sleeping bodies. Someone would wake and call out for sure. If she snuck around in a wide arc and came up the beach, it might work, but only if she stayed out of the moon's rays. Given the amount of light piercing the sky from the glowing beauty, that wasn't a great option. She stared out at the water for a heartbeat, then two, trying to find a solution.

The answer twinkled up at her in the line of silver rippling over the bay. She'd have to swim. If she went out of sight further down the bay, she could leave her cloak and boots within the trees. The curve of the shore would keep her close enough to make the swim to the dock. The supports underwater would be slippery, and the walkway sat high above the water. There wasn't another way, though.

A small cloud passed over Lungol once more, and the light overhead blinked. At first, she thought it might be the moon itself mocking her, but as she dragged her gaze from the water to her hiding place, she wanted to shout for joy. It took a great deal of willpower to keep herself only to a lip-biting grin. Among the nets and fishing supplies lay a coiled rope and several hooks. She chose a large hook, hoisted the rope over her shoulder, and backed herself out of sight of the beach.

"Thank you," she whispered to Lungol when she darted into the trees at the edge of the bay.

As she raced along, the thought hit her that the rope should weigh her down, but it seemed lighter than it had originally been. Odd, but with the way her pulse raced through her body, her muscles were probably extra strong. She'd seen it with her father's warriors before. When they played crackendash or were excited to leave on a mission, their strength would reach levels where they could practically lift a wagon by themselves. It was a new sensation to her, but she relished it.

The bay swept around in an arc, but the trees grew closer to the shore a hundred feet past the docks. That would be the best place to enter the water unseen. She dropped the rope and her cloak, plopping down to remove her boots.

Before she stood again, she ripped a chunk of fabric from the hem of her cloak to wrap around the dagger blade. She didn't have a sheath, so she'd have to hold it in her mouth as she swam. If she tried to keep it in her belt or anywhere on her person, she feared it would drop to the silty bottom of the bay. She wasn't about to leave herself weaponless.

With the rope secured and snug across her body, she tucked the hook under her belt and raced for the bay. The moment her feet touched water, she slowed so as not to splash, clamped her mouth over the dagger, and lowered herself to a crawl. As soon as she couldn't touch the bottom, she swam as hard as possible in a direct line to the ship.

Rowena rarely swam and surprised herself at how quickly she made it to the end of the dock; she'd felt so buoyant and light. She treaded water below the ship's carved dragonhead, growling down, ready to spew fire and boil the bay like a pot of stew. Above those realistic-looking teeth would be where she aimed the rope. The hook had to either dig into the wood or get caught on one of the deep grooves of the scaly face.

She hadn't actually thought about how she'd toss the rope

from so far below and mostly submerged. It proved a hard enough task to tie the hook. She swirled the rope around her head to build momentum, though when she let it go, it landed five feet in front of her. She pulled it back and tried again. This time, it went farther, but still fell short of her goal. She closed her eyes, leaning back to float and settle herself. When she smoothed her breathing, and visualized the rope catching on the sharp mouth, she tried a third time, and then a fourth. On the fifth try, she finally hit the dragon. The hook splashed back into the water and she reeled it in again. Once more—she'd give it one more time before she had to give up. If she kept throwing the rope without success, she would tire herself too much to swim back to shore. So, she would have to figure out a new tactic.

Whatever it took, she would not slink back to her room in defeat.

Her muscles were screaming. Even if she secured the rope, she still had to climb it. One thing at a time.

She swung the rope in a circle over her head, letting it build speed, and then let it fly. The hook bounced once and slid around the wooden tooth. Rowena leaned back, breathing a sigh of relief and allowing herself a small grin of celebration. Then she tugged the rope to make sure it would hold and began her climb.

Again, the games in the forest with her father came to mind. How they would use ropes to climb high into the branches of an oak tree to have a picnic. Her father would talk about Taesing and Skandan, and stories of other lands he'd visited. They were some of her favorite adventures. Now, as she wrapped the rope around her foot to give herself a boost, she understood more than ever how it wasn't just a wonderful memory. Her father had taught her more necessary skills than she'd ever realized.

When she reached the top, she rolled over the edge and slid down the dragon's neck until her feet touched the platform built at the stern for someone to stand watch as they sailed. Rowena let go of the rope, but left it hooked for her trip back. She unwrapped her dagger and hung the cloth over the gunwale.

They had already loaded the ship for the morning. Benches sat along the edges for the rowers, and cargo lined the middle. She snuck along one side, scanning each pile for her box. Near the tall mast in the center, a corner of the carved cover poked out from where someone wedged it under two other small trunks. She reached her arm between the two trunks to see if she could remove it without dismantling the pile, when a noise made her freeze.

A snort followed by a loud snore rumbled through the ship. At least one person slept aboard, which made sense. She kicked herself. With all the cargo, of course, Uther had guards positioned on the ship.

She'd stop for nothing now, though. The box was within reach. She'd have to hurry and hope she could grab it before she woke up whoever it was. The top box slid quietly out of the way and onto a crate, but the second one wouldn't budge. It would take both hands, but she would have to let go of her dagger. Or she could cut the ropes holding down the cargo. Not that complicated! The tight ropes were easy to cut, except the second one made a loud popping noise.

The snoring stopped, she halted, held her breath. For what seemed like an eternity, the only sound she heard was the rush of blood through her ears. Finally, there was a shift against the wooden floor and the snoring resumed. With shaking hands, Rowena set down her dagger atop a crate and eased the long box out of its hiding spot.

She glanced over each shoulder and then unhooked the latch on the cover with ease. A polished silver sword glittered in the double moonlight. Magnificent didn't describe the weapon longer than her arm. Its cross-guard had a woven leaf design and there were runes etched down the blade. It was much larger than any sword she'd ever practiced with. How would she manage it?

She tilted the box, trying to read the runes. The weapon called to her heart like nothing had ever done. Every instinct screamed for her to take the blade into her hand. Her mouth went dry and her hands shook, but she reached out. Her finger poised over an empty oval on the pommel—a setting for a missing jewel.

"Hey, get away from there!"

Whoever called out startled her into action. They were going to take her prize away, but not before she held it. Not before they understood it was hers. As soon as she reached for the hilt, something hard hit the back of her neck. A heartbeat later, her knees gave out, and she fell as everything went dark.

TEN

Fingers dug into Rowena's arm as she fought to get her feet to hold steady on the ship's floorboards. Wet and disoriented, she blinked and shook her head, clearing her vision. The fallen box lay upside-down, splayed open, on the ship floor; the sword peeked out from underneath.

"What are you doing here, princess?"

The smell of ale mixed with onion punched her in the face. She shivered, more because of the cool air against her wet clothes than the vile-breathed threat at her side.

What had happened? The last thing she remembered, she'd tried to grab the sword. Then, someone had hit her on the head and still held her arms pinned to her sides.

"Let go of me!" She swung her foot backward, kicking only the air. That only increased the pressure on her arm. She tried a new tactic, letting herself go limp.

Both she and the man behind her stumbled forward, but they didn't fall. Instead, he stomped a heavy boot onto the floorboards, bracing himself, and brought them both upright. Rowena found herself caught tight against the foul man's chest.

"Thought you could topple a man who spends his life aboard a ship, did ye?" A hearty belly laugh rumbled against Rowena's whole body as he turned them toward others who'd arrived on the boat.

"Oh, Rowena." Daenon clicked his tongue as he hopped off the edge into the boat. "I wish you wouldn't have done that."

They had pushed the ramp into place at some point and made it easy for the prince to come aboard, along with several others. Rowena counted five before she no longer cared and held her stare on Daenon. "Why are you here?"

A grin slid across the prince's face, but he shook his head at the same time. "I'd hoped you'd prove him wrong, if I'm honest. All that talk of fate and prophecy sounded like a bunch of nonsense. But here you are, going after the one box no one else could open, just like they said you would."

They? "What are you talking about?"

Daenon sauntered closer, leaning down to pick up the box and sword. The moment his hand wrapped around the hilt, Rowena's stomach seized. The need to drag her nails down his face for being a traitorous arse flooded through her.

As did a burst of power. It rolled through her chest, into her shoulders, and down her arms. She almost screamed from the pressure, begging to fly out. She wiggled, trying to get her hand free. If she could touch the warrior holding her with her palm, he'd go flying like Daenon had in the cave.

"Be sure to keep her from touching anyone," Daenon called to the man behind her, and motioned with his head for another guard to come help. The second one snatched her wrists and grappled to force her palms together before he wrapped a rope tight around her hands and wrists.

Daenon continued to examine the blade as if nothing else took place. "This is fine craft-work." He rolled his wrist one way, then the other, examining the blade and weight. A bead of sweat rolled down from his temple, and a flush crept over his face. Daenon returned the sword to its place within the luxurious lining and he attempted to seem unaffected.

Once the guards had Rowena thoroughly tied, she pinched her lips tight, fighting the urge to vomit from the two men handling her. She redirected her disgust to focus her glare on the prince. He met her gaze as he closed the lid and tucked the box under his arm.

Afterward, he leaned toward her until they were nearly touching. She turned her face, unwilling to give him the satisfaction of reading how difficult his presence was for her to bear. Her throat burned and a bitter tang seeped into the back of her mouth. Daenon ran a finger along her jaw, forcing her to meet his gaze.

"Allies are scarce, Rowena. Can you be who they think you are? I guess we'll find out." He glanced over her head at the brute. "Tie her arms to her sides and make sure she stays put."

"Are you serious?" Rowena fought to free herself. "Let me go."

Daenon twisted back, but spoke to the guards. "She's under the king's protection. Don't forget that."

With that, he climbed off the ship and left. His heavy boots echoed down the wooden docks until he reached the shore.

A moment later, a scratchy rope wrapped around her waist, locking her arms even tighter. Shoved to her backside, she leaned against a crate while they secured her feet.

"Are you comfortable, princess?" The man sneered and turned to his companions with a loud guffaw. "Get some rest, boys. We head home at dawn."

Rowena tipped her chin to the skies, staring at Lungol. She shook her head; never had she felt so lonely within the light of either moon. Tingles washed over her and seeped into her veins. If only she understood how to draw upon her newly budding abilities better. She tipped her chin, hoping the amount of hair that had pulled free from her braid was enough to hide her tears.

* * *

Something heavy smacked against Rowena's foot, jolting her awake. Flustered, she tried to stand, only to have a sharp pain stab through her shoulders. Dull predawn light washed the ship in full view and quickly reminded her of the situation. She'd vowed not to fall asleep, but she apparently hadn't managed it.

She cried out in pain when rough hands hauled her to her feet. Different aches flared through her from sleeping in an awkward position on hard shipboards.

"Untie her."

Rowena blinked away the pain and met her uncle's gaze. She pursed her lips and refused to speak, willing her glare to burn a hole through Uther. Fidessa stood at his shoulder with a mocking grin, but Rowena ignored her, as well as the prince at her uncle's other shoulder.

"I'm surprised at you, Rowena," Uther said. "From what I've heard, you long for adventure. Why such defiance?"

The rope at her waist fell away, but she didn't acknowledge the relief it gave. She kept her glare aimed at her uncle, despite the tingles racing up and down her arms as the feeling returned. Opening and closing her fists helped. She waited until all the ropes were gone before speaking.

"You've taken what's mine." Her throat rasped with need of water.

Uther nodded, as if concerned. "I have, yes. And that will be difficult for you. You're going to need your strength, but I believe you'll manage."

Rowena's chest tightened, cutting off her air for a moment. How could he act so casually about killing his own family? And what did he mean she'd need her strength? "You'll pay for what you've done."

Fidessa chuckled. "If I were you, I'd watch my tongue when you speak to your king. You aren't in a position to say such things."

"He's not my king."

"Rowena." Daenon stepped around Uther and held open his palm out as if she'd rest her hand in his. "Don't make this harder on yourself than it has to be. Uther is king now. Join him with me."

She slapped his hand away. "Never."

Daenon dropped his hand and raised a shoulder. "Suit yourself, but you'll do better if you accept that."

"You've been working with him the whole time." She scoffed at herself for not seeing it. How could she have been so dense?

"Don't look so upset over it," Uther said. "It's good that you enjoyed his company since the two of you are to be married."

"What?" Daenon and Rowena said at the same time.

"Uther." Fidessa twisted and rested her hand on Uther's arm. "Are you sure that is the best option?"

"I listened to your reasoning against her, and it had merit." Uther kept his gaze trained on Rowena. "However, there are other reasons to consider. Lendan has already agreed as well."

Fidessa dropped her hand to her side and said nothing more, but her chest heaved like she struggled to keep her composure.

A sour taste burned at the back of Rowena's throat as she slid a glance to Daenon. She'd let herself become charmed by his handsome face and gentle speech. But that was over. The sight of him made her stomach curl in on itself. She clenched her fists at her side. "I will not marry him."

"My king, you've never mentioned a betrothal." Daenon spoke with respect yet, his brows pinched too close and his posture had turned rigid. "I'll be taking my place back in Velmeg within a month, and expect to make my own choice of bride."

"You'll both comply, and I'll discuss it no further. Follow me." Uther spun and barked orders to make the ship ready to sail.

For a heartbeat, none of them moved. What about the rest of her things? Where was her trunk? She wasn't ready to go. The Ibernian who'd untied Rowena shoved his hand into her back unexpectedly, causing her to stumble forward. Daenon snatched her elbow to steady her, but she yanked it back.

"Don't touch me." She darted a glare to the prince, but his gaze followed Uther as he climbed off the ship.

Fidessa hurried to follow her husband, blocking Rowena's path to stomp off, so she had to file onto the dock in measured steps.

Uther stopped at the edge of the docks with Fidessa and Daenon taking their place behind him as they'd done before. Rowena hung back, refusing to stand next to any of them.

Dawn brightened the overcast skies to a bright gray, giving a clear view of the shore. Yet there wasn't any activity. Fishermen weren't checking their nets. Nor were there women carrying buckets for water; no one herded sheep to their pastures for the day. Instead, every citizen of Taesing crowded the open spaces near the docks, spilling among the silent nets, crates, and barrels. Most stayed squished as far back as possible, but a group, perhaps twenty, stood huddled together, facing the docks. Among them, she caught sight of Hann's father, Wigg, and little Malia, held by her mother. Rowena's chest grew tight.

"Goetz, have you done what I asked?" Uther called out from where he used his higher position like a dais.

The former councilman stepped forward and dipped his chin. "I have."

One of Uther's men jostled Rowena as he hurried close and set a stool on the dock behind Uther.

Her uncle sat upon it and rested his sword on his lap, keeping the blade under his right arm and extending the hilt toward Goetz. "Then make your oath as my Stallari."

Olve's former advisor eased up the gangplank and dropped to one knee. Rowena sucked in a gasp as she watched the man remove the oath ring from his arm. The one he'd sworn allegiance upon to her father. Goetz set the ring on the dock near Uther's feet, and then rested his hand on the pommel ring of Uther's sword, in the Ibernian custom for oaths.

"You'll die for that," Rowena hissed. His duty remained to her father. "Your vow requires you to avenge your true king."

"My father and his father before served their kings as Stallari, as I will do in honor of you," Goetz began, ignoring her. "My blade has destroyed a band of Jotnari, and at night slain Neredi of the ocean depths. I have suffered great pain against foes and administered justice to those who asked for trouble. My loyalty now serves only you, as does my sword. I will battle to vanquish your enemies and follow your commands, even though it may bring my death."

Uther rose to his feet and sheathed his sword. Goetz remained on his knees. "Rise and bring forward those you've gathered."

Several warriors stepped forward from the crowd and forced those crowded in the center closer. Goetz retreated backward off the walkway, keeping himself facing Uther.

"Olve is dead. If the gods had truly chosen him to rule Taesing, he wouldn't have fallen," Uther called out.

"That's a lie," Rowena yelled. "He offered you guest rights and welcomed you home. You are a traitor."

"Rowena, hush," Daenon whispered.

Uther kept his gaze forward but spoke to the man behind him who'd brought the stool. "Silence her."

The guard jerked Rowena backward, and a leather-gloved hand wrapped around her mouth. The stench mixed with the swirl of emotions churning in her gut caused her to retch.

"Stay still or it'll be a knock to the head," the brute growled.

Uther continued his address, ignoring her struggle. "I'm a generous man. I give you one last chance to bend your knee and pledge your loyalty."

Wigg stepped from the huddled mass to stand at the front. Rowena couldn't stop her tears when she met Hann's father's red-rimmed gaze. He dipped his chin to her and then faced Uther. "You have killed your kin and restrained the rightful heir to the throne. I pledge my loyalty to Rowena, daughter of Olve, Queen of Taesing."

Shivers rolled over Rowena, and she whimpered at his declaration. Not because of how endearing his statement was, but because of what would undoubtedly come next. She tried to shake her head, to tell him not to risk his life for his loyalty, but her captor held her too tight.

"What say the rest of you? Are you all of the same mind? Speak now and there will be no harm to you. Bend the knee and all will be well." Uther's icy tone belied his sincerity.

No one moved. Malia sucked on three fingers, unaware of the danger. Rowena could still feel the soft warmth of the elfling from when she'd held her; could hear the infectious giggles when she'd tickled the girl's tummy. Internally, she pleaded with them to bend the knee. It wouldn't mean anything. They could still be loyal to her in their hearts.

"Suit yourselves." Uther waved his hand to Goetz as if brushing aside a bug from his glass.

Uther's new council leader turned and signaled for warriors to encircle the group. Many pleaded for mercy, both within the crowd and from those standing beyond.

Uther lifted his hands for silence. "There is another matter we must address. That is Rowena's claim to the Skandan's crown."

The man behind her squished his hand tighter over her mouth. She had no intention of arguing. No one would dispute her status.

"No one denies the princess was born during the Burning Moon. My brother has forced you to accept his daughter as if her presence will not bring danger to all of Skandan." He paused and several nods and muttered agreements skittered through those listening.

They couldn't believe such nonsense. Her father had forced no one to accept her. What did Uther hope to accomplish with his lies?

"Now, some would raise her to queen. Giving her honor even though she killed her own father to gain the crown—"

Rowena screamed from behind her gag, kicking and wriggling to defend herself and tell everyone the truth.

"If you don't stop, I'll knock you in the head again and leave you in a heap," the man growled in her ear.

She didn't care and continued to fight.

Fidessa stepped near, whispering in Rowena's ear. "You'll never be queen. Somnum Etsi Suscito."

Rowena's body stilled, slumping against her captor as if she had no bones. The mage had spelled her. She couldn't speak or move except to blink, yet she could hear and see just as well as before—though her gaze stayed straight ahead, fixed on Uther.

"There were several witnesses to this crime," Uther went on, flashing her a grin before facing the villagers again. "Goetz fought near Rowena, did you not?"

She'd grown up surrounded by friendship and love, yet fear and something more—anger, disgust—simmered among those listening to her uncle's tale.

"I did, my king. She drew her bow and carefully took aim at her father. I raced to stop her, but I was too late. I'll never forget how he stared at her, knowing his own daughter had struck him down."

Goetz should remember that, since he sent the arrow. Yet, her father's furrowed brow, questioning her from across the battle, would haunt her forever. She sent another prayer that he'd learned the truth in the afterlife.

"And what say you, Prince Daenon? You helped Rowena run away. Why would you do such a thing?" Uther motioned for Daenon to step to his side.

"It's true, I helped the princess escape the battle along with her friend, Hann," Daenon curled his lip as if saying the name bothered him. "Unfortunately, I didn't see who had loosed the arrow. However, later I learned of the conspiracy. Even though I cared for Rowena, I risked my life to help Hann when his feet slipped from the trail and fell."

Someone strangled a gasp in the crowd. Rowena could guess it was Wigg. He shouldn't have to hear details of his son's death.

Daenon went on. "I lay in the mud, hanging over the edge with a branch for Hann to grab. He tried to pull me to my death, claiming it was his right to sit on the throne next to Rowena. I believe she had his emotions entangled from her Lunara enchantments."

Murmurs rolling through the outer crowd increased.

"She's dangerous," some called.

"No! She's innocent," another cried.

Thank you. Rowena imagined her supporter hearing her words, but it meant nothing.

"Rid us of her," another yelled.

Rowena wanted to shout at them, but no part of her body would rouse. It was as if she was asleep, yet awake.

"What happened next?" Uther asked.

"I had no choice but to let go of the branch. It pained me to see him fall."

Daenon had let go. He'd let Hann fall to his death on purpose. Inside, Rowena screamed and cried and fell apart, but outwardly she did nothing more than blink.

"It's clear they'd worked together to take the crown. You're lucky to be alive." Uther squeezed Daenon's shoulder in support.

The prince nodded. "It's with a heavy and confused heart that I stand here. Later, when we were alone overnight in a small cave, she confessed to me she craved the crown. She'd used Lunara powers to make her arrow lighter to sail farther and strike true."

"She's evil. Born as she was," a woman cried out.

"Save us," came another plea.

The knowledge that so many detested her crushed Rowena. If she didn't already hang like a doll from an abhorrent oaf, she'd fall to the ground in sorrow. She'd been blind, no—ignorant.

Uther once again quieted the villagers. "It's clear that the princess is guilty. She is a king-killer and I should not show mercy.

However, I'm afraid that for the good of the realm, I must. She is a royal of both Skandan and Penumar blood. Because of such ties, she must live."

"And I must add my plea for her life," Daenon added. "Since we are now betrothed, I can't allow her to come to harm. Even if it is by her enchantment, I love her and wish to redeem her upon our marriage."

Lies. Disgusting, outrageous, sickening lies. Daenon didn't want to marry her any more than she wanted to have needles stuck in her eye. He'd die like the rest of them when she had the chance.

Though, beyond Uther, there were those staring at her limp body with hatred lining their faces.

"The leaves only one option. Someone must take her place. Offer themselves as her surrogate. Should I choose, or is there a volunteer?" Uther scanned the faces of those staring at Rowena. Those she'd believed would stand by her no matter what, not that she wanted anyone to die in her place. It was a sad custom. She'd witnessed an elderly mother volunteer once, to save her son after he'd killed a man in an argument.

"I will."

"There. It is done. The penalty for treason and the murder of a king is death." Uther nodded to Goetz and to the guard still propping Rowena against his chest.

The man grabbed her hair and turned her head. Wigg kneeled alone on the shore. Hann had been his only child. She shared his grief, but couldn't endure his death on her conscience. She silently begged for him to rise.

A guard stood over the kind man, sword raised. After one heavy swing, Wigg joined his son in the afterlife, his head rolling to a stop before it reached the water. If Rowena could have vomited, she would have.

"Take the others to the longhouse and lock them inside. Let it be a reminder to all what happens if they defy my rule," Uther commanded the rest of the guards surrounding the group he'd marked as traitors earlier.

Uther's men herded the group like sheep away from the bay. At the edge of her vision, Daenon appeared. He whispered something to a guard, who bowed and raced away alone. Nothing good would come of that.

When they were all out of sight, Uther called to Goetz. "You will rule in my stead until I can return."

"Yes, my king."

Traitorous shite.

Fidessa twisted and blocked Rowena's view, leaning near her once again. "I don't want to miss your tears. Amor Savium."

Sensation rushed through Rowena once again, allowing her to move. "I did not kill my father! This is wrong," she cried.

Uther spun, striding past them. "To the ship."

The guard grabbed Rowena's arm, dragging her alongside of him when her legs at last recovered from Fidessa's spell.

Minutes later, freed onboard, Rowena stood at the stern of the ship, her eyes trained on the village as the oars hit the water and the ship pulled away. By the time the first wisps of blackened smoke rose from her home, her tears had dried.

Whatever it took, she'd fulfill her vow of vengeance—for her parents, for Hann, and now for those who kept their loyalty to her.

ELEVEN

The ship battled through Siren Straight for most of the first day. No one could speak over the howling winds in the narrow passage, which suited Rowena fine. Daenon had convinced Uther to take the perilous route, which made no sense. Most ships didn't dare the temptress-filled waters where beautiful songs would lull entire ships to crash against the craggy rock at the western end. However, the sirens also considered leaving by heading east toward the open ocean an insult, so they used their wrath to churn up the waves and winds.

When they finally reached the Kelson Sea and put up the sail, all the exhausted oarsmen cheered before they fell against the side of the ship to rest.

Rowena sat on the top deck near the prow, where she could stay turned away from the crew. The dragon stayed high over her head, mocking her failed efforts, and left a hollow emptiness in her chest. Stinging tears battled to fall down her cheeks, but she denied them, careful to keep her hands away from her face so no one guessed how badly she hurt. She brushed her fingers over the brooch, pinned at the top of her stocking. Remember.

In the early afternoon, a mark appeared on the horizon, forcing her to her feet. She twisted to make eye contact with her uncle at the stern, jutting her chin to what she'd found. "What's that?"

Uther held his hand over his brow and peered for several long breaths. When he finally dropped his hand, he clamped his mouth together and said nothing. Fidessa, who'd also scanned the horizon, hurried from his side to sit below the deck, shaded from view. Others had followed his line of sight and turned to him, awaiting orders, it seemed.

"We could turn and meet them. I hear they're led by a woman," one of his men said with a sneer.

Rowena huffed at the insulting comment. There were other female warriors onboard, and they'd been as skilled with their blades. If Rowena had a sword, she'd cut the dreg down for making such a statement. At least she'd try. They'd captured her so easily, she wasn't sure her skills were really as strong as she'd always thought.

"One that will gut you as easily as a fish," an Ibernian shield-maiden answered.

Rowena twisted to hide her grin. Maybe she could find an ally after all.

"We stay on course for Forsa," Uther said. "Back to the oars."

The square black sail of the approaching ship grew more distinct by the moment. Rowena had heard the stories of pirates sailing the eastern waters. None had ever stopped in Taesing, but her father spoke of them once, saying he simply knew their leader as V. No one had ever learned her real name.

The oarsmen to returned to their benches, adding their effort to the sail. They turned the ship, so the pirates were directly behind them. From the look of it, the pirates would board them long before they reached Ibern.

Rowena shivered and gripped her cloak tighter around her

shoulders. Perhaps they would help her take vengeance. She'd offer them whatever riches Uther had left behind if they would return her to Taesing.

Nausea surged through Rowena, and she leaned over the rail to vomit. She's spent most of her time sitting, but the rocking motion as she stood made her stomach suddenly betray her. The salty air mixed with the drizzling rain, stinging her nose as she heaved.

"If you keep your eyes trained on the horizon, you will adjust to the motion of the waves," Daenon said from where he sat below her on a crate.

So casual, as if they were on a fishing trip. Like everyone else, he'd put the events in Taesing behind him, forgetting Malia's mud-streaked face, sucking on her fingers as her mother cried and the skies blackened from the burning longhouse. Death meant nothing to him. He'd change his mind when the pirates caught up. Perhaps vengeance would come sooner than she expected.

"I should focus on the approaching ship, then?"

The prince didn't look up from where he worked on braiding a new rope. "They're no trouble. If they try to board us, they'll learn not to attack anyone from Ibern again."

She turned, bracing her back against the side of the ship, studying the crew and their frenzied attack on the oars, willing her insides to calm. Her uncle stood at the stern, staring at the threat behind them. "I suppose that's why everyone is lounging as calmly as you."

A smirk played at Daenon's lips. He paused his work and met her gaze, a slow grin tilting up his lips. "There are many reasons to hurry home. What if they are bringing me a Prime Day gift? Or coming to see us wed?"

His smugness prickled against her skin like ice pellets. She'd never let him lay a hand on her again. "That will not happen."

Darkness wafted over Daenon's blue eyes. "Do you think either of us has any choice to stop it?"

Rowena slumped against the rocking sideboards for a heartbeat, and then two. He'd be free of his foster treaty in another month. Why did he act like they trapped him, too? "When you're released from my uncle, you can do whatever you want."

"It's not so simple." Daenon focused on his rope again.

Whatever his struggles, they weren't the same as hers. He sauntered around, treated like the royal he was, with freedom nearly upon him. She didn't know what awaited her in Forsa, or how long she'd have to endure.

She slid down to sit on the platform, keeping her back against the curved sidewall. There wasn't any reason to stare at the pirates—she'd meet them soon enough. Her uncle had his back to everyone. His gaze fastened on the looming threat.

"Heave faster," he called over his shoulder to the oarsmen.

Uther turned and rubbed his face, resting his palm on the pommel of his sword, tapping his fingers.

She leaned over to peek around the ship's tall dragon head at the approaching pirates. They were considerably closer. The ship appeared similar in size to her uncle's, but it had a bigger sail and cut through the waves faster.

It was a bold move to attack a king, even for pirates. She scanned the ship and mast. Perhaps they didn't know Uther was a king? There weren't any telltale signs of where the ship hailed. Her father always flew his banner at the top of the mast.

"Hmm."

"Why are you so perplexed?" Daenon asked, not meeting her gaze.

She sighed and brushed her hands over her knees, ignoring him.

The prince snickered. "You'd better ask me about whatever has you so fidgety or you're going to burst."

Another guard sitting close enough to hear the comment snorted a laugh, but kept scraping a whetstone on the edge of his axe. His motion seemed more for something to do than sharpen the weapon.

"Why didn't you bring more men?" She finally blurted out. "If Uther planned to take over Taesing all along, why did you only bring one ship?"

"It was enough," the man answered instead of Daenon.

"And why isn't there a banner on the mast?"

"Perhaps he doesn't need one," the prince said.

She leaned back, reining in her questions. He wouldn't give her any correct information anyway, and she didn't need to listen to his grating voice. As she dragged her gaze away from Daenon, she glimpsed the box containing her sword. She shivered and adjusted her cloak again to hide it. A buzzing sensation in her chest grew stronger. The need to grab the sword and hold it made her fidget.

"Pull in the oars. Ready your weapons," Uther called, interrupting her thoughts.

Rowena jumped to her feet, but a wave tilted the boat suddenly and she smacked against a wooden rib, falling off the platform. Pain tore through her shoulder as she landed. She screamed and kicked when someone grabbed the back of her tunic, dragging her under the high decking.

"Stay down, and keep out of sight," Daenon yelled.

A moment later, a grappling hook clunked against the gunwale and dug into the wood. Several more bit into the ship's edge, followed by a sudden jerk sideways. The taller black sail loomed as the pirates reeled in Uther's boat.

Several elves, she assumed Telana, hurtled the edge, engaging with the Ibernian crew. Metal clanked and wood clunked as swords and axes met shields or ship. Rowena eased out from under cover, searching for an opening to bolt for the sword while everyone focused elsewhere.

A rough hand wrapped around her upper arm and dragged her to the floorboards. She twisted and swung her fist, missing her target.

"I told you to stay back," Daenon hissed. A moment later, he lunged to engage with a female pirate who spun and slashed with such speed, Rowena could only stare.

Someone fell next to her, forcing her to scramble out of the way. One of Uther's guards had fallen; his dagger clattered to a stop near her foot. She glanced around as she snatched it into her palm, but no one paid attention.

All around her, fighters punched and kicked as much as they used their weapons. She'd never trained like that. Her mouth went dry. The sight of so many bodies slamming together, dodging and lunging in a chaotic scrum, made her heart pound. Her ribs squeezed too tight. She couldn't breathe. Then, somewhere deep inside her chest, an intense spark flashed, raising the hair on her arms and neck as if lightning filled the air. Rowena fell to one knee, gasping. Energy pulsed within her, urging her to move—to press through the crowded bodies.

Like a beacon, her gaze latched onto the sword box. One pirate bent over, ignoring the melee, and tried to pull it free.

A growl rumbled from her throat. She leapt into the fray, ducking and elbowing her way through the fighting. An Ibernian warrior swung at one of the female pirates, missing and nearly smacking Rowena in the jaw. She leaned away, but caught the pirate's fist in her gut. A burst of air escaped and she couldn't reel in more for several heartbeats. She fell to her knees, clutching the dagger. She crawled to a crate lashed near the mast, gasping. The pirate still wrestled to free the box just out of her reach. Still wheezing, she used the ropes to pull herself to her feet.

The rumors had to be true. Every pirate that boarded them was a female, but they had more strength and skill than she would have believed. The pirate she sought had her back toward Rowena, so she lunged and wrapped her arm around the female's throat. A deep, hearty laugh rumbled against her chest when she pulled the pirate close.

"Leave that alone." Rowena struggled to keep hold of the powerful invader.

"You need more practice," a deep voice taunted. Male?

Momentarily confused, it gave her captive enough of an edge to grab her arm and swing her over his shoulder. Her back landed against the mast and the side of a crate.

She squealed, clutching her side. Her ribs ached and her vision swirled, but she lashed out with the dagger she refused to drop. The sharp tip dug into the male's forearm. It would do nothing but leave a scar, but he wouldn't care about that judging from the one he already had next to his eye that traveled under the mask covering the lower half of his face.

He snatched her wrist and pounded it against a barrel, forcing her fingers open so the dagger fell. She tucked her elbow into her side to staunch some of the pain, but flung herself at the box. It slipped from its wedged position, and she curled herself around it. If the pirate wanted it, he'd have to haul them both to the other ship.

The dreg grabbed her hair and pulled until her eyes watered. "Let go!"

"No!"

Rowena clutched the box harder, ignoring her ribs, her shoulder, her scalp—nothing else mattered other than saving the last connection she had to her family.

A boom reverberated through the air, forcing everyone's attention to the pirate ship.

"You fool," the man hissed. "I must have that."

Rowena peeked at the figure looming over her. He had a scarf wrapped around his head, so only a few dark curls poked from beneath and sharp green eyes seared through her skull.

The din of battle had reduced to grunts and a few choice curse words from Uther's crew. Rowena dared a glance to find out why, detaching herself from the fury-eyed stare of her combatant.

Uther stood at the prow with two pirates holding him at bay, one sword poking under his chin and another digging into his side. Both females turned their gaze to the pirate ship. Like the male, still grappling with her, they covered the lower half of their faces.

Rowena followed their line of sight to see another woman standing on the railing of the taller ship. She held one of the bracing lines, commanding everyone's attention though saying nothing. It had to be V, their leader. Even with the distance, the woman's eyes sparkled with energy. Enchantment radiated through the air with a familiarity like Rowena's mother . . . the captain had to be royal. No one had ever said that.

Heat radiated through Rowena's chest, spiking her heart rate. She couldn't tell if the box heated her, or the other way around. Neither made sense, but it didn't matter. She wouldn't let go.

A moment later, eight archers fanned out from their leader and pointed their nocked and ready arrows toward her uncle's crew. Uther's men lay their weapons on the deck and either backed away or kneeled.

The women gathered the weapons and any crates they could carry and formed a line to pass the goods to the black-sailed ship.

"Time to give up, elfling," the male still standing near Rowena said.

How dare he call her that! She was no child. "If you want it, you'll have to take me with you."

She meant the statement as a deterrent, but as soon as the words left her mouth, she latched onto the idea. The pirates were all female, with an enchanted leader. She would probably welcome Rowena. What could it hurt? She'd rather take her chances with them than her uncle's plans.

The male sheathed his sword and used both hands to haul Rowena to her feet. She hugged the box tighter. When she stood before him, she lifted her chin and met his glare with one of her own.

"I can knock you out, if you insist."

"Take me with you and you can have it." She whispered between her clenched teeth, hoping no one else had heard.

The male's eyebrows pinched close, and he held her stare. Confusion seemed to swirl in his green eyes. His gazed hardened a heartbeat later. "You're not my problem."

He reached for the box, and Rowena swung her shoulder around to knock into his chest. It didn't even make him sway. Instead, he snatched her arm and wrenched it, forcing one hand to fall away from her hold on the box.

Rowena screamed and dug her fingers into his shoulder. The man instantly flew backward and crashed against the side of the ship. He moaned and raised to one knee, only to fall to his backside. His eyes flared wide so that the whites showed all around the green. When he got back to his feet, he climbed to the pirate rail and disappeared over the edge.

The rest of the pirates hurried away with whatever they held, but stole nothing more. One of them flipped through the air, landed lightly on the gunwale of the Ibernian ship, and then gracefully leapt to the pirate ship like nothing Rowena had ever witnessed.

Moments later, the raiders released their lines, and Uther's ship bobbed free. The pirate leader remained in her spot on the rail as her ship sailed away, her unwavering gaze on Rowena until she disappeared from view.

Rowena shook so hard she fell to her backside, with the box landing in her lap. What happened? She had to believe it was her enchantment. It acted the same as when she sent Daenon across the cave. The pirate had acted like he was terrified, but of what? His leader had enchantment.

"You're getting good at that." Daenon said flatly.

Rowena's muscles clenched at his voice, still disoriented from the attack. "I . . . did nothing."

"Ye whispered something. I couldna hear it, but ye did," an oarsman said. "Did ye spell him like the queen can?"

"That's what happens from untrained enchantment." Fidessa

scoffed from behind Rowena's shoulder. "She's dangerous. You should keep her restrained."

At least she'd done something other than cower under cover. If her aunt had such better skills, why were so many of Uther's men hurt? There were at least three dead. Some mage she was.

"You made him panic?" Uther asked, squatting in front of her, moving the sword out of her reach. "Is that what happened?"

"I couldn't have. Lunara magic can only enhance what someone already feels." Or wants to, perhaps. Her mother had explained her powers many times, hoping it would spark Rowena's. She understood the rules . . . well enough. If his alarm had been her doing, she didn't understand how.

"All the more reason to keep her tied," Fidessa insisted.

"Something struck fear into him." Uther shifted to the rail and tracked the retreating ship. "Perhaps now he knows what's in the box."

Why would a pirate fear a sword? Rowena huffed. "He dug the box out of from between the crates as if he knew what to look for. He planned to knock me over the head to take it."

Uther turned back to scan the ship. "And how would a pirate determine what's in our cargo?"

"Maybe you don't have the devotion of everyone onboard this ship." Rowena smirked. "A crew is as good as their leader, and we all understand how you feel about loyalty."

Uther nodded slowly, staring over Rowena's head at nothing. "Give tribute to Ran and get back to the oars. We make Ibern by nightfall." He swept his hand toward one of the fallen guards near Rowena. Then Uther leaned near to her face, holding her gaze. She leaned back, unsure why he'd gotten so close, and didn't blink. Her uncle touched the tip of a small blade to her throat, making her go still. He lifted the box and headed back to the stern. Instead of stacking the box with the others that remained onboard, he leaned it against the ship's hull near where he stood.

Several oarsmen hurried to slip the dead over the side of the ship. After the dead were gone, the oars dipped into the water with haste toward the Northern Island.

Rowena crawled back onto the platform at the prow, staring at the small black dot still visible on the horizon. She should have followed the pirate to the other ship with her sword. Instead, she'd lost her chance at freedom and returned the blade to Uther. Whatever she had to endure in Forsa would be temporary. She'd only be there long enough to end the other royals, as she'd vowed.

TWELVE

No one spoke when they got back under sail after the pirate attack. On the prow deck, Rowena ignored everyone. Though the continual glances from her uncle and Daenon bore into her skull in her peripheral vision.

How would a pirate get information about a sword from a foreign land, locked away for over thirty years? Nothing made sense any longer. She focused on the waves and tried to block everything else out. Occasionally, a sea bird would fly overhead and she'd follow its path, pretending she could soar through the skies along with it. It was the only time she could block out the images from the last few days.

Ibern rose in the distance two days after the pirate attack. An excitement sizzled through the ship from the warriors, making them restless. Rowena's knee bounced incessantly. She couldn't sit still, watching the rocky landscape draw near. There were so few trees or mountains; nothing but disjointed hills with patchy grass marred by too many rocks. Only one rickety dock jutted from the shallow bay, without another ship in sight.

Uther had more ships, didn't he? The queasiness in Rowena's stomach grew worse. She hadn't expected to like Ibern, but the way Fidessa had acted, it seemed she hailed from a thriving village. There was nothing to greet them at this shore other than a desolate outpost. How far would they have to trudge to find the town? After so long on a rocking boat, she didn't relish a long hike on her unsteady legs.

The crew pulled down the sail and settled in at the oars to maneuver near the dock. There wasn't a shore to speak of; only piles of sharp rocks biting into the waves. Perhaps that explained why the small trading post sat farther back, by at least two hundred feet. It seemed odd for the place to hide behind a high circular palisade, however. It wasn't very welcoming for merchants or weary travelers.

The ship bumped the dock, and wood squealed in protest against wood.

"Welcome to Ibern, princess," Daenon muttered and held his hand out wide for her to exit the ship ahead of him. His lip curled, out of distaste for her or the surroundings she couldn't decide, though it meant nothing—she felt the same.

"How far is it to Forsa?"

Daenon blurted out a hearty laugh, nodding to the encircled buildings. "I suppose you could drag your feet to make the walk last longer if you desire."

That ring of hovels was her uncle's kingdom? She bit back a moan and climbed over the gunwale. When she landed, the wooden planks wobbled and shifted like the ship's deck. Her knees buckled, and she stumbled sideways, only stopped from falling into the water by digging her nails into an oar port.

"Better get your legs under you quick," Daenon said.

She sneered at him, forcing herself to stay balanced on the shifting boards.

Several of the crew had already disembarked, unloading the cargo, while others cared for the lines and sail. She scanned the crates and barrels for the sword box without success. Preoccupied by their hustle, the others ignored her. Or so she thought.

A heavy hand shoved against her spine. "Get goin'. I'm for a hot meal and a bed that stays put."

It was the guard who'd tied her up originally. His voice grated against her nerves, but she rolled his touch off her shoulder and marched on. If she had to stay in this horrible place, she'd not give anyone the satisfaction of showing her fear.

Daenon held up a hand, and the man grumbled, but said nothing more. The prince had proven himself her enemy in the cave. If he expected her to cower or be grateful for his help, he would find out differently. Whatever plans Uther had for them to marry would never happen. She'd die first . . . or they would. Either way, she'd forgive none of them. The guard's footsteps plodded behind, staying close as they fell into step behind Uther and Fidessa.

The village, though it didn't deserve such a grand description, rose from the dirt and rocks of the barren land. Dull green moss dotted the landscape that appeared to have sprung up between sharp gray lava from long ago volcano eruptions. Rowena scanned the horizon. The three white-capped peaks of The White Fang mountains rose in the far distance, their smaller offspring cutting through the bleak landscape toward the village. In between, there was an unforgiving tundra that left few hiding spots before reaching a small forested area. She'd never be able to escape without being sighted easily. She bit into her lip to keep it from quivering, but her vision clouded.

"Keep your chin up, dear. It only gets worse inside." Daenon matched her pace. "This place will drag you behind a cart without a second glance."

She hitched her cloak higher, swiping at her face in the motion. She didn't dare snatch a glance at the prince. He'd only have that mocking smirk on his lips, reminding her of her weakness. Though she wasn't entirely sure he'd spoken to her or himself.

Rowena lifted her chin and focused on her destination. A circle of stout poles, towering over two men high and sharpened to points at the top, created a palisade. A set of heavy wooden gates opened onto a path large enough to drive a cart through. On either side of the entrance sat tall towers, open on all sides under a thatched roof. In each, two guards kept watch, yet no horn signaled the king's arrival.

Odd, Rowena thought, craning her neck to glimpse Fidessa's face. But the queen kept her gaze forward, head held high.

Outside the palisade, a few horned bauruns and two shaggy mountain horses grazed freely on the moss. Once they entered the village, the wide muddy path ran through the center with goats, sheep, and chickens wandering aimlessly about. The arriving party had to scoot out of the way for a wagon laden with hay lumbering down the middle. A single elfling walked alongside, prodding the harnessed baurun pulling the load; he gave no greeting. Nor did anyone as they strode toward a tall center structure. The few Telana milling about continued their tasks without acknowledging their king or queen. They kept their heads down, shoulders slumped, working at a joyless pace. Neither Uther nor Fidessa seemed to notice the disrespect or care.

"There are more animal pens than homes," Rowena mumbled to no one. They were in better repair as well. The wattle and daub round huts had rotting thatch and patchy walls in need of repair, where the woven pens for the creatures held together tightly, displaying careful construction.

The tallest structure anchored the circular village, equal distance from the palisade on all sides. In the same round shape, like most of the buildings, it appeared more like a giant haystack than a home. At least double the size of any other structure, it spanned as wide as twenty warriors, rising to a sharp point. Thatching covered the entire conical shape and touched the ground with a single wooden door at the end of the path. Gray smoke curled out the top, disappearing into the low clouds of the same color.

Frustrated there wasn't anyone else to ask, Rowena edged closer to Daenon. "Why doesn't anyone greet their king?"

He inhaled a deep breath through his nose before answering. "You will find many differences from what you're familiar with."

It didn't answer her question, but increased the growing ache at the back of her throat. She had to swallow three times to clear out the sour taste forming with each heavy step. It had been a long journey; she needed a bath and a bed. After a rest, she would figure out what to do next.

Uther strode through the doorway, ducking under the thatch overhang, but Fidessa stopped abruptly. She spun and faced Rowena, forcing her to halt as well. Daenon followed the king, ignoring Rowena and brushing the queen's shoulder with his own as he passed.

Fidessa said nothing for several heartbeats until finally a woman, wearing a scarf over dark hair streak with gray, scurried out of the dwelling. The woman twisted around to Rowena's side and bowed quickly.

"Welcome home, my queen," the woman said.

"Rowena will be in your charge. See to it she learns her duties well." Her aunt grinned at Rowena in a way that sent shivers down her spine before pivoting back to the doorway and disappeared inside.

Rowena hesitated, considering the situation. It was common to assign a servant to a visitor, but the way Fidessa had spoken raised the hair on Rowena's neck. She took a step to follow, embracing Daenon's words that many things would be different.

"Not you. This way." The woman snatched Rowena's arm and dragged her sideways around the building.

Rowena yanked herself free and halted. "What are you doing?"

"Don't sass, girl. Follow me before you force me to take a stick to you." The woman grabbed her again and jerked harder.

Stunned, Rowena stumbled along. A stick? Girl? "Do you know who I am?"

"Having troubles?" A tall, plump woman sauntered over, lines creased between her eyes in a sneer. She, too, wore a kerchief and the same shapeless, rough spun serk as the woman near Rowena. Both women also had stained-covered aprons pinned to their fronts. It hit Rowena just then that they weren't servants, but thralls.

"None that requires your assistance, Hedda," the first woman said, lifting her chin to hold the stare of the woman towering over her.

"I can find my quarters myself." Rowena tried to slide away, but the smaller woman's ironclad grip belied her thin frame and older appearance.

As quick as a viper, the large woman's open palm struck Rowena's cheek.

Shocked, Rowena reached up, cupping her warmed face. "How dare you—"

"Keep quiet," the smaller woman hissed, shoving herself in front of Rowena. "Hedda, no more. She'll learn fast enough and she's my charge."

Hedda curled her lip, glaring at Rowena. "Watch your tongue. You'll get worse than that next time."

"Come." The first woman dragged Rowena away, out of view of Hedda.

Near the backside, they entered a dwelling, jutting out like a short thumb from where it shared a wall with the thatched tower. The low ceiling, catching in Rowena's braids, created too much darkness to view her surroundings. Only a bundle of small embers glowed in the center of the dirt floor. The woman released Rowena and kneeled, blowing until the flames burst to life within a small ring of rocks.

Afterward, the spry woman hurried to a trunk along the far wall and sifted through it while Rowena absorbed the sights of the now illuminated room. Her cheek still burned. She rubbed it, taking in the small pallet covered in patched woven blankets of undyed wool along one wall. A simple wooden table with one chair sat on the remaining wall. It took only a few moments before a trickle of sweat dribbled down Rowena's back from the heat. She waved smoke out of her face, moving away from its path to the door.

The woman straightened, holding in a bundle of fabric in her arms that she shoved at Rowena. "Put this on and I'll see how much I can let out of the hem. You're taller than me."

On instinct, Rowena accepted the offered clothing, then tossed them onto the woman's sleeping pallet. "I brought a trunk of my own things."

The two of them stared at each other for a moment. The woman finally dropped her chin with a sigh. When she met Rowena's gaze again, there was a softness to her face. "If you had a trunk, it will not be arriving."

"But I packed it. The queen ordered me to make sure I had my finest gown." Bia. Rowena folded her arms over her stomach. She had seen no one load the trunk and had thought it buried somewhere within the other possessions loaded onto the ship. Fidessa had mocked her and made sure Rowena lost her finest things. Her life in Taesing was truly over.

"Come, sit with me for a moment." The woman gestured to the bed. "It won't hurt much to make her wait."

Rowena's head ached and though she wanted to stomp away, she plopped down onto the thin, straw-filled bedding.

The woman lowered herself to sit near enough to place her hand over Rowena's forearm. "I'm Muriel. I serve the queen. You must change out of those clothes or we'll both suffer the consequences."

Rowena glanced at the dress. Muriel's gentle tone had a calming effect, yet nothing made sense. "That is a thrall's dress?"

"Yes." Muriel patted her arm. "Where are you from?"

"Taesing." She couldn't breathe, couldn't think past the rust-colored dress with an apron peeking out from within the folds.

Muriel jerked her hand away, though she caught herself and gently clasped both hands together in her lap. "The Skandan princess."

Rowena nodded, ignoring a tear dribbling down her cheek. The heat in the room became stifling. She wanted to scream, to race away, to go home. But her body remained motionless, numb.

The two sat in silence for several moments.

Finally, Muriel twisted and placed two fingers under Rowena's chin, forcing her to meet the older woman's gaze. "This is the queen's decision, and you must obey it. You will endure, and I will help you. But for now . . . it will be safer to do as you're told and not make things harder on yourself."

Safer. From what? Death? Everyone she loved had already died. Perhaps she should join them.

"Don't despair. It's written all over your face," Muriel said. "There is a time for everything. Everyone rises eventually—even thralls. Until then, this is how you'll live. Do as your bid. Speak only when spoken to by your superiors and stay out of the way. Now, change."

She had a calm voice, reminding Rowena of her mother. Fresh tears filled her eyes, and she squeezed them shut.

"Take a moment, but not too long. I'll be back to collect you." The straw rustled, and the air swirled from where Muriel had been.

Rowena swiped at her tears. "Muriel."

The woman stopped halfway out the door and leaned back into the room.

"Thank you."

"I'm not doing you any favors, dear. This won't be easy, but neither of us has a choice." She glanced at the dress. "Hurry. And avoid Hedda as much as possible. She is the overseer of sorts."

Rowena stared into the flames for a heartbeat after Muriel left, clenching the dress between her fingers. Muriel was wrong—she had a choice. It might start with wearing a thrall's dress, but it would end with a dead king and queen.

THIRTEEN

Death didn't scare Rowena—she lived by the sword and would no doubt die by it.

But to exist as a thrall, ordered to carry out mundane tasks . . . forever . . . that terrified her.

The thought crossed her mind as it had every day for the last month she'd been in Ibern. She shifted the yoke across her shoulders, balancing the empty buckets on either side. It was the third trip to the well to haul water for the laundry cauldrons. It would take another three before she could start washing.

They gave Rowena all the tasks that required no mental ability. Which was fine by her because it kept her strong and freed her to plan her vengeance. Which she'd hoped to have already carried out, but Uther and Fidessa made a point of keeping her far away from them.

Forsa only had about forty inhabitants, and they were all unenchanted Telana, like everyone from Skandan—except her. So far, she'd had no interaction with Daenon, which helped ease her mind. There were a handful of other thralls, and the rest were poor farmers or fisherman too busy and tired to care about anything, or guards who wandered around causing trouble. The royals seemed to have no interaction with anyone other than Uther's top two commanders.

"Out of the way, thrall," someone yelled.

A shove to the end of the stick sent her hurtling sideways. The buckets swung and knocked her off balance until Rowena's feet tangled and she slammed against the ground. Her back jarred from the awkward landing and she fell into the middle of a shepherd's flock on their way out of Forsa to graze for the day. The sheep scattered and raced into a table, tipping it over and spreading beads everywhere.

Rowena rolled to her knees, only to fall back again when a boot landed in her stomach. Unable to catch her breath, she clutched her middle in pain and shock. Another blow landed against her shoulder blades while more pummeled her thighs. All she could do was cover her head and wait until her attackers wore themselves out.

"Leave her be," a voice, Muriel's, rang out.

Rough hands hauled her to her feet, but try as she could, her legs wouldn't comply.

"Take her over near that cart, Tuck." Though Rowena was positive it didn't show on her face, relief flooded through her. Muriel was the only person she could count as a friend. Tuck, the seven-foot tall, half-Jotnari everyone avoided, was another outcast her friend had gathered under her wing. Most mistook Tuck's silence for dull wits, but they were wrong. He'd learned to stay quiet and avoid confrontation. A skill Rowena hadn't mastered.

Rowena's feet skidded through the dirt as Tuck dragged her to where Muriel ordered. When she could crack her eyelids enough to see where they headed, she didn't have time to protest before the lovable oaf leaned her against the wheel of the cart, just like Muriel had ordered. Unfortunately, he didn't care about the pile of sheep dung she landed in. He released Rowena and hurried back to help with the buckets and the yoke.

"Thanks," Rowena croaked, her ribs too sore to get out much more.

"Is anything broken, do you think?" Muriel asked, handing Rowena a cloth to wipe her face and hands.

"No, just bruised."

"What happened? Did you mouth off to Ivar again?"

Off to the side, Tuck grumbled words too low to understand. Stories varied about why the half-giant left his homelands, but no one dared to ask him.

"Is that who did the beating?" Rowena huffed. "At that point it was cover my face, or have to work blind. I don't think I said anything to him out of the ordinary."

"So, yes, most likely."

Rowena lifted a shoulder and rolled her eyes. It bothered Ivar that she'd never backed down to him. Nor would she, whether he was the son of Uther's top commander or not.

Her situation wouldn't last and one day he'd pay for how he treated her. That thought got her through all the days in Forsa. Her uncle expected that if he forced her to become a slave, below that even, a slave to slaves, then she'd finally accept his rule.

It would never happen.

Instead, she envisioned different scenarios where the king and queen died, followed by Daenon. No one else mattered, though if Ivar or Hedda got in her way, she wouldn't mind dispatching them as well. If she could figure out how she'd called up her enchantment before, it would make her plans much simpler. As it was, she had to count on her might alone.

Rowena pulled herself to her feet with help from the wheel and Tuck. Her legs were steadier, and she had to get back to work or suffer more than a beating. Bruises and aching muscles would heal, but some guards favored less savory methods of punishments. She'd avoided them and planned to keep it that way. After her experience with Daenon, she cringed at the thought of any man touching her.

Except for Tuck, who eased the yoke over her shoulders. With Muriel's help, they balanced the empty buckets on either side once again.

"Thank you," she said to her friends, and trudged back onto the path toward the well.

"Please, be careful," Muriel called.

"Always."

Fidessa had separated Rowena from Muriel after she witnessed how quickly they had bonded. Instead, the queen assigned Rowena to Hedda directly. But it didn't stop Rowena or Muriel from remaining friends.

Rowena spat some remaining blood from her mouth.

As soon as she destroyed everything the king and queen valued, then her time as a thrall would be over. As it would for her friends as well. Soon.

Barrels, crates, and assorted farm tools crowded the narrow paths through the village. Dogs and goats, farmers and guards, thralls and one princess all got in each other's way. No one cared about anything but their own tasks. Rowena did her best to squeeze by sideways to keep her buckets from knocking into something or someone. It didn't always matter. Arguments erupted over the smallest things.

The only well sat in the center of town. Muddy but drinkable water came up from the deep, craggy pit on the northern side of Forsa. The cavernous hole, dug by Osric's grace before she arrived, wasn't large or smooth. Rocks jutted out of the sides, creating dangerous obstacles to weave around as she pulled up a bucket. One bump would cause the precious water to spill so the process would have to start over.

The well was in sight when an elfling, nearly grown but still gangly with youth, fell on his knees directly in front of Rowena. Hedda shoved past a moment later to stand over the boy. She smacked the boy with a rod across his back. He tried to scramble away, but she yanked him back by the boot. No one moved to help the child. Including Rowena. She had a job to do, and the kid had to toughen up. No one in Forsa had a peaceful time.

"I'll leave you to the Seeker for sure. If he'd even take the likes of you," Hedda yelled.

Rowena twisted sideways, shimmied past the ruckus, and continued to the well.

The woman's brazen use of the dark druid seemed to instigate a frenzy among those who crowded around.

"She shouldn't use that name. It'll call the beast down on us," a male said.

Rowena squeezed between him and his barrel-chested companion.

The second man spat and hit her boot. "If that dark laggard shows his face, the king will to do him what he did to the Jotnari. I say let him come."

Uther used the long-ago battle he won when he'd first settled Forsa as a ploy to keep everyone living in his debt. Fear of the giants kept them willing to live in his squalor village, believing they needed his protection. His rule was a charade in Rowena's mind. The Forsans were sheep ruled by a toothless wolf.

Two women, daughters of a farmer and a guardsman, were drawing water by the time Rowena arrived at the well. It meant she had to wait until they finished. The trip had already taken twice as long as it should have. She'd find herself under the rod like that boy when she returned to the cauldron, most likely.

Neither woman cared that she waited, either. They chatted, ignoring Rowena after they filled their pails, letting them rest on the top ledge. Finally, Rowena turned one bucket over and sat down off to the side. No use letting her shoulders suffer if they didn't have to.

"Mind if I share the other one? Looks like they might be awhile?" A male voice startled her. First, because he acknowledged her presence, and second, because he actually sounded considerate.

She peered up to see who had dared such a drastic action, but the bright day shadowed his face.

"As long as you don't stop me from using the well as soon as they leave." She blinked the spots out of her eyes while he arranged himself next to her.

"I appreciate the respite, even for a moment," he said. "I'm passing through and it's been difficult to find anywhere to stay for the night. There doesn't appear to be an inn."

Where did this guy come from? It was obvious no such establishment existed in Forsa. "Anyone visiting would receive the king's hospitality and must have his permission to be here. I'm surprised you've made it this far without one of his guards hauling you in to present yourself."

Other than Muriel, she hadn't spoken so many words to anyone in a month. She glanced at the stranger and met his warm brown eyes. The kind that made all the chaos fade away. His long, dark hair pulled away from his rugged face, sporting the perfect amount of beard. A small twitch of his mouth gave away that her stare lasted too long.

Rowena snapped her gaze forward and held her breath, frustrated. Thoughts like that would only give this man the wrong impression. She'd already learned that lesson well enough.

"Perhaps they've not recognized me as a stranger."

A scoff blurted out before she could stop herself. "I doubt that. Strangers are a rare sight."

She wasn't about to make a fool of herself a second time by meeting his gaze, but even from the corner of her eye, his muscles distinguished themselves under his black tunic. And the sword slung over his back, sheathed in fine leather, should have had him stopped at the gate immediately.

"I strolled through the gates without issue," he said. "Perhaps you can introduce me to the king."

"It's not for me to introduce strangers."

"Well, allow me to solve one of my troubles. My name is Bram. And yours?"

No one ever asked her name, because everyone already knew it. Rumors of her identity burned through the village days after her arrival, which Fidessa happily confirmed. Not that it mattered to anyone. They had their own troubles and didn't care about hers.

"Rowena."

"A name of joy and strength."

Maybe once—not anymore. "You haven't been around long enough. There's nothing joyful here." Another woman joined those at the well and they seemed poised to stay even longer. Rowena slumped with a sigh.

"It can seem so, I'm sure. Dire circumstances force many to focus only on their own troubles without care for how it affects others." He kept his gaze forward, seeming as if in deep thought.

"Where are you from?" Circumstances in Forsa would only change after Uther and Fidessa were gone. Though, the women at the well would forget all their troubles once they saw a handsome warrior, with the potential to cart them away to better lands. Why had he approached her instead of them, anyway?

"My travels have taken me to many places." He answered, picking up a piece of straw and playing with it between his fingers. "No one is ever exactly how they appear. They work so hard to hide their struggles. Take those women we're waiting for. See the one in the blue over-apron?"

Rowena sighed and rolled her eyes, deciding not to take part in his conversation any longer. Whatever pain anyone had, it meant nothing. Actions were all that mattered.

He continued, despite her silence. "Her father beats her for no reason other than to make himself feel better for his inferior position within the guard. She then bullies the other women to exert some control over herself. It's quite sad, actually."

How could he possibly have that knowledge? Why did so many

believe they could spout stories with confidence and others would take them as truth?

"She deserves compassion, yet she won't allow anyone to offer it," he continued.

"You need to stop drinking so early in the day. Ale has muddled your thinking. She's cruel because she has a small amount of meaningless power. She craves a better position. The Prince of Velmeg will assume his place next to his father soon. Rumor says he's expected to choose a wife. That's the power she craves."

"You believe she wishes to become queen someday?"

"I know it; she prattles on about it all the time. No one ever pays attention to what they say in front of a thrall."

He twisted and held her gaze, gilded flecks glittered in his warm brown eyes.

"What?"

"As I said, it is a matter of focus. You'll see what I mean when the time is right, but you must be looking."

It was an odd conversation she didn't have time for. Rowena rose from the bucket and Bram followed without hesitation. "I have more trips to make. They're just going to have to get out of my way."

She didn't bother putting the yoke behind her neck as usual, and just slung it over one shoulder. She'd stack the buckets and lug them in her arms for the short distance. When she reached for the one Bram had been sitting on, he already had it in hand.

"I'll carry it. I'd like to help in exchange for your company."

No one did anything without wanting something in return.

She frowned. "It is my duty."

"As it is mine." He turned toward the well and strode off with her bucket.

"Give that back." If he thought he was going to take it for himself, she'd show him he'd messed with the wrong woman.

Her outburst brought attention to both of them by the

women at the well. To her utter surprise, they sneered at Bram. It gave her such pause that he arrived at the well first. The women huffed and left.

Odd.

"I assure you, I'm only offering you a helping hand." The stranger hooked the bucket to the rope.

"Well, don't." Whatever his business in Forsa, she didn't trust him. "What brings you here, anyway?"

"You might say I'm on a pilgrimage of sorts." He'd already tied the bucket to the rope and dropped it down in the pit. He swirled the rope to be sure the bucket filled and brought it back hand over hand without a struggle and in half the time it would have taken her. After he set the first one down, he held out his hand for the next.

Rowena prided herself on being independent, even within her current situation, but she wasn't stupid. The speed that he worked would help make up for the time she'd waited at the well—and during her beating. She shrugged. "Better your muscles than mine."

He made light work of the second one as well, having no issue with the irregular sides that could catch the bucket and spill its contents before arriving at the top. But when he tried to take the yoke from her, she drew the line. "I'll manage. You've done enough."

"There's no shame in needing help sometimes."

Bram confused her. How could he think that someone in her position would benefit from having someone else do her work? She had enough trouble from those like Ivar and Hedda. "You realize I'm a thrall, right? I'm in enough trouble for taking so long."

"I'm not one to care much for anyone's station. Every living being deserves to be cared for and treated with respect."

She'd grown up with the same sentiment, but it didn't fit her reality any longer. "You're a stranger who's helped a thrall before announcing yourself to the king. Your decision-making skills are suspect."

He burst into a hearty laugh. She'd not heard genuine mirth in so long, it made her breath catch. It almost appeared there was an inner glow coming from him.

She needed to get far enough from the traveler who made her pulse speed up annoyingly.

"I've heard many in the village believe they owe the king their lives. He saved them from the Jotnari and is kind to everyone. Do you not believe he'll welcome me?"

She was about to duck under the yoke and call the conversation over. Until he said that. "Is it kindness to put someone into slavery? Or do you think I chose this for myself?" If he thought that, he was no better than Uther.

"I've seen many strange things. That wouldn't be the worst of them." The way he spoke gave Rowena pause. How long had he wandered? He couldn't be more than a few winters older than her.

He turned his stare on her so intently it made her shiver. Her palms itched. She had buckets to carry, chores to do, and revenge to plan . . . not entertain his nonsense.

She slipped the yoke over her shoulders and hefted the full buckets into the air. She'd have to hurry through the crowd without another incident. Much to her chagrin, Bram followed.

"You need to go mess with someone else. Declare yourself to the king and see if he's who you think he is."

Bram laughed again. "I'll see the king in due time. But you fascinate me. The king saved his subjects from the giants. Do you not think he deserves their loyalty?"

Saved his subjects. The statement enraged her more than the man could have guessed. She slowly squatted enough for the buckets to relax against the ground and removed the yoke. "You're an idiot if you believe he saved anyone. Uther agreed to terms with King Lendan in order to stop the Jotnari invasion." Uther's deal saved himself, and no one else. There wasn't any other explanation.

"Now, I have work to finish. I didn't ask you for your help and I don't want your company. If I were you, I'd turn around and wander somewhere else."

With that, she set her load and stomped away—as fast as she could, with a heavy yoke across her shoulders.

FOURTEEN

Rowena dumped the buckets of water into the cauldron from her fifth trip to the well.

"Are you still fetching water? You should have shirts on the line by now," Hedda yelled, shoving her big bosom into Rowena's space to gawk at the nearly full vessel.

"The fire has been going for a while, so it won't be long." Rowena bit her lip and inwardly cringed. Her words hadn't been wrong, but they'd come out too quick and sure. She focused on emptying the last bucket, hoping Hedda would move on and let her be.

The woman pinned Rowena too close to the fire. She didn't dare step back. Hedda leaned close enough for her chicory-stained teeth to brush against Rowena's cheek. "That wasn't very smart. Because I see dirt along the inside rim of this cauldron, and that means you didn't clean it well enough before you began. Empty it and clean it properly."

There hadn't been a single smudge on that kettle before she started, of that Rowena would stake her life. "It's only for laundry."

Rowena clenched her jaw. She tried to squirm out from

between the hot iron pot and the squishy woman. The bucket still in her hand banged on the edge and sprinkled water into the air. Some of it landed on Hedda.

"You ingrate!" The overseer screamed as if the liquid had seared off her skin. A little water certainly wouldn't hurt her. "Now, you've done it."

Hedda rammed her elbow into Rowena's side, sending her stumbling sideways. A boot snaked out and swept her off her feet. She landed hard and her breath whooshed out. She didn't move and tried to suck in a trickle of air. A screaming grunt rang through the room. Before Rowena could move, the dirt under her turned to warm mud.

Rowena rolled to a sitting position in time to catch sight of Hedda, letting go of the cauldron as the last of its water drained onto the ground.

The woman heaved, sweat dribbling down her puffy red cheeks. Despite the effort it cost her, she grinned. "Start over."

Mud squished between Rowena's fingers as she pushed to her feet. Her muscles tensed and her fists curled, begging to lash out at the woman. She gagged on her response, forcing it down her throat.

"Do you have something to say?" Hedda stepped closer. "If you were smart enough to do things right the first time, this wouldn't have happened."

A vision of slamming her fist into the side of Hedda's face clouded Rowena's mind. Even as her collarbone took the brunt of the bigger woman's jabbing finger. Fighting back wouldn't help. Lash marks itched where they healed from the last time she had argued with Hedda. The woman lived to make others' lives miserable.

Commotion at the gates drew Rowena's gaze sideways. The entrance to Forsa partially hid behind a row of rabbit hutches and a home. Four strangers—warriors—called up to the Ibernian guards who manned the watchtowers. One guard rushed away a moment later, while the others welcomed the newcomers inside.

"Who's that?" Rowena snapped her gaze back to Hedda's in time to see the woman's nostrils flare.

"Don't you turn away from me," the woman growled.

Rowena pointed at what she saw, effectively distracting Hedda from continuing her rant.

"Clean up this mess and then stay in your quarters. Don't show yourself until I release you." Hedda didn't wait for Rowena's answer; she hurried away.

The horrible woman was barely out of sight when Rowena's name rang out. A moment later, Muriel stood in front of her, scanning the area and Rowena's muddy clothes. She shook her head before meeting Rowena's gaze with understanding. "Quickly, come with me."

"I have to get the cauldron back in place before I go anywhere." Rowena spun and marched to the large black kettle. Not that heavy without the water. She gripped the edge and pushed it back upright.

However, the fire ring had standing water in it. She'd have to rework the stones and haul some dirt to soak up the mud before she built another fire. Then, she would have to wash the carrying buckets and the cauldron before she started hauling the water once again.

"Leave that. There are more important things happening right now."

Muriel snatched her hand and raced the two of them away. When they reached the main road, they had to pull up to a stop.

Guards stood on either side, not allowing anyone to pass. Rowena stood on her tiptoes to peer around the warriors.

Muriel yanked her back to her feet and tugged her arm. "Don't draw attention to yourself. Come this way."

"What is happening?" Rowena curled her lip at all the fuss.

"It's the Fianna," Muriel said. "Hurry."

She led Rowena to her room and barred the door once they were inside.

"Don't the Fianna pledge themselves to protect the king? Why all the concern?"

"They are nothing but mercenaries now. They come once a month to collect tribute from King Uther for protection against invaders, or some such. Honestly, I'm not sure, but there's talk the king might refuse to pay them this time."

Rowena flicked her eyebrows up. "Why should he? If you pay a group like that, you're just empowering them to bully you. My father never would have allowed that."

"Well, your father sounds like he was a decent king." Muriel sucked in a breath and her eyes widened.

"You won't get any arguments from me." Rowena chuckled.

"I should be more careful. And so should you." Muriel grabbed her bed coverings and messed them up into a pile. "You need to stay hidden. It's too dangerous for anyone to see you."

"Why?"

"Everyone knows who you are, which means the Fianna probably do as well. If Uther doesn't pay, those mercenaries may decide to ransom you."

Rowena's blood turned cold. She would not let those men put their hands on her. Muriel must have seen the fear on her face because she rushed over.

"Here." Muriel slid a knife into Rowena's hand. "Keep this and get under the coverings until I come for you."

"Muriel!" Hedda's voice called from outside.

"Hurry!" Muriel whispered and shoved Rowena toward the pallet.

Muriel had just flipped the blankets over Rowena's head when she heard the door bang against the wall. "Why are you in here? The queen is calling for you."

"I'm on my way." Muriel shuffled her feet to the door, but Hedda must have stepped inside.

"What were you doing in here?"

Rowena held her breath, tightening her grip on the knife.

"I had a sliver in my finger and I wanted to take it out where I could concentrate."

"Hmm."

"I'd prefer you leave my quarters."

Rowena's heart pounded so hard that she was sure Hedda would hear it.

"Hurry. The Fianna will stay for a while, and the king must offer hospitality."

The door closed, and both voices faded in the distance. Rowena still didn't move for a long time. The coverings became stifling, and her hair plastered to her cheeks with sweat, but she stayed.

Who could the Fianna ransom her to? The question kept pestering her. Did they think Uther would pay for her return? Perhaps the complete story hadn't reached them. If they understood that Uther and Fidessa had killed the king and queen of Skandan, perhaps they would turn against them. Stories of the Fianna said they used to be guided by justice.

When she had heard no voices pass by for a long while, she dared creep out of her hiding spot. If Muriel was right, it was important for her to stay put. But what if the Fianna could help her?

She had to at least see who the men were, watch them interact. Then, she could determine if she might be able to make them her allies. She had to take the chance. Tucking the knife in her belt, she listened at the door and slowly cracked it open to peer around. When no one seemed around, she raced toward the closest structure and skidded to a stop behind a pig pen.

There was a back door to the king's home that gave access to the larders. It would be busy, but she could hide nearby and listen —or peek. She darted to the next home and ducked around it.

Chunks of daubing had dried and fallen away, leaving gaps in the walls where anyone inside could see Rowena.

She hurried from house to pen to crate until she made it to the larder. The rare, rectangular structure stored vegetables, dried meats and fish, as well as barrels of wine and ale. Like she suspected, there were many thralls and others going back and forth.

She'd only seen four men enter the village. Who was eating and drinking so much? She crept closer.

"What are you doing?" A woman Rowena had never interacted with before, a guard's wife, stood with her hand on a hip. "Get what you need and get back inside. Don't keep them waiting."

Rowena ducked her head. A piece of hair fell over her face and she only then realized that she no longer had her kerchief. Most of those in Forsa had brown hair; a few had a coppery sheen, but no one had her blonde coloring. If she went inside, it would be moments before someone discovered her.

She nodded to the woman and scurried into the larder. There had to be a way to hide. Two barrels of ale sat flush against the back wall. If she could move one, she might slide behind it. She grabbed the top and tried to scoot the round container. It wouldn't budge.

"Rowena."

She spun and found Tuck staring at her. "Help me, please. I need to hide."

"I have to bring more ale." He glanced over his shoulder and then back. "There's a place, but you have to stay right next to me."

"Thank you." She could have hugged him.

"When I go inside, you slide behind the weaving loom sitting there. A blanket is nearly finished and no one will see you."

"I can't go in there." His plan would get her caught for sure.

"Muriel told me to watch out for you. Said you'd ignore her order." He cocked his head with a small grin. "It is the best place. Stay close to me."

She should have stayed in Muriel's room, for no other reason than to avoid being so predictable. Tuck maneuvered around her and lowered the barrel to its side, rolling it toward the door.

"I'll put this on my shoulder. You stay right here." He put his hand on the back of his right hip.

She inhaled and gave a quick nod. A few moments later, Tuck had the barrel she couldn't even move resting on his shoulder. She licked her lips and forced herself to take hold of his tunic so she would stay as close to him as possible.

Exactly as he'd described, a tall loom stood near the wall two feet from the doorway. Tuck crossed his feet, making it seem as if he staggered under the barrel's weight, moving both of them close enough that Rowena could slide into her hiding spot unseen.

Tuck continued on as if nothing were amiss. That sweet giant.

The weaving went low enough that if she stood still, no one would notice her. She slowly shifted to where she could lean her face slightly to see between the frame and fabric. It quickly became apparent why they needed more ale.

Every warrior in Forsa sat at tables scattered throughout the space. They feasted as if it were King's Day. Uther sat with Fidessa and Daenon among his commanders. The four Fianna sat nearby with the traveler at their table, conversing like they were all friends.

The band of mercenaries stuck out wearing animal-skin sleeveless tunics over loose-fitting trousers. One of them had wild, bright red hair with loose curls covering his ears. His bushy beard and mustache hid his mouth, so he appeared to only have a set of bright blue eyes alongside a sharp nose. He belly-laughed like it was his nature, slapping the man who sat next to him on the back.

The others were much more subdued, but also seemed deeply engaged in jovial conversation. A trim, lanky looking man sat with his back to her, with a bow and quiver full of arrows on the floor near his feet. The other two seemed the most subdued. One man with close-cropped dark hair and umber skin sat next to the thin man so she couldn't see his face, but the one across from him had a serious expression. Thin dark brows angled as if continually angry over a hooked nose and tight mouth. He gave her pause. The others were enjoying themselves without concern, or able to hide their intentions better. She suspected the latter.

It would be too difficult to get close to them, and she didn't dare stay any longer. As she ran through different options for slipping out unseen, a crash sounded in the main room. She tipped to the side and found a thrall on her knees, cleaning up from a dropped pitcher of ale. It was the perfect opportunity to run. When the woman glanced over her shoulder directly at the loom, Rowena's heart jumped. It was Muriel. She'd purposefully caused a distraction.

Dear, wonderful Muriel. Rowena glanced around, ready to sprint away, but had to jump back behind the loom when she met the narrowed stare of the red-haired Fianna.

Rowena's pulse sprinted as she tried to stay still, breathing in and out slowly. When no one arrived to wrestle her from behind the weaving, she dared another peek. The Fianna had twisted to speak to someone else. She didn't waste her chance and darted out of hiding, through the door and around the thatched building. When she peeked back to make sure no one followed, she smacked into someone and fell. On her knees, she watched two sandal-clad feet scuffle backward.

Her gaze traveled up a long, brown, cowled robe with a simple rope belt and into the expressionless stare of a woman with silver crystalline eyes. A heavy copper medallion hung around her neck, emblazoned with the symbol of an Oraku. Muriel had spoken of the druid, Yralissa, who occasionally came to Forsa.

Rowena's mouth suddenly grew dry. She rose carefully to her feet and cradled both her elbows into her palms. Her father had taught her to respect druids, regardless of their status because of their close connection to the Primary fae realm of Caelus. She wasn't sure if she should speak or stay silent.

Disavowed druids had done something against the code set for them by the Heptad. Because of that, it stripped them of their Primary fae powers and kicked them out of their homeland. But they still held far more skills than any enchanted race. If the druid had the ability of an oracle to see fragmented parts of the future, they could mark someone for collection at the Reaping. Rowena had grown up with Asta, but this woman had a much more severe countenance. Her stark white unbound hair made her seem wild.

"Excuse me, I didn't see you." Uncomfortable with the silence and with little time to wait, she hoped the woman would be kind, but the words came out squeaky. She cleared her throat. "I apologize."

"You are not where you belong."

"I . . . I was going back there."

"That's not what I meant. Uther has called for me to perform the wedding ceremony."

Rowena backed up several steps, out of the druid's reach. It was supposed to be after Daenon's return to Velmeg. Her chest caved in. "I won't do it."

Yralissa lifted her hand, but suddenly pulled it to her chest, staring wide-eyed at something over Rowena's shoulder. If something frightened a druid, Rowena wasn't sure she wanted to find out what it was. But she twisted slowly to find the ground covered with a writhing black mist. A black cloud grew taller, rising from the center. It billowed with twisting shadows, rising like ribbons of thick smoke, becoming more defined, until a figure took shape. The wind picked up, whipping Rowena's hair around her face. Thunder rolled, and she expected everyone from inside to spill out to see the terror forming in front of her, but no one showed.

A heartbeat later, everything went deathly silent and still. The darkness faded to reveal a horned figure looming where the shadows had been. Eyes, like molten gold, locked onto Rowena's gaze where she stood, gaping in awe and terror.

It had to be the Seeker. The dark druid had come just as some had feared, because Hedda had called out his name. He turned that haunting gaze on Yralissa.

"Leave and warn the king she is not to wed," a deep voice rumbled, sounding strangely familiar within the command.

Yralissa made no comment, only hurried away, leaving Rowena to face the most terrifying individual she'd ever seen.

"Come, and you'll be safe."

A mirthless laugh erupted from Rowena. Safety was the last thing she'd expect to find with the strange druid. His tall horns glistened like black jewels in contrast to where white runes flashed on his pale skin. Was it a trick of light, or did they glow like his eyes?

Whatever happened, she could not allow the monster in front of her to take her. In the most craven move possible, she spun and raced away. She darted into Muriel's room, shoving a small table in front of the door and dove back under the pile of coverings, waiting for the Seeker to find her and tear her to pieces.

FIFTEEN

Rowena trembled on Muriel's pallet, peeking out from under the blankets. She decided that when the Seeker found her, she'd rather know right away than let him surprise her. Time passed. No one screamed outside. She wondered if she'd dreamed up the entire experience.

Then the door rattled.

She raised the knife Muriel had given her. It was such a puny weapon compared to the horns and claws she'd faced earlier. The situation was laughable if she wasn't so terrified.

The door banged against the table, once, twice, and a third. Rowena sat up. The dark being she'd witness come alive within the shadows wouldn't have trouble with a rickety door and wobbly table.

"Rowena? Are you in there?" Muriel called.

She threw off the covers and hurried to move the furniture away. Muriel opened the door and Rowena flattened her back against the wall, peering beyond her friend to scan for anyone else following behind her.

"What is wrong? You're pale and sweating." Muriel wrapped her arm around Rowena's waist and moved her over to the chair, helping her to sit. "Were you caught after you left the feast? It seemed like you'd gotten away."

Had she not seen him? "Did Yralissa tell everyone?"

Muriel squatted in front of Rowena, clasping a hand between both of her calloused ones. "The Oraku made quite a stir, speaking to the king and queen. She announced that Daenon is not to marry you. Isn't that wonderful?"

"Did you see him? Did everyone see him?" Her eyes burned and she couldn't hold back her tears.

"See who? Daenon? He seemed as relieved as I expected you to be. What has upset you so? You're trembling." Muriel stood, bringing Rowena with her. "Come rest. We'll sit together for a while."

They crawled onto the pallet and leaned against the wall. Rowena lay her head on Muriel's lap, while her friend ran her fingers through Rowena's tangled hair. She missed her mother so much. The tears fell, turning into deep sobs. Muriel cooed gentle words until Rowena cried herself to sleep.

* * *

Rowena startled, jumping to her feet when Muriel shook her awake the next morning.

"I hope you're feeling better. We have no more time for you to rest. After the Fianna left, King Uther announced we are heading to Velmeg today instead of next week."

"Today? Why?"

"I'm not sure. But it's best to get outside and not make any trouble." Muriel left to help the queen pack.

That was an understatement. Rowena had had enough trouble for two lifetimes. She quickly plaited her hair, though every noise made her jumpy. Before she left, she adjusted the ties on her stockings. Her fingers glided along her mother's brooch she'd kept. If anything happened to her, she wanted to ensure that something of her family survived. A month in Forsa had forged enough reminders as motivation for her vengeance. She removed the brooch and hid it among the box of Muriel's things waiting to be loaded onto a wagon. Her friend would find it later and understand.

She left the safe room and headed outside, her head swiveling in search of shadows rising from the ground. Why hadn't the Seeker hunted her down? Why had he come? Based on how Muriel acted, no one else had seen the dark druid. Except for Yralissa. She told Uther what the Seeker commanded her. That was at least proof he'd been real. Whatever it was all about, and whatever he wanted, she had to face the day. A small grin formed. With everything else, it finally hit her she didn't have to marry Daenon. That small favor gave her some peace as she left the small room.

On the main road, wagons and carts lined up to prepare for the journey. Uther shouted orders for the largest wagon to move to the front, just inside the gate, forcing Rowena to move out of the way of four larger males hurrying to pull it into place. Others moved smaller carts that goat power or Telana themselves would pull.

"Get working, girl," Hedda yelled, shoving Rowena in the back. "Go gather eggs and pack 'em with straw. Any you break will come out of your hide."

Rowena stared at her for a heartbeat, debating for a split second whether to comply or rush forward and shove her shoulder into the blustering woman's midsection. The image of Hedda coming off her feet and landing on her backside with a thud brought a flash of humor to Rowena.

"Did you think I was joking?" Hedda stepped closer.

Rowena smirked. "Not at all." She let out an exhale and marched past the haughty woman to grab a large basket. The easy task allowed her to relax. Chickens roamed free and eggs could be anywhere, so she'd be able to ignore everyone and everything for a good while.

After grabbing some clean straw from the corner of an empty goat pen, she set about searching the nooks and crannies between stacked crates and barrels. Anywhere with space for a chicken to be safely out of the way for a few hours, there were nests.

A typical drizzle had begun and the gray skies helped Rowena put aside her worries and pretend she was at home, doing chores with her family nearby. A wave of wistfulness soaked her more than the rain. It struck her that for all the times she'd spent wishing to be anywhere other than Skandan—it had now become the only place she wanted to be.

A glimpse of teal caught her eye, and she kneeled down into the mud, stretching her hand between two empty crates at the bottom of a pile. There were three of the opalescent eggs in the nest. It was a simple pleasure she'd learned to give herself—noticing the small pieces of beauty wherever they appeared. In the middle of the mud, drizzle, and suffocation of Forsa, there were sparkling little jewels left around like treasure. It was almost a shame to use them for breakfast.

She rested the last egg in the basket and rose to her feet, stretching her back. Down the lane, the frantic preparations of the growing line of hand-carts, small wagons, and supplies bustled about. Bram crossed by carrying two small barrels. The traveler seemed to have gained Uther's approval to stay. What made him want to remain in the oppressive village begged for an answer, but she refocused on her task.

There were a few more spots to check and those last few would finish filling her basket. She rearranged the straw to give more padding for another layer and finished her perusal of the area.

By the time Rowena made it back to the main road, the caravan of supplies stretched from the front gates and past the large meeting house.

Tuck rushed along on the other side of the hubbub from where she stood. His cheeks were ruddy and his hair plastered to his head from more than just the rain. They always worked him hard because of his size and strength.

Rowena ambled closer to the main wagon to drop off her

basket. Through the gates, two herdsmen led the baurun that would pull the heaviest load. A woman stashing something inside the wagon hadn't seen the pair of horned oxen arrive behind her. When she turned their direction, it must have startled her because she screamed. The normally passive animals, despite their humongous size, lurched back and let out a loud snort and then an ear-splitting bellow.

As tall as a man and twice as wide, the beasts could be deadly, but not from their sharp, curving horns. The acrid stench from the poisonous dung they sprayed when agitated could burn the flesh off someone.

One of them thrashed its head side-to-side, throwing the handler to the ground. Even though the Telana wouldn't let go of the lead-rope, the beast charged in fear, dragging the fae, and leaving a trail of venom-tainted spray. The woman darted out of the way, jumping onto the side of the wagon, but an older man stumbled as he tried to twist and flee at the same time.

Rowena lowered her basket, but let it fall about a foot to the ground. Several of the eggs cracked, but she'd deal with that later. No one else stood between her and the man struggling to get up from his knees. She raced for him, tugging him along in a half-crawl, half-run until they both landed in a heap off to the side, out of reach of the noxious poison. The ground vibrated from the pounding hooves thundering past.

The baurun charged down the line, sweeping aside a hand cart and then a small wagon with a vulugoat already in harness. Screams rang out as the scared animal raced blindly toward the meetinghouse. At least three Telana lay writhing on the ground in pain.

An orange misty plume erupted in front of the baurun's path, forcing it to drop its hindquarters into a skid. It came to a stop and sat dazed for a moment before toppling over onto its side.

When the mist settled, Fidessa stood only four feet in front of the massive animal's trajectory. She still held her hands high from where she must have discharged a charm. The baurun's sides heaved up and down, proving it still lived, but it no longer terrorized the caravan.

Several men had wrangled the second baurun out the gate to race over the rough terrain until it settled and began grazing safely in the distance.

"Are you alright?" Rowena disentangled herself from the man. She shoved herself to her feet, helping the man to stand at the same time.

"It appears so," he said, running a hand over his chest. "That thing would have killed me for sure."

A small trickle of blood dribbled down the side of his face. Rowena pointed to it. "You'll need some physics for that."

They both scanned the ground and found a small rock near where they fell. "I'll take a knock to the noggin' over a horn through the chest any day. Thank you, princess."

Rowena scoffed with a shake of her head. "No one calls me that anymore. I'm not even sure it's safe for you to say aloud."

She stepped over and squatted next to the dropped egg basket, gingerly sifting through the straw to find out how many eggs she'd lost.

"Outta the way!" a booming voice yelled.

Rowena picked up her basket. She and the man she'd helped scooted backward as the revived, yet still groggy, baurun ambled by them. Bram had helped collect the other one, and they neared the gates. The traveler ran his hand up and down the side of the beast's face as if soothing it. He was an odd individual. Tall and handsome for sure. Anyone would say so. The way he carried himself, shoulders back and confident, distinguished him from the others who scuttled around hunched over.

"Rowena." Muriel rushed closer, bringing her attention back to where she stood. "Did you get injured?"

"No, but this man has a cut that needs attention."

"Nonsense." He waved Muriel away. "I'll be fine. It's best not to draw any more attention to ourselves."

The man gave a quick nod to Rowena and hurried away. She watched him go and her gaze snagged on Hedda, stomping her way.

A scoff mixed with a muttered curse left her throat. "You should go too. That one will find an excuse to make this your fault as much as mine."

Muriel snatched the egg basket from Rowena's hands. Mud clung to the bottom, keeping the broken eggs from oozing out. "I'll take that. But fear not. I've heard she has to stay behind to care for what we aren't taking with us."

A smiled broke across Rowena's face, but she said nothing. Muriel winked and hurried away.

"Bring that basket over here," Hedda called.

Muriel picked up her pace. A slight limp affected her gait—Rowena would ask about it later.

Fidessa, Uther, and Daenon strode to the front of the caravan line, cutting off Hedda from pursuing Muriel or saying anything to Rowena. She dropped her gaze and waited for the royals to pass. Rowena stood taller, staring past all of them.

Fidessa kept her head high, as if no one else existed. Daenon focused on the bustling line of those eager to get going.

But Uther paused and beckoned her over. "Come. You'll walk next to the wagon. If you tire, you can sit in the back."

Fidessa twisted. Her smug look soured at the offer.

Rowena rolled her eyes, but settled her gaze on Hedda. She gave the woman as fake of a pleasant smile as she could muster and dropped into a mocking curtsy before following the other royals to the front of the line. If she never saw that woman again, it would be too soon.

Uther offered a hand to Fidessa as they climbed aboard the

wagon. Behind and higher than the where the drivers sat, a bench perched under a tattered cloth cover for the royals. At one time, the fabric might have been a regal detail, but in Rowena's opinion, it only highlighted a sad effort to seem better than others.

"Rowena," Uther called down to her. "In case you've heard otherwise, you're still betrothed. The wedding will take place at the end of the prince's prime day celebrations."

Daenon flashed a searing glare her way and stomped to the other side of the wagon to settle onto the bench next to Fidessa. Uther waved his hand to the two Telana drivers to get going. Each man held the braided reins of one of the baurun, controlling them separately. It was doubtful even one with Jotnari blood like Tuck could manage both of the massive animals alone.

He would not listen to Yralissa . . . and would defy the Seeker's command. What would that mean?

Without ceremony, the caravan eased out of the gates, wheels and feet squelching through the mud. Rowena stood rooted to the ground until someone jostled her, shouldering their way ahead. Whatever it took, she would not marry Daenon; not just because he disgusted her, but also because she never wanted to face that horned monster again.

* * *

The road meandered in a serpentine path because of the rolling ground embedded with boulders outside the village. The baurun team plodded along at such a maddeningly slow pace. After an hour they were just arriving at the edge of the forest.

"At least this pace isn't bothering my knee," Muriel said over the rattle of wheels, and murmurs of those trudging behind them.

Rowena stretched her arms. "What happened?"

"Nothing to worry about. Just tripped."

Rowena clamped her mouth tight for a moment, sure that it wasn't an accident. "How far is it to Velmeg?"

"I've never been."

Rowena halted for a step. "Never?"

The wagon jerked and tilted precariously as one wheel hit a big rock. Tuck raced to help, bracing the heavy load so it didn't topple over.

"Oh, he worries me." Muriel held her hand over her heart. "He's always rushing in without concern for his own safety."

"If others learned from his kindness, what a difference in the realm that would make." Bram eased closer and fell into step with them, giving Rowena a quick nod of greeting when she raised her brows.

She twisted her neck to scan for other groups. The nearest to them were at least ten paces back, distracted by a gaggle of goslings wanting to scatter. It unnerved her how easily the traveler approached unnoticed. She would take more care to watch her surroundings from that point.

"That is a fine dream, but could never happen."

Rowena gaped. It was a statement she didn't expect from Muriel. The woman always seemed to find the good in others. "That sounds like you've been around me too much."

Muriel chuckled. "No, I've just watched too many things befall such a sweet boy to believe others can be kind to those they fear."

"Sometimes fear can be a motivator for change. When life is easy, no one concerns themselves with the plight of others," Bram said. "It's when they fear a personal loss that they take notice of larger needs. At least, that's what I've seen too often."

"Perhaps that's why the Heptad created the Seeker?" She spoke the words more to herself than the others. The image of the massive druid, swirling in shadows, haunted her thoughts too easily.

Muriel snatched Rowena's arm, twisting her so they came face to face. "Never mention that name. Some terrors are real. There's no way the druids created such a creature. It rose from Mortus—another way for the king to find his way out and snatch victims for his army."

White showed all around her friend's brown eyes. She believed saying the name of the being would draw him, just like those said when Hedda did it. "You really believe that?"

"Do you?" Bram asked. Lines etched across his forehead as he waited for her answer.

"The stories say the Heptad created him. Who knows? One rumor says one thing, another something different. I don't care who created the being, but nothing good can come from such a terror."

Bram's nostrils flared, but then he seemed to force himself to speak low and calm. "Rumors grow from a fear of the unknown and wither from the truth."

Muriel let go of Rowena's arm and swiped her hand through the air. "The two of you are going to bring disaster upon us if you don't stop talking about this."

What had he meant by that? His amber eyes seemed to spark as he spoke. Or it was just a trick of light? Being that they'd entered the trees, that seemed unlikely. She scoffed aloud at herself for even noticing such things and twisted to watch Tuck as he helped an elfling onto a wagon.

"Don't believe me and see what happens," Muriel said, misjudging the noise to be about the comment. She hurried to catch up to Tuck, leaving Rowena alone with Bram.

"I didn't mean to offend," Bram said.

"That's not . . . ugh." Rowena mumbled. She glanced at Bram and suddenly didn't know what to do with her hands. Of all the times to be free of a task.

"She shares the same opinion as many I've come across," Bram said. "And she's not wrong."

Rowena pinched her eyes closed and inhaled. It wasn't a topic she wanted to discuss any longer. It made it impossible to ignore the memory of shadows coming to life the night before. She'd rather occupy her mind with the sounds of bleating goats and creaky wheels, enjoying a moment of freedom by herself. "Wouldn't you prefer to speak with someone more interesting?"

"I find you—"

Bram threw out his arm, and Rowena slammed against it to a halt. A heartbeat later, an arrow sailed out of the trees and stuck into the side of the wagon.

SIXTEEN

The quivering fletch that could have embedded into Rowena's side instead of the wagon's wooden plank.

"What . . . where?" She glanced at Bram and then at the trees.

She didn't have to wait long because a group of screaming men, with faces painted like warriors, rushed from the trees. They crossed the ten-foot open area next to the road and attacked. Elven males, wild and crazed, swarmed the caravan, shoving whoever they met to the ground. They wore rough-spun trousers and, if they wore a shirt at all, they made it from animal hides. The Fianna.

Some knocked over carts, broke open cages of chickens and spilled produce. Others engaged in Forsa's guards on the opposite side of the road from where they'd come. It shocked Rowena that they'd share a meal with the king the night before, and attack him the next day.

Tuck tackled a man trying to untether a goat and Muriel sprinted as fast as her damaged leg would allow to help him. Bram pulled the sword he kept on his back and engaged with the same red-haired man Rowena had seen him speaking with in the hall.

The man grinned, wiggling his fingers for Bram to engage, and seemed excited, as if they were only sparring.

A woman beat on one warrior with a pan as he tossed her belongings out of the hand cart she pulled. Rowena raced to help, coming up behind them, and buckling the man's knees so he fell. She kicked him, but he hopped to his feet. The woman attacked from one side, swiping at him with a pan, while Rowena spun and landed a kick to his gut.

He caught the woman's arm and used his free arm to backhand Rowena. She twisted and ducked enough that he hit the back of her shoulder, but it was enough to make her stumble. He shoved the woman to the ground and ran to engage in a fight with Ivar. Good; she wouldn't mind seeing him receive a beating.

Rowena scanned the area. Something wasn't right. Uther and Daenon engaged in the fighting with Bram and the guards, but otherwise, the rest of the attackers were only creating chaos. They weren't stealing anything, or killing anyone, so far. Why attack at all?

She twisted and glimpsed someone climbing into the back of the wagon. With everyone else engaged with the warriors, no one noticed. That was where Uther had loaded the sword, among other items worthy of a thief's attention. Rowena sprinted to the wagon. A small buzzing skittered in Rowena's chest, making her vision blur for a moment and then two. She opened and closed her fist, willing the sensation away.

Two sneaks had climbed aboard and searched through the packed cart.

"Get out!" Rowena punched the closest body in the side, earning a grunt.

A male spun to face her, and she gasped in recognition. A scar trailed next to his eye and down his face, unmistakably familiar. There was no doubt he was the pirate she'd battled before.

"You?"

"Go away. We'll take what we came for and be gone. Do nothing stupid." He held up a knife as if in warning.

"Got it," the other invader called. Dressed in trousers and a cloak, the voice was distinctly female. When she turned, her light gray eyes snagged on Rowena's.

The two stared at each other for a couple of heartbeats. Her eyes were familiar somehow, though Rowena had surely never met her.

The distraction gave the pirate an advantage, and he knocked Rowena off her feet. The two thieves scrambled over the other crates and boxes in the wagon to escape when Rowena glimpsed the sword box under the woman's arm.

"No!" Rowena twisted and snatched the invader's foot.

She stumbled and fell against a barrel, swiping at Rowena with her free arm. "Ah, let go."

Rowena scrambled up, half crawling onto the other woman's back, and took hold of the box's end.

"No, you don't," the pirate called, trying to pull his accomplice and the box out of the back of the wagon, but Rowena held on.

The woman let go of the box, leaving Rowena to battle the pirate for it, but a stinging slap across her face loosened her grip enough the box slid from her grasp. She hustled to her feet, racing after the duo.

Halfway to the trees, Rowena launched herself at the pair, falling between them so all three fell to the ground. The pirate dropped the box, and the lid popped open in the grass.

"It's empty," the woman said with a gasp.

The pirate growled and slammed his fist into the ground. "Leave it. Come on."

He grabbed the woman by the arm and the two of them sprinted for the forest, while Rowena remained still, dumbfounded. Just before the villains disappeared, the woman twisted and met Rowena's stare once more.

There was something about her that gave Rowena pause—a recognition, familiarity, but she couldn't pinpoint what.

Seconds later, a shrill whistle sounded, and the attackers disengaged, swarming back the way they'd come. The guards gave chase but, moments later, only silence reigned among the trees rather than shouts of combat.

Uther, Daenon, and Bram rushed to the wagon.

"What happened? Did they take anything?" Uther peered into the wagon, ignoring Fidessa, who crawled out from under it.

Rowena stared at her as she tried to brush her skirts. Apparently, her mage skills didn't include combat.

"Are you injured?" Daenon asked the queen, and then turned to Rowena. "Either of you?"

Rowena scoffed at his attempt at false concern and didn't answer. She had nothing more than a scrape or two, mostly from banging against the barrels and crates. Bram found the empty sword box and lifted it from the ground.

"Did they take it?" Daenon asked.

Rowena started to speak, but bit back her words. While Bram inspected the lining, Uther didn't seem as upset as he should have been about the empty box.

"It was nothing of value," Uther said. "A sentimental piece, nothing more."

The crackling in her chest rose again, and Uther's comment only made her sure of what she suspected. He'd moved the sword, but it was still nearby, calling to her.

Bram closed the box and set it gently into the wagon, flashing a glare at Uther.

"Did you know this would happen?" Rowena asked her uncle.

"The road to Velmeg is dangerous for merchants, but I am surprised at their boldness to attack a royal caravan," Fidessa said.

"That is why we have guards," Uther said, but it didn't answer Rowena's question.

"Other than that," Daenon gestured to the box, "They seem to have only cost us time." He twisted and scanned down the line of scattered goods and tipped over hand wagons. Those who'd hidden from the raiders emerged and began cleaning up broken crates and other various items strewn about. Chickens, geese, and goats all made a ruckus as thralls chased them down and re-secured them with ropes or crates. No one shouted out in pain or called for physics.

"Interesting indeed." Bram's nostrils flared, but he said no more. It struck Rowena as odd that he'd care at all. This wasn't his home, or kingdom. Their business had nothing to do with him.

Branches cracked and scabbards rattled in the brush where the guards had given chase. Rowena spun, along with the others, to face whoever emerged, but she let out a slow breath when it proved to be the Forsan guards.

"They're gone. Disappeared without a trace," one man reported to Uther. "We spread out, but couldn't find a hint of them."

"They were Fianna," Bram answered.

Daenon shook his head, giving a grunt of what seemed appreciation. "They're rumored to move as quick as deer without breaking a single twig. Apparently, they've earned their reputation justly."

"How is that possible?" Fidessa asked. Her fingers drifted up to the golden torques around her neck. Rowena didn't stop herself from openly glaring at her mother's stolen jewelry.

Uther raised his brows. "It doesn't surprise me after I refused them last night. However, I thought leaving so quickly would avoid their tactics."

Bram scratched the side of his jaw. "They seemed to have had a specific target. What is it that would draw them to you?"

Uther ignored Bram's question. He surveyed the area and then turned to his guards. "Hurry everyone along. We leave in half a mark. Anyone not ready to travel is left behind."

The guards jogged off and called out the orders down the line.

Rowena scanned the area as they went and discovered Tuck helping to herd goats and chickens so others could round them up. She followed him to help, but a hand wrapped around her wrist.

"Where are you going?" Daenon asked. "You should stay near the front."

Rowena yanked on her arm, but could not release herself. Her chest tightened and her breath quickened. "Unhand me."

Bram maneuvered closer, his eyebrows bunched tight. "I'm sure that's unnecessary, prince."

Both men crowded too close. She had to get away. With extra effort, she yanked harder, until a small hole ripped open her sleeve.

Daenon let go. "If you're taken for ransom, we'd be obligated to rescue you. I rather not waste any more time."

Rowena shuffled away, putting space between herself and both men. "What an inconvenience that would be."

"And you have work to do," Fidessa added, tugging Daenon to follow her.

A scoff left Rowena's throat before she could stop it, but she ducked her head and spun to go. No one called after her, but Bram fell into step at her side.

"Can I help you?" She wanted some time by herself. It frustrated her that every simple touch or hint of entrapment would force her into such fear. She needed to focus and Bram following her wouldn't help her find out why the Fianna wanted her sword. And who was that pirate turned Fianna?

"It's odd. They only seemed to want the one item. Why do you think that was?"

At least he didn't want to make a big deal about how her sleeve tore. "The raiders attacked for a purpose and it wasn't to disrupt their travels—that was a distraction."

The sword was the real reason they'd come, and it was the second time she'd faced the pirate. How was one man involved with two such dangerous groups? That was a question she didn't want to discuss with Bram. He'd seen enough of her cowardly behavior; she didn't need to describe more.

"Agreed. Do you know much about that sword?"

She halted and blew out an exasperated sigh. "It was my mother's. She brought it with her from Penumar when she fled the lands."

"She was Lunara?"

"Yes." She spotted Muriel bent over a goat, tying the bleating animal to a small hand wagon, while Tuck rushed off to round up more. She hurried away, explaining over her shoulder as she left. "I'm needed for my duties. Please, excuse me."

Muriel stood and put both hands on her back, stretching. She must not have heard Rowena approach over the goats because when Rowena touched her shoulder, she startled and spun, ready to fight.

"I'm sorry. " Rowena chuckled at the thought of anyone fearing Muriel, peeking behind her to make sure Bram hadn't followed. "Did anyone get hurt?"

Muriel shook her head. "Mostly, they just knocked things around and scattered every beast. So much for the stories of the Fianna as a fierce bunch. Seemed like nothing more than elfling imps from my angle."

"That's what I find odd as well." Rowena twisted and peered at the trees. "They were after something specific. I want to know why."

"Don't you go thinking that way. I can see it all over your face—"

A flock of chickens flapping their way interrupted them. Both women bent over and spread their arms to keep the birds from getting by. An elfling girl, perhaps only ten winters, herded them from the other side. Between the three of them, they wrangled all the squawking hens into their arms. The girl's mother raced over with a crate to fit four. She and her daughter carried the rest, thanking Rowena and Muriel as they hurried off.

"Things will smooth out quickly. We'll be ready to go before Uther commanded." Rowena scanned the area again. She had to find out what the pirate wanted with the sword. And who that other woman was. Even though it meant leaving before she found out where Uther had hidden the blade, she had to do it.

"And you're coming with us," Muriel said, crossing her arms over her chest.

Rowena held her stare, nibbling the inside of her lip. "I know what they wanted, but I don't know why."

Muriel pursed her lips and dropped her gaze to the ground.

"I recognized one of them. It's the second time he was after the same prize. If I can find out who he is, I might stop him from attacking again." Rowena reached out and rested her hand on Muriel's wrist. "Will you help cover for me?"

"Will you see the folly in this action?"

Rowena shrugged. She couldn't tell Muriel about the sword. The less she knew, the better for when Uther questioned her later. Rowena could only hope they wouldn't punish the woman.

Muriel blew out a heavy sigh and glanced over at the goats, who'd quieted to munch the sweet grass at the edge of the road.

Tuck hurried over, leading two more goats by the horns.

Muriel sprang forward, wrapping her arms around Rowena's shoulders. At first, she tensed to push away, but recognized the hug as genuine and slipped her arms around the woman who'd become a friend.

Muriel pulled away first and met Rowena's gaze. "Be careful."

Rowena's throat grew thick and the back of her eyes burned. All she could do was nod.

"Tuck, we're going to help Rowena, so I need you to release those two. Help me untie these others." Muriel worked on the rope holding one of the becalmed goats. "Quickly."

The gentle man stared at Rowena with lines etched on his forehead.

Rowena stepped closer to the large man. "Keep her safe."

He bounced his gaze between the two women, but he let go of the goats as Muriel bid. Both animals hopped sideways and then kicked up their heels. The others, excited by the activity, started making a racket to join them. Muriel and Tuck quickly untied all of them. The goats bounded away with the rest. Rowena's friends waited a couple of moments and then gave chase, calling out for others to help.

The activity created the distraction Rowena needed to sprint into the trees alone.

SEVENTEEN

Rowena didn't expect the heavy underbrush as she fought her way deeper into the forest. Most of the trees appeared to be birch and should have been easy to navigate, but brambles plucked at her clothes, limbs caught her hair and scratched her arms. The ruckus she made would wake the dead, but she couldn't do anything about it. She had to get as far as she could into the forest before Uther called for a search.

When she finally made it into a small clearing, she clenched her fists and huffed. After a few breaths, she assessed her torn clothes and picked twigs, leaves, and bracklebug from her hair. Her shin bloodied her stocking, but it didn't hurt enough to cause worry. If she found a stream, she'd investigate the wound. For the moment, she needed to get her bearings.

Muriel had been right. Chasing after the Fianna was a fool's mission. She no longer even knew which direction she'd traveled. If she found the Fianna, what then? She had no weapons and had proven that her skills weren't as solid as she once thought.

Rowena dropped her hands to her sides and scanned the area for anything she could use a marker of direction. She huffed a laugh—everything looked the same. The trees wore moss like soft green coats, covering their trunks and limbs on all sides. The high canopy blocked out much of the sky.

She'd been a fool. Of course, she could run away and no one would chase her down. It wasn't more stripes on her back or even her life she'd risked. Uther would punish someone else. Rowena wrapped her hands around her middle and bent over. Muriel or Tuck—they'd be who he'd choose. They were the only ones close to her. Muriel had to have known that, but she'd agreed to help, anyway. Her knee would become the least of her pains.

Rowena had to go back. She spun in a slow circle. Which way was back? She made it halfway around when a man stepped out from behind a tree. The same one who she'd witnessed in the hall and fighting with Bram. A nasty bruise blossomed on his cheek just above his bushy red beard.

"You're a little too far from your friends," he said.

"I got lost. If you'll point the way to the road, I'll be going." She didn't expect him to believe her, but the sparkle dancing in his eyes confirmed she was right.

The three other fae she'd spied at the table rose from the surrounding bushes, pinning her into the small clearing. They were all armed with swords or axes or daggers. One had a quiver of arrows slung over his shoulder.

"You were in Forsa last night." Rowena bent her knees, ready to fight.

"I don't recall your lovely face. What made you leave the protection of your king?" The man who had seemed angry asked.

Perhaps if she charged at one of them, it would surprise them enough that she could grab one of their weapons. Which one offered her the best chance?

"How about you tell us why you're really here? There's no escaping, lass," Red Beard said.

She gave a second glance to a willowy man in a torn tunic.

"It's me, is it?" The man lifted his palm and stared at one of his compatriots. "Why is it always me?"

"I've told you, Seamus." The man with the darker skin chuckled. "You need to put some weight on. Who wouldn't choose you?"

The willowy man, Seamus, returned his gaze to Rowena. "I invite you to try. But know that I'll give you the same respect I'd give any warrior."

That gave her pause. He'd treat her as a warrior? She glanced down at her ragged clothing—

All the men laughed.

She kept her gaze on the ground, squeezing the side of her dress between her fingers. Things would be different if she wore her fighting clothes. No one would take a thrall seriously in a fight.

"I didn't say I believed you to be a warrior," He paused with a smirk as she glared. "But I believe in giving respect where it's due and if you're going to challenge me, I'll respect you enough to beat you fairly—as I would anyone else."

Rowena's blood turned to a horde of ants skittering through her veins. She curled her fingers into her palms, itching away the sensation, and tried to hide the slight glow. Her enchantment proved too unpredictable. Muriel had worried about Rowena becoming a hostage. She couldn't let this group know her true identity. Though she also wouldn't let them intimidate her.

She charged forward.

The undergrowth that had seemed so full and annoying earlier suddenly grew too thin and spindly. She dodged left and then grabbed a leafy bush to propel herself to the right, but it only bent over and got in her way. Worst of all, Seamus hadn't moved. He stood calmly where he'd been before with a hint of a grin twitching his mouth.

She gritted her teeth and spun the other direction. There wasn't a need to go directly around him; she could go further into the woods and hide among the brush. Just like the games with Far. His training would serve her well once again.

Two steps later, a solid arm snaked out in front of her,

smacking against her ribs and sending her to the ground, gasping for air.

"I told you." Seamus offered his hand but Rowena slapped it away. "You did well, considering."

"I don't need your help." She rolled to her side and pushed to her feet, refusing to groan about her aching ribs. How fast she'd lost hurt more.

Red Beard entered the clearing. "If that were true, you wouldn't have entered the forest at all."

"Perhaps I can be some help here, Conri."

Rowena spun toward the familiar voice. The pirate, his distinctive scar in clear view, stepped out of the brush to within reach of her if she lunged.

"This maiden and I are acquainted."

"So, you don't deny it?" She gaped, flabbergasted that he would be so bold.

He shrugged. "Why would I? I have nothing to hide."

"You're a thief."

"Are you sure?"

Yes. "Taking something that doesn't belong to you is theft."

Again, the group surrounding her laughed at what she didn't understand. The man before her had attacked and tried to steal the sword twice. That made him a thief and denying it made him also a liar. What was amusing about that?

"A bold statement, all things considered," said Red Beard—known as Conri, according to the pirate.

Rowena met his gaze, confused. "That man worked with pirates to attack our ship a few weeks ago. Now, he's here with you, doing the same. It seems a proper accusation."

"Proper? Hmm. Interesting, you'd have something to say about that." The pirate ambled closer. "Though, to be honest, I've not met a truly proper princess yet."

"Insulting." The woman Rowena had battled on the wagon stepped out from the shadows. "But true."

How many more mercenaries hid among the trees?

Rowena squared her shoulders and stared at the woman again, with more intent to discover why she seemed familiar. Then it hit her in the gut harder than Seamus had. The ash-brown hair and gray eyes, despite a spark in the ones staring at her right then, had an uncanny resemblance to Fidessa.

"You realize we're cousins, don't you?"

Rowena blinked and burst out with a snort of recognition. "You're Safi."

Her cousin grinned and swept out her hand in agreement. No taller, yet slimmer through the hips than Rowena, Safi held her shoulders back with a confidence. Dressed in leather trousers and a tunic covered with a hardened leather brigandine, she radiated the same warrior energy as the others.

"Why are you here?" Rowena didn't ask about her attire or that she was a single female in the company of a large group of men.

"I no longer found Velmeg to my liking." Safi adjusted the vambrace on her forearm with the hint of a scowl on her lips. Curiously, the men all seemed to grow uneasy and sullen at the same time. "However, the bigger question is, why are you here?"

The excuse that she got lost seemed too ridiculous to repeat—better to go with the truth, so she pointed at the pirate. "I recognized him and wanted to know why he has tried to steal from me . . . twice."

"From you?" Conri asked.

"Yes."

"I'm positive that's not true," the pirate answered.

Rowena arched a brow.

"We are becoming inundated with runaway princesses around here," another of the Fianna said. Rowena glanced sidelong to determine it was the last man she'd seen at the feast. The one who seemed the most dangerous.

"Perhaps we should find a more suitable spot to talk. We can share a meal and properly get to know each other." Conri cocked his head, studying Rowena. His face had a jovial appearance. However, the air about him gave no doubt to his leadership over the group.

Rowena glanced at her cousin and forced herself to stand a little taller. If she could be with such a group and be safe, then Rowena would do the same. "That sounds acceptable."

"But first, we will need to form a pact in order for you to be among us. We are a private group. Anyone who we invite will learn much and must share something with us equally important."

That sounded reasonable, yet they already knew all of her secrets. Or did they? If they had learned, she was a cursed moonborn, they certainly wouldn't allow her to stay among them. She masked her face into a bored expression. "What do you want to know that you haven't already deduced?"

"You say the sword is yours, then you'll know about the stone it holds." Conri's eyes glimmered.

It was a test. How had they known the hilt was missing a gemstone? She'd figure that out later, but that was all the information she had as well. What else could she say? "The gem that's missing, you mean?"

"I knew it," the angry man said with a few mumbled curses to punctuate his frustration.

So, they hadn't known that. It gave her an idea. One that would help Muriel stay safe as well. "But I know where it is."

The forest grew silent. None of the mercenaries twitched a single muscle, training their eyes on her.

She had no intention of staying in a camp full of men, despite her cousin's acceptance of such. But she could hide among them until she could get away from Ibern—she'd figure out where to go later.

"I left it with my friend. Help me get her free and I'll give it to you." Rowena raised her chin, trying to seem confident as she lied.

"A bargain with the Fianna is no minor issue, lass. Are you sure?" Conri arched his brow, pinning her with a stare.

"Rowena," Safi said, her eyes wide.

Rowena turned her full focus to Conri. "Yes. Muriel must stay safe no matter what."

"Done."

"It is not."

Everyone spun and faced the stranger who no one had heard approach through the woods, despite the silence. The traveler stood with his fists curled at his side, but his sword remained sheathed behind his back.

EIGHTEEN

Two sensations assaulted Rowena at the same time. The first was how her arms tingled, ready to fight. The second was how her insides fluttered upon sight of the traveler. "How did you follow me?"

Bram's lips twitched as he fought a grin. "It was not difficult."

Rowena rolled her eyes. She was tiring of everyone telling how bad her skills were.

"You have the skills of a Fianna, Traveler." Conri turned to face Bram, as did all the others. Even Safi, who held herself relaxed, but in a stance ready to grab her dagger.

Rowena rose slightly onto the balls of her feet and bent her knees. Although she'd lost all her weapons, or that Seamus had shamed her, she had abilities. Her cousin wasn't the only one who could fight.

"I'd never claim such an honor," Bram answered. "I'm not looking for trouble, but the princess cannot agree to that bargain."

"That would be her decision." Safi held Bram's stare.

Even though they'd never met, and her parents were Rowena's enemies, that Safi would stand up for her when they'd just met, and it wasn't to control her, made her throat thicken. She swallowed once, and then again, to keep herself steady.

"It's important for your safety, and of many others, that you do not," Bram said directly to Rowena.

"I'm in no more danger here than I was there." Probably less.

"I thought Errol was joking. You really are a princess?" Seamus asked. "Why is it you're dressed like a peasant and weren't riding on the wagon earlier?"

"And what business is it of yours?" Rowena continued to address Bram, ignoring the mercenary. "You're not from Forsa or contracted with my uncle—are you?"

Bram released a deep exhale. "I'm hired by no one."

"Yes, a traveler." Rowena tipped her head to the side. His skills equaled the Fianna's, yet he was not much older than her. "I can handle myself. Going off alone with you would not be my best option."

"Well, I'm curious to know you better. Will you join us for another meal?" Conri asked Bram.

Rowena huffed and looked away from Bram's deep gaze.

"I accept."

Conri strode up to Bram and extended his arm. The two clasped forearms.

None of them had offered her such a greeting.

"Our camp is this way." Conri gestured to his right and immediately began striding away, followed by Bram.

Rowena jumped when someone touched her elbow, so she dropped lower in her stance.

Safi held up her hands as if in surrender. "Nothing meant."

Rowena stood tall and waved her away. "It's fine."

The pirate ambled by, grazing his fingers across Safi's back as he passed. Rowena pinched her brows, which garnered a huffed chuckle from her cousin.

"Stay close to me and I'll help you navigate your way with these tricksters."

Rowena nodded and followed in her cousin's wake when she hurried after the others.

* * *

The campfire flickered against the darkened trees. Stew bubbled, filling the air with the scent of carrots and rabbit as it hung over the flames. The Fianna had made their beds of layered twigs covered in greenery, but they were more like nests in Rowena's opinion. However, Safi had helped her make one while the others settled in and waited for the meal. It calmed her somewhat to feel as though she fit in, despite the deal she made.

No one spoke of anything of substance. They laughed and enjoyed simple conversation like it had been any other day. Rowena wanted to ask Safi how she came to be among such rabble, or question Errol about his twice-failed attempt to steal her sword. But in the relaxing atmosphere, her confidence waned. The words got stuck in her throat. She admired their camaraderie. It reminded her of her life before. Before all the deaths. Before Forsa. Before Daenon. She shoved her memories deep down and focused on the present.

The orange flickers glowing against the faces of those surrounding the camp's central fire conjured memories of Rowena's longhouse in Taesing—a place to gather in warmth and friendship, a place to share stories, a place to laugh, a place to belong. Except it wasn't. It was in the middle of the forest with strangers who had more skill with weapons than she did.

Though, calling the group around her strangers wasn't exactly true any longer. She'd learned all their names, but she only interacted with the four she'd met earlier out of over two dozen men crowded around the campfire. Well, other than her cousin and the pirate Errol, who rarely left the woman's side.

As leader, Conri regaled everyone with boisterous conversation and a commanding presence. Second in command, Hywel, had proven her first impressions of him valid. He had a calmer presence, thought-filled, but one that brought with it an unease, like she was always being watched, judged. He did not question Rowena, yet she had the feeling he gathered more information from her with a single look than most would with a dozen questions. She'd positioned herself next to Safi so she could use her cousin to block herself from Hywel's scrutiny.

"There I was, crawling on my hands and knees, bleating with the rest of them, hoping the blasted dog would believe me." Conri slapped his thigh as he recounted a tale of sneaking through a herd of sheep as he ran away from a village.

Rowena could barely listen. She rubbed the back of her neck for the third time, wiping away sweat that wasn't there. Her knee bounced continually. What had made her cousin join these men? She had to ask. It was ridiculous that she couldn't just say the words. And what of the pirate? Who was he to Safi? The two were obviously close.

"Why are you with these men?" The words blurted out in the middle of Conri's sentence.

Safi slid a cocky grin across her face. "I enjoy the company of men, don't you?"

Rowena settled back, eyes wide. That's not what she meant. A sudden chill ran down her spine. Daenon had been but one man she couldn't fight off well. Bile rose in her throat and her hands shook.

"It was a joke." Safi leaned forward and brushed her fingers over Rowena's.

The slight touch forced Rowena to scramble to her feet. Every other side conversation taking place halted, all eyes firmly placed on the stranger making a fool of herself.

Safi rose, standing directly in front of Rowena, blocking the others from view. "You're safe here." Her gaze held Rowena in place without touching her again.

Rowena let out a shaky breath and threw her shoulders back. "Of course. It's fine. I'm fine." She twisted her fingers around themselves, unsure if she should sit or continue to stand.

"No one will hurt you in this group." Safi continued to hold Rowena's stare.

If she could have fled into the trees in that moment, she would have. Her chest ached from keeping it still, forcing her breath to flow in an easy pattern. In. Out. Rowena's focus wavered, fuzzy at the edges while she fought to keep Safi in view; her light brown hair, her gray eyes, fierce and piercing. Strong. Safe.

"Rowena." Safi tipped closer, slowly, gently, taking Rowena's fingers into hers. "You can trust me, I promise."

The words filtered through her haze like the hum of bees in summer. A pleasantness that hinted at something sweet and free if she'd only follow. Rowena nodded, slowly, and then with more vigor as she inhaled. The breathing righted her senses and shook off the shell she'd created around her. She squeezed her cousin's hand.

"Thank you. I don't know what got into me." Rowena forced a tight smile.

"Mmhmm. We can speak later about that. We may have more in common than our family."

Rowena doubted that. If they did, her cousin wouldn't purposefully surround herself with so many men. Safi shifted, prepared to settle down at the fire, still holding Rowena's hand. From across the flames, Bram's pinched stare latched onto Rowena's. His mouth was tight and his posture was rigid. She could have sworn his eyes sparked with gold, burning into her. She dropped her gaze and her body to sit cross-legged next to her cousin.

She'd caused such a spectacle it wasn't any wonder he would be angry. Some warrior she turned out to be, weak and emotional. Rowena glanced up at the now dark sky through the trees. So much for blaming her behavior on Lunara powers. There was nothing but stars twinkling in the darkness. She dropped her gaze to her lap, careful to avoid the brooding traveler.

"So, now that we have everyone's attention," Safi chuckled, as if nothing out of the ordinary had taken place. "Perhaps now's a good time to discuss our plans."

"I'm sure there are more interesting topics before we get to all that," Conri said. "We still have much to learn from our new guest."

Rowena had nothing to tell them. She needed answers for herself. Despite her outburst, she still needed to find out why her cousin had joined the Fianna. If she'd made a deal with them like Rowena had, what was it?

"Another princess enters our forest, willing to make a deal with a group of mercenaries. To live rough rather than stay in her pretty dresses." Hywel leaned on his knees and scanned Rowena. "We were just in Forsa and didn't see you there."

Rowena didn't shy away from Hywel's penetrating green eyes. "My father is . . . was . . . King Olve of Skandan, Uther's older brother. My uncle returned to his homeland under the guise of friendship and then killed my parents and many from Taesing."

"For what purpose?" In the flickering firelight, the lines on Conri's forehead plunged into darkened furrows. "Why would he do that, yet not stay to keep the throne?"

"And haul you here instead of killing you there?" Errol joined the conversation. He'd been quiet, not engaging too many in conversation, so his voice startled Rowena.

Rowena didn't fully know the answers, either. Though she believed it involved her mother's sword, but she would not discuss that. The less they spoke of it, the fewer lies she'd have to tell about how to find the stone.

"I've known King Uther for a long time, albeit not well," Conri said. His voice rumbled low, making a shiver roll over Rowena's shoulders. "It is surprising that he would make such a move without provocation."

"Fidessa killed my mother. The commander he left in charge killed my father afterward." And then blamed it on her. Another piece of her story she would withhold. It was all she could do to keep herself from folding into a tight ball. She could still feel how her mother's fingers had grown cold the last time she touched them. The clash of swords rang in her ears, churned up mud and sweat replaced the campfire smoke in her nostrils.

"How did she die?" Safi asked so quietly it nearly didn't register through Rowena's memories.

"It was King's Day. We had games and contests. Most of the villages of Skandan came to celebrate my father's ascension." Fidessa's comments about Rowena's curse and destiny to destroy her kingdom choked her. Silence filled the camp as everyone waited for her to continue.

"Fidessa used a spell to send an axe into my mother's chest. My father had no choice but to avenge her. As I must now in his place."

Safi leaned back, staring into the flames. "Why would she do such a thing?"

"She believed her husband to be in love with my mother." Rowena plucked a leaf from her skirt. From what she'd witnessed, that seemed likely. "Though I believe it was their intent all along. They hadn't come in peace, but to destroy my father's rule."

"That doesn't answer the question of why leave and bring you here." Bram echoed Conri's confusion.

Rowena snapped her attention to him. Why did he insert himself into her issues? He had no home, no desire to belong anywhere—it gave him no rights to concern himself with anyone.

"He had to be here to bring Daenon home." She spat the prince's name and darted a glance at her cousin. "His prime day at the end of the week satisfies the treaty between Forsa and Velmeg."

Safi snorted.

"You failed to mention that part to us, Safi," Conri said.

"Why is that important? I expected you to be more interested that I left my position as the king's commander."

"Usually, treaties such as that are concluded with betrothals,"

Errol added. "King Lendan was adamant that he would not agree to a marriage with Safi. Uther needed a different princess."

Rowena stared at her lap, entwining her fingers until they turned white. It had never occurred to her she was the aim of Uther's plans. She'd believed it was the sword alone. A cold sweat formed on her neck.

"Is that true, Rowena?" Bram asked.

She snapped her face to meet his sparking inquiry. "How do Ibern or Skandan issues concern you?"

"Perhaps I wander the realm because I care about all of it. What happens in one kingdom affects all the others."

Rowena held his stare, guessing that his flaring nostrils matched her own.

The others continued, ignoring their deadlock.

"They exchanged me with Daenon to live in Velmeg at five years old—I barely remember my parents. Queen Dewan has been a true mother to me. Uther was mistaken to listen to Lendan. It would be better with no treaty at all." Safi sounded incredulous.

That her cousin would find her too unworthy for the treaty sent a fire through Rowena that burned through her chest and down her arms. She squeezed her hands into tight balls. "Is it so preposterous that he would think me worthy? Not that I would marry that dung heap."

"That's not what I meant," Safi said. "If the son is like the father, they are both shite."

"A betrothal with his niece would make sense," Errol said, ignoring either woman.

"Especially if Uther controls her. Both kings of Ibern would then have a claim on Skandan," Conri said.

Conri's comment drew Bram back to the conversation. "Why would either king agree to the arrangement? It's too likely to go the other way. If Daenon uses a match with Rowena to call himself King of Skandan, as soon as either Uther or Lendan die, Daenon would claim their kingdom as well. He'd become high king of both islands."

"I can't see either of those men allowing for that possibility," Hywel added.

"Stop speaking about me as if I'm not right here." Rowena rolled her neck, her muscles begging for some activity. When she tipped her chin back, she discovered the tip of Lungol's crescent edging into view over the trees. More energy than usual pulsed through her. Her knuckle bones crackled as she moved them. When she stretched her hand, the tiniest flash of silver came from a fingertip. She quickly fisted her hands once again.

"Especially because you're wrong," Rowena said, hoping to distract away from whatever happened to her hands.

"How so?" Bram asked.

Again, she wondered why her troubles seemed so interesting to the traveling stranger.

"Because I won't be returning to Taesing to take over the crown. Uther left his Stallari to run things. I'm no longer a princess." Rowena hopped to her feet, needing to move.

"From what I've heard, Taesing was a thriving village. If everyone loved King Olve as it seemed, they'd welcome you back," Errol said.

"My father was a perfect king. Never think otherwise." The outburst startled Rowena as much as everyone else, perhaps more.

Everyone around the fire sucked in a breath, and Conri's eyes widened. He slowly raised his hands as one would to an angry dog. "I meant no dishonor to the king. Now, lower your hands, lass."

Rowena glanced at the men sitting near their leader. They had their focus on her hands. She swallowed hard, not understanding the rising concern rolling through the camp. Except when her gaze roved to Bram, his lips curled up slightly. His gaze traveled from Rowena's face to her hands and back again.

She glanced down and wobbled, as if suddenly very exhausted. Silver enchantment glowed brightly from each palm.

NINETEEN

Safi sprang to her feet and rushed closer, peering down at Rowena's hands. "What is that?"

Rowena stared at the silver glow twinkling between her fingertips. It rolled from front to back as she turned her hands one way and then the other. Her vision tunneled and her mother's words echoed in her mind.

'The moons influence our power. It's like coin from different lands; both spend equally but have different values. We can draw energy from either Masah or Lungol, but all Lunara feel pulled more by one than the other.'

Rowena tipped her head back to find that Masah now also twinkled his rays down on her, showing half of his face, yet seeming to wink his approval. The impatient Lungol had already crossed in front of the slower, larger moon. What did it mean that they were both in the sky right then? She longed to ask her mother for advice. How would she learn to control her power if she didn't have anyone to help?

"Rowena." Safi shook her shoulder and forced her gaze away from the skies.

"My mother was Lunara. We weren't sure if I had inherited her abilities." It also meant that she really had used her abilities in the cave.

"Can you . . . turn it off?" her cousin asked.

"She will struggle with that until she learns control," Bram said, standing near her other shoulder. When had he gotten so close?

"Do you know of enchantment?" Conri asked.

Everyone had closed in. She needed space, needed time to figure things out, needed to be alone. A sudden urge to both fight and run away gripped her. She clenched her fists and dropped into a fighting stance.

"Whoa, there." Conri threw his hands out to halt two other Fianna pressing closer, forcing the three of them to step backward. "Give her some space."

"Stay away from me," Rowena called. She twisted one way and then the next, ready to lash out at anyone who dared get too close.

"They are just curious," Bram said, inching closer. "It's doubtful anyone has seen such a sight before."

His tone carried a peaceful resonance that warred against the churn of building fear mixed with defensiveness swirling inside of her. It was as if an unfamiliar voice whispered into the back of her mind, coaxing her to lash out and attack, while Bram's dulcet tone sought to have her do the opposite.

"They want to control me. Keep me trapped, just like Uther." Rowena slid her foot back a step. "Fidessa said my mother was dangerous and then she killed her. They want to do the same to me."

"That's not true," Safi called out. "No one here wants that."

"You don't know that." The urge to find Uther and Fidessa, to kill them, flared through her chest and she spun to race away.

Strong arms wrapped around her, pinning her arms to her sides. It was exactly as she thought. They would not help; they were going to kill her too. She screamed, trying to touch whoever dared to restrain her.

"Shhh. You're safe. Raise your eyes overhead to Masah, big and peaceful. Draw on that to calm your fears."

It was Bram. She kicked and bucked and tried to free herself. He held tighter.

"Lift your eyes, Rowena. Absorb the bigger moon's energy. Allow it to fill you."

Her entire body shook with the need to break free and run, but also with the need to drop to her knees and weep. Her father had regaled everyone in the longhouse once about a voyage he'd taken where a tempest arose while he sailed on a small ship. The waves rose and crashed in from all directions. They could only ride it out and try to keep the bow pointed at the next wave.

Her insides were that ship.

Bram's words slipped past her fear, and she tipped her head back. Masah shone his brilliant light down on her, overpowering the smaller moon's energy even though the volatile Lungol also begged for her attention.

"Concentrate. Choose. You can decide this for yourself." Bram once again spoke calmly into her ear.

Like a soothing balm, peace settled over her. She sank back, leaning against him, feeling her anger and fears abate. Her chest lightened and she could breathe easier once again.

It was at that moment she realized how Bram's arms no longer pinned her in place, but cradled her gently. His embrace offered comfort without control, and she didn't fear his intentions. He was tall, well over six feet, so her head rested against his chest without having to duck under his chin. She inhaled the mixture of oak and spices radiating from him.

In the distance, someone chuckled. "I guess we don't have to worry that she'll kill us all now."

It was Safi.

Rowena still stood in the middle of the Fianna camp. Her rational thoughts returned.

She broke free from Bram's hold, instantly cold from the loss of his body heat. A new set of emotions sizzled through her, adding to the confusing mix. With great effort, she forced herself to turn around. Everyone in the camp stared at her.

"How are you feeling now?" Bram asked.

Heat surged into her cheeks. "I'm fine."

Bram maintained a calm expression, though he had to hear the way her heart pounded. Hopefully, he didn't understand how difficult it was to keep herself from flying right back into his arms. That little golden glow sparked through his gaze again.

Everything was getting too jumbled up.

"It's the mix of both of the moons being close together, most likely," he said.

Her mother had said she might have struggles with that as well. But what was he referring to exactly? "How would you know that? Are you Lunara?"

Several of the Fianna shuffled their feet and glanced around at the others, though no one said anything. Safi eased closer.

Bram raised a shoulder. "I'm not, but I've traveled through Penumar and learned much."

"Conri," Hywel stepped closer. "I'm of the mind that we don't need this kind of trouble. I say we take her back."

"I agree," Liam added. Rowena remembered him at the table with Conri and the others in Forsa.

"What if they're offering a reward? We should check first," someone in the crowd said; Rowena couldn't tell who.

Several of the men started calling out suggestions about what to do with her, as if she didn't have any say in the matter for herself.

"No one will use me as chattel. Not to marry the prince, or to be traded for a reward." Their plan was exactly why Muriel had forced her to hide. She still didn't believe anyone would pay for her, anyway.

Conri stared silently into the flames while everyone else waited for him to respond. "We should gather more information. If she is part of a deal between the kings, it will change Ibern, and that affects us greatly." He turned his stare onto Rowena, searing and contemplative.

"I know nothing more than I've said."

"I believe you." His face softened and her shoulders lightened a smidge. He scanned those standing near him. "Hywel and Errol, go scout around Velmeg and report back about what's happening there. We'll wait to make any further decisions until you return."

"We'll be back soon," Hywel said. Without hesitation, he and Errol jogged into the dark.

"After all this, I'm famished," Liam said after the silence grew fidgety. "I can't wait to hear more about all of this while we eat."

The Fianna turned away and set about gathering a pile of bread and hard cheeses near the fire.

No one used trenchers or bowls. Instead, they ripped portions from the loaves of bread and broke off chunks of cheese with their hands. It didn't bother Rowena, but it reminded her of how particular her mother had been about sitting down to eat. She viewed it as time well spent with family and friends, and that 'one should take their time to eat civilized.'

She blinked away the sting in her eyes and scanned the group. Hopefully, her mother would understand because though she'd barely known the Fianna for a few hours, she already counted them as friends.

Conri reached out to her with a cup in his hand. "To settle the nerves."

She accepted the offer with a nod. The powerful aroma singed her nose as she brought the cup to her mouth. Whiskey, not the ale she expected. "Not my usual drink."

"The taste grows on you." Safi raised the cup they had handed her in a toast.

Rowena sipped slowly, letting the biting liquid sear down her throat. A few moments later, she rolled her neck and her muscles lowered at least an inch.

"Go easy, though. There's much to happen in the next days." Bram had settled across from her.

How would he know?

"So, Traveler, I can't place your accent. You're not from Ibern, so where do you hail?" Liam asked with a mouthful of bread.

"My travels have taken me to many places."

That was the same thing he said to Rowena when she first met him. "Did you leave your homeland in shame? Is that why you won't say?"

Seamus choked with a laugh. "Bold, that one."

The others chuckled as well, but Bram arched his brows as if the question intrigued him. "It wasn't like that. Since I make the entire realm my home, it's unnecessary to remark on one land."

Silence descended on the group for a short time while they ate. Why didn't he want to speak of his origins? Why keep such a secret? If the others were like Rowena, they were busy trying to figure it out as well. Once again, she lamented never having left Skandan. If she had more experience, she could determine friend or foe easier.

"Are you from Farradar originally?" She blurted out the question without thinking, sitting tall, and then clamped her mouth closed.

A few of the men chuckled. Safi grinned at her and raised a shoulder, showing she wondered the same thing.

"No, but I've been there. It's a beautiful land." Bram's evasive answer didn't help. What was he hiding?

"It is a wonder you're a traveler at such a young age," Safi said.

Bram held a piece of cheese in midair and grinned. "As it is that you're even younger and yet the captain of the King's Guard. The twists and turns in life don't always bring expected outcomes."

Safi raised her cup, and a look passed between them that made Rowena more curious about both of them. She slumped, stuffing some bread into her mouth as she continued to ponder their comments.

"Ho, the camp," someone called out.

"Ho there," Conri answered in the way that would offer the caller safe entry.

Hywel stepped from the bushes a moment later. "Didn't want to startle anyone's blade."

"You've returned quickly. Where's Errol?" Safi glanced over the Fianna's shoulder into the dark trees.

"We ran into a contact for our patron. Errol went on ahead to scout alone until I could catch up. However, after my meeting, I couldn't delay the news I received."

"Which is?" Conri asked.

"If we don't fulfill our contract and provide the item we failed to collect, they will fire the forest until they flushed us out to hang, or we burn."

"How long do we have?"

"The end of the week. Before the prince is married."

"The prince is not getting married." Rowena had made herself clear on that issue. There was no need to keep speaking of it.

"That's the other part." Hywel ran his hands through his hair. "Because of our failure on the road, we are to bring the princess when we deliver the other item."

TWENTY

Rowena would not allow the Fianna to deliver her to Uther to increase his power and control. She'd die before she allowed it. "I won't go."

"How do they know she's even here?" Safi asked.

"They didn't. They expect us to find her," Hywel said.

"And you agreed you would?" Bram asked between clenched teeth.

"And draw ire that we could have delivered her earlier? No."

But Hywel had been the first to suggest they send her back. She wasn't sure she could trust his answer.

"We'll just move to a different camp," Liam offered. "They can't burn everything."

"This patron can do so and would without reserve. We would eventually wish we'd volunteered to be hanged," Conri said, running his fingers over his beard.

Branches cracked in the dark, halting the discussion. Every warrior spun, weapons drawn, except for Rowena, who dashed behind a wide stump, long ago broken and covered in vines.

Errol emerged from the brush a moment later, skidding to a halt near Seamus.

The Fianna smacked the back of Errol's shoulder, sheathing his dagger. "You're back earlier than expected and nearly got a hole through your belly."

The pirate stumbled. "That might have been better than this." He lifted his trouser leg to show two deep puncture wounds in his calf, already red and puffy, with streaks darting in all directions.

"Errol!" Safi screamed, as he collapsed in a heap.

"Rattlerock bite. Get the konferia herbs," Conri ordered, and the camp sprang into action.

Rowena came out of hiding and found a waterskin, handing it to Safi who'd cradled Errol's head in her lap. Her cousin dribbled some of the water over his lips, but he didn't respond.

"We must keep the poison from spreading." Conri wrapped a rope just below Errol's knee and twisted it into a tourniquet.

Liam retrieved some broad-faced, green leaves from a bag and handed Conri a handful, but the large man swatted them away. "Mash them, at least. Get a pot to boil for more."

"Please, let me help. There won't be time for the herbs to work," Bram said, lowering himself to Errol's side.

"What can you do?" Conri asked, the konferia bunched in his hand.

"Hopefully, enough." Bram held out his hand for the herb, which Conri relinquished. The traveler layered the leaves on top of the poisonous lizard bite, placed his hand over them, and closed his eyes.

The leaves curled, and the stench of burning hair and flesh forced Rowena to cover her nose.

"You're hurting him," Safi said, pushing against Bram's shoulder, but the man didn't budge.

A small wisp of smoke rose from under the traveler's hand. Rowena had never seen her mother's enchantment work like that. Though she'd witnessed Asta use her druid powers once, that went beyond what her mother could do, yet nothing so remarkable as what was happening to Errol. She studied Bram's ears, but he wore no druid rings, nor were his hands marked by runes. Every druid had those. Who was he?

He finally released Errol's leg. The crumbled pieces of herbs drifted away like ash, and to everyone's astonishment, Errol's flesh was no longer swollen or red. There were only two faint spots where the holes had been. The hair was all that had burned, not the leg.

"How is that possible?" Rowena asked. "I distinctly smelled burning flesh."

Conri released the tourniquet. "As did I."

Bram sat back with a heavy sigh, and then twisted and heaved the contents of his stomach onto the ground. When he'd finished, he turned his gaze back to everyone. No one spoke, waiting for him to explain how he managed the feat.

"It is a skill I possess, yet one I cannot use frequently."

A putrid scent filtered into the air. Rowena wrinkled her nose and glanced at the ground where Bram had vomited. "Did you absorb the poison?"

"That is how it works, yes." Bram closed his eyes for a moment.

Errol moaned, drawing attention away from the traveler.

Safi offered another drink when Errol licked his lips. He swallowed several drops before cracking his eyelids open. "Hey, Beautiful."

"You're an idiot," Safi answered with a gentle tone in contrast to her words, while stroking his hair away from his face.

"True."

Bram sighed. "He'll recover fully with time and rest to regain his strength. The poison was deep within his muscle."

To Rowena, Bram's warm golden coloring seemed ashen, but so far away from the firelight, it was hard to judge. "You should rest, too."

Rowena offered her hand to help Bram to his feet. He grinned and took her hand in his large palm. Despite the tingles that ran down her neck, or the flutter inside her chest, she tried to seem casual. She realized the ridiculousness of her offer, but she leaned back and did her best to appear helpful, echoing what Bram had told her once. "Everyone needs a hand sometimes."

"That they do," he whispered near her ear after rising, causing her shoulder to lift with a shiver.

She pulled her hand from his and hurried to stand near Safi. Her cousin helped Errol to his feet and let him lean on her shoulder as all four of them shuffled to the fire.

"That's a fine skill you have there," Conri said to Bram after he settled onto the ground.

Bram rested his arms against his crisscrossed legs. "It was bestowed upon me."

"Are ye a witch, then?" Seamus asked.

"Not at all." Bram broke off a piece of bread. "Nor a mage, before you ask."

"If you're a druid, where are your markings?" Rowena pinched her brows, waiting for his explanation.

Bram gave a quick grin that didn't meet his eyes. "Gifts are not always what they seem."

Silence descended on the group for a short time while they ate. If the others were like Rowena, they preoccupied their minds with figuring out Bram's secret. Except for Safi, who kept insisting Errol drink more water and have small bites of bread and cheese.

Her cousin attended him so intently and with care, and he kept touching her in small ways—a brush across the back of her hand, a finger down the side of her cheek, scooting the knee of his good leg so it rested against hers. Safi's actions reminded Rowena how her parents had done similar things. So had Hann. The realization hit her in the gut. She'd never paid attention, or she had, but thought it annoying. Never had she returned his gestures like Safi did with Errol.

Hann had loved her. She wasn't sure what her feelings had

been for him. The memory of her life in Taesing seemed so long ago.

Conri clapped his hands and then rubbed them together. Rowena nearly squealed from the suddenness of the noise, but thankfully swallowed the sound.

"Now that Errol will recover," the leader gave a nod to Bram, who returned the gesture, "we need to discuss how we're going to finish our mission."

Rowena glimpsed Errol's eyes widen and quickly glance around the circle, but she brushed it aside. He'd just nearly died; he probably didn't want to discuss leaving camp so soon.

"There are celebrations with games and dancing all week," Hywel said. "The wedding is still being planned as if nothing is amiss."

Conri squatted near the ground, poking a stick into the fire to refresh the flames. "That is beneficial."

"Three days?" Seamus asked. "It took us nearly a month to plan last time."

"It wasn't the plan that failed. We can try again." Conri dropped the stick into the fire pit. "Besides, we have extra help this time."

Rowena rose to her knees, suddenly very interested in their plans. "Are you speaking about my sword?"

"From our reports, Uther stole the sword," Hywel said.

Rowena clenched her fists. "That's correct. From me! When Uther and his queen killed my family and turned Taesing against me with lies."

"Did you kill the king?" Safi spoke in a low, gentle tone, but Rowena twisted her neck up to stare wide-eyed at her cousin. She'd heard of what happened?

"Of course not." Her memory flashed to the last time she'd seen her father, his eyes staring at her, questioning. 'How could you do such a thing' written all over his face. The arrow had come from Goetz. Of that, she was positive. Hopefully, her father learned the truth in the afterlife.

"Who should or shouldn't own the blade means nothing; it isn't in our possession. We work for our patron, who will pay us a hefty sum to bring them that prize. Though now, I'm more concerned with staying alive than earning coin." Conri stood, his height towering over everyone else. "The good news is we have the advantage now, with the sword being in Velmeg. Safi knows the city's layout, and there will be ample ale and dancing every night."

"Too many visitors to keep track of for the guards," Seamus added, nodding as he seemed to ponder the situation.

"I know where the guest bedchambers are, but I can't guess where they will keep the sword." Safi rose and left Errol's side to stand near Rowena. "And every guard will recognize me, no matter my attire."

"We don't know the sword is in Velmeg. The box was empty." Errol rose on one elbow to join the conversation. "It could be anywhere."

"True." Conri narrowed his eyes, staring at nothing. "But it's the best place to look. My bet is the box was a decoy. I don't see the king leaving such a possession behind. It must be with his things somewhere else."

His speculation made sense. If they were going to be so adamant about stealing the sword, perhaps it wasn't a bad thing. Once they found her family heirloom, she'd take it for herself. Whoever their patron was, they had no right to it. Rowena glanced around the group, her gaze snagging on Bram's across the fire. He stared at her with such intensity, as if waiting for her to do something. But what?

Safi was right. Everyone would recognize the captain of the guard. They needed someone unknown. Someone who understood how to move through a crowd unnoticed. Someone like a thrall.

"I'll find it." The words burst out of her like a startled bird flushed from the trees. "No one pays attention to a thrall, and I have plenty of practice at it."

Conri grinned. "A fine idea, but King Uther's men will be about as well. No matter how they treated you, it doesn't change that you're still a princess. And a missing one they need for the wedding at the end of the week."

Rowena glanced toward Bram without meeting his gaze, remembering something he'd said when they first met about moving through the shadows to learn secrets. "They wouldn't expect me to be in Velmeg. Besides, if I got away, why would I return to my duties as a thrall? No one will pay any attention to me."

Conri narrowed his eyes, making her fidget. "It could work, lass."

"Will King Uther's chambers be near the feast hall?" Liam asked Safi.

"Aye, but around to the back and up one or two levels," Safi answered.

Several of the Fianna glanced at each other, grins sliding into place as if they enjoyed the challenge.

"Well, then. What we'll need is a distraction," Hywel said.

"First, we'll need to get through the gates. The defenses around Velmeg are formidable," Bram said, apparently counting himself into the group's plans.

"Visitors will come and go along the road throughout the week." Seamus tapped a hand excitedly against his leg as he spoke. "We could disguise ourselves as merchants with a load of supplies for the revelry."

"If we steal a wagon, Rowena and I could hide inside the back." Safi rose onto the balls of her feet with a slight curve to the side of her mouth.

No one had made a single comment about the danger or about what might cause them to struggle. None commented on Rowena joining them. Their concern for her capture was only due to how it would affect their plans. Their sense of fair play differed from anything she'd experienced, but it sent excited tingles through her. She was finally going to get the adventure she'd craved.

"We can get inside through the kitchens and then blend into the crowd at the feast. Once we're all in place, we'll give a signal to cause a ruckus. Then, the girls can rush up the stairs to search," Conri said.

"One maid trudging up the stairs for her duties would go unnoticed. Two racing up during a commotion would be," Bram said. "Even if no one stops them right away, someone will go check."

"True," Hywel added.

"Rowena should stay here. The maid should be Safi," Bram said.

"What?" Rowena glared at him. They had already decided. "Why would you think you have any say in what I do or don't do?"

"You're not as skilled at deception, nor where to look once upstairs."

Rowena remained vaguely aware of the others, but her focus narrowed on the man across the flames. "I have plenty of skill. Keep to your own business."

How dare he make such a declaration? She would be part of the plan and retrieve the sword for her family—whatever it took to get it.

"If Rowena goes up the stairs inside the hall, she could signal out an upper window and I could climb up with a rope." Safi gently touched Rowena's elbow, offering support and breaking her glare aimed at the stubborn, handsome man trying to hold her back.

How dare he imply she was the weak point in the plan?

"I assume you've never snuck into a second-floor window at night?" Safi asked.

"Or out of one?" Errol chuckled, winking at Safi.

Hard as she tried not to let them, Rowena's shoulders slumped a smidge. "No."

"Then it's settled," Conri called out. "We'll follow the same plan we had on the forest road. Cause a distraction to give Rowena time to get upstairs. You'll have to be quick."

"There should be two that search, like before, but Errol's out," Liam said.

"What is the plan if things go wrong? What happens if she gets caught?" Bram jerked his head in Rowena's direction as he spoke to Conri.

"I won't." Rowena would let no one down. She would not fail.

"Then I'll take Errol's place," Bram said.

"I'll manage." To prove his point, Errol pushed up from the ground, but as soon as he got to his feet, he wobbled. Safi twisted back to his side and helped to lower him gently back down. "Or not, but I'm still going. I'm good at being distracting."

"That's the truth," Safi offered.

"Do you think you could handle the wagon?" Conri asked.

"Absolutely."

Conri nodded; the matter closed.

"Now, we wait until dark tomorrow. That leaves lots of time to see what fighting skills the newest princess says she has." Liam slipped his short sword from the sheath on his belt and lifted his brows.

Within a heartbeat, a circle had cleared away from the fire, and the men beckoned Rowena forward.

"Fine by me." Finally, she would prove her best skill set.

TWENTY-ONE

Rowena's shoulder ached as she squatted in the bushes next to the road into Velmeg. She'd missed blocking Liam's blow the night before. It would be worse if she hadn't had time to rest. At midday, the group had taken time to pick wild strawberries and relax under the trees while they swayed in the breeze overhead. She'd basked in the peace of it, yet it also reminded her of all she missed in Taesing.

It also gave her time to contemplate her previous training. Liam hadn't pulled his swing, and he'd knocked her off her feet so she had landed on her side. While she'd done a decent job, it only proved that her skills were like watered down wine compared to what they needed to be.

She couldn't deny it any longer. The guards she'd trained with for years had coddled her. Safi had stepped in and offered some tips, especially on how to use their bigger size against them. Despite her likely bruises, she longed to try the technique for throwing someone larger over her shoulder. Unfortunately, they'd had to go over the evening plans once again, and she couldn't practice more before they slipped through the forest to Velmeg.

"Are you clear on your portion of the plan?" Bram asked, startling Rowena as he kneeled beside her.

Instead of complementing his prowess in being able to slip silently through the brush, she wrinkled her nose. "It's easy. Act like a thrall, pretend to serve the meal until I can get up the stairs. Turns out, I'm well trained for this mission, after all."

"Skill with a blade is overrated. The nerve to head into a dangerous situation, knowing you could be injured, takes far more courage." Was he giving her a compliment? "Remember, there will be guards who might recognize you, so don't get complacent."

She scoffed. "Just do your part and leave me to mine."

They had divided into four groups of three before they left, three of which huddled in the bushes alongside the road, waiting. Rowena, Bram, and Safi kneeled together as the only group on their side of the road. The wagon would pass Conri's group first on the other side, and Hywel hid his group directly across from Rowena's. Seamus would arrive with Errol, driving a stolen merchant's wagon.

If they didn't show soon, everything would fall apart. They had to arrive while there was still a need for more supplies. Otherwise, the kitchens would make them wait until the next day to enter the hall.

Rowena tapped her fingers on her thigh, releasing some of her nervous energy. She'd wanted to go on missions for so long. Now that she was part of one, the waiting ate at her nerves. What if she messed up like Bram expected? What if she wasn't capable? She had to do everything right. No mistakes. Otherwise, she would get everyone captured . . . maybe killed.

She had to succeed, and return to Taesing—she was queen. Whatever happened, if she retrieved the sword or not, she would return home and take her rightful place on the throne. After she proved she deserved it.

Wooden wheels from a rattling wagon broke through the silence, creaking over ruts and rocks along the road. It hadn't rained in nearly a day, but all the traffic had dug into the soft earth, creating deep groves.

"You ready?" Safi asked, bumping her shoulder. Her cousin's penetrating gaze seemed to read her thoughts.

More than ever, she would let no one down. "Of course."

Mud had seeped into Rowena's knees from where she rested behind a jumbled collection of greenery. She rose to the balls of her feet, remaining squatted and ready to race out of hiding. Safi did the same. From the corner of Rowena's eye, she could see Bram crouching, muscles coiled, ready to strike as well.

The wagon lumbering toward them had a single hooded driver who swayed with each side-to-side lurch. Errol said he could drive, but if that was him, he needed a healer—or he'd consumed a large amount of ale or whiskey in a very short amount of time. A single baurun pulled the load, leaning hard into the collar, which seemed odd for what should have been an empty cart. Rather than being open, an arching canvas covered the wagon's back.

A whistle sounded from the bushes across the road where Conri waited. Bram answered back, then held out one hand to Safi and Rowena, placing his other hand out to stay put, followed by a finger to his lips for quiet. Hywel sent out a trilling sound, different from the others.

Rowena shuffled through all the signal calls she'd learned while they waited out the daylight. There had been so many. The sound meant . . . Hywel would climb a tree to get a better view, open a gate—which made no sense—or investigate and return. She'd have to count on the others to understand. She darted a glance at Safi, who remained silent while tracking the wagon with intense focus.

There was something odd about the situation. There were only a handful of wagons that had left Velmeg. Once they delivered their goods, most merchants stayed in the town to avoid the risk of traveling in the dark. Some in a hurry to gather another load of goods to sell had left in a rush—but few. This wagon ambled along as if there was plenty of time, or that there was something wrong.

Rowena guessed the latter. The air crackled against her skin, charged with aggression as if it held a grudge.

A hint of movement across the road drew her attention at the same time she sensed Bram tense his muscles. Even the shadows seemed to grow darker. Rowena's insides drew together into a tight ball. She peeked over each shoulder.

Whatever hid in that wagon, danger came with it. She held her breath as it rumbled by.

After the cart had rolled only ten paces, someone lunged from the bushes and rolled under the wooden belly, clinging to the underside like a barnacle on a ship. Rowena gasped. Safi squeezed her wrist. Surely, no one could have heard that over the creaking wood and jangling chains? Yet the baurun's pace lagged slightly.

An agonizing moment later, whoever rode under the wagon dropped and rolled back into the forest, while the wagon continued.

The rattle of beast and cart faded in the distance before another whistle came from Conri.

"Stay here," Bram whispered, leaning closer. His warm breath near her ear made Rowena shiver. He left a heartbeat later, as silent as a wraith.

Bram slipped back to their side not long after. She needed him to show her how he could move so easily without rustling a single blade of grass.

"That was a trap. The wagon was full of guards looking for brigands who raided some merchants earlier," he whispered. "We'll wait another quarter hour by Masah, and then head to the gathering point."

"And hope Errol is waiting for us," Safi said, then quickly added, "and the others."

Rowena bit back a grin. "Of course."

They resumed their watch on the road, close enough that both Bram and Safi brushed against her shoulders. Bram's scent—oak with hints of spice—filled the air, encircling Rowena like a scarf with a confusing mix of power and danger. Her nerves sizzled, and her breathing quickened.

Bram peered out at the road, alert to any signs of danger, yet his hulking size crowded her. The space closed in and she was back in the cave, Daenon looming over her.

"Will you scoot over?" Her words snapped louder and sharper than she'd intended, yet she couldn't help it. She was close to bolting out of the tight space and putting everyone in more danger.

Safi wrapped a hand around her mouth, yanking her closer. "Quiet."

The action combined with her charged emotions and exacerbated everything. The dark, the close quarters—she was back in the cave. Not again. Her chest heaved. There wasn't enough air. She was being smothered. Rowena twisted her face just enough to dig her teeth into the fingers over her mouth.

"Ow. Shite." Safi dropped her hand.

Rowena fell to her backside and scrambled backward. Branches cracked and hands reached for her. She had to get away.

"Rowena," Bram's voice hissed through the dark.

He couldn't grab her. She'd die before she let him trap her. Not again.

"You're going to get us all caught." Safi's fingers grazed Rowena's ankle.

"Don't touch her," Bram growled, jerking Safi away. "Rowena, no one is going to hurt you."

"What's going on?" Another voice, male.

Rowena couldn't breathe. Spots floated across her vision. Strong arms wrapped around her, hauling her to her feet and pinning her arms to her sides. She kicked and bucked. Growls and grunts mixed with hot breath in her ears.

"Stop fighting, lass," Conri said.

There were so many. They surrounded her. Not again!

"Let her go," Bram called.

Conri's arms squeezed harder for a moment, and then he let them fall away.

Rowena dropped to the ground, curling her arms around her knees, rocking. Nothing. She could do nothing. She could do nothing to stop him.

"No one will touch you," Bram's soft voice floated near her. "We must leave here. Can you hear me?"

He sounded sincere, but he was a man, just like Daenon. She couldn't trust him.

"She's puttin' us all at risk." Hywel spoke from somewhere nearby. "Leave her to the guards. Let's go."

"He's right," another Fianna said.

She couldn't distinguish them all. There were too many.

"Let me try." Safi. She was safe.

Tears squeezed out of Rowena's eyes. What was happening to her? She shouldn't have needed so much help. She had to pull herself together.

"Rowena, it's Safi. I understand what you're going through. Look at me."

Her cousin didn't grab at her. How could she understand? No one would understand. Rowena peeked over her knees to meet Safi's gaze, glistening in the moonlight.

"I understand," her cousin said again. There was a truth on her face. The way her lips pressed together as if trying to stave off her own tears. "Take my hand, and I'll keep you safe."

Rowena glanced at the offered palm and swallowed. Embarrassment flooded over her. She dared to glance to her right and left, angry Fianna both directions. She nodded and clasped her cousin.

As she rose, she caught sight of a sliver of moonlight peeking through the trees. Lungol had arrived, chasing Masah through the dark. The smaller moon exaggerated emotions. It would be her luck that her enchantment had a stronger connection with the more volatile moon.

"Make haste," Conri said, spinning and racing away through

the bushes. The others followed without a word, leaving Bram, Safi, and Rowena alone.

"Go," Safi whispered to Bram. "I'll get her there."

Bram flattened his lips. Rowena averted her eyes, unable to witness his disgust at her behavior.

"He's gone. They all are." Safi squeezed Rowena's hand she still held. "When we're done and we finish the task, you and I will talk. But for now, we need to focus."

Rowena nodded. She wanted to thank her cousin for understanding, for making the others leave.

"Concentrate on each step. Make no noise." She used a finger to turn Rowena's chin to meet her stare. "Right now is all there is."

Rowena inhaled deeply through her nose and let it out slowly. "Yes."

Safi patted the back of her hand, spun, and raced away. Rowena didn't hesitate, keeping near her cousin's heels while watching each step and branch. Her mind cleared of all else.

They caught up to the rest of the men after only a short time. They were crouched in the brush at the edge of the trees, Bram already with them. Safi and Rowena joined in the back. There was at least thirty yards of cleared ground between where they hid and the stone-walled city. The gates were wide open, carts and individuals came and went with sharp-eyed guards monitoring everything.

"What are we waiting for?" Safi whispered.

"Liam went ahead to find Seamus," Bram answered, glancing at Rowena with a question in his eyes. She ducked her head, unwilling and unable to assure him she would be fine.

She would have to be. There was a job to do, and she had a part in it. If she didn't get up the stairs to open a window, they might never find the sword. Whatever it took to keep herself steady, she had to find the strength. It shouldn't have been so hard. She would not allow what the prince had done to her to hold that much power.

Two men, arms slung over each other's shoulders, came

wobbling through the gates. They slurred a bawdy song horribly out of tune. The hooded cloaks pulled over their heads left their faces in shadow.

"Farewell, fine men of the watch!" one of them called to the guards closest to them.

"Be off with you," a guard commanded, yet his voice held a hint of humor.

The two continued by the rest of them, but Seamus lifted a hand, showing three fingers as they passed.

Three guards? Three minutes? What had he meant? Rowena leaned closer, about to ask Safi, but Conri turned.

"Fall back thirty paces. We'll be out of view to enter the road."

The Fianna had so many signals. It would take years for Rowena to master them all. Since she and Safi arrived last, they turned and led the group, counting out thirty paces through the greenery. They found Seamus and Liam first.

"Errol's got the wagon. We positioned it behind a cooper's shop to wait," Seamus said after everyone had gathered. "I also brought you this, lass."

He pulled a bundle from under his cloak and handed it to Rowena. It was a thrall's serk and apron. A bitter tang burned the back of her throat. It wasn't something she ever wanted to wear again, but she understood the need and swallowed hard to steady herself. "Thanks."

"We'll have to go in shifts. Five at a time should be fine." Conri nodded to Rowena. "Hurry and change."

She clutched the clothing, ripe with the odor of ale and sweat, and ducked deeper into the trees for privacy yet close enough to still hear the others.

"How's it look?" Hywel asked.

Rowena listened to the others as she shimmied out of her trousers and tunic, holding her breath as she donned the serk.

"There are extra guards, but with the music and revelry, we should do well," Seamus answered.

Rowena slipped the apron over her dress, tying it at the sides. Once finished, she set about replaiting her hair in a thrall style, hesitating when she heard Liam speak.

"What about the lass? Is she well enough?"

"She's fine," Safi answered in a clipped tone. "Worry about your part and she'll do hers."

With an extra inhale, Rowena squared her shoulders. Uther, Fidessa, and Daenon had taken enough from her. They would not have her sword as well. She slipped through the brush and rejoined the others.

"I expect you can get these to the wagon for me?" She shoved her folded trousers and tunic toward Seamus with an arched brow.

The Fianna warrior smirked, holding out his hands. "Of course, my lady."

He was joking, but she hadn't heard the title spoken in her direction in a month. It felt like years.

"Everyone ready?" Conri asked, eyes only for Rowena. When she nodded, he gave a quick perusal of the others, and the first group snuck onto the road toward Velmeg's gates.

Safi and Bram led the way, striding next to each other comfortably. It shouldn't have bothered Rowena, but it did. She hated walking behind, ignored. Seamus and one of Hywel's men spread out on either side of them, with Rowena trailing as a thrall would. The churned-up tracks on the road had her dress muddy to her calf. It wasn't hard to don the expression of a lowly slave by the time they arrived. Guards in high watchtowers on either side of the heavy wooden gates barely glanced at them.

It only took a few words from Bram, and the entire party strolled into the busy courtyard without concern. Warriors sat around fires together in groups, off duty and enjoying ale and roasted meats. Merchants, servants, and children rushed about without giving their party a second glance. Bram and Safi casually turned to the right, heading toward the dark side of the feast hall.

Seamus and his partner turned to the left, leaving Rowena to enter alone.

The open bailey led to a prominent tower with the town radiating out from there. Ibernians didn't use longhouses like those in Taesing. The king lived in the round stone tower, conical shaped, shrinking in diameter as it grew taller, and topped by a tightly woven thatch. Slender windows, carved from the stone, some with open shutters, some closed, spoke of several levels inside. Even the smaller living quarters and merchant stalls were circular and made of stacked stone with thatched roofs.

Rowena steeled herself, ducked her head meekly, and strode the open wooden door to the king's tower. The entire floor was a large open space filled with scattered tables and benches randomly placed around a fire in the center. Its smoke twisted up through the opened hole in the center of the roof high above.

Huge tapestries hung on the wall—four of them spread around the room. Their images told a story of Ibern, it seemed, but Rowena couldn't study them. Between the heavy fabric, the fire and the number of bodies, the air hung thick and warm. A dribble of sweat ran down Rowena's back almost immediately.

Along the edges of the circular room were tables of food and barrels of ale, mead, and wine. She hurried over to one, grabbed a pitcher, and filled it with ale, assuming her role as thrall so as not to draw attention to her observance of the room. She'd expected one set of stairs, but there were two. On either side of the front doors, in a dark corridor, each rose along the curved wall. Guards monitored each opening.

Safi had turned right, so she chose that direction, staying near the tables closest to the wall to fill cups as she observed the guards. They didn't seem too concerned about their duties, laughing with others as they stood near their posts. King Lendan and Queen Dewan stood talking with guests rather than sitting on a dais.

The queen fascinated Rowena. Statuesque with dark hair, a girdle—embroidered in gold—encircled Dewan's emerald green gown. She held a goblet in her hand, laughing casually, in a way that seemed relaxed, natural . . . confident.

Rowena closed her eyes, picturing her mother in the same pose. The warm memory faded as soon as she spotted Uther on Lendan's far side.

With a foul taste seeping into the back of her mouth, Rowena returned to her task. A pressing sensation, similar to what she'd experienced in the wagon on the way to Velmeg, passed through her. Her hands trembled. The sword was somewhere nearby.

Rowena had emptied her pitcher, leaving it on a table to begin her climb, when she froze. At the far side of the room, Daenon and Fidessa sat at a table alone, heads bent, speaking to each other while somewhat hidden in the shadows.

Rowena's pulse quickened, and sweat increased on her neck. There they were, two of her enemies, so casual . . . so secluded. Cutlery sat on the table from their meal. She could easily make her way over there, unnoticed. Slip behind the table as if to fill their mugs. They wouldn't even look at her. It would be quick. A knife from the table in Fidessa's neck and the one from her boot would slide along Daenon's throat. In the uproar that followed, she'd melt out of sight and be up the stairs before anyone saw her near the bodies.

Her feet carried her closer, mindless to anything but her new task. Follow the edge of the room. Stick to the shadows. Her chest tightened. Her palms itched.

Fidessa had softened her usual sour, pinched expression. Daenon's lips moved and his head tilted toward her. The queen dipped her head . . . her hand raising to cover a grin. Rowena halted. What could the prince say that would cause that? Was he recounting how he'd acted in the cave? How he'd disgraced and humiliated Rowena? They'd surely get a laugh out of that. She clenched her hands into fists.

One more table and she'd be behind them. They had paid no attention to her. She recalled how Daenon questioned why she'd spoken to her servant at the feast in her longhouse. How he'd scoffed at treating everyone with kindness. She didn't have to worry about being seen—they considered her invisible.

The next step put her behind Fidessa's left shoulder. She eased another step, ready to lunge. Grab the knife. Fidessa first—avoid spells.

She hesitated. Why? They'd taken everything from her. Her parents were dead. Hann was dead. Daenon had attacked her—made her afraid in a way she'd never experienced.

Tingles sizzled down her arms.

A loud clatter of falling dishes and crockery startled Rowena, and she spun to face the open hall. Her body chilled as if an early morning bucket of river water had doused her from the inside. Everyone else also turned toward a serving woman who'd dropped a tray.

"What's the meaning of this?" someone yelled.

"Look what you've done," cried another. No, not a nameless voice—Seamus.

Rowena lifted her gaze to scan the crowd, but she need not search far. Conri glared at her from five feet away. He motioned with his hands toward the stairs.

From the corner of her eye, she saw the prince slide his glance in her direction. She threw herself between Daenon and Fidessa, bumping both out of the way as she snatched an empty pitcher on their table and hurried off as a thrall they wouldn't care about.

"Watch yourself!" Fidessa yelled out.

"Are you injured?" Daenon asked, nearly out of her range of hearing. His question was so full of concern. He seemed rather different from the hateful creature who'd snarled and clawed at her in the dark.

The guards at the bottom of the stairs were involved in sorting out the mess of what wasn't just a tray that had fallen, but an entire table tipped over. Rowena squeezed past them and up the stairs, stepping lightly on her toes up each step.

When she reached the top, she leaned against the wall, chest heaving. She'd almost ruined the Fianna's mission, but it would have been worth it—perhaps. In the quieter hall, while yelling and laughter filtered up the stone corridor, she wondered if she could have truly done as she'd planned. Wouldn't that make her just as wicked as they were? But wasn't that what she wanted?

Her mind flip-flopped like a fish hauled onto the shore. She had to pull herself together. Concentrate on the mission, one step at a time. Safi's words came to her. She balled her fists and continued up to the next level.

A shuttered window sat not five feet away from the top of the stairs. One closed door shone ahead to the right, but the hallway continued around to the left. She unlatched the window and threw open the shutters. A heartbeat later, a hook swung through the opening and latched onto the stone ledge.

Rowena backed away, swiveling her gaze one way and the other for guards. Moments later, Safi hopped over the edge with Bram right after her.

"What was all the ruckus?" Safi asked.

"Tell you later." Rowena jogged down the hall, unsure of how she'd explain. She couldn't understand herself right then. Why had she failed at avenging her family?

She wouldn't fail again.

"Uther's room will be on this floor or the next," Safi said, standing tall and confident. Sconces hung on the wall, creating a small glow a foot to either side of where they hung. Though the hall was dark, Safi knew where she was well enough.

The three of them stopped at the first door, listening. Safi tried the handle. It popped open with an audible clink. They froze. No noise. Safi peeked in.

"Not one of the royal's rooms. Too small. Their rooms are probably further around," her cousin said and hurried away around the curving hallway.

A few steps later, Rowena stopped abruptly, her breath seizing.

"Are you unwell?" Bram asked, halting next to her. He touched her arm and Rowena startled, jumping out of his reach. He lifted both palms into the air, a fierce pinch to his brows.

Rowena didn't have the vigor to deal with his anger. A sensation bubbled up inside her chest, and her skin tingled. There was a feeling like her body had a string attached to it, being reeled closer to her prize by instinct . . . faintly. She may have counted the swirling in her belly as the aftereffects of being so close to her enemies, but this pull was different. Similar to the cave, just before she sent Daenon sprawling, if she allowed herself to think of that moment. And the time in the wagon. The sword was in the building, but where?

"I can feel it," she whispered aloud, partly to Safi, but mostly to herself.

"What?" Safi spun and met her gaze. "What can you feel?"

"The sword. It's here." She pointed to her chest, rubbing her sternum. There was no mistaking it now—she recognized the sensation. Her enchantment had developed, and it connected with the sword. The blade wasn't just a relic of her heritage. It was something more . . . much more.

TWENTY-TWO

The dark hall closed in, while Rowena touched the sizzling spot in the center of her chest.

Safi stared in silence, bouncing her glance between Rowena's face and her fingers.

"The armor is calling you," Bram stated, as if it was a natural thing.

"Why? What kind of sword is this?" Safi bounced her gaze from Rowena to Bram and back.

Rowena shook her head. "I only know it was my great-grandfather's. My mother brought it with her when she fled with my grandmother." At least, that was the only part of the tale she'd been told. Clearly, there was more to the story.

"Listen, and let it draw you closer." Bram's direct command pierced the dark expectantly. His face had the serious expression she realized he carried most often.

Rather than argue with him for telling her what to do, she closed her eyes, hoping she'd understand where the pull wanted to take her. The sensation filled in the air all around her, but nothing became clear.

"I can't . . .I don't know which way." She couldn't process all that was happening.

"Let's just keep looking, and if you—"

"What are you doing up here?" A guard surprised them when coming around the bend in the direction they headed down the long, narrow hallway. He gripped the hilt of his sword but didn't yet unsheathe it.

Safi drew her dagger at the same time Bram drew his shortsword. Rowena froze in place, indecision rolling through her like an overloaded wagon. A mental image flashed into her mind. Her mother calming the rowdy warriors at the King's Day celebrations. Did she dare? She'd never attempted the skill, but her body nearly begged her to reach for it.

Rowena slowly lifted her hands, trembling as she fumbled for the right sensation to grab hold of, and stepped in front of the other two. "We're just looking around."

"With naked blades? No one is to be up here," the guard said.

"It was a reflex. You know how it is." Rowena made a motion with her hand, hoping Safi and Bram would understand. They needed to put away their weapons if she had a chance. She ambled closer to the guard. "We meant nothing by it."

The guard trained his gaze on the warriors behind her, giving her time to move within reach. She laid a hand on his forearm. "We're no danger. You can relax and go enjoy an ale. Watching a door is keeping you from the fun, anyway."

Her palm tingled like she had a hundred ants itching away at her skin, but she held steady. The guard's eyes softened, and his face slackened. "It ain't fair. I got to hear the feast without even seeing it."

"Very true. We're no threat. You can go." Rowena held her breath, hoping the tremble in her arm didn't ruin her efforts.

"I suppose you seem safe enough. I'll be down in the hall." The guard strolled away, passing a gaping Safi, and squeezed by Bram, who angled sideways. "The others can keep watch."

The three of them watched the man round the curve and waited until his heavy boots clomped down the stone steps before anyone spoke.

"What was that?" Safi whispered.

"Enchantment. That was why she can feel the sword," Bram answered. "We need to go. There are more guards."

Rowena wanted to give a shout and jump, but she pulled her shoulders back, and stood a little taller, biting her lip to quell her grin. She had her mother's enchantment, and would act like the queen had as well. "There could still be more guards. We should forge ahead, prepared to fight as well."

"We'll talk about this later," Safi answered, but grabbed Rowena's elbow as she moved to continue around the corridor. "He said there were others. Can you spell, or charm, or however it works, more than one at a time?"

That doused Rowena's flames of excitement as if she'd been tossed into the bay. If her enchantment worked like her mother's, and it seemed to, then she had to touch whoever's emotions she needed to influence. And she could only enhance what they already felt. That guard hadn't pulled his weapon; he hadn't wanted to fight. He'd wanted to be at the feast. The others would not be similarly minded, most likely.

"I'm not sure." If she was honest, that was best because the power that had welled up in her seemed drained—still there, but a trickle rather than a torrent.

"The Lunara must spend time in harmony with the moons. It will take time for you to develop your skills. You will not be ready for another guard." Bram didn't ask her anything, just made statements. He couldn't understand how she felt. His all-knowing attitude was becoming too irritating.

"I can still feel the enchantment." She curled her hands into fists, willing the sensations to rise once more. "You don't know what's happening to me."

Bram let out a heavy exhale. "We don't have time to argue. Let's go."

He nodded to Safi and spun to leave. Her cousin didn't even glance at her before following. Rowena scoffed and glared down the hallway, where more guards waited. It was her chance to prove herself—and get the sword by herself—but she hesitated.

"Rowena," Bram said, suddenly at her side. "You must come away."

She started at his closeness. The dark and his looming oak-scented presence forced all thoughts from her mind. Her breath hitched. She opened her mouth to speak, but no words formed.

The golden flecks in Bram's eyes glowed like she'd seen in the forest. He slid back, giving her space. "Come."

The surrounding air cleared. Her chest relaxed. She closed her eyes, clamping her mouth tight. When she refocused on Bram, he'd furrowed his brows, and his expression sizzled with anger, but he kept his distance from her. He'd better stay that way because, this time, she had her seax and wouldn't hesitate to use it. No man would grab her in the dark again.

Her nostrils flared. "Fine."

Without a word, Bram raced away, and she followed.

Safi waited at the top of the stairs, leaning around the corner. A commotion in the feast hall sounded as if the place had erupted into a battle.

"What's going on?" Rowena couldn't get close enough to look for herself with the traveler blocking her path. How did they get stuck working with him, anyway?

Safi faced them, shoving Bram toward the window. "Jotnari!"

Giants?

Bram didn't wait or give Rowena time to think. The next moment, he'd hoisted her through the window and flipped her around so she dangled from her armpits. Frantically, she scrambled to grab the rope. As soon as she held tight and started rappelling, Safi came over the ledge above her.

Rowena's palms burned from sliding down too fast, but her feet barely hit the ground before Safi landed without a sound. Bram arrived a heartbeat later, and they were off.

It all happened so fast, it had Rowena in a state that she could only follow.

Outside, they raced toward a small alleyway. A thin woman, with a long brown robe, crossed their path, darting a glance their way and then skidded on the loose soil. Bram halted, extending his arm out, forcing Safi and Rowena to stop as well. It was the druid, Yralissa. She turned slowly, head tilted, ignoring Safi and Rowena, striding in a slow, methodical manner with her gaze locked on Bram's.

"It's not safe. We must hurry to shelter," he said. It wasn't clear if he spoke to all of them or just the druid.

The druid bobbed her head without breaking her gaze.

"This way." He pointed to the alley, and they hurried past Yralissa, who seemed too stunned to move.

"What was wrong with her?" Rowena tried to sneak another peek at the woman, but she'd already moved on.

"I'm sure I don't know." His words didn't match his tone, but there wasn't time to figure it all out.

They rushed to a small cart, normally pulled by a vulugoat. Safi flipped it and they huddled behind. In the streets, women and men raced in all directions. Some to find cover, others with weapons drawn, but even a few of those ran away from the hall.

Then, four Jotnari stomped into view and Rowena's mouth fell agape. They were huge, at least eight feet tall, or more, but their size wasn't half as shocking as their appearance. Large-boned and well-muscled, they only wore woven fabric around their waist and flat sandals with long ties that wrapped around their lower legs to tie just below the knee. Raised tattoos covered much of their skin: chest, back, arms, neck, legs, and even their heads. They either shaved their heads or wore it in thin, tight braids, bound in a small knot at the base of their skull.

Armed with spears, bone-knives, and axes, they paid no care to who they struck down. Male, female, warrior, or thrall—they all fell.

No other Jotnari were visible outside of the hall. Such a small number to cause so much destruction.

A body hurdled over the cart, causing a yelp from Rowena as she ducked low. Conri scooted close after he landed, with a precision that didn't match his robust size, joining their number.

"Did you get it?" He directed his question to Safi.

She lifted a shoulder and shook her head. "There were guards."

"How many Jotnari have come in total?" Bram asked, diverting Conri away from their failed mission.

Conri grumbled under his breath before answering. "Nine. Ten. I didn't stop to count. But it's a scouting party, no more."

"Scouting? For what?" Rowena couldn't guess what would draw the Jotnari to attack so far away from the northern Frost Flats.

"They've been clashing with King Lendan's forces for months as he tries to gain more lands. My guess is they decided Velmeg might be vulnerable with all the celebrating going on."

"It looks like they were right," Safi said, peeking over the flipped goat cart again before falling back down to rest her back against the rough wood. "A full-scale attack would be devastating."

Conri nodded. "We need to pull back. Meet in the forest near the three hawthorns."

Safi reached out and clasped his forearm in agreement. "Be safe."

"So far." Conri winked and rushed into the dark.

"We can't stay here either," Bram said.

"Where is he going? Why don't we go with him?" If Conri had a plan for where to meet, why would he leave?

"He'll be the last to leave, making sure all the groups get out first," Safi answered. "It's his duty as leader."

"We should head to the palisade; find another place to get

out." Bram gripped his shortsword with ease. He didn't seem rattled at all.

"Good thing I know my way around," Safi said with a grin. "The postern is this way."

Bram waited, lifting his hand for Rowena to follow her cousin. She arched a brow at him. He'd been arrogant enough already, and she didn't want him behind her.

He hissed through his teeth. "Keep up."

She gave a satisfied humph as he passed, but she stayed close. The chaos and potentially getting spotted by one of the Jotnari had her unsettled—not that he needed to know that.

Safi led them through a small alleyway to keep out of sight, though they arrived still too near the back side of the king's tower for Rowena's comfort. She kept swinging her gaze left and right, sometimes walking backward. After choosing to watch the rear, she had second thoughts.

Then, down a small pathway, she saw the rope, still clinging to the open window in the tower. The surrounding area had stayed empty, with the fighting concentrated near the front doors. She glanced at Bram, who'd gotten a few steps farther ahead, Safi beyond him.

The guards were probably gone, invested in the fighting. It would be the best time to search for the sword and leave on her own. Perhaps find a ship to take her . . . where? She exhaled. That was a problem for later. With a quick second glance at the others, she darted toward the tower. Decision made.

A pile of crates sat near two tipped over barrels near a tall rabbit hutch. Rowena ducked behind them, waiting. Her pulse raced like thunder in her ears. Between the slats of the top crates, she spied Bram and Safi. Her cousin turned left, toward the outside city wall. Bram followed, but glanced back as he did. His feet slid in the path's soft dirt with a furious growl on his face.

Rowena watched as he scanned the area and turned his face toward where Safi had disappeared. His indecision clear—turn one way and leave Safi alone or turn the other way to find Rowena. She pleaded internally for him to follow her cousin. There wasn't any way he could know if Rowena left on her own or a giant had picked her off...

The last thought lingered in her mind, forcing her to scan her surroundings once more. She turned back in time to see Bram leave, following her cousin. Rowena wasted no time, bursting out of her hiding place to race toward the rope—only to come face to face with a Jotnari rounding the tower.

Rowena yelped despite herself, flailed her arms to stop her momentum, and spun. She willed her shaking legs to move faster than she'd ever gone. Heavy footsteps combined with a deep growling chuckle rumbled through the air behind her.

Whatever happened, she couldn't lead the giant toward the wall and bring danger to Safi and Bram. Rowena darted between two rock structures with thatched roofs, snagging her hand on the corner to help propel herself around the corner. She only gained a step or two on her pursuer. As she sprinted, she tipped over anything loose, tossing baskets, barrels, and boxes behind her. From the snarled words, it seemed her efforts helped. She didn't have to understand the Jotnari language to know the man hurled curses as he smashed through her obstacles.

She rounded another corner and darted inside an open door, kicking over a stack of crates to make it seem as if she'd kept going. Huddled in the dark, the giant ran past her. Silently, she ducked out and raced the other way, zagging around an outdoor blacksmith area.

A heartbeat later, the Jotnari's scream reached her. She glanced over her shoulder to find the ruffian had spotted her.

Rowena raced wildly, heedless of nothing except escape. A dark corridor appeared between a goat pen and a tiny hut that reeked of onions and garlic. When she reached a dead-end, she slapped her hand over her mouth, squelching a scream. The rocky palisade loomed ahead of her, twenty feet tall. She launched herself onto it, determined to climb up and over.

The giant entered the narrow passage moments later, calling out words in his language that had unmistakable amusement woven within. Rowena's foot slipped, leaving her hanging, scraping her feet on the rough stone to find another toehold. She clung to the wall in her desperate search, when the Jotnari yelled out. A heartbeat later, metal met metal in a clash behind her.

She balanced a toe between two smaller stones, trying to thrust herself higher, but her fingers lost their grip at the same time. All the air whooshed out of her body when she hit the hard-packed earth seconds afterward.

That was where she lay as a dark shadow loomed over her.

TWENTY-THREE

The strange fae she'd seen before in Forsa leaned back enough to view him properly in the moonlight. He stretched out a hand with runes etched along pointed fingers. Obsidian horns protruded from his skull, curling back and up into sharp, deadly spires. His face was as pale as the Jotnari, but without the hint of icy-blue. Long white hair fell over his smooth face, emblazoned with runes on his chin. More glowed from his forehead, between the base of the horns.

Rowena shook her head, smashing the back of her skull into the dirt, trying to get away, but he hopelessly trapped her. She'd escaped from him before, but this time she had nowhere to run.

"Come!" a rough voice that sounded gravely from disuse commanded her. Molten-gold eyes swirled with a mesmerizing quality.

"No," Rowena squeaked, grappling with her hands and feet to inch away from the terror in black leathers. It was the Seeker from the tales.

"Save yourself." Another command, but with it, the beast seemed to school his features, softening them.

Something inside her stilled, questioning. Similar to the first time the sword called to her, a force sparked through her arms. Transfixed and curious, she ignored every screaming impulse to run and lifted her hand into his waiting palm.

Immediately, black clouds billowed around their feet, growing larger and rolling up from the ground. Rowena's eyes grew dry from holding them so wide open. She shivered as if the shadows encased her in ice the higher they climbed. When they reached her waist, she yanked on her hand, no longer interested in the hauntingly handsome fae or where he wanted to take her.

"Steady."

Rowena couldn't decide if his voice settled on her like a skittish horse, or if she'd chosen to leave too late. Her vision faded and her body became lighter than air, floating on a cloud of darkness.

When her feet touched the ground again, she wobbled, but didn't fall. Black fog swirled all around her, keeping her upright, yet left her blind to her surroundings. Moments later, it dissipated, revealing a small room with a comfortable high-back chair, which sat in front of a flickering fire that burned from a hearth carved into the wall. She'd never witnessed such a construction.

One slow step, and another, and then she squatted in front of the flames. For a moment, her only thought focused on getting herself warm.

A small voice in the back of her mind warned her to be on guard. She'd left her back exposed. She pushed the advice aside, favoring ignorance. Perhaps she'd die. It would only hasten her to her loved ones. Peace washed over her while she stared into the flickering orange glow. The warmth against her cheeks spread into her bones, melting away her fear. A few moments later, her shoulders lowered. Until she remembered what she'd done. How she'd willingly given herself up to her terrifying captor. Though he hadn't killed her yet.

"Where am I?" She didn't move from her position or glance the at horror waiting behind her. There wasn't any noise, save for the crackling wood, but she could feel the fae's presence.

"A safe place," came the raspy reply.

Gruff as it was, his voice somehow soothed her, which created a new sense of confusion. What had broken inside of her to accept such a situation? There was another question, the one about who the man might be that she refused to ask, but feared she already knew.

She rose and scanned the rest of the room, purposefully avoiding the horned threat. Beyond the strange hearth and chair sat a plain table with two straight-backed wooden chairs. Another table, running the length of the far wall, had neatly stacked bowls, trenchers, and other supplies for preparing meals. Moonlight streamed onto a simple braided rug, cushioning the floor beneath her feet, angling in from the windows on either side of a solid wood door. Stunned at the simplistic surroundings, she couldn't figure out which moon provided the light, so she might decipher where he'd taken her.

The uncomplicated arrangement offered a smidge of comfort. This couldn't be his home. Such a dangerous being wouldn't live in such a humble place. Perhaps a palace made of black stone, hidden high in a vale or some such would suit him better. Or maybe he lived nowhere, and everywhere within the shadows he'd conjured to bring her there. She swallowed, clutching her fingers to the edge of her over-apron.

"Why did you bring me here?" She kept her gaze trained on the rug.

"We'll discuss it later. I must see to a situation. Remain indoors until I return."

She gathered the courage to meet the Seekers's golden gaze. "Am I free to leave?"

"You're not a prisoner." He crossed his arms over his chest and tightened his lips into a fine white line. "You're free to move about . . . Just keep everything in its place."

Rowena leaned back, narrowing her eyes as she studied the fae better. His dark shirt fitted him well, stretching tight over his muscled upper arms and shoulders. He tucked it into his matching black trousers in a way she'd not seen others wear their tunics. It suited him—made him seem normal, despite his other attributes.

"Are you finished gawking?"

"I wasn't." Rowena huffed and crossed her arms, mimicking his stance. "Where are you from?"

"We'll speak later." His tone was irritatingly cool. "I'll return soon."

He disappeared. No dramatic shadows or billowing dark mist . . . just gone in a wisp. After a startled moment, she threw her arms up. He'd transported her to this place, yet his attitude seemed as if she'd arrived as an invader.

Confused and annoyed, she picked up a small log from a basket near the fire and tossed it into the flames. She flopped onto the chair and sank into its softness. Nothing made sense.

He'd implied he would provide answers, and instead, he'd created more questions.

* * *

Rowena startled awake. Disoriented, she sat up and tried to get her bearings in the dark. Chills ran up her arms and not just from the cold. The blackened logs in the fire had burned down to barely an ember, but they reminded her where she was.

How had she fallen asleep? Her body ached, as if she'd trained all day for a week straight. It couldn't be from the short time she sparred with Liam. Even with the danger in Velmeg, she'd not done that much to warrant such exhaustion and pain.

She pushed to her feet and shuffled across the darkened room to peer out the window. Nothing in the view seemed familiar. Moonlight glowed in the meadow. She craned her neck, but the small window didn't allow her to determine whether it was Lungol or Masah in the sky. Hadn't the Seeker said he'd return soon? He'd also said to stay inside, and she wasn't a prisoner. She nibbled at the inside of her lip.

She scanned the surroundings out the window again. A small

meadow stretched to a forest of trees heavy with leaves and filled tight with underbrush. It seemed serene. However, if she went out, she'd expose herself to anything that might hide among the grasses or trees, watching . . . ready to pounce.

Rowena spun and chastised herself. "You're a proper warrior alright."

She wouldn't wait around for danger; she'd rather die fighting a creature with her bare hands. Her mind made up, she stomped to the door. The handle wouldn't budge. She leaned her shoulder against the door, hoping to wiggle it and perhaps free the lock. No use. So much for being free then.

If she planned to stay put, the first thing to do was get the fire going and then find some candles. The last thing she wanted was to sit in the dark until the shadows came to life again.

It didn't take long for the flames to catch and roar back to life, illuminating the room better. She snatched a taper from the basket of logs and lit the sconces she hadn't noticed hanging on the walls when she first arrived. Soon, she had all corners of the small home dancing with a cheery orange glow. Her nerves relaxed into a pleasant hum rather than a pestering rattle.

She inspected the small bed chambers. The mattress seemed comfortable, and no straw rustled when she sat on the edge- a feather bed. Her mother used to speak of having one like it as a girl. She rose and continued her perusal. Two trunks sat side-by-side on the far wall, but nothing else occupied the room. He'd said she was free to wander around—but he'd lied about being trapped. She peeked out to the living area, verifying she was still alone. Perhaps she'd find clues to why such a powerful fae would live in such a tiny, ordinary place.

She clenched and unclenched her fists, then hurried to the trunks. If he didn't want her to look, he should have given her the idea. The first trunk held nothing but blankets and extra linens. She pulled out a quilt to take to the chair with her. It had gotten cold when the fire burned out and she still wore the thread-bare thrall dress Seamus had given her.

The second trunk was nearly empty, except for a pair of black trousers, a short black tunic, long warm socks, and a pair of soft leather knee boots—all in her size. She stared at the clothing. There weren't any other objects she'd seen to show another woman lived there. Had he planned to take her before finding her in Velmeg? A shiver rolled over her shoulders and trickled down her spine. The items in her hands seemed to say so. She put them back, but then stared at them. They would be more practical than the gown. He'd also said to leave everything in its place. She grumbled at her indecision.

The serk reminded her of Hedda, and Fidessa, and Uther—they all wanted her to cower under their rule. She set her shoulders and hurried to change. There were no mirrors or combs to be found, so she used the window glass in the main room to re-plait her hair. Either the events in Velmeg, or traveling as a wraith through the shadows, had her hair in a tangled mess.

"Ouch." Her fingers caught within knots, pulling against her scalp.

Distracted with her eyes squeezed shut as she worked on a particularly troubling snarl. When she peeked at the glass again, she screamed at the fae's reflection in the window. Shaking, she spun to face the Seeker where he stood behind her.

He stared in silence at her efforts.

"You shouldn't show up without announcing yourself!"

He raised his brows into high arches.

She's just scolded someone who could probably turn her to dust. Her insides melted, and she sunk into a cringe. "I mean . . . it's just . . . " Wait, why should she have felt bad? He stood there in silence, watching her! "Don't be so sneaky."

"Do you require assistance?" he asked, unbothered by her outburst.

Uh. Hmm. Even her thoughts stuttered at his offer. She lifted a shoulder, unsure of what to do.

He slid closer and peered at the mess she'd made of herself.

She dropped her arms to her sides. "I'm afraid I'll have to cut that one out."

"That shouldn't be necessary." He slowly lifted his fingers to examine the situation, tugging the tangle slightly. A warmth spread through her chest, tingling in a way that she tried to shove aside, but couldn't.

Washed in a charred oak scent, she focused on the beads in his hair. Scattered among his white locks were ones in gold or silver, each marked with a different rune. She nearly reached out to touch one, but stopped herself.

"There you are." He dropped his arms and stepped back.

She absently touched her hair, pulling a strand in front of her to view. It appeared brushed and smooth, but she'd felt nothing. "Thank you."

"I see you found the clothes I arranged for you." His tone turned icy again. "Even though I said to leave everything in its place."

"I would have sought permission first, but I didn't want to stay in that gown." Her voice wavered, then she clamped her mouth closed. Her time as a thrall had left a stain on her confidence. One minute she wanted to apologize for everything, cower and shake. The next, she wanted to reach out and grab the man's tunic, forcing him to listen to her. He had horns, for Caelus' sake!

"Permission wasn't necessary."

He'd taken her away from Velmeg yet spoke as if she were a burden. "Why did you bring me here if you're going to be angry about it? I'll happily go on my way if I'm so free."

"I'm not angry."

She flicked her brows and twisted to the fire, crossing her arms over her chest.

"You are not a prisoner here, nor a thrall as before."

He'd lied about the first part before. "I'm not a thrall."

"Not anymore, that's true."

She turned slowly, meeting his gaze with narrowed eyes. "How did you know that?"

A corner of his mouth tipped into a wry grin like a predator who knew the game was over. "Am I to believe you don't know who I am?"

The harder she tried to control her breathing, the more pronounced her chest rose and fell. Sweat dribbled down her back. She had to calm down, or she'd give off a prey scent. With a long, quiet exhale, she accepted her fate. She opened her mouth to answer, but the word wouldn't release. Seeker. She couldn't say it.

"If you wouldn't insist on getting yourself into danger, I wouldn't have had to step in at all." His stance shifted slightly, relaxed.

But his commanding tone had an overriding effect of snapping Rowena out of her fear. "I can take care of myself."

"That Jotnari would have killed you."

"You don't know that."

"I do." He shook his head slowly, as if in pity.

Was he always in the shadows, watching everything? "Where? How?"

For the first time, he seemed uneasy. Interesting. The stories she'd heard told of a mindless beast sent to destroy those who no longer followed the Heptad's rules. One who tore flesh with blind rage. That contrasted with the one in front of her.

"It's complicated."

"Why bring me here? Why didn't you take me home to Skandan?" Even though she didn't know where she was exactly, the lush green view from the window proved it wasn't her homeland.

He twisted his lips to one side. "You're not safe there either."

"I will tell everyone the truth. They'll see that Uther lied." They had to.

"That's not the issue. They fear you because of your birth."

Rowena's mouth went dry. He knew she was moon-born. She wasn't part of the cryptic prophecy or associated with the final Reaping. She couldn't be. Then she remembered Asta's message to her father about how the Seeker had to find those like her.

"I'm not part of the prophecy. You've made a mistake!" Whatever it meant, she wanted no part of it. She had other plans for her life.

"You are." He stalked over to the wooden chairs next to the table, picked one up, and moved it near the hearth. "Your birth during the Burning Moon shook Saganus. As it did with each of the others."

"Others?"

He shook his head and gripped the back of the chair. Then gestured to the softer seat. "Come sit. I will explain."

TWENTY-FOUR

Rowena waited for several heartbeats. The idea of calmly discussing the prophecy or how she may have a part in it seemed ludicrous. It had to be a mistake, yet the only way she'd find out was to listen. She straightened her shoulders, making a wide berth around the Seeker to the chair. She wouldn't put her back to him. No other druid could do what he'd done. He'd swallowed her into his dark magic and taken her somewhere. She did not want to do that again.

"Are you going to sit as well or stand over me?" She'd cowered enough for others. This would be worse.

With a graceful ease, he settled his hulking frame onto the wooden seat, crossing one leg over the other as if the chair wasn't two sizes too small for him. "Better?"

Rowena perched on the edge of the oversized cushioned chair. "Much."

"What do you know of the prophecy?" His golden gaze bored into her like he could read her mind if she tried to lie. Which might have been true for all she knew.

She dropped her gaze to her lap and fidgeted with her fingers. "I've heard it. It's confusing, but some believe it's connected to the

Burning Moon."

"No one told you more than that?" He slid his leg to the floor and leaned his elbows on his knees. "That explains why those in Taesing mistrust you. Fear thrives without truth."

She met his gaze and held it tight. Some of her fear slid away at the mention of her home. "You've been to Taesing?"

He made a grumbling sound in his throat, rubbing his fingers along his brow bone, under the base of his horns. "That is of no importance. If not your parents, someone must have shared more with you? Did the disavowed say nothing either?"

"Asta?" She shook her head, having barely ever spoken to the druid. "Do you have a name? Both of the Oraku I'm familiar with have them. You're a druid as well, correct?"

"Yes."

"Then what are you called other than Seeker? And how can you travel through the shadows like that?"

"Are you always so full of questions?" He arched a brow.

She waved away his annoyance. The calm conversation had settled her nerves. If he was going to tear her apart, he would have done it already. "I gave you my trust. The least you could do is answer some of my questions."

"Fine. I have a name, and I'll answer to it." He leaned closer. "But if you don't know it, I'll not tell you."

"Why not? How could I possibly know it?" Her curiosity outweighed the last of her fear. "Would I have power over you if you tell me your name, like a djinn?"

"You would not. Nor would anyone else." He twisted to glare at the fire. The glow highlighted the runes on his forehead and chin. Ethereally beautiful.

Rowena sucked in a deep breath, forcing herself to stay focused. "When were you in Taesing?"

"Recently."

"Looking for me?" She flopped back into the chair. "What is happening there? Is everyone alright?" Did they believe Uther's lies? She couldn't voice that question because she wasn't sure she could accept the answer.

He rubbed his forehead again. "The village is . . . functional. The citizens appear unharmed."

"So, it's like Forsa, now. No more laughter or music or joy?" Her parents had filled her village with camaraderie and fun. Goetz had enjoyed the peace and comforts alongside everyone else. Why would he side with Uther and destroy so much?

"There is a similar quality." He resumed his earlier posture and tapped his fingers against his bent knee. "We must discuss the prophecy."

"I've told you all I know. Why is it so important?"

"Listen, and perhaps you'll understand." He waited for her to look him in the eyes. "The sparrow of silver fire will strike the owl from above and below when thrice the seven gather before the prime goes dark."

"I know what is says." She stared at the stacked stones around the hearth.

"During the Burning Moon, all realms in Edenia were dark. It was a convergence of all three celestials. There are some who describe it as Masah swallowing Lungol. Then, when the larger moon tried to do the same to Sawcl, she would not have it. Sawel burst forth as a ring of fire until Masah spit out the smaller moon and moved away, releasing both."

Rowena laughed. "The Solara might say that. Masah is too peaceful, and Lungol is too clever to permit such things."

He nodded, firelight glittering along his obsidian horns, reminding her they were there. While they sat together, speaking like anyone would, she almost forgot who he was. "The three aligned in perfect unity, joining during the fury tide and remaining locked until the Reaping began. Both light and dark, sun and moon conjoined over Edenia."

"That would be incredible to witness."

"I agree." He folded his hands together and caused the simple chair to creak when he leaned against the wooden back. "Though it was also a time of turmoil. The lands shook and waters churned because of the disruption of the cycles. It destroyed some coastal villages from excessive tides and giant waves. It covered others in landslides from the quakes. In Eridar, Mount Hraun erupted after lying dormant for centuries. A new age had begun. It was many years before life resumed within the realm as it had before."

Rowena stared into the flames. She'd heard none of that, but she recalled how there were no buildings in Taesing older than she was. Her father said a village in good repair kept everyone safe. "It wasn't my fault."

"Not at all. It is what some call fate and others say destiny. It is part of the design to unite the fae. To bring Edenia back as it was in the beginning during the Limitless Age."

"And you're here because the druids believe I'm part of this design?" She forced herself to breathe steadily, despite the way her stomach curled in on itself.

"The Sword of Justice drew me here."

"I'm not meant for anything so grand of purpose." She plucked at a string on her trousers. "Everything my life was to become is lost. Taken. My duty is to avenge my family. After that, perhaps I'll be queen . . . or not."

"That thinking will lead you down a dangerous path. One of pain and hardship. To follow your destiny, you must forgive those who've wronged you. Otherwise, you will trap all of Edenia into a life of ruin and sorrow. Every realm will suffer because of it." He placed both feet on the floor; his harsh, commanding voice returned.

A scoff left her throat before she could stop herself. She'd dreamed so many times of glorious adventures and of being a hero who could save the day. Like climbing the mast to fix a broken line or shooting an arrow at a raging erymanth before it killed someone. Not being responsible for everyone's safety throughout every realm.

Hann's face entered her mind and forced tears to spring. In all of those dreamed escapades, he'd been there at her side. Yet, when the time came to be that hero and save him, she'd failed.

She wasn't anyone special. Hers were visions of a foolish child. What the Seeker claimed had to be for someone else.

Wait. He'd said something else . . .

She swiped at her cheeks. "What did you mean before? About there being others?"

The Seeker inhaled and kept his simmering gaze steady while he let it out slowly. She hadn't a clue what to guess for his name. Brute? Terror? Mysterious? Beautiful? Exciting? She broke their connection.

"The Scrolls say there is only one who will unite the fae. One who will bring the armor and heartstones together and close the rift between Edenia and Caelus. After the Chasm, the Mirror Age lasted centuries. Most have forgotten what divided us, let alone how to mend the realms together again. They did not recognize the first Burning Moon ushered in a new age, the Spindle Age. A time for preparation before the threads of fate are rewoven in unification, yet some heartstones are missing—dislodged from their proper place; some pieces of armor lost."

"The Heptad has them, don't they? That's why they control the Primary Spring . . . to channel enchantment through the heartstones to all the lands." That had been the only teaching she'd received on the subject.

"That is a misconception, not a fact." Shadows swirled on the floor near his feet. He stood and paced toward the door and then back. "The Heptad protects the Spring, and the enchanted power does flow to the heartstones as conduits, but they are not in Saganus. They are to be kept secure within each piece of armor and within the proper realm."

Rowena scooted deeper into the chair and tucked her legs beneath her on the seat. She might have grown comfortable with the Seeker's presence, but she didn't want to get caught up in his shadowy snare again—whisked off to somewhere else. "It's odd that the Sword of Justice is considered armor instead of a weapon. Are the other pieces swords as well?"

"Each piece is different, and they are to held by royals from the six original fae races. They are more symbolic than true armor. In fact, the Sword of Justice is the only weapon, and there is a baldric that would be among a warrior's kit. The others are: a ring, a crown, a scroll, and a pendant."

"Why is that?" In all of Rowena's studies, even if she'd listened better, she'd not had any training on the heartstones or armor—not even the one she was supposed to hold. Her tutors considered the subject a secret for The Heptad alone.

"It is just the way they were designed; I suppose. The seventh is simply a loose dormant heartstone, waiting for the Telana after the final Reaping when the Merging takes place." He leaned his hands on the back of his chair, digging his long nails into the wood. The iridescent runes on his fingers glistened.

Rowena shivered, rubbing her hand over her opposite arm.

"Through the centuries, some heartstones have become separated," he continued. "The enchantment flowing through the Primary Spring is only a trickle of what it should be. We must reunite the missing gems with the armor before the next Reaping or instead of uniting the fae, the Primary Spring will go dry. Instead of a new Limitless Age, the gates of Mortus will fling wide, releasing Ha'mon to rule Edenia."

Rowena searched her memory for stories of the Netherworld king. She couldn't recall much. Osric had imprisoned him for leading the rebellion against Caelus that led to The Chasm. Once a year, the Fearolc left Mortus for the Reaping, gathering Ha'mon's followers to live in the Netherworld kingdom he ruled. Anyone out that night risked being captured if they were spotted.

"There are those who wait for the Reaping, excited to follow the king." Her father had mentioned it once after meeting a group from Bethon during his travels.

"They are foolish or deceived. Ha'mon cares only for building mindless sycophants to worship him. He desires to destroy all Primary fae, bringing them under his control—as vengeance for his imprisonment. Edenia would rot. There would be little food. The elves would be engaged in a never-ending war with the other fae. Death, destruction, pain . . . It would spare no one." The Seeker let go of the chair to cross his arms over his chest.

It made no sense why anyone would wish that. "Why have a way for the gates to open at all? Why not just keep King Ha'mon locked away? What is the point of the Reaping?"

"Osric would not lock his son away forever without offering him the chance for redemption. He set this condition in motion at the end of The Chasm, and he must fulfill it."

Rowena shook her head. "But there is a way to stop it—if someone figures out the prophecy and fulfills it? The others you spoke of . . ."

The Seeker stepped around the chair and sat once again. "We believe the sparrow of silver fire refers to the one born during the Burning Moon. That one would gather the seven stones seated within the corresponding armor and unite the fae. Thus locking Mortus forever."

"And you think it's me?" Rowena sat up straight.

"That is unclear. Rather than one birth, as expected . . . there were many."

Many. He'd said there were others, but the way everyone spoke to be moon-born was rare.

"It is my duty to find the armor and all those born during the eclipse, like you. Then determine who is the one to possess all seven pieces, ensuring they have them before the Reaping after the second Burning Moon, which will take place on your next prime day."

Three months. It wasn't much time to do all he said. "You decide who is to have the armor?"

"There is only one who fulfills the prophecy. It's not my choice."

"But you've come for me."

He rose, towering over her. "You are one of the potential chosen. Which is why you must comply with what I say, so I can move on to find the others."

"I want to go with you. I want to meet them." Perhaps her desire to travel through the realms came because she needed to help him. She huffed a quick chuckle and turned to the fire. "It's what I've always wanted."

"It's not that simple. I must find all the pieces of armor and heartstones first. It was convenient that you were near The Sword of Justice, and your royal lineage connects you with the onyx Lunara heartstone—the Lunastone." He hesitated. "Yet there is your curse."

He may as well have doused her in a bucket of water. She sagged into the chair. She'd always tried to believe her parents that her birth during the Burning Moon had held no such consequence. "Then others were right to fear me. My father should have left me in the forest after my birth."

"I'm speaking of the mage and the curse she placed on you during the feast. Fidessa is unenchanted. It's impossible for her to make an unbreakable curse. However, if you are the chosen and you act upon your vengeance, wielding the sword for harm, it will be as she says. You will bring destruction to Edenia." He paced again, encircling the small living area. "You have already unlocked the box, allowing anyone access to the armor. There is too much at risk. You must put the needs of the realm ahead of your own."

It made sense why he'd think so. Except what did he propose—that she did nothing? She was to live as a thrall, passive and weak, until he determined who the true chosen was?

As far as Fidessa's curse, it seemed only a madwoman's rant. She couldn't remember the exact words the queen spoke. Something else he said made little sense and prevented her from concentrating on other details. "How do you know what Fidessa said?"

He halted and stared into space, seeming unsure of how to answer. It wasn't a hard question.

"From my time in Skandan. Others spoke of it." He stared at a blank spot on the wall.

That couldn't be. The only others who'd heard Fidessa's speech were Daenon and Hann. A stab of pain went through her again. She'd been so stupid. If the Seeker had heard of the curse, it could only have been from the prince.

He could go anywhere with his mist, shadows, or whatever that was. It made sense he could have gone to Skandan, but he couldn't have gotten that information from others.

"You're working with Prince Daenon." Rowena jumped from her chair, racing to put it between her and the fae. The mists had retreated for the moment, but she would keep a wary eye.

"He is a fool of little consequence. I would not have endured what I did to become the Seeker for one such as him." He huffed and glanced at the ceiling.

"No one else heard what the queen said to me." No one still alive. Her fingers dug into the soft fabric. She raised onto the balls of her feet, ready to dart either direction.

"I spoke with Asta."

"They disavowed her. No druid speaks to her." She had to get away.

"My travels have taken me to many places. The Heptad removed all restrictions so that I may complete my task."

Rowena lowered to rest heavy on her feet. The traveler, Bram, had told her nearly the same thing . . . twice.

"And yet, I'm the first moon-born you've discovered?"

His mouth twitched, going from a flat white line to pursed lips. She hadn't asked a tough question.

"Yes." He crossed his arms over his chest and paused before speaking again. "Osric forged each piece of armor for a specific heartstone. If they become separated, the armor and the gem have an attraction toward each other. Not physically, but the power within each draws toward the other, as if pulling a curtain closed. I can sense it, as have you. In the moments when you've described feeling the sword nearby, that is why."

"It's not there now." Rowena rubbed the spot in her chest where the ache occurred. "I think I must have to be close to it."

"That's because of the lessened power coming from the Primary Spring. Which also says the Lunastone must not be within the sword, which is troubling."

"It's not. When I opened the box, there was only an empty golden setting on the hilt."

"The Lunastone could be anywhere, then."

"What about the others, the armor pieces, I mean? If I'm only connected to one, aren't you connected to all of them? Don't you feel them?"

"I do and do not. The box's seal kept the sword hidden. I suspect it is the same for the other pieces as well. It was only recently that the sword's signal became strong enough to follow."

"How long ago?" Rowena had an idea about it, but she needed more information.

"Mid-winter, perhaps." The Seeker tilted his head. "Why?"

"That's when my grandmother died." She'd gone with her parents to the funeral, and her mother brought the box containing the Sword of Justice back with them to Taesing afterward. Then Uther came and destroyed everything. "Did you see my home? Did it burn to nothing?"

He hesitated before answering. "One wall partially remained. Many have left offerings there in honor of those who died in the blaze."

It surprised her that Goetz would allow that. Wait. "You walked through the village?"

He said nothing.

She stared at the Seeker, taking in his profile, the set of his eyes, the sharp cheekbones. So familiar . . . she gasped. He couldn't be. Or could he? "Do you always look like this?"

He snapped his gaze to hers. His golden eyes glowed.

Just like the traveler's—that's why his oak scent seemed familiar as well.

Rowena sucked in a deep breath, holding it until it whooshed out in a burst. "Bram?"

TWENTY-FIVE

The Seeker stomped to the window, standing with his back to her. His broad shoulders rose and fell in spurts, forcing Rowena to notice how his muscular back angled down to a fit waistline. And that his trousers were snug against his backside, causing heat to flood her cheeks. She spun toward the fire and stepped away from him. Her pulse sped after the flock of starlings taking flight in her stomach.

He hadn't answered her question, which was answer enough. The Seeker was Bram, the traveler—the man who'd introduced himself in Forsa, followed her in the caravan, and then to the forest. She whirled around to face him again, her insides deadly quiet.

"You are Bram. Explain yourself!" She threw her hands into the air.

"I left Saganus and started my search for the armor in Penumar. Stories of your grandmother's flight with your mother abound, albeit in different versions, but they all end with her arrival in either Skandan or Ibern. From there, I followed the trail, which led me to you." He spoke into the window, matter of fact, as if it were a scouting report.

"That's it? That's all you're going to say? Nothing about how you lied. How you can be,"—she hesitated, waving her hand up and down—"this! And yet hide yourself as a Telana!"

The Seeker, Bram she had to remind herself, spun and stalked closer. Rowena balled her fists and clamped her lips tight, refusing to move an inch. She wouldn't let him intimidate her, despite her sudden urge to run.

"I did not lie. I never said I was a Telana. My identity is not for everyone's knowledge. It wasn't for you—yet!"

They stood for moments, glaring, muscles twitching. Finally, Rowena spoke. "You trapped me, just like the others."

"I did no such thing. That Jotnari would have killed you, and you cannot die."

Her breath hitched. She leaned away slightly. His words tumbling around inside her head like a bee with nowhere to land. She could die. Everyone else had.

"You are the moon-born who must connect with the Sword of Justice. It is my duty to ensure your safety until I've completed my task."

"It's mine."

"Yes." He inhaled and wiped his hand over his mouth, his fingertips appearing less like claws than long, dark nails. "First, I must secure the sword, which is why my identity had to remain hidden. Others will not trust me, nor provide answers about the armor if they recognize me. I might as well stomp around in this form all the time."

"You've been helping me?" She thought of the times Bram had given advice or protected her. The times he grew angry or frustrated unnecessarily. "No, not helping. You used me to find the sword."

"You may be part of the prophecy as well. It is my first duty to collect all the pieces of the armor. After that, I must ensure they are in the right hands. Knowing where you are is crucial, yet the moon-born are not my first priority."

"So you go about the realm, spying in other forms to steal the armor?" She ignored the prophecy part. If she was part of it, there would be more signs. Like being able to access her enchantment when she willed it, not waiting for it to show up whenever it wanted.

"I do not spy, nor do I take other forms randomly, as you suggest." He wrinkled his nose as if the air had turned sour. "There is just this one and the other."

"You are spying."

"I'm not."

"You hide your identity, listen to other conversations, sneak around searching for others' property. That's not only spying, but thievery." Perhaps it was the close quarters, or the fact she could make out Bram's features among the rune marks, horns, and molten glares, but she no longer feared for her safety. Indignation and a need for answers backfilled her emotions like a swift tide.

He leaned closer. "You are difficult and do not listen."

True. She shrugged.

"The safety of the chosen royal is important, but since they should be easy to find within their realm, the Heptad didn't place that task higher than the armor. You could be the one, yet I struggle to believe it at this moment."

"You said it wasn't your choice. Why must you find all the armor first? How many pieces are there? Who decides who gets to keep it? If there are many of us, perhaps we all must keep our own piece." A distant niggling in her chest shoved against the idea of the sword belonging to anyone else. But she needed it to avenge her family—not for some prophecy. He called it the Sword of Justice, after all.

"Osric has already made his choice. I'm only to find all those born during the Burning Moon. You are the first." He rubbed his fingers across his brow. "Your studies should have taught you the answers to your questions."

Perhaps they would have—if she had listened more. She'd

wanted to be outside, learning to fight. Once she had to stay home to rule, there would have been more time to read scrolls and listen to stories. Osric certainly wouldn't choose someone like her to save the realm.

"I find it doubtful I'm part of this prophecy. My enchantment comes when it wants, it seems. I have no control over it." She threw up one arm, planting the other on her hip.

"You must train. Enchantment is volatile until you learn to control it. It seems you are more influenced by Lungol, which is unfortunate." Bram—she preferred to call him by a name—stretched his neck, nearly scraping his horns on the ceiling.

"Why did you conjure such a small place?" She brushed her free hand through the air.

"I am not a witch. I don't use illusions."

She stared at him for a moment. "Then whose home is this?"

"Why must you question everything?" He squeezed his eyes closed, then took two exaggerated breaths. "I found this place abandoned during my travels. I liked the coziness."

The answer surprised her, especially with how he spat the last word. The idea of a massive man with horns relaxing by the fire with a cup of tea challenged her to hold back a laugh.

"Your horns would hit the doorframe if you walk through it."

"I duck."

She wasn't sure what to say to that. The conversation needed to shift, anyway. She was growing too comfortable around him. "What did you mean when you said I unlocked the box?"

His nostrils flared, yet he answered. "When properly stored, the armor has a shield of protection. It wards away others who may abuse it. If the royal to whom the piece belongs reveals the piece, the shield breaks."

"How could I have known that?" Perhaps that was also part of her studies? She wouldn't think about such things. It was best to forge ahead. She could do nothing about the past. "I'll just have to get it back and all will be well."

"That is imperative." He glanced over his shoulder. "We must use what's left of the night."

"For what?"

"To train." He spoke slowly, as if she were dumb.

In his Telana form, he'd spoken with kindness and seemed . . . normal. She tired of his grumbling, brooding nature. "Must you be abrasive in this form? Is that how it works? Because if so, I'm not inclined to train with you like this."

"I am the same in both forms. You are exasperating, and I no longer need to pretend otherwise now that you're aware of the situation." He leaned closer.

She slid her foot nearer to him, craning her neck to pin her glare to his. She wasn't sure what to say now that she'd faced off with him. His charred oak scent washed over her, muddling her thoughts. Had his cheekbones been so sharp before or his chin so strong?

His gaze broke from hers, only for a moment as he glanced at her hair and roved about her face, hesitating the briefest heartbeat on her lips. Her mouth went dry. But then he seemed to collect himself and returned to their battle of wills with increased vigor.

"You will train. It is essential that you are efficient in your enchantment to hold the sword."

So, it wasn't for her to protect herself or to accept her Lunara heritage. It was for his duty. "Will you switch forms?"

"No."

She rolled her eyes. It didn't matter—he no longer intimidated her. "Do you understand Lunara enchantment?"

He tilted his head, as if the question was unnecessary. "Outside."

"Don't tell me what to do."

"Please." He drew out the word through his teeth.

"Fine."

He spun and marched out the door, ducking under the lintel. Flutters caged within her belly spun in all directions. She blew out a slow breath, trying to calm herself. Her emotions kept swinging around, like she dangled from a rope in the wind. She had to keep her wits. He was dangerous.

Daenon had seemed kind until he wasn't. So had Bram until he grew horns and whisked her away through the shadows. Not that the Seeker had done anything to frighten her other than how he appeared. He'd also pulled back and avoided touching her when she panicked in the forest. He confused her.

She needed to understand how to call upon her enchantment. If he could help her, then she'd train with him . . . because she decided for herself.

"Are you coming?" he yelled from outside.

She huffed a mirthless laugh. Yes, she'd train with him. Then use her powers to keep herself free from control by anyone. With a grumble under her breath, she stomped outside.

TWENTY-SIX

Sweat rolled down Rowena's temples as she tried for the tenth time to summon her enchantment. Nothing had happened since the first time she stood in the middle of the meadow under Lungol's light.

Her body had sizzled with strength, shining with silver sparks. Bram had directed her to aim her power toward a tree. The one she hit uprooted and knocked over two more behind it. She'd fallen to her knees, heaving for breath and exhilarated at the same time.

"Do it again," Bram told her, folding his arms with a scowl. It distracted her, all that brooding disapproval.

Nothing happened again. Not even a tingle.

"You're not trying."

"I am doing the best I can. You're not an outstanding teacher." She fought the urge to roll her eyes. "Do you have any advice? Or are you just going to stand there puffing out your muscles?"

He dropped his chin, and she wasn't sure, but it seemed like he fought a grin. How dare he laugh at her troubles!

"Close your eyes." He dropped his hands to his sides and strolled closer.

"Why?" Rowena slid her foot back.

Bram halted and raised his hands.

Rowena crossed her arms over her chest, doing her best to seem casual. It wasn't his size or black clothes, or even his horns, which gave her pause. She hated that what happened in the cave still made her tremble in the dark. "What do you want me to do?"

Bram glanced away, licking his bottom lip before returning his gaze to her, acting as if he had something to say, but stopped himself. He took several measured breaths before speaking. "You're trying too hard. Lunara enchantment is enriched by time spent absorbing the moonlight, not forcing it to do your bidding."

That rang true with what her mother had done. In all the nights Rowena spent with her, they picked flowers, or mushrooms, or sometimes just strolled. "Where are we?"

"No harm will come to you here."

She rolled her eyes. "I ask to know if maybe there's some primrose or phlox to find." Rowena fiddled with her fingers, unable to look at Bram. "It's what my mother would do."

"That's a fine idea. Nothing like that grows in this area, but I know a place where it does."

Rowena scurried back several steps out of his reach as he strode her way. She would not allow him to take her through the shadows, or however it was he traveled. "I'd prefer to walk."

"So would I. This way," he called without breaking stride.

After a momentary huff at his commanding tone, she strode after him, hurrying to catch up as he entered the trees.

Rowena kept close enough to follow Bram's footsteps through the brush. After they'd gone perhaps a mile into the trees, a restlessness rolled through her body. "Why won't you change into your other form now that I know who you are?"

He paused for a moment before moving on. "Do you want me to?"

Did she? She'd gotten used to him with his broad shoulders

and tall horns, though he wasn't small in his elven form either. The way he stood there all brooding, his mouth clamped tight when she couldn't do as he expected, but never coming nearer to intimidate her, made her smile. She sucked in a quick breath. "It makes no difference. I was just asking."

"My true form is intentionally daunting, to spur compliance. I can change if it bothers you." There was a hint of sadness in his voice. Like he wasn't sure of himself.

That wasn't how she expected the most dangerous being in the realm to respond. "It doesn't."

"Fine, then."

They walked in silence after that. Rowena's mind played with different scenarios, trying to make sense of her swirling emotions. The Seeker looked terrifying. Why didn't her heart pound harder or her body tremble in such terror she couldn't move? What did that say about her?

It was true. And for whatever his reasons, he stayed in his Seeker form. They traveled farther than Rowena expected, not that she expected much.

"It's just over this ridge," Bram said.

Was that the way to think of him? There were too many questions in her mind. "Should I call you Bram, or Seeker, because you are in this form?"

He said nothing for several moments. "Bram is fine for both."

That made things easier. "Is that your real name?"

"You ask too many questions. The place I recommend is just up ahead."

He parted the vines of a long willow-like tree and Rowena gasped. A pond, small and private, came into view. Moonlight sparkled on the water and all around, grew various wildflowers.

"I've never seen such a place." Rowena wandered closer to it, marveling at the perfumed air and the soft grasses. She kneeled at the water's edge, running her finger along a carmine flower's feathery petals, and released its peppery scent. She stifled a sneeze.

"Few have," Bram said quietly.

She peeked over her shoulder. The silvery light coming from Lungol glittered off his horns. An intense desire to touch them overcame her. She returned to examining the flowers. Warm tingles zipped through her body, just under the skin, creating goosebumps. She rose and crossed her arms over her chest, rubbing her upper arms.

"Are you chilled?"

"No." Quite the opposite. "There's so much power. It's overwhelming."

"That's your enchantment reacting. Let it fill you before you reach for it."

"I'm not sure I can wait." The sensation washed over her like a rainstorm, and her only shelter would be to call upon it, to let it out.

"You must. Try collecting the flowers, as you said your mother would." His tone remained steady, yet it didn't calm her.

"Don't talk about my mother. You didn't know her." Tears pooled in her eyes faster than she could stop them. She swiped at them. It wasn't the time for such nonsense.

"Your emotions are reacting to the power as well. How you're feeling is much like it will be for others when you influence them toward an emotion."

Ugh. "Stop that. You don't know everything."

"I'm a druid, Rowena. You understand that means I'm a Primary Fae, correct?"

She stared at him. His molten gold eyes glowed in the low light. His white hair flowed in the slight breeze, causing the rune beads to clink together so lightly it surprised her to hear them. There was a beauty in his form, a grace in his sharp cheeks, a strength in his full lips, which quirked up at the corner. She dropped her gaze to the ground, searching for anything to avoid acknowledging what had just happened.

"Of course." She thought of him as a Telana when he appeared as Bram, but he'd healed Errol, which now made more sense. She plucked a small purple flower she'd never seen before.

An uneasy amount of time went by in silence. Rowena kept perusing the ground, waiting for him to say something. Anything. Where was his know-it-all attitude now?

A small clearing opened near where a stream flowed out of the pond. As soon as Rowena entered it, the full strength of the waxing Lungol flowed over her. It happened before outside the cottage, but this time, it hit her like a hammer.

Too many emotions to process spiked through her heart and mind in all directions while her arms buzzed, as if a thousand angry hornets raced through her veins. She spread her fingers wide, dropping the flowers she'd gathered and staring at the silver sparks bouncing from her palms.

"Take it slow," Bram warned.

Sure, he had to say something right then. She spun and faced him, pointing her finger. "Stop telling me what to do. You show up and act like a kind traveler, all about his own business, but you were spying on me. For what? To find out if I had powers? If I was the one to fulfill the prophecy? You claim you're not working with Daenon, but that's what he wanted as well."

Her pulse screamed and pounded against her chest as if her heart needed to escape. Madness closed in on her. Uncontrollable rage followed by searing sadness. She dropped into a squat, wrapping her arms around her knees, and sobbed. Everything was wrong. Her family, her home, her life . . . all gone. And for what? Nothing. She wouldn't be the one to hold all the armor like the one who the Seeker sought.

"Rowena, breathe."

Words floated into the back of her mind. She didn't want to listen. She couldn't be anyone special. If she was, then she'd have saved her family. It was better if she gave up. Lay down in the grass, the soft, perfumed grass, and let herself stop breathing. That would be best.

Hands grabbed her shoulders, and she screamed out a shrill, terror-filled sound. Rowena fell backward, flipped over, and crawled on her hands and knees as fast as she could. "Get away. Get away!"

Her arms shook too much to continue forward. Her chest heaved in and out. Deep and painful compressions rattled her entire body. If she died right then, no one would avenge those she loved. A moan escaped her throat, followed by a long wail that echoed in her ears as if it came from somewhere in the distance—from a pitiful being far away, tortured and alone.

"Listen. Hear my voice and let me help you."

There wasn't anyone who could help her. She pounded her fist against the ground. There was no one left. No one to take vengeance. That was her destiny. She braced her hands, dragging one foot, then the other until she could rise, knees wobbling but secure.

"Look at me." The Seeker stood in front of her, out of reach. Rowena blinked once, twice, several times. "I can help."

How? Her palms itched. Bitter winds and freezing cold would dry her skin each winter, but this was a different chapped. It was her pain. Hers alone. But something else hid within the turmoil churning through her. An urgency, a yearning that cooed over her.

Let it go. No one can stop you.

"Settle your emotions to control the enchantment. Lungol is powerful and erratic."

The Seeker no longer frightened her. Bram, the traveler, the druid. He had his duty, and she had hers.

"I don't need your help. I don't need anyone." Her shoulders lowered an inch.

"That's the smaller moon's influence. If you release all your power right now, it will devastate all the beauty surrounding this pond. Expand your thoughts outside of yourself." He stepped closer.

"So noble from someone who hides in the shadows and lies

about who he is." She turned her palm to the sky, letting the sparks grow and sizzle until they crackled. Lightning of her own making wavered in the air and danced along her fingertips.

"I've never lied," he spoke between his teeth.

Rowena chuckled. A small huff of a laugh that grew and grew until she doubled over, one hand over her stomach. Tears squeezed from her scrunched eyes. The ridiculousness of his stoic response collided with her anger, and it erupted in mirthless amusement.

Every inch of her body, inside and out, screamed to let her raze the realm. She could do it. And there in front of her, dark and growling, stood the most dangerous yet hauntingly handsome fae —a druid—trying to stop her.

Who was stronger? Enchantment came from Caelus. Didn't that mean she could equal his force?

"Don't do it," he warned.

"You're full of commands. Are you as strong as you claim, or is it all a bluff?"

"Rowena." He closed his eyes for a heartbeat before leveling her with a golden glare.

She lifted her palm at the same time a wall of swirling darkness surrounded her. It wasn't cold this time, and she stayed fully aware of how she became weightless. She floated, melting into the shadows and being cradled by them at the same time.

A moment later, her feet touched solid ground, and the shadows retreated to expose the Seeker.

"Don't do that to me!" Rowena pressed the heels of her hands against her forehead, nauseated from the mixture of travel and power still coursing through her.

"I led you to the pond so you could relax and allow your enchantment to emerge gently. You are not in control of yourself. There is nothing in this meadow you can destroy." His tone softened somewhat. "I won't get in your way again unless you ask."

She glanced around. They were in the meadow outside the

cottage once more. Shrubbery dotted the grasses, but it wasn't the beauty of where they'd been. Part of her wanted to thank him, but he'd taken her without asking. She'd had enough of others controlling her, forcing their will upon her.

Without another word, she lifted her hands and screamed, allowing the silver glow to rush out of her palms in sizzling streams. Ropes of destruction swung one way and then the other, snapping branches and scorching grass. She continued until her voice grew hoarse and she heaved for breath.

"If you're ready to try something else, I can direct you."

She could see the outline of his form in the moonlight when she peeked sideways. "You said you'd wait until I asked."

"True."

When she glanced his way again, he was no longer there. Rowena straightened and searched the meadow. For the first time, the swath of destruction she'd caused came into view. Much of the meadow appeared as if it had been in a recent fire. Uprooted bushes piled upon each other near downed trees. She thought of the twinkling fireflies and the cypsela bouncing over the grasses near the pond. He'd been right to take her away from there.

Sheepish and more clear-headed than before, she understood why he'd tried to help her. "How do I control it?" She spoke no louder than if he stood within reach, believing he would hear her.

"It's not a matter of control but of partnership. Learn to listen—allow the enchantment to flow through you. It is as natural for your body as breathing." As she expected, he sauntered near, having heard her request. He didn't scold, even though he could have. "When you spend time with either Lungol or Masah, it will open the conduit for you to access your abilities. The strength you gain will store away until you need it."

Rowena wiped her fingers along her brow. "My head aches."

"That will lessen with time. Think of it like learning to wield a sword or swing an axe. Your muscles ache as they grow stronger.

And what seems awkward and unnatural becomes an extension of your arm in time. This will be the same." He could have chastised her—remarked on how she hadn't listened or how she'd destroyed so much. Instead, he remained calm.

"What of the bruises that blossom after training sessions with a weapon? What will happen here?"

"It will be similar; however, the pain will not be visible on your body but within it. Heartstones are called such because your heart is where you will gather and hold your power. There will be some chest pain and along the path through your arms and hands. Therefore, you must learn discipline in how much, and when, you use your abilities."

She inadvertently rubbed her breastbone, aware of the deep ache developing there.

"There is something else," Bram continued. "If you release your power with such force as you've done here—without the ability to replenish—it will drain you, leaving you exhausted and vulnerable. You will be without enchantment until you can recuperate in the moonlight. And it will leave your physical strength impaired as well. Regular weapons will be difficult to wield."

What good was being enchanted if it left her weak in battle? "That's not a fair trade! I won't cower to others in fear when I am stronger than they are." Disgusted, she threw up her hands and stomped a few paces before returning.

"It is best to train under Masah first. His gentle influence will make it easier. With Lungol in the skies alone, it may be best to rest for now."

"I can't stop. This is what I've longed for, and now I need it to avenge my family. Fidessa will pay for what she did to my mother and how she tried to place a curse on me. Uther will find out what it's like to watch those you love perish." She clenched her fists, chest aching, but she relished the pain. This was her destiny. She had everything she needed to exact her revenge.

"You have a higher purpose than that." His voice hardened, shadows licking the air around his feet.

Rowena straightened her spine, pulling back her shoulders. "I will become nothing other than what I say for myself. Everyone has controlled me, made my choices, held me back—never again."

"Your obstinance will be your undoing."

"Assist or leave."

"Choose a bush you uprooted. Make it lighter." He crossed his arms over his chest, still glaring.

She turned her back to him, rolling her neck from side to side. Make it lighter—with no explanation. He needed to work on his training techniques, but she'd figure it out.

Inhaling slowly, purposefully, she calmed her mind and focused only on a tumbled bursta bush. The idea of using her enchantment immediately sent a surge of buzzing tingles down her arms. She lifted her palm.

A stream of silver light glittered across the darkened ground and hit the bush. The already damaged plant flew, landing against a broken stump. She dropped her hand with a huff.

Twisting her neck, she arched a brow at her supposed instructor.

"That was incorrect."

"Clearly."

He met her expression, waiting.

"Help me . . . please."

He ambled over. "It would be easiest to show you. May I touch you?"

Her insides tightened, but she needed his help. She swallowed hard, willing herself to calm. "Yes."

Light as a feather, the Seeker's hand covered hers, facing her palm to the ground and curving his hand so that hers rounded. His long nails hung over the edge, out of the way. Her breath caught at the same time quivers plagued her belly. His charred oak scent whispered over her, making it harder to concentrate.

"Aim your hand toward the object you wish to influence and slowly lift your hand." He did not stand close enough to touch her back, though his voice caressed her neck in a way that made her eyelids flutter. "Understand?"

She nodded, not trusting her voice.

He kept his hand in place. "Try."

With great effort, she chose another bush, aiming for it as his hand moved with hers. No visible sign gave her insight that she'd connected, yet there was a recognition in her chest that she had. Slowly, forcing herself to ignore the warmth of Bram's hand, she lifted her palm.

The bursta wiggled, then floated off the ground to hover in the air. Her body had a sense of lightness to it as well. She lifted her hand higher and the leafy underbrush rose higher. A squeak left her throat as her heels left the ground.

"You will become lighter, as well. Allow yourself to embrace the sensation," Bram whispered in her ear, removing his hand from over hers. The hair on her neck rose with goosebumps on her skin.

The higher she lifted her hand, the more she rose, until her toes dangled at least a foot off the ground.

"Now, bring your hand down."

She jerked her hand to her side. The movement slammed her feet back to the soil and sending a jolt of pain through her ankles and knees.

He stepped further back from where she landed. "You'll want to lower your arm more slowly next time."

The cool night air surrounded her, and she shivered. Unwilling to show how much he'd affected her, she sidestepped farther away. "You could have said that."

He harrumphed, but she almost caught a hint of mirth in it.

Inhale. Release. She tried again. This time, she lifted a cluster of plants connected by tangled roots mixed with soil. It was easier to manipulate than controlling the streams of power. She moved several fallen objects. A broken tree trunk caused her some extra effort, but she managed. Sometimes, she rose and at others she was careful enough to stay grounded. She found she could move whatever she influenced and toss it, creating a game of sorts, and perfecting her aim.

"Now try the opposite," Bram said when she took a break. "Turn your hand over, keeping it cupped. Start higher, dragging your hand toward the ground."

He didn't offer to show her. She hesitated, considering whether she should ask, and then thought better of it. This was like training with the guards. His effect on her had to be because of her heightened emotions. Nothing more.

She did as he instructed and forced a sapling that had fallen across another downed tree to roll off the other side. The sensation in her legs, however, forced her to double over. She felt as if someone had captured her in a net, forcing her to her knees against her will.

"That is not enjoyable."

"It is helpful. You could prevent a warrior from lifting a weapon against you, or keep a wagon stuck in mud. There are reasons to master this skill, yet it is more difficult to manage."

She gritted her teeth and tried again. And again. Each moment, she gained a better understanding of her limits and how she could push them.

"Save some of your strength and practice again tomorrow." Bram had called the warning to her several times, but she'd ignored him. However, she finally allowed herself to glance around.

They stayed in the meadow until Lungol had gone to rest. Streaks of lavender and brilliant tangerine lifted their fingers along the horizon. She dropped her arms to her sides, suddenly dizzy. Her knees hit the ground with a thud. All her efforts had drained her more than she'd thought.

"Come. You need rest." He held out his hand.

Her arms had turned leaden and shaky. Exhaustion washed over her and tears pricked her eyes, making her frustrated, which caused them to roll down her cheeks faster. The next moment, she found herself surrounded in shadow. A comfortable, welcoming cocoon cradled her.

"Take me home." Her voice wobbled, and she leaned into the darkness that held her like a child, her head tucked into the hollow of the Seeker's shoulder.

TWENTY-SEVEN

When Rowena's feet touched the ground again, the same nauseating sensation rolled over her from how she'd traveled with the Seeker. Dark shadows swirled and retreated to reveal a forest all around her, filled with more birch trees than pines. The Seeker had brought her back to Ibern, not her home.

She whirled around to argue, but wobbled and nearly lost her balance. Strong arms wrapped around her, keeping her upright until her vision cleared, and she stared into Brain's face. He was back in his elven form, and it made her forget for a moment where she was. His warm brown eyes, heavy with concern, bored into hers. She glanced quickly at his chin, now covered by a light beard, and his forehead was smooth—without runes or horns. His hair had turned brown once more, pulled away from his face in the Telana style. It seemed sad almost, like there was something missing. She blinked once, then rapidly, and shoved out of his embrace.

"So, is your other form only meant to terrorize me? This version is for everyone else?" She lashed out, more to distract herself from comparing his two forms and how each affected her. The slight wince that crossed his face at her words sent a pain through her chest, creating another layer to her confused state.

"It's best if I keep my true identity hidden," he said with a growl. "I expect you'll honor that?"

She shrugged, doing her best to seem casual. "Everyone already believes I'm cursed. Explaining how I know your secrets will only be worse for me."

He snorted.

She changed the subject. "Why did you bring me here? I asked to go home."

"There is still much to do here."

"And you get to decide that?" She planted her fist onto her hip.

He pursed his lips for a heartbeat, then leaned closer. "Yes."

"Wha . . .?" His insolence shocked her. "I decide what I do and where I go."

He crossed his arms over his chest, forcing his tunic tight over his muscled arms. "You're not a princess anymore, or so you said. You don't get that privilege."

Her arms sizzled, and she narrowed her eyes, raising her palms, enchantment ready.

"You need to save that." He didn't bother to drop his gaze or seem concerned.

Rowena clenched her fists, covering the soft glow. He was right, and she hated it. The surge in her emotions pushed aside her exhaustion, at least. "Whatever. Let's go, then."

He had the audacity to give a smug grin before he strode by her into the undergrowth. She had half a mind to turn the other way, but dawn peeked through the leaves, and she didn't exactly know where she was. She gave a whispered grumble and hurried after him.

Not long afterward, they were at the Fianna camp. Rowena had been so distracted with all that happened with the Seeker and discovering his true identity, she'd forgotten that the last time she'd seen anyone, it was in Velmeg during a Jotnari attack. It didn't take but a moment to realize something was wrong.

Errol stood near Liam, arguing with Conri and Hywel. The

rest of the Fianna either stood near them, patiently giving them space or milled about, trying to seem like they were busy.

"Ho, the camp." Bram called out, seemingly to bring attention to their awkward entrance into the tense situation.

"Traveler," Conri said in greeting, keeping his arms crossed over his ample chest, with none of his usual exuberance.

"What seems to be the trouble?" Bram asked, stopping next to Liam.

Rowena hung back a few steps and scanned the camp. "Where's Safi?"

Errol twisted toward her, glaring. "Lendan's men took her."

Rowena hurried to his side. "Where?"

"I don't know, but she can't be there." Even in the low, early dawn light, Errol's face flushed with anger. "It's not safe for her, and that's not getting through to these shites who won't go get her."

"It's not that we won't," Conri said. "It's that we need a plan. We all barely got out of that place. Every guard in the city is on duty and ready to slice apart anyone who tries to come near."

"Not to mention," Hywel added, "we don't know where the Jotnari went. They don't give up, so we're not even safe here."

"Safi is strong, and she knows how to handle herself." Conri relaxed his arms and rubbed a hand over his beard. "She'll understand—she's a warrior. Besides, I'll bet she still has support among the guards. They won't do anything to her."

"You know the guards aren't the issue." Errol dropped his chin to his chest, some of his vigor waning. "It's the king."

"He won't have her executed?" A shiver rolled down Rowena's spine. She'd just met her cousin, but she was the only family Rowena had. "Surely not without a trial, and they wouldn't do that while they're concerned about the Jotnari returning."

Errol wouldn't meet her gaze. Then she glanced around. None of the men would look at her, not even Conri.

"What did King Lendan do?" Bram spoke in a low, menacing tone—the Seeker's voice.

She snapped her gaze back to Errol. The surrounding air suddenly became hot and stifling. The King Lendan hadn't raised his son—they barely knew each other—but somehow, Rowena suspected they might be too much alike. "Did he attack her?"

"Tell them," Liam said.

Errol stared at the sky for a brief time, then lowered his gaze to the snuffed ashes of the campfire. "The king and queen raised Safi as their own. According to her, they were kind and fair. Yet they are warriors, even Queen Dewan. Safi trained from a young age in weapons and tactics. King Lendan praised her and groomed her early on to take leadership of his army, which she did as the youngest commander ever."

"Was she respected by the warriors?" Bram asked.

"It seemed so," Errol answered, kicking his toe at a small branch. "She'd trained among them and fought beside them from the time she was only ten summers. She's fierce and determined." His expression softened, a slight grin lifting his lips.

Rowena could picture her cousin in the middle of the seasoned warriors. She'd done the same thing.

"It wasn't a secret that Lendan wanted her to be in charge, and there wasn't any way Safi would have accepted the position if she hadn't earned it. That's not how she is." Errol finally met Rowena's gaze. "I met her two years ago, during a summit in Bethon. She charmed me instantly, but told me she didn't associate with someone she'd have to put into the stockades. So, I joined King Lendan's army."

Memories of sparring with Hann flooded Rowena's mind. He would have gone anywhere with her. "I had someone that would have done that, too."

"So how does this explain the danger you feel she's in now?" Bram rested his hand on the hilt of a dagger he had in his belt.

Rowena took in the dark handle, the glittering silver—it was the same blade he'd worn as the Seeker. She raised her eyes to meet his, making sure he saw that she'd noticed.

"As our relationship grew closer, King Lendan became more and more agitated with the time we spent together. He started insisting she stay longer at his table during the evening meal. Then it was long tafl matches where he would send me away, along with the queen. Eventually, they assigned me to the overnight gate watch. It took several months before I found out he'd forced her into his bed. After that, it turned out that my previous skill set had value after all."

Rowena's stomach turned over, and she had to swallow several times to keep herself from vomiting. Daenon had pushed himself on her, but the king . . . for months. Rowena couldn't comprehend how her cousin had endured. "She's so at ease here. With all of you. How does she do it?"

"She has nothing to fear here, lass," Conri said softly. "We may bend the rules to fit our interest, but we hold to the honor of old. Anyone who willfully harms a woman or child must pay a price."

"When we heard her story, she became as a sister to us," Liam said.

"A royal has a duty to uphold justice for those he, or she, rules," Bram added, darting a glance at Rowena. "We must replace one who rejects that obligation. Poor leadership in one kingdom will burrow in and influence other areas of the realm."

If he didn't mean to direct his statement directly at Rowena, she understood it as such. Forsa was a ramshackle village because Uther loved the power of his crown, yet not his obligation. Lendan deserved to be tied out during the Reaping like a sacrificial goat. The Telana of both islands deserved better. But was Rowena any better? When she followed through with killing Uther and Fidessa —and now Lendan, if she could get to him—she'd truly be the king-killer as Uther accused.

That was why he'd been so insistent she put aside her

vengeance. Could she if it meant making a better land for those like Safi? Like Muriel and Tuck? Her family had done nothing to deserve a premature death. Hann certainly didn't. And Safi shouldn't have suffered what happened to her. Someone had to stand up for them, too.

"That's fine to say, but the only way we replace a king is when he dies," Hywel said. "I'd prefer to keep my head than entertain talk of making that happen."

"No one is speaking of assassinating the king," Conri said, holding his hand up to stop the murmurs spreading within the rest of the Fianna standing around.

"I make no promises for myself on that matter, but that's not the issue." Errol shifted his weight and grimaced. "We can't let Safi stay inside that city. As soon as things settle down and they've prepared Velmeg for the Jotnari to return, Lendan will find her."

"You're still not healed enough to make a charge or sneak through the streets with the day getting brighter as you go." Conri glanced at Errol's leg.

"I'll do well enough."

"I'll be at his side," Liam said. "As I said, she's our sister."

"If we stick with a small group, we could move quick." Seamus stepped up next to Conri. "It'll barely be full daybreak before we're out. The three of us can get the job done."

"Four," Bram said.

"Five!" They would not keep Rowena from going.

Conri scratched the back of his head. It was clear he didn't want to agree, but he couldn't deny the importance of going, either. "If you want to go, I'll not stop you. But if you're caught, don't be looking for us to come. I'll not put everyone at risk with those giants lurking about."

"Understood," Liam said.

"We can check the sally port?" Seamus offered.

"They'll guard it, but not with as many," Bram said.

"Let's get going." Errol didn't wait for an answer and strode off, though he couldn't hide his limp.

Everyone followed without looking back.

As expected, the front gates were closed and extra guards stood in the watchtowers. It took longer to work their way around the palisade because of the patrols they encountered. Though each time it was only a pair of guards, they could have easily overtaken as could any Jotnari. Especially since they carried torches with them as they patrolled, even with the skies getting lighter.

When they reached the sally port, they spied a group of five guards huddled together in discussion just outside the wooden door built into the rock wall.

They stayed as far back as they could to keep the gate in sight and keep themselves hidden.

"We wait here," Liam said. "They've been in pairs. These are probably reporting in and will move on."

It made sense. They huddled low, blending into the brush. Bram insisted on being near Rowena, though he didn't crowd her, but she could still smell his oak scent. She had to force herself to ignore its intoxicating aroma and not let her mind drift into remembering how it took on a charred perfume as the Seeker.

Errol sucked in an audible breath, snapping Rowena's focus back to the group near the narrow back entrance. Dawn had brightened the skies enough for the guards to extinguish their torches, and they no longer stood with their heads bent in conversation, which gave a clear view of Daenon. He gave three quick raps on the wooden door, and moments later, it opened. A tall, thin figure slipped out to stand with the others.

"Fidessa?" Rowena brought her fingers to her lips, ashamed she'd whispered the name aloud.

The queen spoke with the guards briefly, and then she and Daenon disappeared back through the door. The guards split, each pair hurrying away in different directions.

"Let's go," Errol said, ushering them to the entrance after the torchlight faded into the distance.

"Should we wait to make sure the prince and queen are gone?" Rowena asked. The last thing she wanted to do was slam into Daenon as they snuck into the city.

"Whatever they're up to, they won't stay near that area long. It's near the midden," Errol said and jogged away.

They all followed, and Rowena hoped he was right.

TWENTY-EIGHT

Errol had a fine skill in picking the lock that impressed Rowena, yet Seamus and Liam seemed to have expected no less. As Errol explained, the rank odor of the midden heap assaulted their nostrils as soon as they snuck through the sally port. No one would want to linger nearby.

They'd made it past the blacksmith forge, when they had to rush to hide from a four-member guard crew jogging by. It split their group on either side of the path. Bram had ducked right, pulling Rowena with him against the rock wall of a small home. His head tucked under the overhanging thatched roof. When he pressed her into the darker corner, she'd given him a quick jab to the side with her elbow, yet only ran into a well-toned midsection. He had the most irritating way of distracting her.

Errol and Liam found cover behind some barrels, and Seamus had jumped into a sheep pen. If the guards hadn't been so focused, they might have investigated what caused all the animals to erupt into a bleating chorus.

Bram motioned to the others that they should split up, go separate ways to the king's tower where they'd agreed they'd most likely find Safi. Huddling in the dark, tight space—while they gave all their hand signals—should have made Rowena uneasy. Instead, Bram's presence gave her more confidence. No challenge would be too large for the one who lurked within the traveler.

The trio veered to the left, following a path behind the sheep pen. Wordlessly, Bram motioned for Rowena to follow him around the building to the right. He didn't wait to see her roll her eyes, but she did it anyway, staying close behind. When they reached a wide cart path, Bram slowed them to amble along the side as if they were in no hurry.

"What are you doing? Someone will see us!"

"And decide we must belong here, unless we act as if we have something to hide." He raised both eyebrows, waiting for her to understand his tactic.

It was the same as hiding in the woods. If they stayed calm, they could hide in plain sight. It was a good plan. She nodded, and they continued. Except, the paths were mostly empty. It wasn't the bustling city they'd been in before.

"Do you think they have ordered everyone inside?" She bit the inside of her lip, trying to remain as casual as Bram.

"That is a possibility."

They moved closer to the side, staying in the shadows that grew dimmer while Sawel took her place in the sky. "Can you do something? Wrap us in that mist you make, perhaps?"

He glanced sidelong at her. "It doesn't work that way and would only bring more attention, not less."

She twisted her lips. That was unfortunate. While she contemplated asking if he could move them closer like he'd done with her before, unsure if she really wanted to use that option, an older woman scooted out of her home. She dipped a pitcher into a rain barrel outside her door. Then the old woman halted, peering closer at them as they strolled to the far side of the road and adjusted their cloaks.

When she didn't call out, but went back inside, Rowena exhaled a slow breath.

"Agreed," Bram answered, to her unspoken relief. He pointed to another path cutting to the right. "Let's go through there where it's less traveled."

The undisturbed moss between the buildings proved they'd found a little-used trail. As they neared the end, another woman, in a thrall's dress, hurried across the opening.

Rowena gasped and raced after her, darting out of Bram's reach. She called out in a whisper. "Muriel?"

The woman skidded and spun to face Rowena with wide eyes, dropping a basket she carried onto the wide path. "Oh!" She came racing to Rowena and jerked her into a tight embrace. "A guard reported seeing the Seeker steal you away."

"I'm here and safe." Rowena relished the momentary comfort of Muriel's arms. Her chest caved a little with wistful memories that she had to shove aside.

They pulled apart and Muriel gave Rowena a questioning grin as she recognized Bram when he moved to their side. "I was sure that beast had devoured you."

Rowena snuck a peek at Bram, who pursed his lips and lifted his gaze to the skies.

"As much as I love that you're safe, you can't be here," Muriel said. "Some are saying you summoned the Seeker. That you created a gate within Velmeg to Mortus because you're moonborn."

"That makes things more difficult," Bram said.

Muriel nodded. "There are guards going through the streets with orders to capture you if you return. King Lendan believes that's why the Jotnari attacked."

"He has my cousin. Do you know where they're keeping her?"

"I haven't heard." Muriel took Rowena's hand between her own. "Please stay safe."

"After we free Safi, but you must come with me." Rowena pulled free and put her hands on Muriel's shoulders. "I was so concerned after I ran away that Uther would punish you on my behalf."

Muriel huffed. "Your absence riled him up, but he hasn't bothered with me. I'm sure he won't. You are dear to me, child, but I must remain here for Tuck. After the attack, things are very dangerous for him."

"You can't protect him on your own," Bram said, stepping closer. He'd stayed silent as Rowena had her moment with her friend, but he was correct.

"He can come, too. I'll convince the Fianna to protect him as well."

"The Fianna? You expect me to hide within a group like that and feel safe? You need to get away from them." Muriel leaned closer and whispered. "What if they find out who you are?"

"They already know." Rowena gave her a soft smile.

"They are honorable men, despite how it may seem." Bram's gaze softened on Muriel.

Rowena had to agree.

Muriel inhaled, shaking her head. "The king has sent scouts, including the prince, into the woods to search for the Jotnari camp. If they found Tuck outside the gates, they'd think he was working with the giants. They'd kill him instantly as a traitor."

She wasn't wrong about what they'd do to the sweet half-giant. But . . . Rowena twisted to meet Bram's gaze. "The prince?"

"They believe the prince is out scouting with the others?" Bram asked Muriel.

"Yes, they left in the night. No one is to be outside, but the queen sent me to the kitchens to make scones. In the wee hours of the morning! As if I could just whip them up in moments. She'll be ranting about how long I took by the time I'm back." Muriel retrieved the basket she'd dropped, swatting away the dirt that had collected on it.

"Hours . . . with no one to know if she left her rooms," Bram said.

"What would be the reason?" That the prince had been with the queen gave Rowena pause.

Muriel halted and bounced her gaze between Rowena and Bram. "What is it?"

Rowena crossed her arms over her chest. "We saw Daenon outside the sally port, speaking with some guards. Then Fidessa showed up, and spoke to them also before the prince followed her back through the door."

"The guards left as if given orders," Bram said.

Rowena dropped her hands. "Come with me. Something is happening, and it's too dangerous for you here. We'll keep Tuck safe as well."

"No harm will come to him." Bram had a determined set to his jaw. "Even if the Fianna won't accept him, I assure you I'll find him a safe place to hide."

Rowena thought of the cottage—wherever it was. Tuck would like it. If he could accept how he'd have to get there.

"You there!"

Muriel gasped at whoever called out behind Rowena. On impulse, Rowena spun and threw out her hands. Enchantment coursed through her arms and shot out of her palms at the same time she recognized the older woman from before. It was too late for Rowena to pull back from what she'd done.

The woman twisted, knocking herself off balance, so when she fell, the enchantment Rowena had thrown at her only grazed her shoulder. For a split second, Rowena sagged in relief—until the woman screamed.

She rolled, scrambled to her feet, and ran down the path while screeching about the cursed princess' return.

Rowena spun and grabbed hold of Muriel's hand at the same time Bram slid between them and potential danger.

"Please gather your things and leave through the sally port." Rowena squeezed her friend's palm. "We latched the door, but it's unlocked."

Rowena had never been so happy to know a scoundrel pirate. Errol had insisted they keep the door that way, so no one would get trapped if they got separated. Now, it would also save her friend's life.

"Rowena, we must leave," Bram said. A moment later, he rushed to engage three guards rounding the corner.

Rowena twisted one way and then the other, ensuring no one approached closer before she spoke to her friend. "The box you had in your room in Forsa, with extra dresses . . . Is it here with you?"

Muriel blinked slowly for several heartbeats before she answered. "Yes." Deep lines burrowed between her brows.

"I hid a brooch in there. I can't be sure, but I think it might be important. When you pack your things, can you bring that with you? If it doesn't make you linger."

Muriel's face softened, and her lips curved up in a way that seemed more sad than true. "I will see what I can do."

"Don't stay to search. I can figure out a way without it. I can't lose anyone else I care about."

"You are strong. A Lunara princess!" Muriel cupped her cheek, kissing her forehead. "No one is ever truly gone when your love for them lives in your heart."

"Rowena!" Bram called.

"You'll come? Please say you'll come."

"Go, be safe." Muriel squeezed her hand and hurried away, still favoring her leg. Rowena stared after her for a long moment.

All the pain of losing those she cared about, and the anger for those who'd caused it, filled Rowena and crushed her heart. This land. Uther. Fidessa. Daenon. She turned slowly, watching Bram fight with speed and grace. The corner of her mouth tipped up.

She sauntered forward, lifting her hands and sent enchantment into a guard, aiming his sword at Bram's back. The Telana flew ten feet and slammed against a handcart, falling in a boneless heap.

More guards poured around the corner, and Rowena aimed at

those in the lead. Two more crumpled. Their bodies forced the others to make a wider arc or jump over them. Either way, it gave an advantage she and Bram needed against so many.

Forsan warriors had credible skills. They were the only part of Uther's reign he concerned himself with. But the Velmeg fighters had a different level. Lendan had an army of hardened warriors.

Rowena let her enchantment fly, hitting one after another, but she couldn't keep up.

"Slow down," Bram yelled while battling bare-handed, even though he had a sword on his back and a dagger on his hip.

He'd told her to go slow at first. She had to spend more time with the moons, learning, absorbing. The skies lightened to a hazy purple streaked with pink. Her breath grew thicker—her arms heavier.

A guard dodged Rowena's enchantment and made it close enough to swing his sword at her head. She had to drop and roll out of the way, leaving a path clear for more warriors to flood between the buildings. When she rose, she swiped her hand through the air, sending a crate into the feet of the charging warrior.

He had to jump out of the way. She squeezed between the wall of a building and a half-filled barrel. Her chest heaved, and sparkly dots swam at the corners of her vision. A sword slammed against the barrel, missing her by hand's-width.

Other crates and baskets sat nearby. From her position of relative safety, Rowena concentrated on a crate. She held her hand out, changing the weight of the wood until it wobbled and rose an inch. With a sweeping motion of her hand, the crate flew into a guard. She sent two more before realizing she'd left the ground herself.

No longer behind the barrel but hovering above it, only Rowena's knees remained hidden from view. Several warriors halted and backed away from her. She aimed her hands at the barrel, toppling it over, and rolled it into three men at once.

Rowena had to blink several times, landing hard on her feet. She sucked in a deep breath, preparing to call upon her waning enchantment once again, but stopped with a strangled yelp.

Lendan and Uther ambled into view, standing at the edge of the wide path. Their presence meant nothing to her, except that Uther held Muriel tightly to his chest with a knife to her throat.

A guard near Lendan blew a horn, startling everyone.

"Halt for your king!" the man shouted once some of the din had settled. Most of the guards stepped away from Bram and Rowena. Eventually, everyone turned to the kings, chests heaving.

"Rowena," Uther said, loud enough for her to hear, but calmly, as if no one else stood near them. "Did you think I didn't know you'd return? Or that I wouldn't be watching the one person who continually risks herself for you?"

Muriel shook her head slightly. Rowena leveled her glare at Uther. "Do not harm her."

Everything inside of Rowena screamed to charge and call upon her enchantment until she drained herself. She would save someone she cared about, even if it meant her own death.

But he kept Muriel close enough that Rowena couldn't attack.

From the corner of her eye, she could see Bram. Guards had encircled him, keeping him from coming closer. "You're not like him, Rowena," he called.

She tilted her head, contemplating that. All her plans ended with Uther and Fidessa dead. Those in Taesing believed she'd killed her father and wouldn't want her back. There wasn't anything to lose . . . at least not for herself.

If the Seeker had been right, and she was part of the prophecy. Did that change things? She didn't have the sword. Wasn't that what he'd said made the difference? She could kill Uther in other ways.

While she debated herself, the light flickered to her left. A body rushed out of the shadows, headed for Uther. Tuck! One of

Lendan's guards swung a club that landed in the half-giant's stomach. Tuck stumbled back but didn't fall.

Muriel bit into the king's hand. He dropped the knife and let her go for a moment. Rowena sprung into action, charging Uther, but he snatched Muriel's hair, yanking her back to him. Then he kicked her in the side of her bad knee. Muriel crumpled to the ground with a scream that burrowed into Rowena's chest.

Tuck roared. The guard halted his club midway through his second swing. Tuck ripped the weapon away from him and smacked it against the man's skull. The guard fell, blood darkening the soil under him. Tuck bolted toward Muriel.

Someone shoved backward both Lendan and Uther. Guards with swords high created a shield around both kings.

Rowena raced to stand next to Tuck. Muriel lay sobbing on the ground.

The half-giant growled a warning, and Rowena raised her hands.

TWENTY-NINE

The guards pressed forward. Most had hate-filled stares for Tuck. Rowena had to dig deep, forcing her enchantment to form in her hands. The glow made the line of warriors halt.

"Do as your king commands," Lendan called. "Take them!"

Before the guards could react, noise from a battle around the corner rang out. Shouts, metal on metal, and breaking wood, closed in behind the kings.

The guards facing Rowena twisted away from attacking her to defend their king. Then swiveled back again with fear that flashed in their widened eyes.

"Which will it be?" Rowena called out. "Face the enchantment or protect your king?"

Sweat beaded on her brow and more dribbled down her back. The effort of keeping her power at the ready weighed like a baurun on her shoulders. Tuck bared his teeth, waiting.

Bram broke free from the warriors and forced his way to Rowena's side. "Stop. You're draining yourself and won't be able to fight at all."

His words were just loud enough to reach her ears, and he spoke from between clenched teeth. She hated that he always had the right response. Worse, an ache grew within her chest like it had before when the sword was nearby, but there wasn't any chance to look for it.

The fighting around the corner had nearly reached them, and the guards finally reacted. Half split off to help the kings, and the others charged at Rowena, Tuck, and Bram.

Too focused on the guard pressing closer to her, Rowena didn't pay attention to the new arrivals to the battle. Her opponent held a round shield and battled against her power, edging closer. She couldn't hold a sustained effort much longer. The warrior fell when he took a blow to the back of the head, revealing Safi behind him.

A weakened Muriel gasped from where she lay on the ground.

Rowena bent quickly and squeezed the woman's arm. "This is a good thing." Safi was the only family Rowena had left worth fighting for.

Her cousin rushed to Rowena's side. "Miss me?"

"Did the others get you out?" Rowena asked, but couldn't say more when she lifted the man's shield and sword, bringing them to herself. Like Bram had warned, she couldn't continue with her powers much longer.

"I got myself out. What others?" Safi said, then engaged with a warrior from Forsa.

The shield was cumbersome. Rowena had practiced little with one, so she let it fall. The sword was too heavy for her as well. The man had been broader with larger arms, but if she used two hands, it would work. "Errol, with Seamus and Liam," she called to Safi.

"That rat—" Safi got cut off by another opponent. "Errol shouldn't have come."

Rowena dropped low and sliced into a Forsan woman's calf. "We had to keep him from coming by himself."

With Bram and Safi's help, the guards fell back. Rowena glanced at Muriel. Her skin had paled and her hair stuck to her cheeks in a shimmer of sweat.

"Tuck!" Rowena called, dropping to her knees next to her friend.

Safi grunted, stepping into her swing to force away another attacker. "What are you doing?"

Tuck skidded to a stop on his knees next to Rowena. "Muriel?"

"We have to get her out of here. She needs a physic." Rowena brushed the woman's hair from her face. "We'll get you some help. I'm so sorry. So sorry."

"Don't." Muriel shook her head, causing herself to wince in pain. "It's not your fault."

"Take her to her room," Rowena told Tuck.

"No," Muriel reached out a hand to Tuck. "It's not safe for you. They'll kill you."

It was true. Tuck had killed one of Lendan's guards. "Take her and then go. She's right, you can't stay."

"I'll go after." He scooped Muriel into his arms as gently as if she were a newborn lamb. "The Frost Flats. With my kind."

The idea of him joining with the Jotnari pained Rowena. It was doubtful he'd find acceptance there either, but it was at least far away and where neither Lendan nor Uther would follow.

Muriel reached out a hand to Rowena, who held it tight. "I didn't get to your brooch."

"Shh. It's not important." She touched her forehead to the back of Muriel's hand and then dipped her chin to Tuck. The giant raced away from the fighting and down a small alley between two circular stone buildings.

They'd been so good to her. A stabbing pain pierced Rowena's heart.

Seconds later, a rough hand grabbed her arm, yanking her away from where she stood. She had ignored her surroundings. Safi dragged her behind an overturned cart.

"You are a danger to yourself," her cousin snapped.

"They had to get to safety." Rowena bristled at the comment.

Safi raised her brows in a huff.

"We came to find you," Rowena added.

"I didn't need help." Safi glanced to the ground. "But I've learned that you must get away from here. Far away from Uther and Fidessa."

"Rowena?!" Bram called.

"We have to go." Rowena lifted high enough to see over the edge of the cart.

Bram sliced a sword toward another oncoming attacker, who blocked it. With a growl, he shoved against the other blade, which threw the weight of the man backward and gave Bram a moment to stab him while he was down.

Errol, Seamus, and Liam had arrived and became engaged with the guards as well. Rowena plopped down with her back against the wood. "The others are here."

"All of them?" Safi peeked for herself and grumbled under her breath. "He shouldn't have come."

Rowena grabbed her hand. "What did you want to tell me? Quickly!"

"Uther went to Taesing for the sword—the one we're supposed to find—but not just that. He believes you are the key to helping him find a heartstone so he can restore the Telana's enchantment."

Rowena's stomach turned over. A sour taste built near her back teeth. She had to breathe in short bursts through her nose or she'd vomit. "It was my fault."

"What was?"

"I'm cursed. I've brought all of this upon everyone."

Safi shook her shoulder. "Listen, you did nothing. It wouldn't surprise me if my father had this plan since I was five."

Rowena shook her head. "I need to leave. No one else should get hurt because of me."

"Stop that. You are not at fault."

Her uncle had come for her. Not because he loved her

mother like Fidessa claimed. Not because he wanted to rule Taesing. He destroyed her family, her home, her village . . . all because he believed Rowena was part of the prophecy. "He can never get it."

"Agreed. Which is why we need to stop him."

Uther wanted to restore the Telana by using her and the sword. How? The sword connected to Lunara enchantment. The heartstones were specific for each race. Even Rowena knew that much. Uther had to understand that as well.

"I thought Fidessa killed my mother out of jealousy."

Safi rolled her lips together. "My father killed yours intentionally, but your mother's death was an accident."

Rowena stared at her cousin. "Are you defending her?"

"Of course not. It's just . . ." Safi scratched above her temple. "They are my parents. Rotten ones that I barely know, but . . ."

True as that was, they'd also traded Safi away. Rowena remembered Daenon's words from the cave, about how hurt he'd been that his family rejected him. Nausea rattled her stomach, and she shoved those thoughts aside. She had to stay strong. "How do you know all of this?"

"They had me locked in a storage room, as if I couldn't get out of that." She stared at the ground, disgust written on her face. "I snuck out after each meal. No one would be back to check on me for hours, and I searched for the sword. One time, I came upon Lendan and my father talking."

"The two of them are working together?" Rowena pressed her back against the rough wood of the cart.

"Apparently. The treaty ending and Daenon's prime day celebrations are just an excuse. Though they want to bind you to the prince."

"To control me." It was as if no one expected her to put up a fight, or she had plans of her own.

"Yes."

Something, or someone, crashed into the wagon, knocking

Rowena forward. Safi fell onto her hip and raised her arm to keep the heavy wood from tipping on top of them.

"We need to get out of here." She and Safi rushed out from their hiding spot behind the cart and instantly engaged with two warriors.

Rowena's mind went blank, and she used muscle memory to fight. She kicked her opponent in the gut, knocking him to the ground. Then stomped on his hand to wrench his sword free. She cared about nothing except the next blade coming at her.

Jab. Swing. Punch. Kick. She detached herself from all thought, all emotion. Their faces were blank and the motions ingrained. Her senses told her someone fought near her. She avoided them and continued. When she fell, she used her legs to sweep her opponent down. When a blade came too fast, or she moved too slowly, she ignored the pain. Blood dripped down her fingers from a cut across her upper arm. She had to vomit once from a blow to the gut that sent her sprawling in the dirt.

It didn't stop her.

Until . . .

A stone landed at her feet and a heartbeat later, it burst into a billowing green cloud. It had to be Fidessa. She'd joined the fighting.

Rowena squeezed her eyes closed, coughing, and scrambled backward until she tripped over a fallen guard. She kept a tight grip on her pilfered sword, blindly slicing back and forth to keep anyone from reaching her. She continued to scoot until she found a rock wall to keep at her back. Others around her coughed and gagged as well. The putrid scent of vomit permeated the air.

A cool breeze picked up, swirling around Rowena. Her senses cleared. Her eyes dried. She rose and found Bram with his back to a round dwelling nearby. A single trickle of black mist dissipated away.

She met his stare, and he gave her a nearly imperceptible shake.

"Who are you?" Fidessa called out.

Rowena twisted her neck and scanned for her aunt. Fidessa stood ten feet away between a bottleneck in the path between a raised rabbit hutch and a domicile's stone wall. She stared at Bram.

"We met several nights ago in Forsa. I'm surprised you've forgotten." Bram was so calm. How did he do it? He hid the greatest secret in the realm, yet he acted as if he was the same as anyone.

"You are a witch," Fidessa spat between clenched teeth.

Rowena sauntered closer, suddenly full of confidence. "What's the matter? I recall you gloating that your mage skills made you all-powerful."

Fidessa straightened her shoulders and folded her hands together in front of her, perhaps to hide how they trembled. "I don't see either of you helping your friends."

Bram didn't flinch and kept his stare trained on the queen. As hard as she tried to do the same, Rowena dragged her eyes as far right and then left as she could without moving her head. Everyone else was still stuck in the eerie green fog. Though no one screamed any longer.

"What have you done to them?" The cruelty from her aunt and uncle would never stop until someone put an end to them. She had to do it.

"I overwhelmed them with the power to do . . . nothing." Fidessa tried to make a pouty face as if their plight made a difference to her. "I guess your mother wasn't the only one who could influence others to do her bidding."

"My mother never used her power to harm." Rowena lunged, ready to scratch the mage's eyes out, but Bram stuck out his arm.

He was so careful; he didn't even touch her, just made sure she knew to stop. Rowena dragged her gaze over his strong shoulders, over his brown beard. Just a little longer than it was the last time, even though he'd spent the night training her in his Seeker form. Did his hair continue to grow even when he wasn't all dark and shadowy? She nearly reached out to touch him, but stopped herself with a strangled gasp.

Bram twisted, piercing her with a questioning stare. That did not help. Rowena swallowed, buying time as she lifted her shoulders, having no better answer.

"So you've found yourself another enchanted." Fidessa tried to sound unfazed, but there was a wobble to her voice.

So distracted, Rowena had almost forgotten her desire for maiming her aunt. The urge rushed through her with a gale force. "Wrong again."

There was a certain amount of pleasure in the confusion that crossed the queen's face. Her shoulders rolled as if she wore too heavy a cloak and needed it to fall off her back.

"Release the others," Bram said. There was power in his command. The quick widening of Fidessa's glare said she recognized it as well.

The queen raised her chin. "I will release them when they deserve it."

Bram arched a brow, but Rowena rested her hand on his arm. He snapped his gaze to her. "Let me convince her it's in her best interest to stand down."

"You must be careful," he said in a low voice that rumbled through her. "Your reserves are low and . . . the choice you make will affect many."

"I'm aware." She huffed a heavy sigh, covering for the way his brooding gaze made her stifle a shiver. "You've been very clear."

He twisted so Fidessa couldn't read his lips as he whispered. "The others shouldn't stay in her charm for long. If you fall behind, I will release them."

She dropped her chin in acknowledgement, but also to give herself a moment before she met the queen's gaze and strode forward.

THIRTY

There was truth in Bram's warning about her strength. Rowena had to struggle to call upon her enchantment, just like she'd done in the meadow. She needed to relax, not force the power. She barely had enough enchantment to face the queen and make her pay the same price her mother had. Yet, her chest still ached. Her palms itched.

If she wasted time searching for the sword, she'd become too tired and lose the chance to avenge her family. The armor could come later.

The Fianna and other warriors remained stuck in Fidessa's charmed green fog, unable to move or speak. Some remained standing, others had fallen to their backsides. All of them crowded the small space between the round buildings. Rowena didn't want to guess at what was happening inside their minds. The two kings watched the action in the alley in silence from where they stood on the wide cart path, unaffected by Fidessa. Rowena kept her chin high, her gaze severe, as she ignored everyone but the queen.

"So brash. You get that from your father." Fidessa cooed. "It was an accident, you know."

Rowena wrinkled her nose. The stench of the queen's condescending attitude was intolerable. "You meant that axe for me. I won't be as careless."

Fidessa sighed, lifting a palm. "For your father, actually. He bent down, and it missed him."

That gave Rowena pause. Whether the intended target had been her father or her mother or herself, the queen had no remorse for her actions. Uther uttered a mumbled curse, which she dismissed. His turn for her wrath would come later. "Your death will be on purpose."

This time, she wouldn't hesitate. There would be no second-guessing. The queen had to die for her crimes. Rowena would deal with whatever the fallout took place. The realm would survive.

Her blood spiked with power, filling her with a heady sensation. Rowena lifted her palm, raising a barrel, and swept it at the queen.

Fidessa's lips moved, speaking an inaudible spell. A gust of wind forced the barrel to turn and crash against two oncoming warriors. Their bodies slumped.

"Careful, Rowena," Fidessa said. "Any errant power you can't control could cause unintended consequences."

It mattered little to Rowena if she injured Lendan's or Uther's men from her battle with the queen. However, she glanced around to ensure there weren't any innocents snared by Fidessa's charm.

Bram stood, unaffected, near where Safi sat motionless next to Errol, with the other Fianna lying further down the alley. Ensuring there were only warriors nearby, as well as spotting where her allies were, helped lower Rowena's concerns.

She locked her gaze on Fidessa. "I'll make sure you're the only one to suffer."

"Bold statement from one who has no training." Fidessa cupped her hand, raised it, and quickly flicked her fingers open wide.

Small shards of what seemed like broken glass flew toward

Rowena, but in a wide enough arc to hit others as well. Fidessa had intentionally caused pain to others, including those who served Uther, though no one cried out or acknowledged what happened to them.

Without dropping her gaze from her aunt, Rowena plucked one of the skinny pieces from near her elbow. She did her best to swallow down the pain without letting it show on her face before she tossed it aside. "Not much of a threat."

"Rowena, remember," Bram called.

She did. She remembered the blood seeping through the fabric of her mother's gown. She remembered the glimmer in Hedda's eyes as the queen gave the woman permission to punish Rowena. The woman had laid ten stripes across Rowena's back for daring to eat her morning meal before cleaning the goat pen.

Rowena lowered to one knee, digging her fingertips into the pebbled path. Pushing her power to make something lighter came easier, but Fidessa had swatted away the barrel too fast. Rowena had to prove she wasn't weak. Prove that enchanted abilities were better than anything a mage could conjure with spells, potions, or charms.

After a long exhale, she closed her eyes and cleared her mind. Then she pressed against the soil, pulling an invisible thread that led to Fidessa. The force on her own body increased the moment she latched onto the queen. Rowena's fingers sunk below the surface, heavy. When a divot grew under her knee, she opened her eyes, but continued to pull against the queen with her power. Rowena's body slumped, suddenly too powerless to rise. She leaned against her thigh, a grin defying the weight of her power as dirt covered the queen's feet, locking her in place.

In her periphery, an object soared in Rowena's direction. She released her hold on the thread to duck out of the way and plopped to her backside, heaving for air.

Her gaze snagged on Daenon as he stalked between the buildings, closer to Fidessa. The prince smirked. He made her flesh crawl. Behind him, Queen Dewan had also arrived, standing next to the two kings.

The high queen's presence gave Rowena pause. She'd not had any personal contact with the Queen of Velmeg. Even though she wore the same leather-clad style of fighting clothes as Safi, she maintained a regal presence. She also held a drawn blade, tightly gripped, with her lips pursed, and a glare sharper than her sword aimed at Fidessa.

An arrow had landed in the prince's path, halting him midstride. One more step would have impaled him.

Rowena twisted her neck, finding Bram with another arrow nocked from Seamus' bow and aimed at the prince. He kept Daenon from joining her aunt.

His effort to keep the battle only between her and Fidessa sent a pleasant tingle down Rowena's spine. Her strength trickled back, allowing her to stand, while Fidessa yanked her feet free from the dirt.

"What did you hope to accomplish by that little trick? It appears you've weakened yourself more than me." Fidessa tipped her head back and laughed.

It would have been the perfect chance to launch a dagger into the queen's throat. Unfortunately, her aunt had a point. In the meadow, the Seeker had explained that her ability to increase the weight of an object should be a weapon of last resort. It drained her too quickly. She had hoped to throw the queen off-balance; scare her with how strong Rowena could be. Instead, she'd proven herself vulnerable. Yet, Bram had helped her with the arrow—without commentary or reprimand.

And Daenon took advantage of the moment. Just as he had the other time she'd shown weakness in his presence. She wanted to use her powers, to flatten him, leave him helpless in the dirt. If Rowena fought him, she'd lose track of the queen. While the prince made her blood boil, he would have to wait.

"Watch out," Bram called just before a shield hit Rowena on

the back of her shoulder. It knocked her forward, but the wooden circle didn't have enough momentum to force her to the ground.

"You're a poor excuse for an enchanted," Fidessa taunted. "Yet you have my daughter's support. You're betrothed to Daenon. Uther keeps you as a pet. Another pitiful Lunara that insists on disrupting my life."

"You hold your daughter inside your trickery and wonder why she doesn't warm to you," Queen Dewan called out.

Fidessa twisted to face her, giving Rowena a much-needed respite. Sawel's rays pierced the skies as she peeked over the horizon. Rowena could not draw any more enchantment. She glanced at Bram, dipping her chin in defeat.

He narrowed his eyes, as disgusted with her as she was with herself, most likely.

"You were supposed to raise my daughter to be a queen." Fidessa stalked closer to the Velmeg queen. "Instead, you made her a warrior. Pledged to protect you and the king instead of rise to power. And yet, she's here with a band of misfits and thieves. Why is that?"

"Safi is commander of the King's Guard," Lendan growled. "I will correct her mistake in following a pitiful dreg into the woods later."

While the mage kept the royals' focus elsewhere, Rowena watched the shadows crawl out from barrels, crates, wagons, and buildings. The darkness elongated and covered all those within Fidessa's charm. Sputters and coughs rang out as those the queen had trapped revived.

Fidessa spun back to Rowena. "What have you done?"

"You are not as powerful as you believe. Training can only take one so far, but instinct grows." It was a bluff, but she wanted to keep suspicion off of Bram.

From the corner of her eye, Rowena glimpsed Safi trudge closer. "You know nothing about me. Did you think I'd be pining for you all this time? Without a word or a letter?"

"I have loved you every day we've been apart." It was the first words the queen spoke that didn't sound like an attack, and probably were true.

"You can't leave an elfling, only five summers old, for years and expect them to understand that. I don't know you and you certainly know nothing of me." Safi relaxed into an easy stance, seemingly unfazed by the charm her mother had used against her.

"You'll understand the reasons once you're home and have had time to adjust. When you begin your training—"

"As a mage?" Safi interrupted. "I think not. The realm needs fewer tyrants that inflict their will upon others. That kind of power is despicable."

Rowena didn't miss the glance her cousin flicked toward King Lendan.

"It is your birthright. I've dreamed of us training together and combining our skills, to be the most powerful rulers Ibern has ever had." Fidessa's voice almost sounded pitiful.

"Is that so?" Lendan asked.

"Safi is already powerful and brave and intelligent," Queen Dewan said. The Ibern queen gave Safi the same soft, loving gaze Rowena's mother used to give.

"You are not her mother," Fidessa shrieked, then quickly clamped her mouth shut, shaking. She turned to Safi and spoke in a tight, forced calmness. "I agreed to this arrangement only so you could grow in a better place than that midden heap, Forsa. I sacrificed for your benefit."

"Sadly, I believe you." Safi shifted her weight and crossed her arms over her chest. "I'm sure you believe what you did was the right thing to do, perhaps the only thing you could do. At first, I wished you would come back for me. But that's not the way things turned out. I've learned that it is easy to claim love, but rarely true. Loyalty proven by deeds is a far greater measure, not promises."

For a moment, Fidessa stood in silence, pain gripping her face as if someone had slapped her. She swallowed, her eyes misting.

It was an odd contradiction Rowena struggled to understand. The queen lacked kindness, compassion, and honor, but after she'd boasted about Safi's return so often, Rowena had a twinge of pity. But her aunt gave up her child to gain power. The same reason she'd attacked Rowena's parents.

Her momentary sympathy dissolved along with Fidessa's expression. The queen's mouth tightened and her nostrils flared.

"Then I have truly lost you." Fidessa twisted to Uther. "I gave you everything. For what? False promises. All based on some misguided dream. Do you think I don't understand your efforts to gain Lunara enchantment are because of that wretched woman? You wanted to become like her. Perhaps she'd even leave your brother and accept you."

Uther remained silent with a glare aimed at his wife.

"Where did you see that leaving me?" Undaunted, Fidessa continued her rant. "Would you have set me aside to rot? And what of Safi? While you were busy pining for what you couldn't have, you ignored those who would have loved you. Now our daughter is a tool, a weapon, created to use against us. You're too much of a fool to even see it."

"I will remind you to watch yourself," Dewan said. "Safi is to be respected."

"This is between them, Dewan," Lendan added. He seemed to find the entire exchange enjoyable. Though from what Errol had revealed, he was as loathsome as her aunt and uncle.

Rowena slid closer to Safi. Her cousin had been a pawn in the game Fidessa and Uther played since she was an elfling. Rowena had only dealt with their hatefulness for a month.

"As usual, you are overly dramatic, Fidessa." Uther's tone grumbled with disgust.

"I'm better than her! She didn't even want you and yet you ignored me, keeping her between us all these years." Fidessa's face flushed pink, and she clenched her fists tight at her side.

Safi gave a small tug to Rowena's fingers, tipping her head

toward the Fianna. The two of them made a slow step in that direction. The recovered fighters had grouped together, engrossed in listening, with their weapons either sheathed or slack in their hands.

"I cared for you once." Uther rubbed his fingers between his brows. "This was an arrangement of convenience from the beginning, for both of us. You seem to have forgotten that. You were an outcast, selling potions and charms to survive until we met. We made a good pair for a while."

While the king and queen argued, Rowena and Safi arrived near Liam and Errol. Seamus positioned himself a few feet away, aiming an arrow toward the closest guards. Bram sidled over to flank the group's other side.

For a moment, no one spoke.

"If the two of you have finished, it would seem you and I have some things to discuss," Lendan said to Uther. He then scanned the area, gaze halting on Safi next to Errol. "Let's put an end to all this non—"

A horn blasted from the gates, interrupting the king. Chills prickled Rowena's skin. If Velmeg had the same system of calls she remembered from Taesing, one blast meant either a warning or a welcome. Since the celebrations for Daenon's prime day had resumed, there was a possibility of a late guest's arrival. At least Rowena hoped that's what it meant. Another long blast would prove that true. However, a short blast would mean trouble.

Everyone stood still, waiting. The horn sounded again. A short blast, and then another and another. That could only mean a threat to the entire city.

"Jotnari," Rowena whispered.

THIRTY-ONE

All warriors, whether from Forsa or Velmeg, raced into action, darting between the round stone buildings toward the front gates, ignoring Rowena and those with her.

"My men. Hold," Uther called. "Bring me both princesses."

"It's time to go," Errol yelled.

"The sally port." Seamus spun and sprinted that way without waiting for a response.

Rowena and the others dashed after him toward the hidden entrance. Whatever threat came at the front gates, they wanted no part of it. Especially if the Jotnari had returned. If Uther's guards wanted to chase Rowena and Safi, they were welcome to follow. The Forsan warriors were a lesser concern than the Jotnari. Rowena had barely survived the last time.

The group slipped down a bending path. Seamus lead and Safi stayed close to Errol, with Rowena behind them by two steps. Bram followed last as they rushed through broken crates, upturned buckets, and strewn vegetables from all the fighting before.

Rowena hesitated near a fallen warrior and snagged his dropped dagger on her way by. Bram had saved her the last time she faced the giants by turning into his Seeker form. She didn't want to rely on that again.

Only a handful of guards pursued them—perhaps three, from what Rowena could see when she darted a glance over her shoulder. After their public display, it surprised her that Uther still had any support. He cared only about power, and he hadn't resisted saying so.

"Halt," a gruff voice called from behind.

"Sure." Bram gave a sarcastic huff, staying close behind her.

Bram always appeared too steady, serious even. His remark surprised her. She bit her lip to keep a grin off her face that had no place in the current environment.

"There, ahead on the right," Errol called out, guiding Seamus, who increased his speed.

Liam kept up with his fellow Fianna, and the two of them rounded the corner ahead of Errol by several paces.

A moment later, Liam reappeared, arms windmilling as he scrambled to retreat. Seamus came into view right after. He screamed and lurched to his knees, falling face first to the ground. A Jotnari rounded the corner and ripped a spear out of Seamus' back a heartbeat later without breaking stride.

Rowena screamed and grabbed Safi, who was already yanking on Errol's sleeve.

"Jotnari!" Liam hollered, waving his hands for the group to turn around. He hadn't seen his friend fall, but there wasn't time to mourn for any of them.

Rowena, together with Safi and Errol, spun and charged back the way they came. The guards giving chase, halted, then turned to save themselves. Uther's control had its limits, after all.

She glanced back, only to see Liam right on her heels, blocking her view of Bram. The hair on her neck rose, and an uncomfortable twist wound its way through her gut. She darted to the side and let Liam pass.

Sure enough, Bram had halted ten paces back, his gaze fixed on where Seamus lay still in the dirt. Screams rang out on a path to her left, where the Jotnari must have veered.

"Come on!" she called to him. She twisted her neck, debating if she should leave, only to see Liam disappear around a corner. If she ran now, she'd be on her own. Bram was the best one to face the giants. She'd be safest to stay with him anyway, she reasoned.

He hadn't moved. Instead, he stood there with a wide stance and his shoulders back, ready. She sprinted to him. "Stay with us. You don't know how many there are."

"Go with the others." He slid a quick look before returning to watch the corner.

"Come with us." Rowena spoke through gritted teeth, so the words were practically a growl. The Seeker could battle whatever threat appeared from anywhere, most likely, but why should he take that risk?

He rounded on her, forcing her to lean back with a gasp. "I will find you. Now go!"

"Don't expose yourself for this." She clenched her fists and stood her ground. Rowena couldn't accept that she had a part in the prophecy, but Bram did. If he abandoned his duty to find the armor, or wasn't able to continue, the realm would have no hope.

His eyes sparked the way she'd witnessed several times before. When he was angry or charged with emotion, she realized. Confusion and something else, like a restrained fire ready to combust if allowed air, flickered across his face.

"Please." She swallowed, shaking from the raw truth of her plea for him to stay.

He narrowed his brows, chest heaving, but gave a single curt nod.

With the decision made, they sprinted away from the sally port gate. Moments later, growls and heavy feet pounded the soil from more Jotnari behind them. Rowena didn't care how many of the giants chased them. She pushed her legs to go faster because she didn't want to face even one.

"Turn left," Bram called. She darted around a pig pen toward the protective wall surrounding the city.

Bram kept them as close to the base of the palisade as possible, which she didn't understand until they were closer to the front. Archers stood on high platforms, shooting arrows over the stone wall.

"Behind us!" Bram called to the nearest one. The Telana twisted, his brows rising high before he released an arrow, and another at the pursuing Jotnari. Rowena waved her arms and called out to the next archer they had passed, who also turned on their pursuers.

By the time they rounded the corner near the front gates, no more giants followed. They stopped at the edge of the bailey and hid behind a wagon sitting in front of a short stone silo. Rowena leaned over and braced her hands on her knees. Whether she did it out of relief, the exertion, or plain fear—she didn't know or care. She just needed a moment to compose herself.

"There," Bram said.

Rowena straightened and followed where he gestured. Liam, Errol, and Safi huddled near the edge of a building on the side of the king's tower, staying out of sight. Bram ducked and led the way around the back of a goat pen and vegetable larder to join the others.

Liam looked behind them. "Seamus?"

Rowena met Bram's gaze. He settled his hand on Liam's shoulder. "He's in Caelus now."

The Fianna pursed his lips and stiffened for a moment. He turned away, staring at nothing, it seemed. Stunned silent, as activity buzzed all around them, they mourned their friend's death.

Yet the battle raged on, and they needed a new plan.

There were more archers along the walls, and others had joined the guards in the watchtowers on each side of the front gates. Two thralls led a pair of horses harnessed to a small ballista into the open area of the bailey. Others piled melon-sized round stones near the weapon. They would load the rocks onto the weapon and heave them over the wall.

"It's odd that no more Jotnari have come through the sally port," Bram said, turning to study the path they'd taken.

"Perhaps they think the first group is still pestering everyone." Errol kept his gaze on the ballista.

Moments later, a warrior set one stone onto a beam of the ballista. The stone rested against a tight cord that the warrior pulled back until it seemed likely to snap. Then he released it. The stone slid along the groove and sailed high over the gates. Guards and archers cheered at the weapon's success.

Errol gave a low whistle. "Impressive."

"They're pulling back," a guard in the right watchtower called out.

Everyone inside the gates raised their weapons, whooping in victory.

"That didn't seem enough of a challenge to the Jotnari," Safi said.

"If they were that easy to defeat, Seamus would be alive," Liam growled.

Rowena's stomach churned. She agreed; something about the situation didn't seem right.

It didn't take long for the cheering to stop. Outside the gates, a Jotnari called for King Lendan.

"I give my word that there will be peace if you will allow my representative to enter your gates for a parlay." The voice boomed loud and clear to all in the open courtyard and huddled out of sight.

None of the kings or queens were visible. All the royals had to have retreated inside the king's tower when the Jotnari arrived. The wooden door faced the front gates, and a moment later, a messenger slipped out. The door slammed shut behind him as he ran to speak with a guard who climbed the ladder to the left watchtower to announce the king's answer.

"The king declines to speak with you." The words came out with a mocking sneer.

"That's not wise," Bram whispered.

"No," Liam agreed.

The next moment, the bashing thud of sword on shield rang through the air from all directions, proving the Jotnari had most of the city surrounded. The erratic banging morphed into a slow, steady rhythm. A slack tide that portended disaster. The beat grew steadily faster. Thud———thud———thud——thud——thud—thud—thud—thud - thud - thud.

Rowena's teeth squeaked in her ears from how tightly she clenched her mouth. The repetitive sound grated against her spine, clawing its way up her neck and into her ears. She lifted her shoulders, trying to sink into her own skin—and then it stopped. In a heartbeat, the air grew disturbingly quiet.

All eyes turned to see white flags raised high from both watchtowers. King Lendan had entered the bailey and stood halfway between the gates and his protective home, shoulders back. Whatever the Jotnari wanted, they wouldn't get a cowering king.

"The king will hear your proposal," the guard called down.

"We have something to return to your king. We expect a parlay in person, and we'll bring his property," a Jotnari called out. "There is no danger to you. We will enter your gates unarmed."

"Like that will matter," Safi whispered.

King Lendan gave a solemn nod and stared stoned-faced at the gates.

"It's the half-wit," the guard called down a moment later.

Rowena stopped breathing. Tuck. He'd left to rejoin his kind, barely half a mark earlier. They couldn't have done anything to him so quickly. At least, she hoped not. She took a step, but Bram stopped her.

"Wait. You mustn't give them the chance to use you."

At the moment, she didn't care about that. If they'd hurt that kind man, she would kill them all. Why did it have to be daytime? Her enchantment sizzled like a pot nearly empty of water.

"It's Tuck. I have to go." Her voice rose in desperation.

"We'll all get closer, but stay back until we see for sure," Safi said.

Rowena noticed Safi flash a glance to Bram, but she didn't care what they thought of her. Uther had hurt Muriel, and now if they had brutalized Tuck also, she couldn't stand it. Was everyone she developed feelings for to be hurt? It was too much.

They all moved as one, to the next circular building, closer to the king's tower. It gave them cover, yet allowed them a clear view to the center of the courtyard where Lendan stood waiting. Bram and Safi stayed on either side of Rowena, keeping her from running into the open.

The front gates creaked open, and three Jotnari approached. One strode in front, followed by two others with a large, slumped body dragging his feet between them. A strangled moan came from Rowena, but she stayed still, her legs too wobbly to move.

The single Jotnari halted in front of the king close enough to tower over him, but Rowena cared little for their games. She watched as the other two dropped Tuck into a heap to the king's left.

"He's dead," she whispered, too distraught to find her voice.

"No, look." Safi pointed. "He's breathing . . . at least."

He may have been alive, but they'd beaten him so much it seemed more pitiful that he lived. Rowena couldn't see his face from her position, but his shirt hung in tatters from a whip that had cut through the fabric. One leg lay at an odd angle and she could only imagine how many other bruises and broken bones he had.

"It's clear the time has come for your tainted presence in our lands to end. You dare send this abomination to our camp. Your brash disregard for the law must end," the Jotnari said. Whether that was how loud he normally spoke, or if he was projecting so all those in Velmeg could hear, Rowena couldn't tell.

"I sent no one to your camp." Lendan also spoke louder than usual, not to be outdone, it appeared. He didn't even glance at Tuck.

The poor half-giant had hoped to find sanctuary among his kind, and they had nearly killed him instead. Tears blurred Rowena's vision.

"You must surrender or die. No longer will your influence corrupt these lands."

"Well, shite," Errol whispered.

"We should go. We can leave through the back and gather Seamus' body," Liam added.

It was a good plan. In her head, Rowena understood it. But she wouldn't leave until she could see Tuck and ensure he was alive and had proper care.

"That is an inadvisable action." King Lendan's voice interrupted their plans. "I'd suggest you return to the Frost Flats before there is more bloodshed." The king rested a palm on the hilt of his sword, his other hand casually hooked a thumb in his belt.

If Rowena hadn't heard Safi's story, she might have had respect for him.

"We have tolerated your savage race for far too long." The Jotnari representative sneered as he answered the king. "When the realm went dark, it was a sign of the destruction your kind brings upon this land. My father believed it was only a symbol that we must be vigilant to keep our distance, to prohibit your filth from defiling our lands. But he was mistaken. It is time to cleanse ourselves of those who refuse adherence to the proper laws. You keep druids, women, no less, among you to spread diseases and lies throughout the lands, even beyond these shores."

Safi scoffed and sucked in a gasp.

The doors to the main tower opened, and Queen Dewan strode out to stand by her husband. "I thought you had actual concerns. If you have questions about our practices, I'm happy to answer them for you."

King Lendan kept his gaze on the Jotnari. "Your might will not sway me to change our customs."

The Jotnari flared his nose, growing red with anger, but he kept his gaze trained only on the king. "We have grown powerful because of our adherence to the law. It is a sign of our favor with the land. We thrive as our fathers did before you arrived and corrupted this region. I intend to right that egregious mistake my forefathers allowed. It is said that another time of darkness is near unless we purge ourselves of those such as you."

"This is Telana land. We will change nothing to suit you," Lendan said.

"There is no hope for you. I will not suffer this soil to accept your presence any longer. Board your ships and leave, or we will destroy you." The Jotnari sneered at the king, then turned on his heel and strode through the gates with those who came with him.

The guards closed and barred the gates after them and then spun to await orders.

Rowena could not hold herself back any longer. She raced across the open ground, landing on her knees near Tuck. "What did they do to you?"

Tuck moaned and tried to move.

"Shh. Don't move." Rowena helped him move his top arm so he could stay on his side.

"Tell me what you said to them?" Lendan growled, standing over Tuck and Rowena. He ignored her efforts to relieve Tuck's pain.

"He's from Forsa and in pain," Rowena snapped. "Let him rest before you interrogate him."

"He killed one of my guards and led the Jotnari to my gates. He'll answer any question I ask," the king spat.

"I ... am ... sorry," Tuck whispered. "Not spy."

"He needs help." Rowena twisted to the left and right, gazing at the guards who surrounded them. "Won't any of you help? You've seen how he jumps to assist anyone in need. Many of you have received his generosity. Help him!"

"It is true. The boy is generous," the queen added. She leaned down opposite of Rowena. "Why did you kill the guard?"

Tuck tried to speak, but his throat gurgled, causing him to cough uncontrollably.

"He was defending his friend. It was an accident," Rowena said. She left out the part of how it was her fault Uther tortured Muriel. Neither of her friends would have gotten hurt if it wasn't for her. "He's never uttered an unkind word or turned away from anyone in need. Even if they are cruel to him."

"This is pointless," Lendan said. "Ready the ballista and prepare to keep that filth from my city."

Warriors hurried to ready weapons to fight. The king strode away, ignoring the women who helped Tuck, but Uther stepped forward. Rowena hadn't even seen him arrive.

"He has gotten what he deserved. Come, Rowena," Uther said.

Boots crunched in the dirt, stopping near Rowena. She peeked around her shoulder and recognized Safi's stance. "Touch her, and you'll face me."

Bram and Liam arrived to stand on either side of Safi.

Uther grumbled, but slid his feet backward until he spun and strode off toward Lendan.

The queen gave a soft smile over Rowena's head, then laid a gentle hand on Tuck's shoulder. "You sound like an extraordinary man."

"He deserves better." Rowena rubbed the back of Tuck's hand, trying, unsuccessfully, to stop the hitch in her voice.

"And he'll have it." The queen rose, pointing to three guards. "You, you, and you. Come help your queen."

The three Telana guards jogged over and kneeled on one knee.

"This boy is a blend of our cultures. We have just witnessed what heinous beliefs can arise out of forgetting our compassion,"

Dewan called to everyone and turned to the men. "Take him inside and place him in Princess Safi's old room."

The guards gaped, bouncing a quick glance at Safi.

"Do I need to repeat myself?" the queen asked.

"We'll need a pallet," one of them said, looking to Dewan for approval.

"Then, get it."

The guards scrambled to their feet and hurried off to fetch a board to assist them with Tuck's larger frame. Rowena stayed at Tuck's side, reassuring him that help was coming. She met the queen's gaze. "Thank you."

"I've made many mistakes." She moved around Tuck and slipped Safi's hand into hers. "It's time to right a few of them. Stay away from here. I'm sorry I couldn't stop him."

Tears pooled in Safi's eyes. "It wasn't your fault."

"I should have taken stronger measures."

The guards arrived with the board, interrupting the queen. Bram and Liam assisted the guards while the others stepped back.

"Rest, my friend." Rowena squeezed Tuck's hand and made to move aside, but he held onto her, tugging her close.

"Leave. Now," he grunted.

"I will go as soon as I can."

"No." Tuck coughed. "Danger."

The men carted him away when he devolved into a coughing fit.

"You should get inside," Safi told Dewan. "I'll be alright."

Rowena's cousin and the queen embraced quickly, squeezing tightly as the pounding of shields outside the palisade started once more.

The queen rushed away, and Safi kept her back to everyone for an extra moment. Once again, the Jotnari made the slow rhythm of noise meant to instill fear. Their sound turned steady, like a beating heart, and sped up as it had before. Rowena's pulse matched, wavering on her feet.

"I don't like this." Errol rushed up to join them after being absent to help Tuck.

"We should go," Liam said. "Let the kings lose their men."

Safi stood rigid. "Some of them were my men."

"They didn't rush to help you," Rowena pointed out. Goetz flashed into her mind. Loyalty didn't always go both ways.

Like it had before, the Jotnari rhythm came to an abrupt halt.

"This can't be good," Errol said.

"Agreed," Bram answered. "This is not a safe area."

Rowena spun, staring at him. "Do you know what's happening?" She wasn't sure what all his skills included. Perhaps he could see things others couldn't.

He didn't answer her question. "This way." He turned and stalked slowly away from the activity near the gates.

They'd casually made it around the side of a small home when a screech rang through the air, rattling the handle of a bucket sitting on a cart near Rowena.

"What was that?" Safi asked.

"Something that shouldn't be," Bram answered.

A dark cloud passed overhead, blocking out Sawel. It was odd —there were clear skies all morning, and there wasn't any wind to push a cloud that fast. Another screech came from the sky that was so loud Rowena covered her ears and ducked. She tilted her chin and witnessed a gigantic beast undulating a long tail. It made a wide, banked-turn in the distance.

Rowena stared, rooted to the ground, fascinated and terrified in equal measure. "What is it?"

"Hide!" Bram yelled.

He was afraid?

"Dragon!" he screamed out for all nearby to hear. He snatched Rowena's hand and dragged her under the cover of a thatched roof overhang.

THIRTY-TWO

The beast was unlike any other Rowena had seen. Massive enough to block Sawel from sight, it spread its wings. Each one was wider than the front gates of Velmeg, as it curved in a wide arc. With a flick of its long, spiked tail, it was back over the city. A dragon, Bram had called it.

The beast was snowy white with scales that blinded with an iridescent shimmer when Sawel's light touched them. Along its neck, it wore a ruff of plumage, like the collar of a cloak. Its large triangular head swung one way and then the next, mesmerizing bright pink orbs scanning the ground.

It was dangerous, yet brilliant and regal. Rowena couldn't tear herself away from it. Then it opened its mouth and screeched once more, a deafening sound that bore through her skull and rattled her teeth.

Fangs as long as Rowena's forearm glistened just before icy feet ending in talons sunk into the roof of a home, ripping it away. Confused and frightened, Telana rushed from the home, screaming. To where, Rowena didn't know. There was nowhere to hide from a creature like that.

It swooped low and the enormous jaws grabbed a goat from a pen, biting into the animal without slowing.

"We're not safe here," Liam said. "We have to get to the forest." He'd smashed himself against the rock wall on the other side of Bram.

Rowena peered around Bram, searching the other buildings nearby for Safi.

"She's across the way." Bram jutted his chin to where Safi and Errol had their backs pressed against the wall of another stone home.

The dragon flew low, whipping its tail between buildings two paths over. Rocks banged against each other, making a clattering sound like a mountain slide. Rowena's heart pinched as she remembered Hann. She drew into herself at the memory of a different rock slide. Hann's soft smile as he clung below her, propping up her foot so she didn't fall. He sacrificed himself to save her.

In the distance, she heard her name. Then Bram's face came into focus—his warm brown eyes piercing. Large hands cupped both sides of her face.

"Rowena!"

His voice broke her stupor, and with that came screams, panic, and destruction happening all around them. Bitter-cold air snapped at her skin, sprouting goosebumps. Her teeth chattered, and she wrapped her arms around herself. It was summer, it shouldn't have been so frigid.

Telana raced in all directions. Forced from their homes, they called out to loved ones. Some had ice clinging to hair and face, as if caught outside in a winter storm. Others had fallen, blue with cold, dead.

"How?" Rowena's frozen nose hairs prickled.

"The dragon spews an icy frost. We must stop it. Stay close to me." Bram scooted along the rough wall, keeping under the thatch as long as possible, until he raced to the next closest dwelling. Rowena stayed close, with Liam following.

Archers shot arrows, but they bounced off the scales like stones on a lake. One warrior stood his ground, sword held high and ready to swing at the feathered wings; eagle-like except for their size.

Before his blade moved, a stream of frost riddled with shards of ice and hail the size of goose eggs came at him. It hit the powerful Telana, not even giving him time to swing. His body turned a blue-gray to match the fallen stones scattered over the ground, encased in ice.

"Muriel and Tuck." Rowena whispered the names of her friends.

"Can you kill it?" Liam asked. The whites of his eyes showed all around the brown, even in the low light. A seasoned warrior, strong and skilled, begged for her help.

"It's too big—too strong." There wasn't any way she could face such a threat.

Liam exhaled and darted across to where Safi and Errol hid.

"To kill it will require higher ground." Bram scanned the area. "Stay with the others."

"I could help." Or perhaps not. That had to be what he was thinking. She'd nearly used all of her enchantment against Fidessa. He would probably change into his Seeker aspect and didn't want anyone around.

Bram tipped his head, studying the dragon. Its gigantic, feathered wings, so beautiful against the clear sky, brought such disaster. He startled her by spinning and holding out his hand, palm up. "We'll draw it to a less populated area."

She dragged her gaze from his hand to his face. He raised his brows, urging her to accept his offering. Without breaking eye contact, she lowered her hand into his. A sparkle filled his gaze that warmed through her.

Then they were off, dodging frantic mothers carrying screaming elflings, shepherds releasing their flocks to run free, broken carts and dead bodies. Bram dipped his hand to snag an abandoned blade, even though his sword remained on his back.

They sprinted to a pile of rubble that had once been a building and he dropped her hand so she could climb alongside him. At the top of their makeshift mountain, they stood as bastions for the city.

"I know what I said before, but if you have any enchantment left . . . use it. Every bit." He shoved the found sword into her hands. "You'll need more than that dagger."

She'd forgotten she still gripped the blade. It had been a comfort to keep her fingernails from digging into her palm. She shoved the smaller weapon under her belt and gathered the sword with both hands, waiting.

"Are you going to change?" She wasn't sure if she should ask or what to expect.

Bram glanced overhead. The dragon still flew away from them, following the palisade in a circle around the city. "I can draw some of my power without changing forms—I am a druid." He adjusted his feet among the stones. "I should not compromise my identity any further, if possible."

She understood, yet hadn't thought of the power he had to contain just as a druid. That had to be how he'd released everyone from Fidessa's spell. He'd revealed himself to her because she had a part in his duty, or so he believed. That responsibility superseded the trouble for only one city.

Her stomach plummeted, all confidence draining the moment the dragon screeched again. It had seen them and flew in a direct line to where they had made themselves visible targets.

Rowena lifted her sword, but remembered the warrior who died challenging the dragon. She bent at the knees and set the blade at her feet, lifting her hands instead. Better to use whatever enchantment she had left first. Perhaps the dragon wouldn't see her as a threat and she could strike.

The rubble shifted beneath Rowena's feet. She tightened her

stomach muscles to remain in place, envying a solid empty wagon not far off. It was a good idea to be on higher ground, drawing the dragon's attention away from the innocents darting around like fish in a pond. However, her enchantment flickered no brighter than the last bit of a sputtering candle. She had to do the best she could, and ignore the loose, broken stones to concentrate on the threat bearing down on them.

Those simmering pink eyes honed in on Rowena. The beast could sense that she was the weaker opponent. Her hair lifted from her arms, and her hands grew clammy. She forced herself to breathe only through her nose. In, slowly. Out, slowly. In, out. In, out. In, out.

The dragon dipped its chin, maw open, saliva oozing between its fangs. Rowena leaned away, twisting right to send a pulse of enchantment, aiming for the soft underside of the jaw. She missed and hit a scale on the side of the face, bouncing her power off at an odd angle. It had no effect. The dragon roared, tilting its head to peer where Bram lashed out against its side. Rowena thrust her hand out, summoning as much of her ability as she could. The blast hit underneath the mouth, between the jawbones.

With a huge downward thrust, the dragon snapped its wings, billowing dust and debris in its wake. Rowena leaned her face into her elbow, coughing. She bumped into Bram and lost her footing, tumbling off the pile.

"Rowena!" Bram shouted. The sliding rocks, crashing and bouncing off the mound, spoke of his efforts to reach her.

She held up a hand for him to stop. "I'm alright. Stay there."

Her back already stiffened from where a rock had jammed into her spine, and there were scrapes all down her arm—probably in more places that she'd find later. She stood, scanning the sky while she rolled her neck. The dragon wasn't in sight.

"Stay down there," Bram called. "We can squeeze it between us."

That was a good idea. Especially since she didn't think she

could effectively fight without better footing any longer. Her gaze snagged on the wagon. That would work.

"There it is." Bram pointed over her left shoulder.

She spun to find the beast aiming for them again. Rowena gritted her teeth and raced to the wagon, climbing into the flat back, hands up and ready.

Even with the solid boards under her feet, she felt wobbly. Her vision tunneled, forcing her to blink rapidly. She wasn't any help. Bram had been right to tell her to stay with the others. He'd almost left his position to help her. If he'd done that, he wouldn't have been able to fight off the dragon as it headed back toward them.

He had to stay focused, ignore her. The city's hope rested in him alone. She would do what she could, but it wouldn't be much.

As if the dragon either lost track of Rowena or knew she no longer posed a threat, the creature focused on Bram alone. He didn't waver, not a single flinch.

Bram raised his hands. No magic sparked or became visible, but the dragon's flight teetered, dropping like a stone in a heartbeat before catching itself. The beast shook its head, hovering. The massive white feathers on its wings beat wildly only feet from the tops of homes, creating enough force to blow apart the thatched roofs.

Rowena darted a glance around the ground and spied her lost sword stuck under rocks that had shifted when she fell. She slipped the dagger from her belt, the only weapon she had left. If she had any enchantment in reserve, it would be little help.

After a few moments, the dragon roared and resumed its flight, undulating slowly like it was swimming on a lazy summer day. The change of strategy sent a skitter of dread down Rowena's spine. Then, lightning fast, the dragon released a chilling frost. However, Bram had worked his enchantment. If that was what it was even called for a druid, the stream of snow and ice hit against an invisible wall, ricocheting outward.

Rowena ducked behind the sideboards, flattening herself as

close to the side of the wagon as possible. Her breath fogged and the wood at her back and under her body turned to ice, but she stayed immobile until the flow ceased.

She peeked over the edge, teeth chattering, to see the dragon's huge white back once again hovering, this time lower. The wings beat in a slow rhythm, with barely enough speed to keep such a humongous body aloft. It seemed to her. It still made a considerable breeze that made Rowena wish she had a cloak. She could no longer see Bram around the beast.

Instead, she had an up-close view of the sharp spikes lining either side of a center ridge, running from neck to the tip of the tail. It spread its elegant feathered wings wide. Like the scales covering the body, there was an iridescent shimmer that changed from blue to purple to pink. If it wasn't such a deadly brute, it would have been the most beautiful sight she'd ever viewed.

Rowena slid her gaze down the length of the tail, which swayed from side to side like a cat when it waited for the perfect time to strike its prey.

She brought her arm up, blocking the chilly air from her face, waiting. The dragon was so close to the wagon it could knock her over. So close. So close she could touch it. She stared, letting her mouth fall open with recognition.

Rowena swallowed a gasp, dropping back behind the sideboards, her feet sliding on the slick wood. Did she dare? Could her enchantment work on a beast? Influence was the easiest of her abilities to use and cost the least effort. If she could stop the destruction, to save the city . . . she had to try.

She licked her lips, gathered her courage, and peeked once more. There wasn't anyone to give her a signal. No one to confirm she did well. It was her decision and her consequences.

The dragon remained as it had been. If Bram had done something, held it in place with a charm, he might have been waiting for her to act. She had never spent time with Asta to learn about druids or the skills they possessed. Bram seemed to know a lot about how Lunara enchantment worked; he would know what Rowena could do. He'd also told her to use every bit of what she had available. There was no time to wait; she had to act right then.

The floorboards were still slippery, but more like a morning dew, with the frost melting and dripping through the cracks between planks to the ground below. To influence the dragon, she would have to touch it. It was possible to lean over the sideboards and reach the tail as it swung by, but she'd risk falling and alerting the beast of her presence. To touch it and hold on, she'd have to leave the safety of the wagon, risking that tail impaling her if the dragon startled.

She could hide under the wagon. Perhaps hold the tail from one of those spikes so it didn't slam into her, influence the beast to fly away and then drop and roll before it saw her. It was a good plan . . . if she lived through it.

It was her best option. She set her shoulders and rolled onto her stomach, easing her way toward the open back of the wagon. Her feet slid off the edge first and hit the ground softly.

The dragon's tail swung slow and steady, one way and then the other. She timed it through three cycles. When it reached the height of the arc farthest from her position, she sprinted around the corner of the wagon and waited. Her chest heaved. Her pulse pounded through her ears, too loud to hear if the dragon roared.

The long white tail halted at its peak, then glided her way. Rowena lifted her hands, ready to catch it like a rope. Except this would not end with a splash into a swimming hole. She would either influence a massive beast to leave the city—or die.

She waited until the tail reached its zenith and then grabbed hold of the final spike at the pointed end of the tail. The weight and momentum dragged her along with it as it rebounded the other way. For a moment, she lost hope, feeling nothing. It wouldn't work, but then . . . she wanted to cry. A profound sadness overcame her, though it wasn't her own. It was the dragon.

As Rowena skidded along, clinging to the spike as if she were a fly on a goat, she sensed the dragon's heart. It didn't want to be there. It didn't understand why there were so many trying to harm it. It wanted to go home.

Rowena thought of how she'd dreamed of Taesing when she first arrived in Forsa. She'd remembered every home, every face, and every trail of the village she'd grown up in, but over time, she'd forgotten. The memories faded, replaced by frustration and anger. She'd wanted revenge more than she wanted the freedom of home. She'd been naïve and arrogant, thinking of no one but herself.

"You don't have to stay here. You're free," she said, hoping the dragon could understand, or feel, or remember. "Go home to the White Fangs. Live without fear."

Her feet left the ground as the tail reached its apex on the far side. She held on tight, waiting to begin the next swing. Instead, the tail raised higher, snapping with a decisive blow. The dragon had discovered her presence.

Rowena flew, landing hard on her hip and shoulder. The air left her lungs and she could do nothing but gasp. The dragon let out an ear-piercing screech.

Despite her fight to breathe, tears formed, and Rowena prepared to die.

THIRTY-THREE

Rowena stared into the sky. It was blue for once after so many days of gray. It was a fitting day to be her last. Soon, she'd join her family and find out what the realm of Caelus was truly like.

The dragon screeched again, probably warning others away from its latest prey. She hadn't avenged her family. Hopefully, they'd understand. A cloud rolled by, white and brilliant, but it wasn't a normal cloud. It swayed and grew smaller. Rowena followed it as it faded from sight, and silence rained down over her. There'd been no cloud. The dragon had gone back to the White Fangs, like Rowena had told it.

A strangled laugh escaped her throat. Tears flowed down the sides of her temples into the dirt. She would live. It was the only thought that flowed through her mind until a handsome face came into her view.

"Rowena, speak to me," Bram said, his eyes brimming with worry.

Giggles continued as she stared at him.

"Where are you hurt?" He ran his hands lightly over her arms, checking for injuries. The mirth of her situation struck her, causing her to laugh harder until she had to roll to her hands and knees.

She inhaled and held it, forcing herself to slow. When she did, her senses returned and for a moment the tears fell out of relief, out of sadness, out of fear at how close she'd come to death.

A warm heat radiated from her lower back. The sensation grew more intense the longer she concentrated on it. After being so cold because of the dragon, she relished the heat. Except where did it come from? She gasped and arched her back, dislodging Bram's hand, crawling away.

"I'm not injured." It was a lie; she hurt in multiple places. It was too hard to choose which might be the most serious, but she would assess those later, on her own.

"There's blood running down the side of your face." He stared at her with those flecks of gold sparking. She mentally imagined the brown fading away to become molten crystals. She dropped her gaze to her lap, shutting out the image.

Rowena reached up to touch an aching spot inside her hair above her temple and winced. Her fingers came away red and sticky. "I must have hit my head."

"And many other places, I presume. That was not how I envisioned you'd use your abilities." A slight tug at the corner of her mouth sent a wave of tingles through her belly.

In the distance, crowds cheered. "What happened?" She gestured toward the noise, deflecting the conversation away from her battered body.

Bram leaned back, sitting on his heels. "I believe the Jotnari have retreated."

"Why? They could take the city without the dragon." She scanned the area. Piles of rubble, broken wood, and scattered thatch covered the ground. An entire pen held dead pigs, thawing from the dragon's frost. A huge gaping hole in the palisade showed the farmlands beyond. "There must be other spots like that?"

Bram lifted one shoulder, letting it drop with a sigh. "The

others will have to explain what happened." He rubbed the side of his face. "I hope you can see now that you are not ordinary. You are more capable of helping others than you've accepted."

Perhaps. Though she'd used the same skills her mother had. Any Lunara would have been able to do what she did. Wouldn't they? She'd only known two other Lunara—her mother and grandmother. "It doesn't prove that I'm the one from the prophecy."

"Perhaps not, but it shows that you're worthy of the Armor of Caelus. You care for others and protect them."

Of course, she cared for others. That was exactly why it wracked her heart with pain when she remembered those who'd died. Innocents who deserved to be protected, like Malia, the toddler from her village. And others tormented for no reason, like Muriel and Tuck.

"I've done as well as I can, but there are still those we must stop." She tried to move her legs to stand, but they groaned in protest. Instead, she scooted to lean her back against an upturned feed trough.

"It is one thing to bring justice, and another to seek vengeance. They are not the same."

Why was he speaking to her of all this now? Hadn't they just defeated a dragon and saved the city from a horde of giants? "My head does hurt, after all. Perhaps you can spare me your speeches until later."

"There will be others around soon. We may not have time to speak of these things. It's my duty to ensure the sword is in your hands, but you must use it with care. Allow yourself to move forward and forgive the mistakes made in the past."

"Mistakes? You believe it was a mistake that Goetz killed my father and blamed it on me? Or that Uther put me on trial, convicting me so I couldn't be queen? Was my time as a thrall—the beatings, the lashings, the back-breaking labor—all a mistake?" If he expected her to forget those injustices, that was his mistake. The more they spoke of things, the more she boiled inside.

"If you hadn't suffered in Taesing, in Forsa... here, the Jotnari would have won the day. The dragon would have destroyed Velmeg and most of those inside."

"Do not tell me that all those I love died so others can live. I will not accept that. The Jotnari wouldn't have attacked if I wasn't here." She clenched her fists until the knuckles of both hands turned white. "Isn't there an inherent vengeance in your duty? Your other form terrifies to force others into compliance. How can you expect me to forgive and ignore those who destroy innocents?"

His nostrils flared, and his lip curled to show his clenched teeth. "I am not an instrument of pain. You know nothing of how my form came to be. I am not the issue. My duty is to ensure the realm survives, not just one stubborn, insolent, prideful princess, no matter how skilled or intelligent or brave she is."

He'd scooted closer as he spoke, leaning nearer to her face. Her pulse pounded through her ears like a stampeding deer. She pursed her lips and matched his glare. His oak scent filled the space between them, spicy and warm. She swallowed, darting a glance at his lips. He leaned closer.

Footsteps pounded against the ground, and they parted with a start. Rowena's chest heaved, and she scanned the area for anywhere to look other than Bram. A moment later, she sat in a ring of shadows from those huddled around. Bram rose and stepped back, giving way for Safi to kneel next to her.

"That was amazing. You forced the beast to leave. How?" Safi untied the side of her protective brigandine as she spoke, tearing a piece of fabric from the hem of her tunic underneath. She dabbed at Rowena's head injury as if it were something she'd done before. "Many witnessed it. I'm not sure if they're more or less afraid of you now, but I'm thoroughly impressed."

"How did you charm it?" Liam asked from where he loomed overhead. "To make it stay still like that?"

Rowena remained quiet. She couldn't think straight. Bram had been so close, so angry, yet she wanted to kiss him. To feel his beard tickle her face. They'd survived a dragon attack, sending the beast flying away and taking the Jotnari with it. He'd battered her with talk of duty and justice, yet the way he'd surrounded her hadn't made her want to run away. Instead, she'd wanted to close the gap between them. What was wrong with her?

"I've never heard of a Lunara connecting with a beast before," Errol said.

Rowena blinked several times, clearing away her foolish thoughts. "I had nothing else left to try."

"We could see it hovering over the other buildings. How did you get it to stay still long enough?" Safi asked.

She hadn't. That had been Bram. "It was confused."

"That was something new." Conri startled them, jogging up with Hywel and maybe ten others. He slapped the back of Bram's shoulder, then scanned the group. He settled his gaze on Liam, who shook his head in silent answer.

Seamus had always been quick to smile. He'd also shown patience with Rowena when he and Liam gave her lessons. His death added another log to the fire burning inside for those she'd lost.

"It's good to see you," Safi said. "How did you get past all the guards?"

"They broke the palisade in many areas," Hywel said. "We shouldn't stay long since you're no longer in captivity."

"She's not going anywhere," King Lendan's voice came from around a corner before he appeared. Uther, Daenon, and several guards arrived with him.

Rowena grabbed hold of Safi's arm, getting help from her cousin to rise. When she regained her feet, she stood tall, only to have a buzzing sensation fill her chest. It was the same as she'd experienced before whenever the sword was near. Rowena scanned the newcomers, careful to appear casual. Until she found what she sought . . . hanging from Uther's belt. When she dragged her gaze up, her muscles straining against her skin to charge, he met her with a knowing sneer.

Uther had worn the Sword of Justice to taunt her. He'd had it the whole time. Some part of her had wondered if he'd been the patron who hired the Fianna. Obviously not, since he'd never lost it. Who else would have known about it? Daenon, but he stood next to Uther as if he had no cares at all.

"Is there something you want to say, Rowena?" Her uncle smirked.

"That is not yours."

He stared down at the blade hanging carelessly at his side. "Seems it is. Perhaps you should have paid your mercenaries better. Though, did they know you have no coin at all?"

"I hired no one. Now I'll have the satisfaction of taking it off your cold, dead body myself." She didn't have to turn to Bram to feel his disappointment. It rolled over her shoulders from where he stood behind her.

"What I want to know is why the Jotnari suddenly attacked after years of peace," Lendan said.

"Your charming personality?" Safi said. Bold.

"I will deal with your rebellion next," the Velmeg king said.

Uther slid a glance to Lendan. "That won't be necessary. Since the treaty is over, I'll deal with my daughter."

The King of Velmeg stiffened and narrowed his eyes. But instead of at Uther or Safi, he directed them at Rowena. She'd done nothing but help him. What could he find against her?

"You should be careful, Uther," Lendan said, continuing to pierce Rowena with his glare. "I might wonder if you brought this Lunara witch into my kingdom on purpose."

Witch? Rowena gaped. How dare he say such a thing? She didn't have time to set him straight before Uther commented.

"That wouldn't have done me much good to destroy the city

when our families were to unite. That would be like tearing down my house."

That finally broke Lendan's stare with Rowena. He stepped sideways, putting more distance between himself and the other two.

Daenon chose that moment to amble over to a barrel that had somehow stayed upright during all the turmoil. He hopped up and sat on it, finding the king's discussion entertaining, apparently.

"It's no matter who you marry to my son, you'll never have a claim to my kingdom. My son will never rule." Lendan pulled his shoulders back, glaring at Uther.

Rowena shifted her gaze to the prince. He'd been so arrogant that his life would change for the better when he returned home. It didn't sound like it was going to be what he hoped.

"I can agree with that. Perhaps I'll send him to Skandan with his new bride. Bring that island into submission." Uther remained casual, relaxed almost, as if he had no concerns.

"You?" Lendan settled his hand on the hilt of his sword. All around, the warriors from Velmeg and those of Ibern shifted, slowly moving toward their respective kings.

"Now would be a fine time for us to leave," Conri whispered.

"I couldn't agree more," Liam said.

Rowena didn't share their enthusiasm. She wasn't going anywhere until she had that sword away from her uncle.

"Me," Uther said. "Because I intend to be king of all Ibern and Skandan."

Lendan drew his sword, as did all of his men. Daenon jumped to his feet and armed himself as well. Though Rowena wasn't sure which king he'd side with.

It only took one of Uther's guards to shift his feet to kindle the fire that instantly roared to life. Both sides charged, erupting into chaos.

The Fianna turned to leave the kings to their mess, but a

contingent of Lendan's men had silently moved around to block their way. There would be no leaving Velmeg without a fight.

THIRTY-FOUR

Rowena still had her dagger, and she wouldn't let anyone down, but her energy waned. She wasn't ready for a tremendous battle yet after the dragon. Her enchantment had drained, leaving her without the smallest ability except to use her skills with a blade.

"A fight it is then," Safi said. Then she lowered her voice so only Rowena could hear. "We should try to get out of here the first chance we can."

"Fine by me." The faster they left Velmeg, the better for her. The hubris she'd had of thinking she could stand toe to toe against a sword had fled long ago. Now, without her enchantment as well, and only a dagger . . . she may as well lay down and let them slit her throat.

"Keep near to Safi and me," Bram said over his shoulder.

She grumbled under her breath. However, her head throbbed, and a cut on her arm bled again the first time she parried. It would be best to let the others do the heavy fighting. Except she wasn't about to stand around like some weakling. She kept herself on Safi's left, guarding her blind side. As Bram did for her. They became a circle of defense for each other.

The ten guards who'd come around behind them turned out

to be the King's Guard that Safi had led. Half of them had split off to battle the Fianna, but that didn't stop the rest of them from trying to kill their former commander.

"You can move along, you know. It doesn't have to be your day to die," Safi said to the guard she battled.

"Did you really think we enjoyed having an elfling lead us?" He spun around, trying to hit her back.

Rowena dropped low and swept her leg out, tripping the warrior. Safi sliced through his sword arm. It remained intact, but the gash exposed his bone and gushed blood, forcing him to drop his blade. It was a large cumbersome-looking thing, more for ceremony than actual fighting. She kicked it out of his reach.

Two more guards arrived to take his place. Rowena had to battle her own opponent, despite how she flagged. She braced herself to fight the best she could, lamenting they couldn't continue as a team.

"You think your skills are so complete," the next warrior against Safi taunted. "You were too blind to see how many of us coddled you."

His attitude reminded Rowena of the brute she'd fought during the King's Day celebrations before everything fell apart. What had been his name? Trying to recall it helped keep her mind off her pain, though the warrior slashing closer to her kept her occupied enough.

"I'm holding up fine against you," Safi said.

It was true. While Rowena had to retreat several steps, Safi had gained ground in her fight. It spurred Rowena to push harder. In the close quarters, the Velmeg guardsman used his dagger as well, making it a more balanced of a match. She internally chuckled at herself. In her battered state, it seemed easier for her to think of everything as just another competition. It gave her confidence and made her determined to win.

The oncoming warrior lunged, so Rowena side-stepped and stabbed toward his side. He was faster than she expected and he blocked her dagger. He shoved against her, forcing her to stumble backward into Safi.

"How does that work?" She stood over the man she fought as he clutched his arm to his side. "Did you earn Lendan's loyalty when you looked the other way each time he abused me? Do you think I owe you anything?"

Rowena had no time to hear more. The guard she fought charged and slashed toward her chest. She ducked low and swiped at his feet, knocking him off balance. He stumbled to the side, giving her a view of Safi as she slammed her blade into her opponent's neck.

The guard came at Rowena again, sneering. She spun and sliced into his back over a kidney. It didn't stop him.

He sneered at Rowena. "You're not as skilled as the commander, and we've been knocking her around for years. I'm just getting started with you." His words fired up her need to win. She glanced around and an idea formed. It ate at her pride, but would play into the dreg's opinion of her. She jumped back and dropped her arm, making herself vulnerable.

The guard hesitated, giving her a dubious look, but lunged closer despite his misgivings. He should have listened to his instincts, because she'd given way to Bram. He cut the man down in one blow.

The three of them stood, resting for a moment, taking in the battle.

Scattered, the Fianna engaged with either Lendan's or Uther's men. None of the two king's warriors fought together. No surprise. It had rattled her a little to hear the guards' hateful comments to Safi. They'd known what Lendan did, and not only did they ignore his behavior, they didn't seem to care how he hurt their commander. They'd held a grudge her cousin hadn't known about. Given the opportunity, they seemed to relish the chance to kill her in battle.

The pathways between the round homes of Velmeg were

always tight, but the dragon had destroyed so many. It forced the fighting into an open area surrounded by piles of rock, straw, broken wood, and even smashed pottery. It broke the battle into several smaller groups, which Rowena hoped would be in the Fianna's favor. But the crowded conditions required the groups to spread among the debris, making it harder to keep track of everyone.

Ten paces away, Conri fought two of Uther's men. The big man laughed, making it seem as if he was having a grand time. But a bruise bloomed on his cheek that Rowena could see even from her distance.

"Stay near Safi," Bram commanded, and sprinted away. She momentarily huffed at herself over how quickly she complied, scooting closer to her cousin. His intentions were to help, and she understood that.

Safi moved them next to an empty raised pen, probably for rabbits, so it would guard their back side. "How did you make the dragon leave?"

She huffed at her cousin's question. None of the fighting had bothered her. She spoke with a casual ease, though she seemed eager to hear the answer.

"Like I said before, it was confused. Only a scared animal trapped and looking for a way out. My abilities can influence emotions and I just had to tell it to go home. It seemed young."

The Jotnari had sent the dragon in to destroy the city, making it easier for them, but the beast hadn't wanted to be there. What had they done to control it in the first place? How did one capture a dragon and then insist that it fight for them? The beast had only wanted to go home. It hadn't been evil.

"I wonder where the dragons have hidden? No one has seen one for centuries," Safi said.

"Until now." The things Rowena had believed easy to decipher, the clarity between right and wrong, blurred.

Even Fidessa's anger and jealousy made some sense when she

faced Uther. Not that it excused her behavior or made Rowena feel sorry for her. It just muddled her idea of how easy it should be to figure out who told the truth and who told lies. Nothing was straightforward.

Everyone had secrets.

Uther had revealed his—he had the sword. His quest for power was nearly complete. He'd planned the attack on Taesing, her father's murder, and her capture. At least she had disrupted something... She'd never be a thrall again.

Rowena spun to Safi. "Muriel! I have to go find out if she's alright. What if?" She couldn't say the words, just pointed to the rubble from demolished homes.

"I was near the tower while you were speaking dragon. There's a lot of damage, but not much to the quarters surrounding it. The top of the tower is missing, but she was serving my mother, right?"

"Yes, but she had injuries. Fidessa wouldn't allow her to rest in comfort."

Safi snorted. "She wouldn't. But we can't risk leaving that way—I'm sure she's safe."

She couldn't be sure, and they both knew it. But her cousin was right. There was no chance to check on her friends. She had to pray that Osric watched over Muriel... and Tuck.

A guard from Velmeg and one from Forsa battled each other, unaware of how close they came to Safi and Rowena. One of them stumbled, waving an arm to keep his balance and accidentally hit Safi.

She startled him by kicking him in the back. He lurched forward into the other man. Then both turned to face the women.

"Rest's over," Safi said with a grin. "I'd rather be in the thick of it, anyway."

Her cousin relished the battle. Rowena had a much different view of fighting now than before; when all she'd ever done was train. She used to dream of the excitement, the glory. But in training, no one died for real.

She ducked out of the way of a club swung by a Forsan.

"I'll get a prize for bringin' you ta the king," the man said.

She shook her head, dodging out of the way of his hand. In trying to grab her, he'd let the club fall lower, leaving his entire side open. "If you want to earn the king's favor, you should be a better fighter." She shoved the dagger between his ribs.

From there, more warriors crowded closer. The fighting moving like a serpent, winding and writhing through the broken buildings.

Safi and Rowena moved together, careful to guard each other's weak side. At some point, Errol purposefully moved closer to Safi.

"You should take the princess and go. Head to the forest and we'll catch up when we can."

Safi scoffed. "Rowena is not so delicate as to need rescued, and I'm not leaving until everyone else is safely away."

She kicked her opponent in the gut, sending him sprawling.

"Why do you have to be so stubborn?" Errol called from where he dueled with one of Lendan's men.

Rowena dodged behind a barrel, frustrated that Errol's offer sounded appealing. Her strength was failing, but she would continue. She'd keep fighting until she fell.

"Let's go together," Errol called. "Leave now and never look back."

Odd. Rowena could see the stiffness in his leg as he feinted left and then right, fighting a man much larger than his lither frame. Did he fear what would happen to Safi if he fell?

Safi knocked the hilt of her sword into the head of a guard. The man stumbled backward and Rowena rushed up to slash her dagger across his arm. He dropped his weapon and ran.

"I'm not leaving, Errol. What's this about?" Safi didn't miss a strike, even as she grew more agitated with the pirate.

Errol grumbled, but one of Lendan's King's Guard attacked and forced him farther away.

Safi's speed and ferocity increased, but Rowena dug deep and kept up with her.

Bram battled in the distance. His skills were a sight to behold. Between him and Safi, she wondered how any of either king's forces still stood.

Rowena stumbled, falling to one knee. She rolled out of the way just as an axe rushed toward her skull. It buried in the dirt next to her. Still on the ground, she swung her legs into her attacker's knees. He lost his balance, falling. Rowena scrambled up and jumped on top of him, jamming her dagger into the side of his neck, and then stumbled off of him.

She turned and ripped the axe from the ground, searching for Safi. They fought in what would have been a wagon path, but there were so many bodies crowded around all the debris, she lost track of her cousin.

The hair on the back of her neck rose a moment later when she caught Fidessa's stare. The queen seemed fresh. Her hair was still bound in braids with a clean gown. What had drawn her out of safety to join the fighting? She pulled something out of a pouch on her belt and tossed it near a melee of several fighters. A little packet soared through the air and burst when it hit the ground. Three of the warriors crumpled to the ground immediately.

The mage had arrived, bearing charms.

THIRTY-FIVE

Fidessa threw another packet near where Errol fought. Safi screamed and charged toward the queen.

Engaged with one of Lendan's guards, Rowena couldn't follow. She tried to work her fight toward her cousin, but the dreg kept pushing her the opposite way.

It wasn't until she'd nearly stumbled around a tight corner that she realized her mistake. She'd been so focused on getting back to Safi that she'd allowed herself to be cut off from everyone else.

They locked all her allies in scattered battles, most that she could only hear.

"Ah, not as good as you think you are, then?" The warrior tipped his sword to rest the blade against his shoulder, unconcerned with how it left him vulnerable.

Because he wasn't. She had an axe and some ability to use it, but she couldn't reach him. He toyed with her because of his longer blade combined with a longer reach. That didn't mean she didn't have options. He hadn't defeated her yet.

"I wouldn't be so quick to judge." She had to stay on the balls of her feet, ready to force him to leave an opening.

"It's a shame, really. I expected a bigger challenge from a

Lunara witch." He brought his blade down hard and fast. Rowena barely got her arms up in time. The hooked end of her axe caught on the sharp blade to yank it off course.

"I'm not a witch. That's not even possible, you fool." She leapt backward and lifted the axe above her head to build momentum for her next blow. It didn't matter where she buried her axe into the fighter; it just had to slow him down. As long as the sharp edge of her weapon found his flesh, she'd be able to get away. Rowena lunged toward him, bringing the axe down.

Except her move didn't surprise him. He lowered his shoulder, twisted left, and smacked into her side. The blow sent her sprawling into the dirt. Her head hit the ground, reopening the wound above her temple. She sputtered, blinking away the sweat and blood, and rose to her hands and knees. A boot landed against her side, ripping all the air from her body. She fell, gasping, and clutched her arms to her chest as she blankly stared at the sky above.

A blade, glinting in Sawel's light, hovered at the edge of her vision, ready to slice through her. The Telana brought down his weapon. Rowena let out a cowardly whimper and squeezed her eyes closed.

But the blade didn't bite into her exposed neck. It stopped short, resting heavily against her pounding pulse.

Rowena snapped her eyes open, and the brute leaned closer, shadowing the daylight. "You're dead, princess. Not yet, but soon. It's by the king's orders you still breathe. We all know you're moon-born. An abomination from Mortus. You'll not be opening any more gates now."

The man yanked her to her feet and dragged her along, stumbling. Her mind swirled, desperate to understand what had happened. Muriel had told her that some thought she'd brought the Seeker into the city when Bram rescued her from the Jotnari. She wasn't sure how she'd explain that event without giving details of where she went—or with who.

There wasn't any reason for Uther to need her any longer. He had the sword. She'd unlocked it so he could apparently wield it. There wasn't anything left she could offer. Why keep her alive?

The brute shoved her through the crowded space, warriors sneering at her along the way. Blades still rang out at the edges. Her friends still fought for their lives. They should run, get away.

Dazed, she stared at her captor's hand bruising her arm. There were tattoos on his hand. Not runes, but a series of swirls. He was from Velmeg.

The crowd parted, and she was flung to her knees in front of Lendan.

"When Uther explained his plan, I expected better results," the king said, roving his gaze over Rowena with a curl to his lip as if she were diseased.

She rose, refusing to cower at him.

"It's hard to believe you're supposedly so valuable." He stepped forward, gesturing his hand to the guard who'd brought her. The man grabbed both arms, holding them behind her, while Lendan pinched her cheeks. He twisted her face one way and then the other, like she was an animal at the market.

The brute held her tight against him, making it impossible for Rowena to avoid Lendan's touch. Bile grew in her throat, but the guard had not thought of her feet. She waited until Lendan met her gaze, then stomped on the king's foot.

Quicker than a viper, the king backhanded her. The sting took her breath away and made her eyes water.

"You are despicable." Rowena would have spit on him if she didn't have spots crowding her vision. She didn't need to make herself seem any more pitiful than she already did.

"She's a handful, Father. I can assure you." Daenon sauntered closer.

Rowena did her best to control her shiver, but it was impossible with the prince so near and with what the king had done to Safi in her mind.

"I don't mind that." The king leered at her. She held her head high, mouth tightly pinched and her nostrils flaring from trying to keep her breathing steady. "Are you sure she's the one? Doesn't seem like anything special."

"She's the moon-born princess from Skandan. I was there myself," Daenon said. "I even confirmed she had gained her mother's enchantment. The prophecy says one of silver fire. That her Lunara abilities give off a silver light confirms it as much as anything."

"Well, then." Lendan twisted to Daenon. "Where's the sword?"

Daenon nodded and stepped closer to his father. "I survived in that Forsan hovel all this time, expecting that you must have had a reason for exchanging me for some half-wit girl."

The king tilted his head at an angle, casually resting his hand on his sword.

"Then when the druid told Uther she'd seen the way to restore Telana enchantment, I believed you so wise. I was there, learning all of Uther's secrets and he'd given me access to the greatest one of all. You'd welcome me home and together we'd take over Ibern. Then you said I'd never rule."

"You did your part in helping your kingdom. You'll have your reward." Lendan stepped over to lean against a broken wall. "You have done well."

"Are you proud of me, as your son?"

Rowena stilled, waiting. Daenon had been concerned about earning his father's approval when he attacked her in the cave.

"Did I not just say that?"

"I did well—that's what you said, yes—but am I not fit to rule?"

Lendan crossed his arms casually in front of himself. "There are many parts about being a king that you could not understand."

"Because you sent me away." Daenon's fingers opened and

closed into a fist. "You tossed me aside in some treaty that meant nothing. I tried to be everything you wanted."

"I have no need for anything that comes out of Forsa. We must sacrifice for the good of the kingdom. You served your purpose there and now that's done."

Daenon's eyes widened a moment before he answered. "Did you ever care for me?"

"Don't be a child. Learn to distinguish the difference between politics and the truth." The king's cruelty came out in such a smooth tone. Chills rose along Rowena's arms.

"I'm your son. A prince; the future king."

"You are nothing to my kingdom." Lendan's glare could have sliced his son in two had it been a sword.

"Well . . ." Daenon scratched at the sparse beard he had. "I suppose we'll both agree on one thing—I've been a fool, idolizing you, planning vengeance against Uther on your behalf. I guess I'll just have to take over for myself."

During the entire exchange, the guard holding Rowena had gotten more focused on the men and didn't pay attention to her. His grip had gone lax.

Lendan drew his sword. "My King's Guard needs a new commander. I can find you a position of power, if that's what this is about."

Daenon tilted his head as if he considered the offer. "I have another position in mind."

A knotted ball formed in Rowena's gut. There was only one way this conversation would end. The king's dismissive attitude of Daenon, treating him as if he had no value, would fuel his anger. It had done that to her when Fidessa forced her to be a thrall. That she could relate to the prince left her cold inside. She shoved that thought aside for later. Rowena twisted her toes, slowly digging into the soil for leverage for what was about to come.

"Soon, Uther will fall. All of Ibern will be under one crown." Daenon smirked and drew his sword. "Mine."

Rowena threw her head back, cracking her skull against her captor's chin, then used the leverage she'd created to leap free of his hold. Metal hissed along metal as father and son fought each other.

Unsure of whom to support, guards formed a ring around the two, allowing Rowena to race away unhindered. The rough ground tripped her more than once. She grabbed hold of a post that must have been the corner of an animal pen and flung herself around the corner. Straight into Safi.

The two hurtled to the ground.

Safi cried out, then grumbled. "I was coming to find you."

"Daenon fights the king." She pushed herself to a sitting position, wincing from another set of bruises.

"Which one?" Safi rose and offered a hand.

"Lendan."

"Interesting." She glanced over her shoulder, nibbling the corner of her mouth as her eyes narrowed in thought.

"Where's Fidessa?" Last time Rowena had seen the queen, she'd been throwing charms into the midst of the battle.

"She ran out of her little tricks and ran off." Safi seemed to snap out of whatever she contemplated. Rowena hadn't missed how she'd flinched and covered her arm at the sound of her mother's name. "We should, too."

"I need to find Uther." There was no way she'd leave before getting the sword.

Though the hate billowing off the two men she'd just escaped from needled at her. Lendan was a horrible individual, and he deserved to die for what he did to Safi, if nothing else. But that would be an execution based on crimes he committed. Those were facts, not feelings. Daenon acted as she wanted to. If she'd had her way, she would have already killed Uther, Fidessa, and the prince.

What would she have done after learning what Lendan did to Safi? She was her family. Where would her vengeance end?

"There's more fighting this way." Safi pointed in a direction away from where Daenon and Lendan battled.

She pointed toward the king's tower, closer to Daenon and Lendan, but it made sense that Uther would be there. He wouldn't have bothered to traverse through the narrow, filthy pathways. He wouldn't care how anyone suffered. There were two destroyed homes near them. Rowena pictured families huddled inside to avoid the fighting and then becoming trapped under the stone rubble. When the fighting was over, there would probably be more. Whoever was king afterward wouldn't care.

The direction she chose also led them away from where Safi and Fidessa had fought last. There was more to that.

"How's your arm?" Rowena called as she hurried behind her cousin.

"It's nothing, just a little scratch."

Sure. That was what she would expect Safi to say. "Did she hit you with a charm?"

Safi skidded to a stop and slumped before turning around. "I hesitated. She's supposed to be my mother. I can't kill her. A guard died with her next charm packet. He'd be alive if I had done what I should have."

"It's not as easy as it sounds." Rowena stared into space for a moment. "To kill someone, I mean."

"It's just that, I have. Lendan made sure of it." Safi rubbed the spot on her arm where she said had a scratch. "It was a requirement for becoming commander."

Rowena waited, but movement up ahead made her glance over Safi's shoulder.

"We should talk later."

"There's someone ahead." Rowena wanted to stay there and talk about what happened. Safi was the first friend her own age she'd felt so comfortable around, despite how most of their time together had been in battles. Not since Hann . . . "When this is over—"

"Yeah."

Rowena squeezed Safi's hand, careful to choose the uninjured arm.

They could hear shouts and blades hitting against metal and wood, but they didn't come upon anyone until they reached the front near the gates. They stuck close to the tower, which had somehow remained mostly unscathed, and peeked around to the front. The large double wooden doors had splintered, with only a partial section hung from one side. Otherwise, the open bailey in front of the tower had wood shards covering the hard-packed soil.

One guard tower had fallen completely, and the other one teetered on the verge of collapse. A section of the palisade had crashed down wide enough for a full wagon to drive through.

Two separate battles took place. One group comprised four of Lendan's men fighting against each other. "It seems like allegiances are shifting."

"Agreed," Safi said. "And we can't get caught in the middle of this."

In the center, Uther stood against his own men. Three of them circled him like a pack of dogs. Rowena's stomach threatened to revolt. Her uncle called insults to the men who used to fight for him, but it was the sword held high that drew Rowena's notice. Uther fought with the Sword of Justice.

The blade was simple from so far away. It didn't seem like anything special, and it was clean. Uther hadn't used it against anyone yet. Rowena had to get to him before he did. If Bram was correct, and she had been the one to unlock it, then she could be the reason for the entire realm falling to the King of Mortus.

THIRTY-SIX

Rowena scooted closer to get a better view.

"What are you doing?" Safi whispered, grabbing her arm.

She twisted to face her cousin. "That sword cannot be used to kill someone. I'm not sure what would happen if it draws blood at all. I have to get it."

Safi gazed around her. "How do you know?"

Rowena wasn't sure how to answer. She gave as few details as possible about what Bram had explained, hoping her cousin didn't ask too many questions. "I was told."

"By your mother?"

The question caught her off guard. If only Mor were there, so she could speak to her, ask questions, and get advice. That would help with so many things. But she wasn't. "No."

"I'm sorry."

Rowena stared at Uther, at the sword, and at the broken gates. It was all too much. "He can't have that. It's the only thing that matters right now."

Safi blew out a heavy sigh. "We don't have a lot of choices. Any way we go, we're exposed."

It was true. Uther stood in the middle of the bailey, with

guards between their position and his. Sawel was at her zenith, shining brightly overhead. There wasn't time to wait for shadows to hide in.

Rowena blew out a huff. "I could distract him. Go straight out there while you slip through the palisade and come around from behind."

"I'd only end up engaging the guards. We need to get there before they stop dancing around." Safi raised her shoulders. "They're moving closer to the break in the palisade."

Rowena released a long exhale. "If we could climb the rubble, we'd have the higher position." It's what had helped against the dragon.

"We could use the height to ambush them." Safi nodded, keeping her gaze on the fighting.

Rowena squeezed her cousin's arm as the signal to go and then sprinted for the broken wall near the left watchtower, but ten paces into their run, the doors to the tower opened, and Fidessa sauntered out.

Rowena wasn't sure if she grabbed Safi first, or the other way around, but they both skidded to a halt, drawing notice from everyone in the bailey.

For a moment, both battles went silent. Rowena bounced her gaze from Fidessa to Uther.

"I'll take the queen. Get to the sword." Safi spoke in a low tone for only Rowena to hear.

She gave a shallow nod.

Safi sprinted straight for Fidessa and, a heartbeat later, Rowena raced toward her uncle.

Those fighting against Uther turned toward Rowena. They hesitated, glancing among themselves. It made sense they'd wonder if she was coming to help them or Uther. The wise bet would be to stop her, and she couldn't allow that.

The air all around the courtyard weighed heavily with the stench of death and dung, forcing Rowena to control her gag reflex and keep her mouth closed. Splintered gates, scattered rocks, and the bodies of several goats and one baurun littered the ground, and hindered her pace.

Rowena twisted her ankle, stumbling, but she kept upright. She could climb onto the baurun, use it like they'd planned to use the rubble, and jump off of it. Even if she only knocked a guard down, it would provide a small amount of time.

Her plan didn't matter, however, because at the same time she reached the dead animal, the ground shook and a sound exploded so loud it rattled the remnants of the gate. Rowena's shoulders pulled back and her chest arched out like something had hit her in the spine. Then her feet left the ground, and she sailed into the closest fighter.

They both tumbled to the ground. Disoriented, Rowena's ears rang. All other sound was only a jumbled warble, like she was underwater but less distinct. The guard slumped over her legs, and she shoved at him, but he didn't move. She heaved harder until he slid away, leaving a bloody trail on her trousers.

Rowena rubbed her hands over her thighs and knees. She had cuts and bruises, but not enough for what covered her. It wasn't her blood. She shoved the man with her feet, rolling him onto his back. His open eyes stared at the sky, glassy and lifeless, his own axe stuck in his chest. It must have happened when he fell. Still sitting on the ground, she scanned the area. Everything seemed to move at half-speed.

Two of Lendan's men who'd been fighting in the bailey also stumbled around as if they'd had too much ale. The other two were motionless on the ground. More fighters poured around the corner. The clanging metal of their weapons was distant in her ears. She couldn't keep up with their speed, and it made her nauseous.

She forced herself to focus. One of the new arrivals was Daenon, and the other was Lendan. They continued to battle, but other guards flowed in after them. Where were Uther and the sword? She rolled to her knees. There, closer to the front gates, Uther struggled to his feet. The last remnants of the broken gate crashed down, creating a cloud of dust. It rolled over her uncle and billowed into her face. She grabbed her tunic, hiding her mouth and nose, but she still coughed violently. Sound crowded out the ringing in her ears, bringing with it the shrieks of battle.

Halfway to her feet, someone hauled her the rest of the way and spun her around. She blinked rapidly to steady her vision and to keep from vomiting, only to have Bram's wild-eyed gaze meet hers.

"Are you injured?"

She shook her head and wiggled out of his hold. "The blood is not mine. Uther? Where is he?" She'd lost track of the king and the sword in the dust cloud.

Bram swiveled to the left and then the right and pointed. "There."

Rowena trailed her gaze to where he pointed. Sure enough, Uther clambered toward the front door of the tower. Bram kept hold of her hand as they raced away. She wanted to pull away, advance on her own, but dizziness still washed over her and she appreciated the help.

Uther ducked inside, still holding the sword. Next to the doors, Conri leaned against the stone awkwardly, unnaturally stiff. He didn't even try to stop the king.

Bram redirected them the Fianna's way, but Rowena slowed, leaning away so her hand pulled out of his.

"What is it?" Bram asked.

"Uther has the sword. We have to get it back." Rowena glanced at Conri and then the door.

"We will, I promise, but Fidessa spelled Conri. It could be dangerous for him to remain stuck for long. If he's not breathing, or if his heart has stopped beating, he'll die. I have to counter it." Bram's eyebrows narrowed as he waited for her answer.

"If Uther sheds blood, you said it could mean the realm would fall." She slid her foot closer to the door.

"As it will if you do the same. If you wrest the sword from him, you must not take vengeance."

She swept her gaze around the bailey, taking in the destruction and the mayhem. There were so many fights, and for what? Some served Lendan, some Uther. The Fianna served themselves. Bram served the realm—and she had to as well.

While she took in all the madness, she watched Daenon knock his father to the ground, and a moment later, he slowly shoved his sword through the king. That was what she'd envisioned doing to Uther countless times, but to see the prince take his revenge, it shattered her exalted idea of victory.

"The king is dead," she whispered, tipping her head for Bram to follow her line of sight.

"We must help Conri first and then find Uther."

Her instinct was to defy him, to rush headlong through the doors and find her uncle. To kill him and make things right. That was what she'd always believed his death would do. But in reality, her adherence to such a self-righteous position held herself in bondage, far more than when she was a thrall.

Uther and Fidessa had destroyed her life, and they deserved to face justice—by an executioner. A strong queen didn't take revenge; she held proper trials with fairness and served appropriate punishment. That was what those in Taesing would respect and accept her once again.

Daenon stood over his father, no longer the prince, but the king if anyone would follow him. He'd killed his father in combat; most would deem that understandable. Only someone with equal power could stand against his claim.

"This is not right. I can't let my realm continue to suffer." She raised her chin, eyes stinging with tears she held back, and met Bram's gaze. "I must become queen. It's the only way to keep both islands safe. If we lose the sword, all of this disaster will flow over to the continent and beyond. We can't let that happen."

Bram smiled a true and beautiful smile that raised his cheeks and crinkled the lines next to his eyes. "You are already the queen. I will help Conri—you find Uther. Guard yourself and I will meet you inside. It's not only the sword that's important, but the one who holds it as well."

He didn't wait, but spun and sprinted to Conri, trusting her to do the right thing. Whatever it took to secure the sword—all pieces of the separated Armor of Caelus—she would do it. She set her shoulders and strode to the tower doors.

THIRTY-SEVEN

Such a difference one day could make. The night before, the large feast hall had seemed overly crowded and too warm. Rowena had strolled her way to the other side of the room, unnoticed, to stand behind Fidessa. If Seamus hadn't intervened, she would have killed the queen and possibly the prince as well. Now another friend and King Lendan were dead instead.

High in the wall, a hole exposed a ray of light streaming into the otherwise dark space. Dust motes floated in an angle to the floor and hid the cavernous room's edges in darker shadows.

Eerily quiet in its emptiness, the room had no fire that burned. Tall candlesticks lay scattered on their sides, and benches had toppled over. If she didn't know better, it would seem like the remnants of an exuberant night of feasting. She edged farther inside, lifting her hand to shield her eyes, and peering into the darkest spaces.

Something... no someone, sat on the far side, saying nothing. Mutely, they watched her.

"Who's there?" She hoped they couldn't hear the tremble that rolled through her. Rowena would fight if she had to; she still had the axe hanging from her belt.

No answer. They continued their silent vigil.

"I'm trying to figure if you're brave or witless to enter alone," Uther said from behind her.

Rowena spun to face him, the hairs on her neck rising from turning her back on the other threat. "Come closer and find out."

Her uncle strolled through the room, stepping over an iron candlestick and stopping near the cold ashes in the central hearth. His tunic had torn at the shoulder and dirt covered his hair, making him appear more beggar than king.

"I'll concede that you're tougher than I gave you credit for. A month as a thrall hasn't dimmed your spirit in the least." He relaxed his stance, fingers tapping on the sword's hilt on his hip. "You've become so much more of a bother."

"Give me my family's property and I'll leave." As it always did, her blood sizzled within such proximity to the Sword of Justice. The sensation rushed through her like a thousand angry bees, stinging the underside of her skin.

"Have you not figured it out yet? He can't part with it because of her," Fidessa said.

Rowena twisted sideways, keeping her uncle in her periphery while she assessed the new threat. Rowena's back was to the broken wall and her vision had adjusted better to the low light, which helped her recognize her aunt. She'd gotten herself caught between the king and queen. But her gaze snagged on the silent form next to Fidessa—Safi sat on a chair, with a blank expression.

Her cousin didn't move, didn't blink, didn't speak. Fidessa reached over and ran her hand over Safi's head, tucking in a wayward hair behind her pointed Telana ear.

"What have you done to her?" Rowena's fists clenched, but she stayed rooted in place. Safi appeared the same as Conri had. Bram had feared the gregarious Fianna leader would die if he didn't release him quickly. Would Fidessa be that cruel to her own daughter? A shiver rolled down Rowena's spine.

"Let the girl go, Fidessa," Uther called in a flat tone. He seemed more annoyed than concerned. His attitude wasn't surprising. Nothing but power mattered to him.

"She's my daughter. You kept her away from me all these years. It's little wonder she can't see how much I love her."

"If that were true, you wouldn't force her to stay against her will," Rowena shook her head, remembering her own mother. The way she'd brushed her hair and plaited it their last night together. "You'd rather her sit dying at your side than live as she desires."

"She's not dying," Fidessa spat. "She needs time to adjust. Soon she'll understand I'm doing what's best. Her father has robbed us of so much."

"Your sensitivities are exhausting," Uther said. "She's a capable warrior. It would be better for her to serve as your guard rather than your pet."

Rowena struggled to grip whether Uther defended Safi for her sake or just to berate his wife. She'd place her coin on the latter.

"She'll understand!" Fidessa shrieked. "There is no world where I can exist that she does not. Not any longer. It's because of your dealings that she hasn't learned her correct place. She battles because she is confused. You will not take her from me again. She'll understand."

"And Dacnon? How does he fit into your plans? Do you think he'll continue to bind himself to you if Safi is available to him?"

Rowena's stomach rolled. The idea of Fidessa and Daenon together as a couple made her queasy because her aunt was so old. But the idea of Daenon touching her cousin, using her as his father had done, made her burn with the desire to slice the prince's throat.

Caught between the warring couple, Rowena wasn't sure which way to go. Uther had the sword and she couldn't allow him to leave with it. Fidessa held Safi within a charm that could drain her life away, despite what her aunt claimed. She slid her foot back. If she moved out of the light, she'd move against one of them unseen.

"Stay put, Rowena," Uther said.

"Isn't this cozy?" Daenon said, sauntering into the hall. "Is this a summit I wasn't aware of?"

"The king is dead, then?" Uther asked.

"Of course not. He stands here, ready to negotiate a treaty with you. Isn't that the expectation?" Daenon smirked and ambled closer to Rowena. "But who will we use this time to seal the deal?"

"Have you truly killed your father?"

Uther and Daenon spun to face the newest occupant of the room. Rowena tracked Queen Dewan as she slowly left the cover of the stairs to face her son.

"Fathers don't toss their sons away, leaving them to rot."

The queen stopped at the edge of light and folded her hands in front of herself. Rowena could see the lines etched in her face and the way her mouth quivered to stay firm.

"They promised me visits. Once per year at a minimum." She sighed, keeping her head high and gaze on Daenon. "It was a lie."

"That you did nothing to correct." The prince—king, Rowena corrected herself—had such venom in his tone. Like Fidessa, Dewan wouldn't have had any choice.

"It was out of my power to change. So, I did what I hoped was being done for you. I loved the girl in my care. Safi is a fine young woman, full of spirit." Her lips tipped into a tight, mirthless grin. "I'm sorry, my son."

"I did not mistreat him," Uther said. "I gave him power and position, and if you ask my wife, he had much love."

"Do not mistake my patience with meekness, King Uther," Dewan said. There was a low, menacing tone to her words that Rowena wouldn't have guessed she could muster. She could like this queen. "They were children in our care. We all share blame for the tortures they endured."

Fidessa huffed but said nothing.

Daenon let out a mocking laugh. "I assure you, mother, my

choices have been my own. Uther is weak, not worthy of what he has."

"Well," Dewan flattened her lips, her eyelids fluttering for a moment before she resumed. "I am sorry, none-the-less."

Commotion at the door brought in Bram, Conri, and the rest of the Fianna. They rushed into the room, stopping short to assess the situation. Other warriors followed, filtering through the door and blocking the exit.

"Are you well, Rowena?" Bram asked.

"You should never have inserted yourself into Ibern matters, traveler," Daenon said. "Or is it you've taken a liking to the taste of thrall?"

An angry scoff left Rowena's throat before she could stop herself.

Bram strode slowly toward Daenon. Others may not have noticed the way the shadows wavered, but Rowena did.

"There are consequences for what you've done," he said.

Daenon waved his hand in dismissal. "Take her. She's not worth the argument. I have more important things to deal with."

Bram clenched his fist at his side. For all his talk of patience and forgiveness, he seemed on the verge of tearing Daenon's head from his shoulders. She wouldn't have minded. Though she wasn't sure what caused his anger. It couldn't be because of what happened in the cave. She'd never confided in him about that. It had to be because of his Seeker duties on her behalf.

"This isn't your concern. As much as it pains me, I agree with Daenon." Uther stood taller, feet wider apart and ready to spring into action if the situation required it. He pulled the sword free. "This isn't much of a blade, plain leather around the hilt and missing a jewel, but well balanced."

Rowena became dizzy. The restless itching became unbearable. The sword was hers. She had to take it. She didn't remember pulling the axe free, but her fingers gripped the handle tighter. Her chest heaved and her vision tunneled. Nothing else mattered. She charged toward Uther. Her voice broke free, screaming.

Uther shuffled backward, raising the sword high. At the edge of her sight, she witnessed Bram sprint toward Daenon, but she had only one focus.

Uther brought the sword down in a swift arc. Rowena twisted to avoid getting hit. The blade couldn't draw blood. She lost her footing and tripped over a fallen candlestick. The sharp metal pierced through the outside of her thigh. She grunted and rolled to her knees, covering the wound with her free hand.

Uther kept still as she pushed herself up, hopping on one leg until she could settle some weight onto the injured one.

"You're so determined. Just like your mother." Uther shook his head. His face washed in a dreamy, faraway expression. "It's true that I loved her. I've never denied it. When you were born, I'd watch her hold you and wish it was me sitting beside her. That you were my child."

The idea disgusted Rowena. She hated hearing him speak of her mother or dishonoring her father. Yet a twinge of pity filtered through her. "You've wasted your life wanting someone who would never love you. You've chased power to prove your worth, but that wasn't what my mother valued. Honor, integrity, kindness. Those were qualities she admired in my father."

Rowena scanned the room. More guards had entered the hall, lining the walls with the Fianna, watching the royals battle themselves. Daenon still fought with Bram near the fire pit in the center, though it seemed he only preoccupied the newly declared king, unwilling to kill him. Fidessa had moved closer, but Dewan had disappeared.

Rowena let her arm hang. The axe scraped against the wooden floor. "I won't kill you, but you're no longer king."

Uther quirked a corner of his mouth into a wry grin. "That's not for you to decide."

"I am Queen of Skandan, and I declare you an outlaw, unfit to rule. Hand over the sword and I will allow you to go free." She didn't have the authority to strip his crown, but if the warriors around the room thought she did, perhaps she could convince them to hold him for her. She wasn't close enough to take the sword by force, and her leg made it too difficult to fight him for it.

Movement in the shadows at Uther's side caught her eye. A moment later, blood seeped through Uther's tunic right before a blade emerged from where someone had shoved it through his back. Uther stumbled a step, then two. The sword dropped from his grip, clattering and bouncing out of reach. When her uncle reached out, she caught him as he crumpled, falling with him to the floor and revealing Errol holding a bloody dagger.

"You look so much like her." Uther wheezed and coughed, his throat gurgling. Then he went silent.

"What have you done?" Rowena held her uncle's body, shocked.

"Fulfilling his contract," Daenon said, from behind her. "Once a scoundrel, always a scoundrel."

A pouch sailed through the air, caught by Errol, jingling with coin. He stared at his hand and glanced over his shoulder at where Safi sat, oblivious to everything. He turned back, his eyes closed for a moment. When he opened them, there was a cold resolve. "There might have been hope for me, once, but a deal is a deal, and I made my choice. Coin is the only true justice."

In a heartbeat, he slid into the darkness and disappeared.

"You'll not get far!" Conri yelled from where he stood on the far side of the room.

Soft footsteps approached, and Rowena glanced up to see Fidessa staring down at her husband. There was resolution and a hint of sadness in her dry gaze. "You weren't supposed to die."

"Fidessa," Daenon called. "It's better this way. We can rule together."

The queen turned and picked up the sword, ignoring Daenon.

Stuck under Uther and hindered by her injury, Rowena couldn't reach Fidessa. "Do not touch that."

Fidessa turned to stare at Safi. Conri, Hywel, and Liam had moved closer, standing between the queen and her daughter.

"I waited for you, promised that when you returned, all would be well. We'd rule both Ibern and Skandan, all of us together." She spoke to Safi as if no one else was in the room or that she didn't have her daughter bound, speechless. "But you turned on me, too. I deserved so much more."

"We will rule together, my love," Daenon called out.

Fidessa moved her gaze to Conri and lifted the sword. "Since you didn't deliver, this cancels our contract."

Rowena gasped, staring at the Fianna. She'd worked with them to find the sword for the queen?

"Fidessa?" Daenon sounded pitiful.

The queen once again turned her gaze on Uther. "You were my true love. If only you would have loved me back."

A wind blew through the broken wall, whipping around the circular room while Fidessa muttered words under her breath. Bram yelled something, but Rowena covered her eyes from the dust, creating a howling whirlwind between her and Fidessa.

In an instant, the swirling funnel dropped silently to the floor.

The queen and the sword were gone.

THIRTY-EIGHT

For several long moments, no one moved. Bram stood ten feet away from where Rowena sat underneath Uther's body. Shadows shifted behind him that could have been from the commotion Fidessa caused, but Rowena understood differently. Bram's fists were curled tight and behind him, the darkness rippled as if he barely kept it from filling the room.

His duty was to find and keep the Armor of Caelus protected. He'd failed and Rowena didn't know what that would mean—for him, for her, and for all the others standing in the room.

"The king is dead. The queen is gone," one of Uther's men said. He swung his gaze between Daenon, Uther's body, Rowena, and back to Daenon. "What are we to do?"

Bram spun and strode closer to the man. "You are going to decide for yourself who you'll follow. Choose carefully, because you don't want to be on the wrong side."

"Queen Dewan remains," a guard from Velmeg called. "Our duty is to her."

Several of Uther's guards peered around, seeming to weigh their odds. Two near the door ducked away. That created a stream of others who followed. Those who stayed remained at the edges of the room, unsure what to do next.

Rowena could understand since she was of the same mind. Her insides felt hollow. Fidessa had taken the sword, somehow disappearing without a trace. It had to be trickery, but not even Bram suggested how to find her.

"This is all your fault," Daenon hissed between clenched teeth.

Rowena ignored him at first.

"She is a powerful mage. We had a plan. Then Uther brought you here." He'd moved closer.

Rowena yanked her arm out from under Uther and rolled him to his side. Between her blood-soaked tunic that stuck to her skin and the coppery scent, she gagged and held the back of her hand under her nose for a moment. She struggled to her feet and glared at Daenon. "I did not come here by choice. You invaded my home under the pretense of friendship."

Sweat rolled down the side of her face, and her eyes shuddered. It had been a long day, and her body had reached the limits of abuse it could take.

"I have never been your friend." Daenon chuckled. The menacing sound created goosebumps on Rowena's arms. "Like Hann, that . . . What did he call me? Unsket? I told him what I'd do to you before I let go and watched him fall to the rocks below. I wonder if anyone ever searched for his body?"

Rowena stumbled. He'd already told her about how he'd killed Hann. But it was one thing to know, and another to find out how he'd made her friend suffer even more. Memories of that horrible day flooded her mind. Tears rolled down her cheeks.

Daenon rushed over and kicked her thigh where the candlestick had created a deep gash. Rowena screamed out, unable to hold back her pain.

"You aren't even worth finishing what I started in that cave."

A roar echoed through the hall. Shadows billowed and grew in a frenzy of swaying columns. The Seeker strode from the room's center directly for Daenon.

A smile stretched across Rowena's face, even as her tears continued. Her heart thumped a wild, excited rhythm.

"You will not touch her ever again." Bram loomed over the new king, his horns glittering even in the shadows.

Daenon scrambled backward, then halted and stood his ground, though his chest heaved.

All around the room, seasoned warriors had the sense to either flee or press back as far as possible.

"So, the traveler is really the dark druid, the Seeker. All you've shown is that you're no mystical beast. You're a man who can die."

Rowena's jaw dropped open. The audacity to challenge the power Bram displayed didn't show bravery but utter stupidity.

Daenon swung his sword, only to hit shadow as the Seeker gracefully slid out of the way.

"You are no match for me. You're nothing but a bug to squash under a boot. Leave while you still can." The low timber of the Seeker's voice would chill anyone's blood. From the pale faces of those remaining in the hall, it had.

Rowena stood and picked up the axe. She forced her shoulders back and limped to Bram's side.

Daenon's confident expression faded. Faster than anyone could see, Bram closed the gap between them, punching Daenon so that he flew backward and landed on his arse.

"Get up," Bram growled.

Daenon scrambled backward like an awkward crab, leaving his sword. He made it to his feet and raced away. Coward.

Except he sprinted to Safi.

"Leave her alone!" Rowena threw the axe and tried to run after him. Her leg gave out, and she fell to one knee, gasping to catch her breath.

The axe hit the ground and skittered away. Daenon grabbed Safi's arm, forcing her to stand. She complied without expression.

Her eyes remained open but unseeing. What spell did Fidessa create that left someone like that? Rowena could only hope that Safi didn't know how much she seemed like a sleeping puppet.

Hiding behind her cousin, Daenon regained some of his overconfident persona. He pulled Safi so that her back leaned against his chest and brought a knife to her throat.

"Since you're so all-powerful . . . bring me the sword before Masah is full again, or Safi dies. If she lives that long—who knows what spell Fidessa used or what it will do?"

Daenon dragged Safi backward, yanking back a tapestry to reveal a hidden door. The two of them disappeared.

"Find him!" Bram ordered to no one and everyone. Both Lendan's and Uther's guards scrambled to comply. He turned to Rowena, but something over her shoulder made him still.

Rowena twisted to see Yralissa approaching from the stairs. The druid ignored Rowena and strode up to the Seeker.

"You shouldn't have returned."

THIRTY-NINE
BRAM

Bram studied the disavowed. Her audacity to approach him gave him pause. It would make sense that the Heptad would have had spies in place, yet they didn't know he'd be in Skandan. The route he'd taken through Penumar to the northern islands wasn't easy to follow. Not that he'd been evading anyone. Yralissa had a different purpose, but he wasn't sure yet what it was.

"I am not beholden to you." He intentionally dropped his voice to a low growl and stretched his shadows closer to her. He held no obligation to any druid other than those on the council.

"It will upset The Heptad to learn you've concerned yourself with Telana kingdoms," Yralissa said.

He sauntered closer to the woman, forcing out more of his power. Yralissa trembled, though she clenched her hands and raised her chin, trying to hide it.

"I am dedicated to my duty." He locked her in his gaze, testing how long she could last. Three heartbeats. Impressive.

"Then there is nothing to be concerned with." She tucked her hands into her wide sleeves, but he watched how the fabric moved as her fingers fidgeted.

Bram narrowed his eyes. She'd given in too easily. "Is there something else?"

"Will you restore my power?"

So that was it. Bold. He almost admired her strength to ask such a thing of him. He didn't know if he could reverse the Heptad's punishment upon her. Perhaps he could. They'd been so concerned with covering their mistake, they'd not restricted anything from him.

But she'd been cunning enough to think of asking, and that made him question what else she might be capable of.

"It is not my place to override the council. Your loss of position is from your own doing. Appeal to them."

Yralissa narrowed her gaze. Her lips twitched as if she had more to say, but she bowed her head and left, saying nothing.

Rowena hobbled closer to his side. "I have a bad feeling about her."

Bram glanced down at the woman by his side. Her wildflower and pepper root scent muddled his senses. That had to be the case, because why else would he constantly want to take her in his arms and kiss her? Of course, her fierce determination and concern for others had earned his respect, too. She tipped her chin up, waiting for him to speak. Her amber eyes and full lips beckoned him without effort.

"It's nothing to worry about." He had to focus on his mission—she was a moon-born and would play a part in fulfilling the prophecy. That was all.

He had exposed his identity, which could make things more difficult. However, rumors, even though true, had a way of morphing into something unrecognizable. By the time he'd retrieved the sword from Fidessa and secured the Lunastone with it, he'd be free to move on without concern.

Most of the guards had fled, but those remaining loyal to Velmeg and the Fianna remained. All had their gazes trained on him.

"There has been much unrest in this kingdom, and in Forsa. It's time to put weapons aside and lend a hand to those in need of help." He stepped closer to the center of the room, within the stream of light coming through the broken wall above. If they would listen, they'd have to see beyond his appearance. "Queen Dewan will rule now. She is strong and fair. I trust she will lead you all with wisdom."

Conri eyed him with a tilt of his head. Bram could almost see the questions he had floating around him.

"Will the Fianna help restore the city?" Bram asked.

Conri ambled forward, with Hywel and Liam at his side. "That's a big secret you had there, traveler."

"I did not lie. I have been to many places."

Rowena scoffed behind him. He poked his long nails into his palm to keep from grinning at her familiarity. It would serve him better to remain stoic with everyone else.

"I don't doubt it," Conri said. "I think it's best if we leave for now. With the discovery that the queen contracted us to find that sword, it's best if we lie low for a while. Who knows what she has planned now."

"And I'm not risking my neck without pay," Hywel said.

Bram flicked his brows higher. It made sense, though he'd hoped they'd consider doing some good for others instead of taking contracts. Though the battle wasn't theirs to fight, and Velmeg wasn't their home.

"You had no reason to suspect what Fidessa truly wanted, but distancing yourself from her actions would be wise." Bram said. "Be safe on your journey."

"And to you, Seeker," Conri said. "But I'd appreciate knowing you won't be around here much longer. It's unnerving that you could step out of the shadows unannounced."

"I can assure you, I will leave soon."

He didn't have to turn to know Rowena had stiffened at his comment.

As the Fianna left, Liam gave Bram and Rowena one last peek before heading out the door.

A soft clearing of a throat made Bram twist around to find Queen Dewan standing with her hands loosely held in front of her. "Thank you."

"I'm not sure I have helped in any significant way," Bram said.

"I mean, for not killing my son. He is a troubled man who needed a kind father. I'd hoped Uther would do better than my husband, but it doesn't appear so."

Bram wasn't sure how to respond. His instruction from the Heptad required him to ensure quick compliance of the moonborn. Conversations with royals and dealing with the realms' politics were not something he'd prepared for.

Rowena reached out and took the queen's hand. "There's always hope he will come to his senses."

That seemed unlikely, but the queen patted her hand, satisfied enough with the answer.

"Have you seen the thrall, Muriel, by chance?" Rowena asked Dewan.

The queen chuckled lightly. "They are both in my chambers. Tuck is a powerful man and a large one. My rooms were closer for the guards to carry him. I asked for Muriel to sit with him, and they were a comfort to me during the attack as well."

Rowena released a deep breath. "I'm so happy to hear that."

"I must go see to the repairs now," Dewan said. "Please keep me appraised of your search. I look forward to news that Safi is safe."

Rowena's lips quivered as if she tried to offer a confident smile before the queen strode for the bailey. Bram clenched his fist, his nails pressing into his palm to stay calm. Safi had suffered so much, and it pained him that Rowena's cousin was in Daenon's clutches.

After everyone left, Bram wasn't sure what to do. He had to go after Fidessa and the sword, but he struggled to leave Rowena. She limped toward a bench, wincing.

"May I help you with your leg?"

"Like you did with Errol's rattlerock bite?" She lowered herself to the bench.

"Since it's not poison, it's not as difficult." He moved closer, kneeling next to her. "However, I'll have to touch you."

Her eyes widened, but she recovered quickly. "That's fine."

He enjoyed how she forced herself to be brave, but someday, he hoped she'd understand that she didn't always have to be that way, not with him. For the moment, he would enjoy that she didn't fear him.

He gently laid his hand over the wound on her leg. It wasn't a deep gash, but it had torn the muscle.

"Close your eyes," he whispered.

She complied, inhaling and exhaling in a slow, measured way. He could hear her pulse though, and it raced like a rabbit chased by a dozen sandcats. He let his power flood to her other injuries as well. She'd been braver than he'd thought. Bruises, sprains, and cuts—some deep—pestered her entire body. He left none of them unhealed. When he finished, he removed his hand, instantly missing the warmth of her.

She fluttered open her eyelids and met his gaze. He'd drifted closer to her than he'd meant to be. She sucked in a deep breath. He glanced at her lips. Her pulse beat faster, thumping loudly in his ears.

He leaned back slightly, recalling his duty. "I have to find Fidessa."

"And Safi." Rowena's nostrils flared. "We have to get her away from that monster."

"Yes."

"I'm coming with you."

"What if I say no?"

Rowena brought her face close to his again, reaching out to put her hand on his chest. "Don't tell me what to do."

He tried to force himself to seem stern, but she grinned, shredding his resolve. Instead of explaining how it would be dangerous or that his duty did not allow for working with others, he held out his palm.

As soon as she lay her hand in his, he pulled her close, keeping his gaze steady on hers. She'd been through so much, and he could feel the tremble in her fingers. The ones on his chest she hadn't removed. Did he dare? He slipped ever closer. His darkness flickering at their feet.

She squeezed his hand.

He tilted nearer as his shadows swirled and whisked them away.

Rowena and Bram's story continues in
Rune of Thorns, Enchanted Shadows 2

Snap this QR code or enter the site link into your browser for your special invitation
for a free story and extra bonuses

https://www.kellynjane.com/secrets

ACKNOWLEDGMENTS

When I first started planning the Tales of Edenia series, I scared myself. I didn't have one or even two series that came up, but multiple. An entire universe of stories, worlds, characters, and ideas so big, I didn't know if I could even write one of them, let alone all of them. Time will tell on that last part.

Rowena is a strong, stubborn, wonderful young woman who became part of my desire to write this book over a year before I put the first word to the page. She goes through a lot, has terrible things happen, makes mistakes, struggles to deal with life sometimes, but keeps going. There are moments she needs to cry, then she wipes her face and moves forward. Her courage, love, friendship, and inner strength inspire me.

That might be an odd thing to say about a character that formed out of my mind, but she became like a real person to me through this process. Her story had to be told, and to do that, I had to dig deeper within myself.

This book is the biggest, in word count, that I've written so far in my career. It's said that it takes a village to raise a child, but I can tell you, it takes one to make a book come to life as well.

I can't thank my editors more. Every part of my heart goes out to them for all the hard work they dedicated to helping me put out the best book possible. Arielle, you helped me put my feet onto the path in the direction I was meant to go. Your wisdom and advice helped me open up and write the book I needed to write. I wouldn't have put aside my fears without your feedback. I'm so happy we both enjoy copious note taking! Candy, my consummate cheerleader who keeps me sitting down to put more words on the page, then makes sure they are the right ones! Thank you for making me feel special. To everyone at Enchanted Quill Press, especially Jo. You run a wonderful business with so much professionalism. Thank you for taking the time to help save me when I needed a life raft. I wouldn't have survived without you. Jen . . . you are the Jen of all Jens! From the beginning, you have been with me on this journey. You've seen the disasters and the promise and guided me to strive for my very best. I cannot thank you enough!

Rebecca Frank, of Bewitching Book Covers, what can I say? Everyone gushes about your art and I feel privileged to work with you on this series. Rowena came alive under your brush strokes.

Anna, you got me through this last year. I would have been in a black hole without your help keeping me online. You kept me tethered to the real world, and my business afloat more than once. Thank you so much!

Family . . . you are my lifeline. I literally can't survive without you. I don't think I've made a meal on my own for more than a year. You lift me up when I fall; you sit with me when I despair; you dance with me when I'm excited. Nothing you've done has gone to waste—I've soaked in every moment, word, smile, laugh, and hug. Craig, you've become such an amazing beta reader, holding me to a higher standard. As well as being willing to stand firm and make me rethink things when I don't want to. Audrey and Sydney—you push me even when you don't know you are. You're both living life to the fullest and I admire you so much. I'm so excited about our futures. Libby, Bear, and Billie, too, your dedication to keeping me filled with furry kisses, snuggles, and an office full of the cutest little snores makes every day better. Thank you for your steadfast schedules that force me out of my chair regularly.

ALSO BY KELLY N. JANE

Enchanted Shadows
Rune of Secrets
Rune of Thorns
Rune of Oaths
Rune of Blades
Rune of Crowns

The Royal Quest Completed Series
Dragon Prince
Dragon Magic
Dragon Mates
Dragon Betrayal
Dragon Crown
Dragon War

The Viking Maiden Completed Series
Ingrid, The Viking Maiden
Amber Magic
Realm of Fate
Arcanum (A Viking Maiden novella)

ABOUT THE AUTHOR

Kelly is a USA Today bestselling author who writes heroic, royally epic fantasy immersed in elaborate worlds rich with history, myth, magic, slow-burn romance, and fast-paced action.

A lover of sassy chihuahuas and bobbed-tail cats, her coffee mug is always full, and she believes dessert goes with every meal. When not in front of her keyboard, she's probably reading, playing with yarn, or on a wild rabbit chase down an exciting research trail!

www.kellynjane.com

www.ingramcontent.com/pod-product-compliance
Lightning Source LLC
LaVergne TN
LVHW040747250326
834688LV00034B/489